D1471830

THE DEVIL VIRUS

A NOVEL
BY
CHRIS DILEO

Cover Design © 2019 by Don Noble
https://roosterrepublicpress.com

ISBN-13: 978-1-947522-18-3
ISBN-10: 1-947522-18-3

BLOODSHOT BOOKS

READ UNTIL YOU BLEED!

For Jenn

ACKNOWLEDGEMENTS

This book would not exist without William Peter Blatty's *The Exorcist* and Joe Hill's *NOS4A2*. Although my book does not come close to either of those masterpieces, I hope my affection for those stories shines through.

This book would also not exist without my Episcopalian upbringing. I was brought every Sunday to St. Anne's Church in Washingtonville, NY, where I was baptized and confirmed. I thank the good people who comprised that congregation in the eighties and nineties for their compassion, humor, and support.

There are conversations between priests in this book that are, some might argue, sacrilegious. If you were offended, I can only shrug and blame it on my parents. They were both devout Episcopalians, but they were highly educated, and their belief was never at the expense of their intellect. They taught me what it means to be a good person, they shared their faith with me, but they also taught me to question, to ponder, and to form my own conclusions. For that, I am forever grateful.

My heartfelt thanks to the following: Alberta DiLeo, who always believed in me and taught me the importance of work ethic; Warren DiLeo, who died when I was eleven but who left behind a coffin-shaped bookcase of horror novels that seduced me; Marian O'Neill, who read voraciously and taught me the importance of sarcasm; Brenda and Jack Carter, who are as supportive and loving as any parents I could hope for; Jean Bolton, my favorite English teacher, who read my horror stories in high school and told me to never stop writing; LeeAnn Doherty Van Koppen, friend, unflinching literary critic, and ceaseless supporter; Lucas Kane, friend and astonishing writer with whom I talk shop; Karla Herrera, surrogate daughter who is meticulous and brutally honest in her critiques; Mark Williamson, friend and fellow creative; Michael Marshall, who has given me much more of his time than I had any right to expect; Scott Nicholson, who believed in my words and provided professional guidance; Michael Koryta, who took the time to answer my questions and provide encouragement; Owen King and Kelly Braffet, who visited with my creative writing students and encouraged them and me to keep at it; Scott Miller, my first agent, who dared to give me a chance; Stephen King, whose books shaped me as a writer; and the many students I've taught throughout the years who kept saying I should write a book.

I am immensely grateful to Pete Kahle for publishing this as a Bloodshot Book. His faith in my novel is humbling and more inspiring than I can express. Thank you, Pete. Thanks also to Don Noble, who created a kickass cover.

Thank you to my wife, Jenn, who was honest with her critique of this book, is always sincere in her support, and is steadfast in her faith in my writing.

Finally, thank you dear reader for coming with me on this journey. Before I let you go, I must remind you viruses are everywhere, in the very air you're breathing as you read this, and those viruses are predatory and hungry—desperate to live.

Some of them might even be demons.

Chris DiLeo
December 2018

THE DEVIL VIRUS

CHRIS DILEO

PART ONE

THE LAND OF UZ

The night before the accident, before I started on my
personal road to Damascus, I went into the little room off
the kitchen that had once been the garage to check on my
father. I found him in the bathroom on the toilet, his
sweatpants bundled around his ankles, his sweatshirt sagging to
reveal a narrow, liver-spotted shoulder, one arm draped over the
curved lift-assist bar, chin on his chest. Ben Masters appeared to
be sleeping—or dead.

Dead on the toilet: an ignominious end for a once-adored
father and priest.

Relief offered a selfish respite from this life of eldercare
with its constant weight of responsibility, but I thought of
Phoebe asking after my dad's heart attack, *Is grandpa dying?*

and her immense relief when I assured her grandpa was going to be fine, though I had no reason to believe that but as a father and a priest, I knew it was the thing to say.

"Dad?"

The room smelled of disinfectant and old-man odor. The sliding-glass shower door stood open to reveal the plastic seat and the hand-held shower head, a crime scene whose victim was youth.

Naomi had painted the room a light blue and decorated with matching floor mats, towels and a soap dispenser, which was supposed to make it homier, but instead it felt like a cheap, crammed motel room. Medicine bottles were strewn across the counter, his pill case with little boxes for each day of the week open and tipped, pills scattered. The light from the bulbs around the mirror caught the silver edge of a nail file sticking out over the sink.

"Dad?"

He mumbled something, probably Latin. He'd been doing that a lot recently, revisiting his classic seminary education. His doctor said it was part of the mind's regression, reverting without connective logic, and his thinking was going to get more jumbled, an old film reel coming unspooled and entangled.

I shook him gently and he woke slowly in bumbling degrees with guttural chokes and a long trail of white phlegm slipping off his bottom lip.

One eye was bloodshot, a remnant of the stroke, and the other featured a grayish-blue cataract that made everything fuzzy for him. Fuzzy like his brain.

"You okay, Dad?"

He grabbed my arm, squeezed hard, and stared at me for several uncomfortable seconds.

"It's a goddamn waste," he said in a crackly voice. "Resisting like this."

"You're okay, Dad."

I helped him up and tugged up his pants, my head turned away in privacy, as he stood there without helping. Thankfully, what was in the toilet did not require a wipe and I flushed it away.

"You fell asleep."

"I was dreaming."

"Anything good?"

"'Thou shalt not be afraid for the terror by night; nor for the arrow that fly by day.'"

"Sounds like one of the Psalms," I said.

"Well?"

"There's a lot."

He shook his head and started the fragile trek out of the bathroom. This Bible game was a new thing. Biblical passages were the only thing he had no trouble keeping straight.

"'All things are possible to him that believe,'" I said.

My father grunted. "Gospel of Mark. Chapter nine, verse twenty-three."

He stumbled on the next step, fell to one knee, but I snagged his arm before he could go full sprawl.

"Goddamn it." He punched the carpet with surprising force. "What is the point?"

"You're okay, Dad. I got you."

I helped him onto the bed where he sat, hands on his knees, breathing in short, hollow gasps. The hand he used to punch the floor looked a bit strange, darker or something. Maybe dirty. Who knows what he might have been doing with it?

"What's with your hand?"

"What?"

I gestured and he held it up for a moment before saying it was fine and covering it in his lap. Black lines crisscrossed over it and around his knuckles like some bizarre tattoo. It might have been black pen.

"What did you do to yourself, Dad?"

"Do?" he said as if the word were nasty. "What do you mean?"

I huffed like some impatient schoolteacher—Naomi would have been so proud—and told my father he needed to be honest with me. "I won't be mad, Dad, but if there's something wrong with your hand..."

"There's nothing wrong with it."

"Or you did something to it."

4 THE DEVIL VIRUS

He glared at me and I waited. I'd read posts online about eldercare some of which were very troubling, particularly those about elderly parents reverting to almost infantile behavior. Staging tantrums. Throwing food. Hurting themselves or other family members.

"You remember that Quincy Toft boy?" my father asked.

"Doesn't ring a bell. Are you going to show me your hand?"

I thought of yanking his hand free and holding it high for examination, but if he was regressing into childish antics, he probably wouldn't react very well. So, instead, I grabbed the plastic tube connected to the oxygen generator, this bulky thing by the bedside, and my father let me slip it on around his ears and angle the nostril stubs into his nose. I had to reach across the bed to turn the machine on and it came alive with a loud beep and settled into a rhythmic rumbling hum and exhaling sigh.

"Why did you turn this off?"

"I don't need it."

"Dad, you fell asleep on the toilet. Oxygen deprivation."

"You're a doctor now?"

"You're not one, either."

He took a long inhale of machine-produced air and sat a little straighter. His white hair flapped like a wing on his head and he rubbed his feet back and forth across the blue carpet that had been worn thin in a path from bathroom to bed. Crumbled tissues lay scattered around. I started picking them up.

"You can't just decide you feel better and don't need oxygen. And what about your pills? Did you get them confused again? Are you going to show me your hand?"

"He killed himself," my father said.

"What? Who?" I pushed his glass of water back from the night table's edge.

"Quincy Toft. He was a little kid. Scrawny. Kind of kid who fell over swinging a T-ball bat. Never had any friends. Followed kids, begging for them to let him be their friend. Followed them everywhere. Throughout school. On the playground. Down the streets in town. Any time you saw a group of kids, you could bet Quincy was ten steps behind, scurrying after them in a Buffalo Bills jacket that billowed around him like he was a puffed-up balloon. Always following and never included. Must have been like that from the time he was seven or eight until he was about ten or eleven."

I smelled Vicks vapor rub and one of those flower-scented Plug-Ins Naomi added all over the house. Dad said that smell reminded him of Mom. A busted blood vessel had taken her years ago. Phoebe hadn't even been a year old at the time.

"What happened when he was ten?"

He didn't say anything for a moment, just stared at his hands, the one still hidden beneath the other. They had morphed into pale maps of scraggly blue veins with tissue-paper skin. His nails had yellowed, too, like his teeth.

"He swallowed a bottle's worth of Tylenol. Sat there in his bedroom with the pile of pills next to him and swallowed one after the next. If you think about it, you can even see the way his throat must have started constricting after the first couple dozen. But he choked them down. Almost eighty of them. Then he wrapped a plastic bag around his head, one of those with the big stupid smile and Thank You for Shopping printed on it. Strapped duct-tape around his neck. To be sure, I guess."

When he sermonized, my father liked talking around things, using metaphors and anecdotes, preferring an apropos fable to a direct discussion. *A metaphor is a sermonizer's best friend* he told me when I was preparing my first homilies. *And if a metaphor isn't apt, use an anecdote. And if you can't recall one, make it up. But don't make it too direct. People get suspicious of stories that snap together like puzzle pieces.*

Along with a *metaphor is a sermonizer's best friend*, my father also believed *the Devil is in the details.*

"This boy's family attended Saint John's?"

"You don't remember? Somewhere else, then."

He was referring to all those churches he visited as part of his pilgrimages, a self-ascribed addition to his priestly duties that sent him for a week or two on a trek of New York churches at least once a year. He took me with him a few times, but they were dull affairs.

Either Quincy Toft attended one of those other churches or this story was a fabrication, an intermingling of frayed memory frames on the cutting room floor of my father's mind, maybe a lost sermon he never delivered.

A rather macabre one.

"The boy's parents were out. They came home late, didn't check on him, found him the next morning. The bag was stuck to his face. Whitish vomit had hardened around his lips and clogged his nose.

"Quincy told his parents angels were hunting him. They came for him at night. Big, bright lights, enormous things, horrifying. Like the way abductees talk about aliens. Parents thought the boy had a hyper-active imagination."

"That's very ... unsettling, Dad."

"So are angels. Remember what the angel said who appeared before the shepherds? 'Fear not.' Why say that if an angel doesn't look frightening? And how does Saul respond when an angel appears to him on the road to Damascus? He is 'trembling and astonished' and those traveling with him are 'speechless'—and afraid."

"Don't the angels say they bring good news?"

"And Saul is blinded," he said. "Imagine how bright it must have been. How awful that brightness must be."

"But he's not blind for long," I said. "A symbolic blindness. Psychosomatic, perhaps."

"The liberal interpretation," he said.

"New wave Episcopalianism," I said.

He was joking—he'd been a barely disguised liberal, yet since the stroke, his moral compass seemed out of whack.

My father believed, as I did, that a priest's job, an Episcopal priest's in particular, was not to dictate interpretation: it was to offer numerous ways to examine a fragment of scripture, turning it over slowly like a prism in a blade of light to see all the possible colors.

Post-stroke Ben Masters was more of a literal-minded believer. If the pulpit were still his, he might advocate public stoning, as per Leviticus.

"You should get some sleep."

I pulled back the sheets Naomi washed twice weekly and helped him slide in. He kept his hand hidden all the while.

"You're not going to show me your hand?"

"No visit from my beautiful granddaughter this evening?" he asked.

"Not tonight, Dad."

"Is she going to wake the whole neighborhood?"

Phoebe and her nightmares.

When she was in the grip, really letting it rip, her vocals could shake the house, even make the wine goblets in the china cabinet stir. For an eight-year old and someone so small, Phoebe had impressive lung power. If someone were walking by on the street outside, he'd think she was being murdered. Her "screaming fits," as Naomi and I were calling them because that sounded better than "night terrors," though it amounted to the same, had been getting more frequent, yet all the online parent guides assured us it would get better, even if it got worse first.

"She'll grow out of it," I said.

"It's hard to fight it. 'The thief cometh not, but for to steal, and to kill, and to destroy.'"

"Gospel According to John," I said.

He waited for the chapter and verse with full recognition of his continued victory in this little game.

"Goodnight, Dad."

"That Toft boy," he said, stopping me at the door, "was an example."

"Of?"

His ailing eyes rolled up toward the ceiling. "There are worse things than nightmares."

Three nights previously, I woke after two in the morning and for a moment I thought maybe I would get up anyway; I felt pretty good, pretty rested. I could polish up my sermon for Sunday. Almost immediately, however, exhaustion weighed me back into the mattress, the feeling of being rested no more than a tease.

I started to fall back asleep and—

8 THE DEVIL VIRUS

Heard something downstairs. A creak of floor, a faint accompanying murmur. I knew it was my father. Walking around and talking to himself. I almost got up, but my body wouldn't get moving. If he wanted to walk around at night when no one was there to help him up if he fell, I supposed that was his decision.

✝

The road to Hell might be paved with such assumptions.

✝

We lived in a colonial house that still needed some sprucing—the creaky stairs, the raggedy carpet in the bedrooms, and the curling tongues of paint peeling off the house. As a priest, I didn't make much, but Naomi was a third-grade teacher at Warrenville Elementary, which was a good forty-minute drive for her, but her salary kept the mortgage in check and the girls donned in relatively in-vogue clothing. I'm not sure what that means for an eight and a four year old, but any time I had tried to say, *Oh, this dress would look so pretty on you*, either Tamara (the four year old) or her older sister would give me that *get real* expression of incredulity and barely restrained impatience at my ineptitude and say, "You can be pretty dumb sometimes, Dad."

"How's your father?" Naomi asked.

She was in bed, her blonde hair pulled back, her brown-frame reading classes pushed up against her face. She was reading a book about constructivist pedagogical approaches to Common Core learning in the 21st century elementary classroom.

"Drifting," I said.

When I finally got in bed, she put the book aside, tucking a highlighter and a pen in her spot. Her cheeks were flushed red. They always did that when she was reading, speaking animatedly about teaching, or caught in the throes of bedroom P.E.

"It'll be okay," she said and rubbed my arm.

"He was asleep."

"Well, that's good."

"On the toilet."

"Cleaner than diapers, I guess." She thought for a moment. "Unless his pants weren't down."

"They were."

She smiled. "Uh-oh. He give you that Ham-saw-his-father-Noah-naked-and-God-cursed-Ham's-offspring-for-all-time spiel?"

"I hope my father doesn't actually believe that."

"I don't know," Naomi said. "These days, he might get behind the Eve-damned-all-humanity-for-all-eternity stuff. Plays well with the ladies."

"The truth hurts. I can appreciate that."

"You know," she said with a curl of upper lip, "for a priest you're pretty insensitive."

"I do have a tender side." I slid one hand along her sweatpants. She stopped me before I reached the ticklish spot under her knee.

She tugged gently on my ear, which was an inside joke going way back, and we kissed.

"The girls need tucking in." Phoebe was eight, Tamara four.

"Whatever you say, my love."

"That's a bit more priestly of you."

I hesitated in the doorway. "I'm concerned."

"About tucking in the girls?" She'd reopened her book, highlighter in hand.

"He's changed. We make fun of it, but all this conservative biblical stuff is really troublesome."

"A lot of faithful Americans might take umbrage with you on that."

"I mean, he spent his whole life preaching a more, I don't know, gentler gospel, and now he could do tent revivals with Pat Robertson."

"As I said, plays well with the ladies."

"Church was always about laughter and food and being good to each other. It's like he doesn't remember who he was or what he once believed."

"You're worrying too much."

I sighed. "I am worried. Phoebe spends a lot of time with him."

"She loves her grandpa. I think it's good for her. For both of them."

"What if, you know, he really loses it? He's been mumbling Latin, I think he did something to his hand, and he was talking about some kid committing suicide."

She put down her book again. "You want to have this conversation now?"

"I'm not talking about putting him in a home."

"Then what?"

I couldn't quite figure out what I wanted to say. "He's so old."

She laughed. "He's not that old. And, besides, it's natural. We're going to get old too, you realize. Did you say he was talking about a kid committing suicide?"

I thought for a moment, a wistful sensation almost fluttering inside me. "He was a great dad and he's been a wonderful grandpa. It's sad what happens. There ought to be a better way for people to fade gracefully. Something less humiliating."

"It's called dying in your sleep."

Tamara was already asleep in her room directly across from ours. The only window looked out on the front yard and the trees across the street. Her jade plant, the one Phoebe loved but acquiesced to her little sister because Phoebe wanted a purple jade plant (and refused to entertain my point such a plant did not exist), sat on the window sill in a splash of moonlight.

"Phoebe gave me her plant," Tamara said after Phoebe had placed the plant with its tree-like trunks and thick, rounded leaves in its spot.

"That's because she loves you," I said.

She gave me something close to an interrogative stare, close enough for a four-year-old anyway. "Do you love Phoebe more?"

Your child can hurt you so deeply without a kick, punch, or scream—and often do so inadvertently. It's their special talent, especially daughters'.

"She's playing you already," Naomi said when I told her about it later.

"It makes me feel awful. I love them both. I..."

"Shh," she said and sealed my lips with one finger. "She knows you love her. She's learning the fine art of manipulation."

"At four?"

"Phoebe had it mastered by two. I was beginning to worry Tamara was slow."

Tamara's mermaid nightlight cast a baby blue glow up the wall beside her bed and her face was buried in the pillow, hair covering in a mop. I brushed it back from her cheek and kissed her.

"I don't care if it's manipulation," I whispered. "You're my baby."

She didn't stir.

✝

Phoebe was sitting up in bed waiting for me.

She had been a crying baby, a screaming baby. All night long. It's amazing we ever thought to have a second child. Phoebe cried if she couldn't see at least one of us and she went through extended periods where she only wanted Mommy and then only wanted Daddy. Naomi and I took our respective turns and gloated only briefly in the rotation of leg-grabbing favoritism because being your child's favorite is only good for the esteem when you're not needed at three in the morning.

"Hi, Daddy," Phoebe said. She was wearing pink and purple pajamas with flying ponies on them. Her room was done in a wash of pastels and crowded with stuffed animals: they crammed bookshelf space, lined the top of her white desk, and congregated on her bed as if engaged in some stuffed-animal version of smoke-filled, back-room caucusing.

All the lights were on in her room including the overhead one. I turned it out and went to her.

"Little crowded up here," I said as a bunny and a panda tumbled into my lap.

The bunny was Foppy and got its name because although she'd meant to call it Floppy (those dangling ears), she struggled years ago with the l-sound, so Foppy it was to be forever. Sometimes Foppy stalked Phoebe's dreams in giant dinosaur steps. She'd drawn a few pictures that spent time on the fridge— a giant grey bunny, big as a house, with protruding, prehistoric fangs.

"I like them," Phoebe said. She defied me with an impossibly cute expression.

"You look tired."

She shook her head. I yawned in grand, exaggerated fashion until she giggled.

Her room smelled of cinnamon. Another of Naomi's Plug-Ins.

A stuffed animal was on the floor, a big lion we had gotten at the Bronx Zoo. She named it Braveheart. It was contorted in as if it had been stretched and twisted. I picked it up and clumps of white cotton stuffing plopped out of its severed belly. The cut was jagged, like she gutted it with her fingers.

Phoebe turned from my expression and picked up a stuffed animal seemingly at random, but I recognized it as a teddy bear Naomi had picked up somewhere and, for whatever reason, Phoebe took to as if the bear were a missing part of her she'd finally found. She called the bear Ben. When I asked if she named him after grandpa, she gave me that *are-you-serious?* face and said, "No, this Ben has always had that name."

"What happened to Braveheart?" I asked.

"I'm scared."

"What's wrong, honey?"

She pushed down into the bed and raised the comforter until she was a head among a collection of stuffed animals.

"Scared of having another nightmare?"

She nodded.

"They're bad dreams, honey. It's okay. They can't hurt you."

"You promise?"

"Yes."

"They can't hurt me?"

"No. I promise. I'm your daddy. Would I lie to you?"

She looked worried and a bit puzzled liked she'd been asked to solve some intimidating mathematical equation on the board in front of the whole class. "What about as a priest?"

"What do you mean, would I lie?"

She nodded.

"I think God would be very upset with me."

"Can God protect me from the bad dreams?"

The thief cometh not, but for to steal, and to kill, and to destroy.

I caressed her face. She was warm. Like always. When she was a baby, Naomi and I must have taken her temperature a billion times, always warm but never a fever. *Some kids are like improperly set ovens*, the pediatrician told us. *They run hot.*

"Just dreams. Nothing more. They can't hurt you."

Phoebe thought for a moment. "Can I sleep with you and Mommy?"

"You've got a big bed right here. And all your stuffed animals."

"I'll just bring Ben."

"Remember what we discussed?"

She hesitated. "I need to be a big girl."

"Can you do that for me?"

"I don't want to be alone."

"Mom and I are right down the hall."

"If I scream, you'll come?"

"Of course."

"I don't like when I'm alone and no one comes."

I thought of Quincy Toft sitting on his bed in a Bills jacket swallowing pill after pill, the muscles of his throat flexing up and down. The image was there, perfectly clear—I could even see a Bills poster on the wall behind him—and then it was gone.

"I'm always here for you. I promise."

The mauled lion sagged in my hand.

I tucked the comforter around her, kissed her forehead, but when I stood, she stabbed out one foot so it dangled free off the side of the bed.

It looked sickly white.

"Peekaboo," she said.

Phoebe loved that silly infant game so much she played it when she should have long ago left it behind. She liked to run up to me, cover her face and then fly apart her hands and shout the requisite phrase. Of course, bedtime was the perfect moment to resume the game. I'd tuck her in, and she'd kick out a leg. *Oops, peekaboo.* Tuck it back in and, what do you know, out pops an arm. Giggles all around.

This time, all her limbs stayed tucked. I kissed her again.

Before I left, I managed to negotiate the lights being turned off in exchange for both of her night lights staying on. One featured a cow leaping over a glowing moon and the other was a large green-tinted cross Naomi had purchased at Phoebe's request. "She's definitely a preacher's daughter," Naomi said. The cross was one of those forever LEDs that would never burn out. Cute touch, it being a cross and all.

"Grandpa's going to die, isn't he?" Phoebe said as I was closing the door.

"You don't need to think about that."

She started to respond, stopped, and appeared stuck.

"Get some rest, honey. We'll talk about it tomorrow."

"Daddy?"

I peeped through the crack. Even with both lights, she had fallen into darkness. "Yes, baby?"

"I love you."

I paused in the hallway with the mauled stuffed animal. I almost went to the bedroom to show Naomi and then I went into the kitchen and pushed the dissected thing deep into the trash. The lid snapped shut with a hollow echo.

✝

Late that night, waking in bed, I thought I heard something. The floor downstairs creaking, my father out of bed and shuffling around again. He was down there, whispering to himself, and then he wasn't, the sounds absorbed into silence.

The house stood dark and completely still.

He'd gone back to bed.

And that faint groan of wood must have been the house settling because no one was walking up the stairs.

I was sure.

✝

The scream ripped through the night and yanked me from sleep with the sudden smack of a cold hand across the face. I had been dreaming about Phoebe's lion, about its seams splitting with awful popping sounds, its cottony insides spewing out, but I was up and headed for the doorway before I even registered what was going on, and the dream fell away into a hot splash inside my chest. I heard Naomi flipping back the sheets and getting up right on my heels.

The floor was cold against my bare feet. I had fallen asleep in sweatpants and an undershirt; sweat stuck the shirt to my chest.

With the bedroom doors closed, the hallway was dark, only the faintest moonlight stretched out of the open office at the far end of the hall. Naomi's schoolwork was strewn all over the floor in there, everything grouped in piles and labeled with specific-colored Post-Its. The hallway smelled of cinnamon, yet another one of those Plug-Ins.

I moved past Tamara's room as her cries started up. Naomi would get her.

It wasn't until I opened the door that I realized there hadn't been any light floating in the crack beneath it. The night lights were off. Phoebe certainly wouldn't have done that, but what were the odds that the bulbs in both would go out during the same night? Slim, no doubt, but not impossible. Just unfortunate, especially for a little girl prone to nightmares.

Phoebe's scream peaked at ear-splitting decibel and I paused in the doorway as if hitting a wall made entirely of her scream.

"I'm here. I'm here. Daddy's here."

My hand flopped against the wall for the damn light switch, but it wasn't there. I went lower, then higher, Phoebe pushing that scream harder and harder, someone driving a monstrous blade deep inside her.

I found the switch, flicked it, and the overhead light bloomed bright. Someone stood over Phoebe. A large dark figure, back to me. The guy was hunched forward, reaching toward my daughter. My own startled scream caught in my throat. Someone had broken into my home. Someone had slipped in here. Someone was hurting my baby girl.

The figure turned, its black cloak or whatever it was wearing shimmered like water, a rain coat or a silk dress coat maybe, and from beneath a shadowy hood was an aging face with deep-grooved wrinkles and thin lips and yellow teeth. I smelled something sour, my own sweat perhaps.

"Dad?"

The bulb in the overhead light flared super bright—shadows thinning in those wrinkled creases—and popped as if smashed with a baseball bat. The bulb's death was loud enough to be heard over Phoebe's endless howl. And the room fell back into darkness, and even the moonlight failed to reach through the window.

"Dad!" I screamed over Phoebe's cry.

For a moment, I stayed in the doorway with my baby girl screaming her head off in the dark and that smell of something sour, something going rancid, filling the room. My heart thudded madly, and my limbs flushed with heat. What the hell was I seeing? Was that my father?

It couldn't be him. Someone else was in my house and I had no weapon.

There are things worse than nightmares, Dad had said.

Something pushed into my back and for a moment it was some other guy who had crept into my home and was now pushing a gun into my back, but it wasn't some deranged predator in the night: it was Naomi holding Tamara, her foot wedged into the small of my back.

"What are you doing?" Naomi yelled over Phoebe's screaming. "Jesus, Lucas—"

I went for it, hands up. Whatever I hit, Dad or some crazed intruder, I was going to grab him and throw him to the ground. I'd throw a few punches, teach whoever it was he couldn't mess with my family. Priest or not, I was a man, dammit.

The night rushed past me. I heard a strange grunting, growling sound and realized it was coming from my throat. Phoebe screamed even harder and I thought she might burst a blood vessel. Maybe several.

My arms swooped through the darkness, my eyes starting to adjust, and I could see a darker outline of something but as I was about to hit it, it slipped away, oil pushing across moving water.

Naomi turned on the hallway light and a bright rectangle of it fell across Phoebe's bed as I smacked the wooden headboard above her. Her huge eyes stared up at me; tears reflected along her nose. Stuffed animals had fallen in all directions like earthquake victims.

Foppy the bunny stared at me with its red eyes, as if this were all my fault, before it toppled off the bed's edge.

Phoebe reached for me with both arms. Ben-the-bear dangled from one tiny, clenched fist. Her face was impossibly red, like when she was an infant and Naomi and I tried everything to calm her, but she kept crying and crying until we fled to the emergency room because, silly or not, we thought something in her head might rupture. It happens; ask my mother.

In my arms, Phoebe fell into heaving, tortured sobs. She clutched at my shoulders, buried her face in the crook of my neck. I rubbed her back, told her it was okay. Everything was going to be okay. I was her father, cloaked in kingly power, even mystical power, but I had no knights to command, no potions or spells to offer remedy. Just words. That's all we ever have. Even all the prayers and blessings, the pleadings to God, the transubstantiation of wafer and wine, for those who believed—none of it was magic, just words.

I stared around her room at the twisted sheets, the stuffed animals in disarray. Circles of light orbed in beady, plastic eyes. Judging me. No secret intruder. Certainly not my father, who would have fallen several times before making it halfway up here, cane or not. I had stood in the doorway while my baby screamed and now I was trying to comfort her. It's too hard to explain the conflicting emotions of self-disgust, anger, and helplessness. If you've been there, you understand.

✝

Naomi managed to get Tamara back to bed with a motherly ease that was almost a mockery of my fumbling fathering. We took Phoebe downstairs and Naomi gave her some warmed milk with a sprinkle of cinnamon on top. I checked on my dad, opening the door enough to make out his lumpy form on the bed and closing it again without even making the tiny click sound of the bolt sliding into the strike plate.

"You ready to go back to sleep?" Naomi asked.

Phoebe shook her head. She held the milk in both hands with her bear perched against her. Shadows pocketed the bear's face. We were sitting at the dining room table, as far from Dad's room as we could get on this floor.

"Why don't you try?" Naomi said. The microwave clock said it was approaching four.

"It's okay," I said. "I'll stay up with her."

Naomi's face fought between unexpected inadequacy and total gratitude. She kissed us both and went back upstairs. The steps faintly creaked.

"You want to talk about it?" I asked Phoebe.

She shook her head, drank some milk.

"It's okay, honey. Nightmares happen to everyone. They can't hurt you, remember?"

Worse things than nightmares.

"It was dark."

"Your night lights burned out, that's all." *And the overhead light, too*, I thought. *A bit of an anomaly, sure, but stranger things have happened.* That was one of my mom's favorite phrases. No matter what: something stranger has surely happened. Examples were, presumably, unnecessary.

"It was in my room."

"What was, honey?"

"The monster."

"There's no such thing as monsters."

She hesitated. "You saw it."

"What do you mean?"

"You opened my door and you saw it. I know you did."

Something caught in my throat and I had to fight to force it down. "I didn't see anything. I was just scared."

"You were?"

"I was scared because you were so scared."

She thought about that. "It was standing over me. A dark thing. A shadow man."

With my father's face, I thought. "Sometimes when we have bad dreams we wake up and see things. They're not there but our mind thinks they are because we saw them in our heads. Does that make sense?"

I had been having a nightmare, too, something about her stuffed animals.

She nodded a bit hesitantly. Can't ever be too quick to trust adults, not even Daddy. "I'm sorry."

I hugged her, told her not to be sorry, not to ever be sorry for having bad dreams. "Everything is going to be okay. I promise."

She paused longer this time, staring down into the last little bit of brownish milk in her glass. "I want to go to Uz."

I smiled. "Okay. Let's go."

Last summer, Phoebe attended Bible Camp.

Our church was small, a congregation of maybe twenty-five to thirty regulars and an additional twenty-five to forty who showed for Christmas and Easter, which made our financial book rather thin. We offered Sunday School before services every week during the school year, but no one was charged to attend it or paid to teach it—Iris taught it, saying she enjoyed opening children's hearts to God. We made ends meet by renting out the parish hall to a woman who conducted yoga classes Tuesday nights, and something called "Cognitive Introspective Release" on Thursday evenings. I didn't know anyone who attended. Alcoholics Anonymous used the place for free on Saturday nights and the members usually made a good donation around Christmas. Occasionally, someone would pay a few hundred to rent the parish for a Sweet Sixteen, but those were few and very far between. We were no Catholic institution with money trickling down from wealthy families and we never hosted cash cows like Casino Nights and Bingo Bashes. The official Episcopal view on such things was we should not profit off people who may have an addiction. That would be like hosting a Bible Brewery Night and inviting the AA members.

When it came to religion and money in Marguerite, The Word of Christ mega-church was the place to look. Some people called the church The Glass Cross because the place was a sprawling compound with a peaked glass roof where a huge cross radiated sunlight. The church offered hundreds of congregants the pure, undiluted Word of God, all delivered in reassuring absolutes.

Along with undisputed truth, The Word of Christ Church offered daily daycare, intensive Bible study classes, fitness classes, movie nights (G-rated only), courses on parenting, financial planning, and after-school tutoring for all subjects. They also hosted an annual Golfing for God outing. Last year, a state senator and his cronies played. The picture had been on the sports page of *The Times Herald Record*.

The church also offered a six-week summer Bible Camp. It cost six hundred dollars, but Naomi and I thought it might be good for Phoebe. She could make more friends, something she always struggled with for whatever reason, and even though I was a bit concerned about her coming back as a lock-step, indoctrinated True Word believer, Naomi assured me with a wink we could undo any permanent damage.

The damage proved minimal. She made several friends and she talked incessantly about how much fun she had and why couldn't our church have games and food and singing. "We sing," I told her, though our choir was five people who accidentally sang in key from time to time and an elderly organist who played too loud.

"No," she said. "This is fun."

Part of Bible Camp included an extended adventure through Bible Land. The church brought in religious-themed carnival rides like Round 'n Round the Forbidden Tree, The Fall of Jericho Coaster and Noah's Arc Splashdown, and games like the Laser Tag-inspired Judas Hunter or the brain buster Guess that Proverb, something Dad would do quite well playing.

Actors walked around in biblical attire and performed skits—the Nativity, of course, but also Paul's conversion and even the Stations of the Cross. I'm glad I hadn't known about that in advance. More than anything else, however, Phoebe enjoyed a make-believe game called, "Prayer Construction." Sounds like some college-level word-parsing task, but it was something far more interesting.

The kids were asked to find their favorite Bible story or biblical phrase and construct a world around it in their head. This place would be their Constructed Prayer Place. They could go there whenever they wanted. Several times a day or only a few times a year. Whenever they wanted. It didn't matter where they were in reality because they could go to their special prayer place and God would be waiting for them. They could set it up any way they wanted, fill their place with anything.

"The promise of prayer is one of escape and sanctuary," Phoebe told me.

Most kids named their places things like The Garden or Jesus Land, but Phoebe named hers The Land of Uz. The first time she mentioned it, I asked her if she meant Oz, as in The Wizard of, but she said, no, it's Uz, because that's where Job lived. I asked Phoebe what she had been told about Job, but all she said was "he was a devout man." She liked the name Uz and built her prayer place beneath its banner.

"So tell her what prayer really is," Naomi said.

"What's that?"

She flashed me her *stop-screwing-around* expression.

Most people, my wife included, thought prayer was like introspection and meditation mixed together, which is completely fine. They might also see prayer as dropping a Happiness Request in God's inbox or a deposit into the Savings Account of Religious Stock, a sort of retirement fund for people who want an enjoyable afterlife. That's okay, too. Whatever works. For my money, though, I think there's something to this prayer place.

I really do.

✝

Phoebe and I went into the living room and sat on the couch. She nestled in-between the cushions as she'd been doing since she was two. The large cushions closed in around her.

Phoebe had taken me to Uz a few times before, or at least she had gone and I had humored her, as any good father would his daughter's fanciful imagination. The first had been right after Bible Camp ended. She was sugar-overload excited and couldn't quite calm down enough to explain what was going on while she closed her eyes and described a place of multi-colored wonders and rolling hills. I thought of bright, goofy cartoons.

It wasn't until the nightmares got really bad that I actually figured out what Uz meant to my daughter.

"You ready, Daddy?"

"I am."

"I am," Phoebe repeated.

When Moses found the burning bush that spoke with the voice of God, he asked God what he should call Him, and God said, "I am." I don't know if there is greater meaning in Phoebe and I saying the same or not. It was part of her ritual. Yet much of what I did as a priest might also be called ritual.

We Episcopalians love our customs, but we are a thinking lot, and we aren't much for definitive truths, just pastries and questions.

✝

"First," Phoebe said, "we go light."

"Okay," I said.

She didn't say anything for a moment and then opened one eye, turned to me. "You have to close your eyes, Dad. Otherwise it's cheating."

I smiled. "Sorry, honey."

She settled back, closed her eye and I closed both of mine. When she started talking again, she sounded serious, and I had to focus not to laugh, not because this was silly but precisely because this *was* serious business, dammit. People might think it was a foolish kid's gimmick, but in the world of the child, nothing is deserving of more reverence and gravitas than the imagination.

"Ready to go light?"

"I am."

Phoebe's breathing slowed into a steady, gentle inhalation that filled her lungs gradually and then a longer, even slower exhale. I thought not for the first time how amazing it was someone managed to get young kids to actually do this. I knew a few Buddhist-types who practiced a form of mediation and each of them openly discussed how challenging it was to reach that calm center, to find that inner peace, and float in the river of being.

"Feel your feet go light," Phoebe said. "Feel the bones and the muscles go light. Feel it going up your legs, into your knees, and up your thighs. Feel it at your waist."

I tried to match my breathing to Phoebe's and willed my feet to go light, demanded the muscles and the bones lose all density, commanded my body to become a feather, to be able to waft off on the slightest breeze. My feet tingled, but that was it.

"Now, fly," Phoebe said. She inhaled and held her breath. I wanted to open my eyes and look at her, but I kept them closed. No cheating. "Are you flying, Daddy?"

"Yes," I said.

"Come with me to Uz," she said and giggled as if I had tickled her. The sound was so slight, so vulnerable, but somehow so powerful, an indestructible suit of armor made from the wind.

She pronounced Uz as the *uzz* in buzz. Some people pronounced it like *oose* in loose. Those tended to be people for whom fancy-sounding words were like fancy food: things to be praised and gloated over. Phoebe didn't need any such pronunciation to make her world special.

I wanted to go with her, wanted to share in her potent imagination, but my feet were firmly stuck to the floor, tingling there with pins and needles. I was stuck while my angel flew to a world only, she could see.

"There it is," she said. "The Land of Uz. It's nighttime there but the stars are so bright it's like the sun's out. Everyone is waiting for us. Braveheart and Pandy, Chip and Phillip, Sergeant and Foppy..."

"What about Ben?" I asked.

"He's in my arms, Dad. He's flying, too." *Duh, Dad.* "They're waiting for us. They're always waiting for us. We give this place life."

Something about how she said that—*We give this place life*—that tweaked a thing inside me, and I thought I might cry. Before I became a father, I never would have imagined the urge to cry coming so easily.

"They need us. The Monster is loose."

"There's no monsters," I said.

"Yes," she said firmly. "There are. There are monsters everywhere. And even here in Uz there is *the* Monster. He has many names. Sometimes he is Golgotha, but his name is really Abaddon, but we can't call him that."

She said the name, so it almost sounded like *A Bad One.* "It's too dangerous. He is the Uz Monster." *Uzz* with *buzz* again. *The Buzzing Uzz*, another title from Dr. Seuss crowded in among the rest on her bookcase with all her stuffed animals. "He hides in the corners and slips around like shadows. But I can find him. We can put him back in his cave. Will you help me, Daddy?"

I had the crawling skin sensation of being watched and I tried to shake it off, but the sensation spread down my arms. In the Book of Job, Abaddon is a doomed place. In Revelation, it is the name of a demon who rules a bottomless pit and commands an army of locusts who have men's faces and lions' teeth. Episcopalians aren't much for such things. Maybe Bible Camp had demon story time around the campfire; Hellfire Hour, they might've call it.

"Yes, honey. I'll help. I'm here for you. Always."

"I see him," she said in sudden alarm. "The Uz Monster is right there. Back in the Rolling Hills. Do you see the sign?"

For a moment, in the darkness behind my closed eyes, I *did* see something. A green highway sign wedged into the side of a grassy hill. The white letters were not block-style, but scrawled in Phoebe's girly, looping cursive. *Rolling Hills*, it read. A purple-shaded arrow pointed straight ahead.

Rolling Hills, like the hill where Jesus was crucified, a place called Golgotha.

"I see it." My voice sounded faint, not even there.

"The Uz Monster is there, hiding, but I see him. Help me, Daddy."

The green sign darkened. I thought of old Polaroid pictures developing while you watched, the image emerging, growing sharp, becoming something tangible. I was here. In Uz. I could see the sign. *It's not what she sees*, my mind insisted. *You're not in the same place, not at all.* I was nowhere closer to another world than when I looked at the crayon landscapes she created that Naomi hung on the fridge. In those pictures, her stuffed animals were as large as dinosaurs and the trees washed in shades of pink. But I saw the sign. It brightened, hardened, and I could even feel its weight in my mind, something solid blooming inside me. I saw how the ground gave way around the sign's edges, curving grooves where grass grew in crooked tufts. I felt the cool grass beneath my feet. I hadn't walked barefoot through grass since I was a boy. It was so soft.

"I'll help you, honey. I promise."

Behind the sign a dark shape slithered.

"I see it. The monster."

"We can get it, Daddy. We can send it back to the cave."

"Show me how."

A face fought inside that shadow, dimpled into eyes, protruded out a nose, gaped into a mouth, pushed out a bulbous forehead. *This is what she sees*, I thought. *It has to be. This is what comes for her in her nightmares and what she sees when she wakes in the dark and screams for me.*

The thing I had seen hovering over her.

Rage flushed through me. I wanted to seize the thing and beat it, wanted to make it feel all the pain it had inflicted on my baby girl. My hands curled around my knees. I hadn't fought anyone since middle school when kids taunted me with the name "God boy," but I would fight now. I would pummel this horrible thing until it was a disjointed ink blot on a sidewalk. I would not stop until it was gone, gone forever, and my angel was safe.

But how to fight a monster made of shadows?

"Show me," I said.

"Use the starlight, Daddy. Grab the starlight and send the Uz Monster back to his cave."

I reached up into that dark sky but there were no stars. No starlight at all. Only pure blackness. Yet the highway sign radiated light like living things seen through heat-reading cameras. Where was the starlight?

You're not in Uz. You're not with your baby. She's all alone.

"Grab it, Daddy. Grab the light."

"I—can't."

"Daddy?"

"I—"

"Where are you? I don't see you. Where are you?"

"I'm sorry, honey. I'm sorry, I—"

"Don't leave me, please. Don't leave me alone."

Her whimpering cries echoed around me as if from the black sky engulfing this alternate world that was not hers, but my own awful imitation. The cries became sobs.

"Why, Daddy? Why did you leave me alone? You promised. I need you."

I'm sorry, I'm sorry, I'm sorry.

I pushed out from my fake world but the sky pushed me back down, right there before the glowing green sign written in Phoebe's penmanship. I tried again but was pushed deeper into the grass, rough-edged now like blades. My mind constructed this facade and now it trapped me. Trapped in my own imagination. Maybe that was why most children were so quick to disown their imagination. They were smart enough to know if they didn't escape its world, they'd be stuck forever.

The Uz Monster was not here, either. A trick of the mind, no more tangible than anything else in this place. A trick because the monster, the real monster, was going after Phoebe, closing in on her with its shadow tentacles and black-hole mouth.

"Daddy, where are you? Please—"

I'm coming, I'm—

—not speaking. This place wouldn't let me. I was trapped here. Not forever, just long enough for Abaddon (*a bad one*), the Uz Monster, to get Phoebe. Long enough for it to drag her back to its cave and long enough for it to suffocate her with its amorphous, shadow body. I heard her crying. Soon she'd be screaming, but that wouldn't last long. I'd be here, stuck in my own head, long enough for the thing to kill Phoebe, and when I was released, I'd find her slumped back against the couch between the enormous cushions and her lips would be blue like she'd eaten one of those flavored popsicles, only she didn't have a popsicle, she choked to death on a shadow, on a goddamn figment of her imagination that somehow came to life, which was impossible, fucking impossible, because nightmares didn't come to life, they didn't slither from your ears and fill the corners of your bedroom, they didn't rise from nothing and walk, they weren't born of trauma into tangible beasts driven to feed on ceaseless fears—that was superstitious nonsense, that was the Boogyman, the Devil, and those things were nothing because they weren't real, not real, *not real, NOT REAL!*

The black sky descended and swallowed me. Something had my arm, wrapped around it tight enough to cut off circulation. *The Uz Monster. It's got me. It's severed my hand, it's—*

My father glared down at me and I screamed.

✝

I swallowed most of the scream. I hadn't turned on the light in here, so only half of my father's face was lit from the dining room and for a moment it appeared half of his face was missing, as if a shadow thing had swallowed it.

"It's me," Dad said.

His grip on my wrist was surprisingly tight and I gawked at it for a moment, confused. This was not the man who could barely walk ten feet without falling. The man who needed oxygen pumped up his nose while he slept. The man who fell asleep on the john.

"I am," I said. "I am."

He released my wrist and stepped back.

"Jesus, Dad."

"She's crying."

Who? I thought stupidly.

I turned to Phoebe and my own tears threatened to join hers as I yanked her free from the couch pillows and hugged her so tightly you might think I thought I had lost her. To be honest, in that moment with the early morning creeping around me and strange thoughts whirling through my head, my Dad staring at me, and my wrist throbbing from his grip, I thought I had lost her.

✝

Phoebe calmed, sagged in my arms, too exhausted to cry. I rubbed her back and said everything was going to be okay. She wanted to find peace in her imaginary world, but her nightmares followed her there and I hadn't been able to help, yet I thought I could promise it would somehow be okay. No real magic—just words—but it helped.

I told my father to stay put and carried Phoebe upstairs. She nuzzled against me and mumbled something.

"Shh. Go to sleep."

"You were there," she said fighting through her exhaustion, eyes closed.

"Shh."

"You were in Uz. But you didn't realize it."

I tucked her in my spot in the bed and smiled when she turned on her side and buried her face in Ben-the-Bear's fur. The bear stared at me with black plastic eyes.

Naomi remained still.

You were in Uz. But you didn't realize it.

In Phoebe's room, the stuffed animals appeared to have gained some semblance of order on the bed. Most were sitting up facing me, how Phoebe always set them up. Like sentries. The bunny with tiny red eyes and long, dangling ears, Foppy, sat hunched on the bed's edge. Hadn't that bunny fallen to the floor? Yes, it had and then I picked it up without even thinking about it, like so many of the other actions I performed as a parent that became reflex many, many years ago. I'd walk through the house, picking up toys, folding towels, even making the beds and a moment afterward have only a vague memory of what I'd done.

The animals stared at me with plastic eyes and I had the stupidest feeling they could actually see me. That wasn't quite right, though. It was more like something could see me through all those fake eyes, like they were tiny versions of the witch's magic mirror. Something was watching me, daring me to investigate.

Go ahead, come in, pick one of us up, look at us REAL close.

Foppy had fallen but I had not picked him up. I had left him—*it*—on the floor. I was sure.

Pretty sure.

Sure, you're sure, those plastic eyes said in their dead way, *so why don't you come in here and get as close as you can, eye-to-eye, and see what you find. Convince yourself we're merely cotton and plastic. Come on in and take a SUPER CLOSE look.*

I felt immediately stupid. I shut the bedroom door, doing it a little harder than I intended and stood still in the vibrating thud.

The house settled to stillness.

✝

"What was that?" I asked my dad.

He sat in the armchair across from the couch, that one hand still hidden, right over left.

I sat on the couch and adjusted the cushions where Phoebe had been. He didn't say anything, and I thought he might have fallen asleep as he had last Thanksgiving, falling dead asleep before a plate of food. As he had earlier tonight on the toilet.

"Dad?"

He whispered something, a fragment from a dream, perhaps. Maybe not even English.

"Dad?" I said louder.

"What do you want me to say?" He sounded hard-edged, angry.

I flinched, unable to help it. "What's wrong?"

"I was trying to sleep. I heard something going on in here. What were you doing?"

"Phoebe's prayer place—never mind. You shouldn't get out of bed in the night. What if you fall?"

"I'm not incapacitated."

That wasn't the question I wanted to ask anyway. I wanted to know how he'd suddenly gotten so much strength in his hands. Especially his right one.

"I'm concerned, that's all."

"Concerned I'm getting better?"

There was a threatening tone there—or was I imagining that?

I said nothing. Before all this, meaning life since the stroke and the heart attack, my father had been a very even-tempered man. People praised his degree of patience. He could sermonize for a half hour in competition with a chorus of unruly, crying babies and not once show even the slightest irritation.

Four years ago, my father came to live with us. Though he wasn't pleased about leaving the only home he had known for the last thirty years, he was grateful to be around the girls, exchanging hugs and smiles in moments perfect for greeting cards. The girls loved having grandpa at home. Naomi and I were grateful too, mostly. We weren't especially grateful when he decided to do everyone's laundry and dumped a half gallon of Clorox on load after load, and we weren't grateful when he let the toilet in his bathroom stay clogged for three days before telling us, and we weren't always grateful when he offered parental advice ("What you should tell those girls is..."), but mostly it was good having him around. Naomi's divorced parents lived on opposite sides of the county: one in California, the other, Miami. They visited on holidays, but the girls deserved at least one everyday grandparent.

Dad enjoyed being grandpa, he and Phoebe had gotten very close, but he missed being a priest. And of all the things he missed about his time as pastor at Saint John's, it was the pilgrimages he longed to experience again. I figured those were out of the question, and this was before he suffered his physical setbacks—he was getting weaker and growing a bit hairy in the memory department, hence our Cloroxed clothes and his shit-stuffed toilet, but a year ago, my dad seemed like he might be up to it. I was still hesitant until David Javan called to say he was going to join my father, be a human crutch for the old man.

David was a priest and an MD, which he joked was helpful when performing exorcisms. My father met him upstate during one of those pilgrimages and they developed a fast friendship. Nothing unites a pair of priests, apparently, like exorcism humor.

They went on their own pilgrimage and, far as I knew, everything went well.

He returned three weeks later and suffered a stroke. A minor one. It happened in the middle of the night and Naomi and I didn't get concerned until he wasn't up by nine the next morning. His right side was frozen, that side of his face sagging like the skin might slide off his skull. He could talk but most of it was mumbling. I thought this might be it and I was immediately very grateful for the time we had him in our home.

He got better.

Two months of rehab and he made a near-full recovery. Impressive for a man his age. Then came the heart attack. First of his long life. Doctor said had it been number two or three, he never would have survived. But the body was strong. He came out of it okay, at least at first.

God gave him one more chance and Ben Masters recovered. Four months of rehab later, he came back to us. He seemed normal. Then he started getting ornery. Bicker for no reason. He once threw a glass of water across the kitchen in response to some comment I forgot the moment it was out. I casually asked his doctor during one of Dad's routine checkups if such behavior was typical. The doctor said without hesitation dementia was very common. "A blight on those of us who survive long enough," he said. "We get old and then we forget how we got there. Forget who we are, too."

I did not tell Dad what his doctor said, nor did I share it with Naomi, but she worried anyway he might hurt the girls and while possible, my dad could barely get around without help. That water glass toss had crippled him for a good twenty minutes, sitting at the kitchen table wheezing in choking gasps. Since then, he'd only gotten weaker.

Until he squeezed my hand hard enough to cut off blood flow.

He might be old, both a stroke and a heart attack victim, but even the ill have adrenaline. He heard Phoebe and me in here trapped in some late-night hallucinatory exercise and he freaked. Adrenaline gushed through him and he came out here and yanked me by the wrist. Now, he was crashed in the armchair, wheezing away.

Only he wasn't wheezing.

Actually, he appeared to be breathing almost normally with the slightest hitch on the intake. He sounded good. Very good.

"Are you feeling better?" I asked.

"Why? Don't you want me to get better?"

His eyes cleared, clouds parting, but not for light—for the shadowed orb of an eclipsed sun, a burning sort of darkness. *Like some kind of astrological sign*, I thought. Only located in his eyeball where that cataract was.

Or had been.

"I'll help you back to bed."

"I'll be fine."

He didn't move. One of his pajama pant legs was twisted above his calf. The brown-spotted skin and white leg hair reminded me of a deep-sea creature.

"Dad—I ask you a question?"

He waited.

"Why did you tell me about that Toft kid?"

He shrugged. There was something gruesome about it, like his body was sinking into itself, bones grinding against bones. And he was still hiding that hand. If it hurt him, I assumed he'd tell me. If it was serious, I'd found out eventually.

"I was trying to help Phoebe with her nightmares," I said finally.

He looked at me, his face half in shadow. "You can't fight nightmares."

"No? What does God say about it?"

My dad had always been quick with biblical references and especially fast lately with calling up apt passages.

I figured he'd mention the thief coming in the night again.

"God has nothing to do with nightmares," he said. "They belong to the other guy."

✝

After he went back to his room, shuffling steadily with his hands in the pockets of his sweat pants, I went upstairs to the office. Naomi's stuff occupied the floor and bags and crates of colored paper and stuffed folders lined the walls, but she always let me use the desk. The bookshelf featured a mix of theological titles and guidebooks for creating a more dynamic classroom. My books were dark colored and bland; hers, bright and glossy.

I turned on the computer and opened up the sermon I planned on delivering in a few hours, but I closed it again after a moment and opened a blank document. I had a new idea. I always typed the sermon and then cut and pasted it into digestible portions on index cards.

A half hour later, mid-pasting of index cards, something occurred to me and I stopped. I looked around and for a fraction of a second someone was standing in the office doorway. A shadowy figure (*The Uz Monster*) dissipated into swirling dark. For a moment, it unnerved me.

I had been writing about Job, the poor cursed inhabitant of The Land of Uz, and I thought again of my father's heart attack.

Is grandpa dying?

Concerned I'm getting better?

Two months later when Dad came back to his single room that had once been my garage—that very night—Phoebe had the first of the scream-inducing nightmares. The same exact night.

I'm sure of it.

That Sunday morning, the day of the accident, my sermon was about Job and his awful suffering. It was as if I knew what was headed my way. It's a wonder I didn't hear the chatter of devils in the back of the church, all giddy with the promise of coming miseries.

After the service, a man with grey hair and wearing pinstripe pants and a black blazer told me that for an Episcopalian, I wasn't half as illogical as he would have guessed. This was David Javan and he was joking, or so I assumed, considering he was the one who on occasion cracked exorcism jokes. But I hadn't seen him in a few years. He had been a priest in western New York and had gotten his medical degree with a concentration on infectious diseases. He said he wanted to help "all those dying kids in Africa."

"It's good to see you," he said. "I've been remiss."

He was looking at my father who was standing up by the kneeler before the altar, back to us, head tilted toward the giant cross.

"No, no," I started to say. "He's okay. He's had his rough spots."

"But he's all right?"

Concerned I'm getting better?

Dad hadn't hesitated when kneeling to receive the wine and wafer during communion. Not even a slight groan. He held out only one open hand, however.

"This is the body of Christ," I had said as I set the wafer in his open palm. He whispered something to me, but I hadn't caught it, so I leaned in, thinking maybe he needed help back to the pew, Naomi and the girls kneeling to his right, Naomi sipping the wine from Lavon who was serving as lay reader, or that he needed his oxygen.

"You all right, Dad?" I whispered.

"I asked if that's what this is," he said. "The body of Christ."

He gestured with his hands as if he wanted me to take a real, close look. The wafer featured a stenciled cross. His cataract looked almost transparent, as if it were fading. Last night when we were in the living room, that cataract had been an eclipsed sun, but that was a trick of the light and this was no optical illusion.

"If I eat this, am I cannibalizing the savior?"

Catholics believed the bread and wine offered at Communion was the body and blood of Christ, that during the service it *actually* transformed into flesh and blood, even though the appearance didn't change. This was called transubstantiation. At Saint John's, our wine was from six-dollar bottles, and heavily watered, and the cross-tattooed wafers were purchased from a church supply company. We believed in the fine art of symbolism. No magic required.

"What is it, Dad?"

He stared at me and the cataract seemed to fade even more, a cloud thinning across a blue sky. He popped the wafer in his mouth and chewed into a grin. There was something repulsive about how he kept chewing, smiling and staring at me.

Then Lavon was offering the wine and my father gulped from the chalice and I was moving down the line, depositing wafers in open hands.

I shook off the odd memory of communion and nodded at David. "You look good."

He was younger than my father, only in his sixties, and his gray hair reflected the sharpness of polished silver, and he had a strong body, a marathon runner's build.

"I've been away for a while."

"Ministry or medical?"

"You know I'm retired."

"So vacation then. Anywhere good?"

He made a "perhaps" gesture.

"Well, I'm sure you'd like to talk to my father, and I have a vestry meeting I need to get to."

"The Great Reverend Masters," he said with a knowing smile.

"At least around here," I said.

He hesitated, but barely, as if what he was about to add was some kind of secret but trusting me was not really much of an issue. "I'm over at Word of Christ Church now."

The mega-church in its sprawling complex, a veritable compound, a half-hour away, where a flashy, near televangelist-type of preacher named Reverend Roves helped lure in hundreds of people every week. He preached the unquestioned doctrine and people emptied wallets into collection plates.

"Thought you were retired."

He shrugged. "What am I supposed to do? No wife, no kids. Too old for the medical scene."

"So, you're Reverend Roves' backup?"

He chuckled in an uncertain way. "Not quite. It's not my church. Not that one. They got me in an office reading finance reports."

"Exciting way to spend retirement."

"It was good to see you, Lucas."

He waited and it seemed there was more he wanted to add, a hidden something that couldn't be handed out but had to be pried free.

"You didn't take communion," I said.

"I had a big breakfast."

"Bet you saved room for a pastry or two, though, didn't you?"

"You Episcopalians, kings of coffee hour."

I shook his hand again. Naomi and the girls were heading down the center aisle, Tamara skipping with the exuberant joy only a kid can guiltlessly display after church has dismissed. Phoebe smoothed her yellow Sunday dress and assiduously adjusted the butterfly clips in her hair.

David hadn't left. "Your father's been okay?"

"Sure," I said with a politician's grin. "Why?"

"I was just talking to him and we should talk." He leaned in, his stare trying to bore into me. "It may be urgent."

"Urgent? What about?"

"Your father ... He is not well."

"What do you mean? It's his hand, right? I knew something was wrong."

He didn't respond, as if the problem were obvious.

"Should I take him to the hospital?"

"Won't help."

"What are you talking about?"

"May I call you tonight?"

He leaned toward me again, his words insistent, which pushed a "Sure" from my lips. "Can you at least tell me what this is about? Because if my father is sick, I need—"

"It's complicated. I'll call you. I need to see someone first."

"See someone? Who? A specialist?"

"Tonight. You'll be home?"

"Yeah. Should I be concerned?"

He made an ambiguous gesture that could go either way and started off.

"God bless," I said a bit uneasily. There was something urgently wrong with my father, yet not urgent enough to stop David from seeing someone first. An expert, perhaps.

He glanced over his shoulder, eyes trailing past me toward my father. "Let's hope."

He left as Tamara grabbed my leg and Naomi kissed me on the cheek.

"Was that David?" Naomi said. "It's been a while. What did he want?"

Your father... He is not well.

I hadn't told Naomi about last night, about the whole Land of Uz thing. I didn't want her to worry and I didn't want to think about it, either—it was like a strange dream that persisted with its troubling images and could only be discounted with persistent denial; to share it was to actually give it longer life—and, besides, I wasn't sure how to explain the conversation with my father, any of our interactions in the last day actually. Last night's had seemed so bizarre and, I'll be honest, scary, so maybe it was best relegated to the troubling-dream category.

We said perfunctory goodbyes, discussed ordering Italian for dinner, and then they headed out to the parking lot and I went to retrieve my dad. I glanced back once halfway down the aisle and caught my three girls in the late-morning sunshine: the light silhouetted them in the open doorway—Naomi in the middle, a daughter on either side, her hand on Tamara's neck, and Phoebe's arms stretching for the sky as if willing herself to take flight.

First, go light.

Now, fly.

They stepped out of the doorway and were gone.

"Dad?"

I stopped a few feet behind him. My father stood, back to me, still staring up at the altar and the giant dangling Jesus. The altar was simple, the colors muted. Tails of smoke curled from the extinguished candles. The potted white lilies before the altar smelled faintly sweet and slightly rotten.

He'd always been a tall man, a giant when I was a boy, but he'd shrunken since the stroke. After the heart attack, he walked with a noticeable arch in his back. That Igor-hump was gone. He stood tall again, a hair or two above me. He held the cane at his side with the laziness of an unneeded umbrella.

"Dad? Naomi and the girls are waiting to take you home." I touched his arm and the muscles beneath his suit tightened. "You okay?"

"On the cross, Jesus cried out he was forsaken," Dad said in a deep tone very much like his old sermon voice. "In that moment, a demon came to him and offered salvation. It whispered in his ear and into his heart and promised to release him from this misery."

"I hadn't heard that."

"It's there, if you read between the lines. Jesus is beaten, he is weak, and he is tempted."

"And what did he do?"

"What would you do? He was in agony, suffering—he took the deal and gave up the ghost."

"Some people might disagree with your interpretation."

When Jesus was in the desert for forty days, the Devil came to him and tempted him three times, once to make Jesus turn rocks to bread, once to make him plummet from a tower, and once to offer him all the kingdoms of earth. Jesus, of course, resisted each time. There is no mention of the Devil returning while Jesus suffered on the cross, but I think we assume he's there somewhere, hanging back with the heckling crowd.

"I'm all over this church, you know," he said. "My hands have been everywhere. My blood, my tears—all of it—given to this place. This place is me. I *am* this church."

"I know, Dad."

"I want you to remember that."

"What's on your mind, Dad?"

"God sent His only son to save us. He sent him because He wanted us to know the depth of His love. Right?"

"So we say."

He grunted. There were other faiths that believed Jesus' death was a ransom, a perfect life in exchange for another perfect life: Adam's. For me to believe that, I'd also have to believe in a talking serpent.

"You ever wonder what Jesus thought about it?"

"He had a mission. He understood."

"Yes, but did he *want* to do it?"

"Ultimately, he wanted whatever God wanted."

"Never mind the Trinity, the father, son, and holy ghost. I'm asking, as a *man*, did Jesus want to heal the sick and then die on a cross with broken arms and a crown of thorns?" He spoke without the slightest strain or wheeze.

"It was what had to be done."

"Would you do it?"

When I didn't respond, he faced me. His eyes were clear, as if the cataract had vanished, and red swirls blotched his cheeks. "Would you willingly go through all that pain, all that torture, all that denial? Would you do that?"

"I'd do it to save my family."

"But would you do it if I commanded you to?"

I broke his gaze. "Where's all this coming from, Dad?"

His hands were joined, but not in prayer. He was pushing something into his left palm, jamming it in there. But for a moment, I didn't register what he was doing because that hand was almost completely black. A charred scrap of wood abandoned in a fire pit. I was about to comment on his hand (*diseased, has to be diseased*), when I heard a tiny *drip-drip*: blood droplets spotted the railing.

"Dad, what are you—?"

His hands parted, his gold cross lapel pin in his right hand, the pointed back jutting out in a spike, the tip wet with blood.

"Dad—"

He held his left hand out over the railing and squeezed it into a black fist. His skin was frayed in places, like shedding snake skin. Blood pushed between his fingers and dripped from his palm.

"This is my church," he said.

He opened his hand to show the self-made stigmata, a bloody splotch in an unnaturally dark palm, and flapped it down on the railing. He smeared blood over the wood in a paintbrush swoosh.

"Dad, what are you—"

He grabbed my wrist with that black, diseased hand and his fingers dug into my flesh like icicles and he twisted my arm, pain flaring in my elbow.

Don't you want me to get better?

"I asked you a question." It was the same stone face he had when I was seven and he caught me in the garage with anti-freeze. Stone forged of guilt and fortified with rage. "If I commanded you go through all Jesus endured, would you do it? Would you do it because you are my son?"

He twisted my arm and fresh pain erupted in my elbow. *He's going to break my arm*, I thought in stupid shock.

"Jesus, Dad, enough!"

He held on a moment longer, his uncut fingernails burrowing into my skin, my arm twisting, and he grinned at me, a grin like a warped jack-o-lantern rictus, and yellowy phlegm bubbled in the corner of his mouth.

He let go.

I fell back several steps and rubbed my wrist. The pain there faded but my elbow throbbed as if hyperextend. My father was looking at his infected hand, like it had grabbed me of its own accord. Like it was no longer under his control. Blood dribbled on the carpet.

"What the hell is wrong with you?" The word "hell" echoed briefly in the church.

"I'm sorry?" He said it as a question.

"Dad, I'm concerned."

He nodded, glanced at his injured palm, wiped it on his leg. It left a small red streak. "Are you?"

I could have slapped him, but maybe that was my throbbing elbow talking and my injured pride. "Something is wrong with your hand. Why did you do that?"

"All things are possible to him that believe." He walked toward me, and I stepped back. He hesitated a second as he passed, and my hands came up in reflex. Or maybe self-defense.

"Naomi and the girls are waiting."

He grunted something and kept walking toward the doors to the parking lot.

I wanted him to say something more. I wanted him to apologize. Really apologize, showing he understood what had happened. I wanted him to tell me he felt genuinely awful and maybe he should go to the hospital because another stroke or heart attack was coming. I wanted him to be concerned about his hand. I wanted a reasonable explanation.

Your father ... He is not well.

He didn't say anything, just kept walking on the blue carpet and out into the rectangle of door light and was gone. For several minutes, I stood alone in the empty church.

✝

Fractures of lopsided glances, tattered images and ruptured thoughts and I hear half-severed phrases and squeaking sneakers on linoleum, screaming bursts and strangled cries. *You're in shock*, someone says, a woman, I think, and I want to tell her this isn't shock because I know what that feels like. I was fourteen when I jumped into Henry Ruben's pool in the middle of December when the temperature plummeted below freezing. My limbs numbed, my lips turned blue, and the world toppled upside down or maybe only sideways, wrong somehow and Henry's mother freaked, called 9-1-1 and someone, a paramedic maybe, said, *Don't worry, he's just in shock*. I remember what that felt like, pin-pricking numbness, a sense my heart wasn't quite working correctly, pumping so slowly and then galloping in bursts, banging around in there like a rabid fox had been sewed inside me. I knew that well. That was shock.

This is worse.

People tell me to be calm. A woman with a seashell of blonde hair across her forehead says, *You have to try to relax.* And how very much I want to, too, if someone could shut up the asshole screaming his head off around here. Sounds like someone is ripping off the poor bastard's testicles. Give the guy drugs, something. Anything. The woman with the hair on her forehead is shouting at me, as if this is my fault. *You have to calm down. You have to relax.* She smells of antibacterial soap, but the V of her blue scrubs hangs down to reveal the tops of wonderfully shaped breasts and I reach for them and she lets me have them, for a moment, so soft and wonderful, and guilt, an enormous stampeding herd of it, crushes me, grounds me into the dirt, shatters my every bone.

Try to relax.

How can I relax when that guy keeps screaming? Make *him* relax. I don't even know what's going on. What is this place? The floor slips beneath me, everything so squeaky smooth. A boat at sea with a fancy, tiled deck. The light is bright but not sunshine-bright, no those are fluorescent lights, or LED lights like the night lights in Phoebe's bedroom, and I can't shut them out. They burn through my eyelids.

There's blood on my hands—only it's not mine.

This is to help you calm down, the woman with the hair and the breasts says. She looks like my wife, only younger. Like Naomi looked all those years ago, her skin smooth, her smile effortless. We were so young. Untarnished. The woman has a needle, a syringe, and it's filled with something and I don't want that stuff inside me. Why are you doing this to me? I'm not the problem. What about that other guy, the screaming one? Why can't you do something about him? I reach for her and my arms stretch and stretch and wobble in the air before me. I'm falling backwards. Dropping. Why won't they catch me? The woman smiles down at me, a Thanksgiving Parade balloon with an awful, enormous grin of stupidly white teeth and huge, inflated breasts.

You threw yourself on her. You freaked, like Henry's mom, and that's why they're doing this to you. Why you must rest. But I didn't throw myself at her. She could have fought me off. She let me touch her. No one has to know. I'm sorry.

Sorry doesn't cut it down here, friend.

They push me into warm water. It splashes over my face and I choke on it. It burns my throat. I can't breathe. It sloshes like water, but I'm not wet. *You need to relax.* Relax? RE-lax? RELAX? No, what I need is to *know*. I need to know the truth. What is this? Where am I? What is going on?

You're in the ICU.

I SEE YOU what?

No, not like that—like this: *You're in a hospital. There's been an accident. Your family was in a car that—*

She wipes sweat from my forehead and there's a splotch of blood on the white towel. I know without asking and I hate that I know. It's Naomi's blood. She's in here somewhere, in the I. SEE. YOU. Her face is bubbled and crooked, a wax figure left beneath a heat lamp, and her blood is everywhere. When I grab her, try to yank her back to me, to hoist her up and out, to pull off these wires and tubes, like she's a damn machine, her blood wets my face and neck and for a moment it's her soft kisses under my Adam's Apple, her gentle, teasing breath along my collar, her fingers tugging my ear.

Please, I cry but that isn't all of it, no, not by a long shot. Your wife is here, yes, and so are your daughters.

You have to calm down.

Voices cackle all around and something is beeping, beeping, beeping—dinner is done, check the meat, put a fork in it, it's done, done, done and dead. They're all dead.

Don't let them be dead. Please don't let them be dead. I'm sorry. I'm so sorry. I know I thought dark things, bad things, during those long nights when Phoebe cried and cried and nothing I could do would quiet her or when she covered half her bedroom wall in thick crayon, every one of her crayons worn down to little nubs and the drywall warping and cracking, and I screamed at her. I didn't mean those things. I was tired. I was weak. I wasn't the father I wanted to be. Don't let them be dead! Don't take my girls!

"You have to calm down," she says.

Make him stop screaming, I try to say.

But, of course, that's what she's trying to do—calm the screaming man who just saw his mangled wife and tried to drag her out of her hospital bed.

✝

Even before I saw it, I knew it wasn't right. I sensed this was the wrong place, but it was too late to turn back. The green highway sign jammed into the grassy peak. *Rolling Hills*, the sign read in loopy script.

This isn't the place.

No, this was someplace else. The white cursive letters faded into the sign as if into sludge. The sign slumped sideways, crumbled in from the corners with loud, harsh metallic grinding sounds, the squeal of a prehistoric beast. The ground groaned open in a black maw and swallowed the sign. A crevasse with no bottom. Somehow, I knew that. If I fell into that hole, I'd fall forever. I would die at some point and yet still descend. I might fall faster and faster, my body flipping head over feet, arms flailing, but there was no ground rushing upward to meet me.

That's where it lives. It lives in a place with no bottom. Abaddon. A bad one.

In a rapid wave, the grass blackened as if burned, an unstoppable disease killing all the green with no more force than a gentle breeze. I smelled wet, rotting wood and something even more foul. I heard a sound like wind only with a deep white-noise vibration, the sound of living things singing together, the sound of a swarm swirling closer and closer, getting louder, shaking the ground like a stampede of a thousand horses.

Abaddon the Destroyer. The King of the Locusts. The Uz Monster.

Coming for Phoebe.

✝

I woke in a hospital.

I sensed other people there, but I didn't want to see them yet, wanted a respite of solitude—there was something awful waiting for me in this world and I didn't want to know what it was yet, though surely I sensed it, so I stayed as still as possible, my breathing calm, and listened.

"It's so shocking," a man mumbled.

"I don't believe it," a woman said. "I. Don't. Be—*lieve*. It."

"It's going to work out," another man said a bit shakily.

"Yeah," said the first man. "How's that? One daughter dead, and a wife and child in a coma."

"Is it Phoebe?" I said without moving from the top of a made bed. My voice sounded strong and I knew by the voices who was in the room and on whom I could depend for an honest response.

"Oh, Jesus," Iris said in surprise and laughed uneasily. She was twenty-nine, married, and had two kids. She was the youngest member on the church's vestry and as secretary kept meticulous notes on yellow legal pads, her penmanship done in perfect neat little letters. She suffered a miscarriage last spring and her penmanship had become even more rigid and precise.

George and Lavon stepped to either side of the bed. They looked tired, the kind of tired earned after a day's wandering lost in the woods.

"How are you feeling?" George asked. He was closing in on sixty, serving his eighth term on the vestry and acting as Senior Warden, which in Episcopalian speak translated to class president.

"Tell me: is it Phoebe?"

George started to respond and couldn't find the words. Lavon grabbed my arm, squeezed, Mister Reliable. "There was an accident, Lucas. Tamara didn't survive. I'm so sorry."

I heard precisely what he said, each word perfectly clear and unambiguous in meaning, yet somehow, I didn't get it.

And I thought I knew about shock.

As usual, Lavon Solly wore green overalls. He was a semi-retired farmer who once had a huge business in the area—Lavon's Dairy, and his truck even sported a vanity plate, MILK MAN. He was a widower but never had children, though he didn't tote around any regrets.

At the vestry meeting last spring when Iris broke down and wept about her lost child, Lavon hugged her and let her cry until the worst of the sobbing passed.

He squeezed my arm again as I fought through tears. But maybe I didn't fight through those tears. I remember the hospital, the nurse with the blonde hair and the breasts, and all that happened afterward, but I don't know about the crying. I remember the pain—I carry it still as a rock in my gut that weighs millions of pounds—but I don't remember the crying. Maybe I don't want to. People say grieving is messy.

People don't know shit.

"What else?" I asked.

Lavon didn't hesitate, thankfully. "Your father is dead. Naomi and Phoebe are alive but in critical condition."

I nodded as if all of this registered. Had all of it registered I might have started screaming again, maybe screamed so hard I'd blow a vessel in my brain. I could go like Mom: vessel pop and all stations offline.

"Where's Naomi?"

"She's in ICU," George said. He wiped tears off his face as if ashamed.

Iris stood at the foot of the bed. Her expression reeked of pity.

"No," I said. "My *wife*. Where is she? I need her. I need to see her. She has to know about this. Oh, God, I have to tell her. No one else can tell her. I need her."

Lavon tightened his grip on my arm. "Relax."

I wanted to curse him out, curse all of them. I wanted to yank free from Lavon's grip and jump off this bed and punch George right in his tear-strewn face. *How dare you cry,* I wanted to scream. *How dare you fucking cry. You should be ashamed. You should beg for me not to knock in your goddamn teeth.*

"My wife..."

The three of them stared at me not saying anything, but I knew what was going on. George, Lavon, and Iris were my welcoming party.

Welcome to The Land of Uz, where all we know is suffering.

"Doctor," I said.

The three of them nearly fought for the honor to find one.

✝

The doctor was a young man with slight shoulders, light complexion and an Indian name, Patel or Fadi, not those but close. He gave me the rundown as if it were game highlights for some psychotically macabre sport. Naomi had two broken legs, a femur in one and both tibias, a fractured hip, a broken wrist and a right arm fractured in four places, three broken ribs and two cracked; she suffered extensive bruising throughout and inside her body, including on her lungs and along her trachea, a broken mandible jaw bone, a fractured zygoma, and a scleral hemorrhage, which was bleeding beneath the white of her right eye, but all of her internal organs appeared fine. All, save for her brain.

"Your wife has an acute subdural hematoma," Dr. Not-Patel, Not-Fadi said. "Her skull took a massive trauma during the accident and it appears bone fragments have sliced brain tissue. We have sedated her to help ease the pressure and need to operate within the next few hours."

"Wasn't she wearing her seatbelt?"

"In an accident like this, a seatbelt doesn't make much of a difference."

"I don't understand."

The doctor looked uncertain. I was sitting up in bed and the room spun lazily.

"Let me tell you about your daughter," he said.

Phoebe had gotten at least somewhat luckier than her mother. She had only some bruising, including several bruised ribs, and an extradural hematoma. She was in an induced coma while the bleeding in her head was monitored and a cause of action determined. If the pressure eased, no surgery would be needed. If the pressure increased, options would be discussed.

Options. How completely ominous.

"Thank you," I said.

The doctor nodded and went away and I was left with the most absurd of ideas: I had been told my family was in some kind of awful car accident, one of my daughters was dead, the other in an induced coma, and my wife was as beat up as if she fell from a plane without a parachute and, although he didn't say it, the doctor implied, she probably wouldn't make it, and I *thanked* the guy who told me.

I should have punched him in the face. That, at least, would have been more befitting the moment.

✝

Welcome to The Land of Uz, where nothing is real except your fear.

That thought came from nowhere, or at least from somewhere I couldn't yet identify, and if there's any credibility to prognostication, perhaps that was my moment. Not that there was anything I could do about it. My Job-like suffering was rapidly approaching, a meteor descending, and there was nothing to be done.

I was sitting in my little church office, the vestry meeting finally over, and I was trying to process what had been said into a cognizant memo. I leaned back in the squeaky office chair and absently rubbed my wrist.

Don't you want me to get better?

Was my father actually getting better? How had he had so much strength?

What about that black hand? Didn't it hurt him?

Sitting at the ancient computer with the yellow-stained sides as it wobbled on the metal typewriter desk, I thought about faith, which is how I most often spent my desk time.

I was sitting there, typing, the small window beside me looking out on the yard and the woods beyond, the November sunshine bright with the lost promise of summer, sitting there in my Sunday dress clothes I wore beneath those fancy vestments, the wooden cross with the hemp rope around my neck Naomi and the girls gave me last Christmas.

"It's authentic, right from the holy land," she told me.

I had been thinking about faith in some vague way, and I touched the cross as absently as scratching an itch on my temple.

Then the phone rang.

✞

A police officer found me in a room that had two worn couches and four plushy chairs. There were no windows, just generic prints on the walls of waterfalls and fields stretching to the horizon. One was of a corn field with a setting sun lighting the golden stalks.

The cop was tall and thin, his bulky gun slung against bony hips. "Your wife was driving a 2009 Camry containing your father and two daughters. They were driving on Cliffside Road when they crashed head-on with a 2013 Acura. A teenager was driving, speeding. He was the only one in that car. He is in critical condition. He crashed directly into the front passenger side where your father was seated."

I nodded.

"After impact, the Camry ricocheted into the trees lining the road. The trees stopped the car, it tipped, lodged against them but it didn't fall off the shoulder. Police were called within five minutes. I'm afraid that's all we know so far."

Five minutes. My family had lain in a wrecked car, bleeding and dying, for five minutes before another car came along and someone called the cops. Five minutes in which I was sitting on a cushiony chair in a cozy office during a vestry meeting listening to people gripe about service attendance and donations.

"Who was it who called?"

The cop hesitated. "First person on the scene."

"Can you tell me who?"

"The woman's name is Maggie Prescott."

"Can I talk to her?"

"There's a lot you need to deal with right now, sir."

✞

George brought me a vending machine sandwich and a Coke. The sandwich was as stiff as cardboard, tasted like it too, and the soda impossibly sweet. I kept eating and drinking even as my stomach roiled in nausea.

"You don't have to stay," I said to George and Lavon. Iris had left at some point, some people had living families, after all.

"We're here for you," George said and Lavon patted my shoulder.

In the hallway someone burst into startled laughter.

"Must've been a good joke," George said.

Our room hummed with silence.

"I have to call Naomi's parents."

"In time," Lavon said. "Take it easy."

"I can't sit here." My legs vibrated with energy like coiled springs trying to erupt.

"It's the best you can do right now."

"You guys don't need to stay."

"We're not leaving."

Because if we left, their faces said, *you'd have no one.*

A nurse, this one with brown hair pulled tight against her head, tight enough to bulge veins in her temples, came in at some point and asked if I wanted to see my daughter. *The live one or the dead one?* I thought of asking. Instead, I nodded and followed her. George and Lavon stayed behind.

We walked past rooms where people slept, rooms where TVs droned on and on, rooms where families gathered around beds and joked and laughed and hoped no one would say the obvious, as in, *You realize this means something is seriously wrong.* Nurses said hi to the nurse leading me and offered me hesitant smiles. Doctors ignored everyone in the name of the Chromebook or iPad clutched before them like a life preserver. The whole place stank of cleaning products, of the acidic bite of Clorox or something even more potent. I actually longed for the artificial smell of one of Naomi's Plug-Ins. There were no shadows; the overhead lights were steady and blanched everything below.

At some point, in the elevator, descending below ground, it became clear to which daughter I was headed. When the doors opened, I could barely walk. My legs felt heavy and my stomach knotted. *Not the morgue, please not the morgue.* I could think of nothing worse than this nurse with the bulging temple veins pushing open the door to the area marked Morgue and saying, "She's right over there. You can pull back the curtain. Don't mind the autopsy instruments." I imagined the cold of such a macabre place, as if the whole area were one giant freezer storage for corpses. The dim light would reflect in disorienting orbs across the stainless-steel wall of corpse drawers.

Would they really autopsy my daughter? Would they do it without telling me?

No reason to cut her open. Besides, she's pretty much cut up already.

"Please," I said in a voice I didn't recognize. *Can't possibly be me. I don't sound that pathetic, do I?*

The nurse turned, her face morphed into concern and then practiced response. She came to my side, took my arm with one hand and my back with the other and asked if I felt dizzy. We stopped in the hallway. An orderly in a blue uniform pushed a cart slowly past. One of the wheels squeaked.

"I can't," I said.

"Okay. That's okay."

Her pitying look rammed me with another truckload of guilt.

"No, no," I said. "Show me."

A few feet later, however, I stopped again. I put one arm on the wall and then rested completely against it. "I'm sorry. I can't do it."

She tried the pity angle again, but I looked away. "I want to see my other daughter. I want to see Phoebe."

She hesitated and my heart stopped.

No, no, no. She can't be down here, too. She can't be dead. And my wife too, I suppose. Why not? In for a penny, in for a pound. Of flesh. A snippet of Shakespeare came to me from some dusty corner: *All my pretty ones? Did you say all? O hell-kite! All?* And then, a final offering, *Did heaven look on, and would not take their part?*

I chuckled. I thought I could swallow the laughter, but it burbled up and gurgled out. My chuckle crackled hollowly and morphed into something close to a mad cackle. It echoed down the hallway.

The nurse rubbed my back as if I were suffering a coughing fit. It helped at first and then I thought I might lose it and keep laughing, louder and louder, seize with giant, hiccuping laughs that sounded like grunts. I'd fall to the floor, unable to stop. Tears would spurt from my eyes and I'd grip my sides from the pain and laugh and laugh and laugh until I could no longer suck in a whistle of air.

Slowly, the laughing eased and stopped. It felt like I endured a bout of painful vomiting.

"She's been taken for tests. I'm sorry."

"She's okay?"

Her smile was hesitant but enough. I breathed again. My lungs burned but that was okay. More than okay. Give me all the pain. All *their* pain. Give all of it to me and I will take it willingly and gratefully.

Have mercy on us and forgive us.

You take away the sins of the world.

"I know this is hard," the nurse said. The vein in her temple throbbed in a tight squiggle. "But you should see her now. It'll help."

I could have laughed but I didn't. If I started laughing again, I might never stop.

✠

Tamara wasn't in the morgue, but she was close to it. Several floors below ground and down a long, barren corridor there were several non-distinct doors marked with only numbers. My daughter was in room 3.

It was a small room with a couch and more of those generic paintings on the wall. One was an ice-capped mountain top. A

54   THE DEVIL VIRUS

box of tissues waited on the couch. In the middle of the room was a gurney and on it was one of my angels.

She looked so small. Didn't they have gurneys for children? *Sure they do, and don't worry—they have coffins for children, too.*

It was not white cloth on top of her but a thin papery sheet that crinkled beneath my touch. Of course it was paper—the cloth sheets were for the living. It was pulled up to her chin. I wondered if I pulled back the sheet to expose her feet, would there be one of those tags dangling from her big toe? Was she headed for one of those cold-storage drawers?

"I'm sorry," I whispered. What else could I say?

Her pale cheeks made me think of slimy things living in mud. *Which is where she's headed. Into the ground. Unless you cremate her. Is that your plan, Lucas, old buddy, old pal? Burn your daughter to crispy ashes?*

Her eyes were closed. Purplish bruising like punk rocker makeup circled one swollen eye. The swelling had only begun and maybe it would even continue. She was dead but the tissue would still swell. Wasn't it true your fingernails kept growing for days after you died or was that the skin receding making the nails appear to grow?

She could have been sleeping. Her thin lips were parted enough for wisps of air. Her hair needed combing. How she hated that. I would tell her to be still and the moment the brush was in her knotty mess of hair, she would scream and pull back. *Let Mommy do it!* Just be still. *No, I want Mommy to do it. It hurts when you do it.*

I smiled.

Please. Don't be here right now. Don't be in this tiny hospital room under ground. Don't be on a bed beneath a paper sheet. Don't be dead. Please, don't be dead.

The sheet was far too large for her tiny body. *That's because she doesn't have much of a body left.* She was crushed in the back seat. Crushed beneath grandpa. Her legs were shattered in multiple places as easily as a dried stick snapping in a child's hands. Her pelvis was crushed. Her ribcage condensed until her ribs popped. Her heart was in there, squished, a useless reddish blob in a sloppy mess of ruined organs.

"I'm so sorry," I said.

This time, I let it all come out.

✝

The nurse was waiting for me. I wanted to hug her and hold on for all it was worth. We stared at each other and though her eyes flushed with renewed pity, I loved her intensely in that moment. She didn't ask how I was. She didn't offer any words of comfort. That only made me love her more. I didn't even know her name.

"Where's my father?" I asked.

✝

Benjamin Masters was in room 1. Naomi was in surgery. And Phoebe, lovely Phoebe— getting tests done. So, who were in the other rooms? Unless someone was lying. *We needed to ease you into the grief. Loss of this magnitude can be especially debilitating to the psyche and to the body. It's jumping into arctic ocean water. You need to ease into it, adjust your body. If you dive in—*

You'll be in shock.

My father's official cause of death was heart attack. He had not been crushed, barely been hurt.

I had spent a lot of time already thinking about God and, specifically, about Job—*Welcome to The Land of Uz*—but standing before my father, he covered in another papery sheet with a block of wood propping up his head, I suffered the first punch of how cruelly unfair this whole thing was.

My daughter had been crushed, pulverized, but my father, in the direct path of the teenager in the Acura, might have escaped the crash with minor bruising and a broken leg, had his heart been able to hold on. Where was the justice in that? He survived the crash because the seat fell back, killing my daughter. Tamara never had a chance. And that's all this was, wasn't it—pure chance?

After 9/11, I spent days reading witness's accounts, watching videos, becoming ensnared in conspiracy theories. Again and again, the difference between those in the towers who lived and those who died came down to freak chance: stepping onto an elevator or just missing one, going to the rest room or staying at a desk, working on the 77th floor or the 78th. Did God decide life and death upon such arbitrary things as elevator rides?

Or car rides? Had I driven my family home, maybe none of this happens. Or at least I'm with them when the oncoming car swerves and crashes into us. At the very least, I would have been there.

If they all die, you can too. No one will even blame you.

That thought was cold, its voice emotionless, yet I took comfort in it. If they all died, I would go with them. That's what a good husband and father should do. The Episcopal faith doesn't spend much time discussing sin and avoids topics of suicide and Hell, preferring instead the love-thy-neighbor New Testament doctrine. I didn't know if suicide was a stamped one-way ticket to a hot place made of brimstone, but I didn't care. As a priest, I probably shouldn't say that. The priesthood might be concerned with truth, but it gives a wide berth to honesty.

✝

This room had no couch, just a lowly gray metal folding chair set before the gurney where my father laid beneath a paper sheet. The paper appeared to float over him with the way his body had stiffened in an awkward mannequin-like pose, right leg slightly arched, torso twisted, one arm straight, the other akimbo. *Rigor mortis.* As with Tamara, his face was not covered, the paper sheet stubbing his chin, but his eyes were closed. He could have been sleeping.

"Tough break, Pop," I said. My voice sounded quite loud in the tiny room. Instead of the same insensitive fluorescent lights throughout the rest of the hospital, these body-viewing rooms (what else might they be called?) had recessed lights in the ceiling as if this were someone's den. The lights were dimmer than their blanching cousins in the hallway but unlike those lights, these could not fight the shadows pooling in the corners and doming down the plain walls in big, exaggerated frowns.

Staring down at my father wasn't so bad. There was the familiar mole on his neck, looking a little red, as if blood-swelled—a collared dress shirt always concealed the mole, and that memory was a slice of solid footing. The accident hadn't killed him, not directly anyway. This was supposed to happen. Not like this of course, not with my wife and girls, but he was supposed to die. He was old, sick, frail—

Frail enough to squeeze my wrist until the fingers numbed. Frail enough to twist my arm, so frail he could have fractured my elbow.

Don't you want me to get better?

Couldn't his apparent improvement been a pre-heart attack induced incident? Same with his improved walking? His sudden ability to breathe without canned oxygen? His fading cataract?

Could there actually be something known as "pre-heart attack induced incidents of hyper-activity and renewed body function"? I saw some TV show once about a guy who was infected with rabies who was violently ill for several days and then, as if touched by God, completely cured. Seemingly. A day later he died. Maybe heart attacks could work similarly. Like the body was harnessing its remaining energy and giving itself one last *hoorah* before kicking off.

I knew nothing of science, save what I had gleaned from TV. Religion, any religion, eschews science like a scrawny kid evading the schoolyard bully, though Episcopalianism (and maybe Unitarianism) occasionally attempt to reconcile differences. For example, creationism need not refute evolution. Why couldn't God have started the evolution snowball tumbling down the hill? I don't think religion needs to fear science but, then again, I never gave my faith a litmus test.

Someone was standing behind me.

I felt the person there, several feet back by the door, the same way I always sensed when Phoebe tried to sneak up behind me. Even before I heard her minute steps on the carpet, I knew she was there. I did not have some special extra-sensory talent like telepathy or precognition, though maybe those do exist and each of us enjoys a little of such things to varying degrees, which is why we wake up in the middle of the night at the precise moment a loved one has perished or get an inexplicable urge to go to a specific place immediately only to find someone there we haven't seen in years but who happens to need a friend right then, but I knew someone was there just the same. The hairs on the back of my neck stirred with that familiar cold tickle. *That's called horripilation*, I thought. *As in horror.* Where had I learned that?

It was the nurse again. Perhaps she'd been called back to her station or was getting tired of escorting me around or maybe she wanted to offer comfort. I felt guilty, using her time as though my concerns (all of the dead-family variety) trumped any she might need to address involving suffering, *living* people. But I was suffering. I shouldn't feel any guilt. I should be self-centered, self-absorbed, so grieved no one else's concerns could penetrate my thinking. Maybe it's because I was a priest or maybe it was because I had no idea what I was doing. I'd been the comforter many times but that is not the understudy for playing the bereaved. There was no preparation for this. Yet, what the hell was wrong with me, worrying about some nurse? Just my mind trying to distract me from what was going on, using guilt to keep me from understanding what the guilt really meant, that my wife was dead, that I was—

No one was at the door.

Perhaps she had been there and slipped back out because she decided not to disturb me. She might've thought I was administering last rites or something. At least praying. The door shimmered slightly. Trick of the light, of course, but for a second that light made it look like the door might open, like the nurse might poke her head in, flinch back when she saw me staring right at her, and apologize and say something about needing to go upstairs but that I could stay as long as I needed. I'd thank her and she'd linger a moment with a sorrowful, pity-ridden expression and she'd remain even as I turned back to my father and I'd feel her standing there, staring.

The way I had felt her a moment ago.

"Hello?" I offered and immediately felt stupid. I sounded ridiculous, one of those bewildered girls in a horror flick where it's obvious she ought to run, run, run for her very life but she continues exploring the house, even wanders down into the basement where the lights flicker, all the while calling in a tiny voice, *Hello? Is anybody down here?*

The quiet of the room fuzzed in my ears. But there was something odd about the door. On the outside, the door had been the bland, sterile kind like every other door in this hospital, but the inside was a peculiar brownish gray, and looked almost like a large splotch had stained it and then gradually faded. Also, it was crooked. Not warped out of shape, cocked a little, canted to the left, a door on a ship rocking on the open sea.

Naomi had gotten me one of those kinetic, perpetual-motion office gadgets CEOs and executives have on their high-polished desks. Mine was a pair of rotating sticks that swirled in opposite directions while the entire thing rocked from side to side. It swayed one way, seemed as if it would tip over, and then rocked all the way to the other side. If stuck on a sermon, or simply delaying doing any work in my little church office, I would tap it and watch it do its thing. Once, I watched it without looking away for at least five minutes and maybe longer. The more I watched, the more captivating it became and the more magical. With each rotation, I was more and more sure the thing would topple over.

I might have stared at that stupid thing for hours. Once I looked away from it, however, I realized with some alarm I might vomit. The office was rocking, almost imperceptibly, back and forth. That same sensation, the feeling something that should not be moving was so very gently swaying, came back to me as I stared at that door.

The sensation was slight, easily deniable, but still there. Could the door have been constructed poorly, a lazy worker eyeballing when he should have been using a level, and now that askew measurement made it appear like the room was tilting?

Even if a building inspector strolled passed, he probably wouldn't notice. Not one door in a building with thousands. I hadn't noticed, not until I was in here and looking behind me because I thought someone was there.

You're freaking a little, I told myself. Understandable, of course. On an intellectual level, I understood this and accepted it. I *was* in shock. It wouldn't be several days until I could get my head around what was going on. *Once you see all the coffins lined up with matching flower arrangements on top, then you'll understand.* Hadn't I woken up a few hours ago to a house rocked with a little girl's screams? And now that scream was only a memory, a ghost of something forever gone.

There's nothing wrong with the door. No matter how fervently I assured myself it was me, not the door, that was off, I grew more and more sure someone had nailed in the doorframe crookedly. But then the door wouldn't close. But the door looked strange, too, like maybe that same worker, realizing his error, shaved off some inches so it would close.

I stepped toward the door and the floor slipped under my feet. I wobbled, arms going out at my sides in reflex, and I must've looked so ridiculous, a drunk trying to walk the yellow line, a kid pretending to be a tightrope walker. I swayed, a buoy on water.

Must have been a wet spot on the floor.

Paper rustled behind me.

A chunk of ice melted in my chest. I strained to hear more but white-noise fuzz filled the room.

I hadn't heard anything. I was staring at the door, trying to make it somehow be a normal, perfectly aligned door when in reality the door was fine—I was the one who was askew, forever askew from now on—and my ears, wanting to get in on the action, played a little trick. That was all.

I turned back to my father. My stomach twisted like a sopping dishrag.

The paper sheet covered his face.

✝

Several conflicting thoughts battled for control and above, or maybe beneath, all those frantic and tremblingly sane thoughts, dizziness like a lingering ache in the back of my head rocked everything in unsteady rhythm.

The sheet had been down beneath his chin. I hadn't really looked at his face, but I remembered distinctly looking at the little black mole on his neck. It was to the left of his esophagus. He always had it and it was one of the reasons he always wore a collared dress shirt beneath his church vestments. I had been looking right at it a minute ago. I was sure because I had been thinking it curious how the mole looked red, as if filled with blood.

His bare feet stuck out now, the sheet pulled up to his ankles. Dangling from the big toe of his closest foot, a yellowy tag stirred as if in a puff of air. It was made of card stock and featured several lines and boxes for classification, but only the name had been filled in in black Sharpie: Masters, Benjamin.

I reached for the tag.

On the far wall, a giant print of Dali's *Christ of Saint John of the Cross* filled a frowning arc of light. It had always been a favorite painting of mine and I even had a small, framed version in my church office; something about the way it evoked a sense of mystery appealed to me—that whole looking-for-answers thing again. But the print hadn't been there before.

The walls had been bare. I was absolutely sure.

As sure as you are about seeing the mole on your father's neck that you've seen since you were a little boy?

Was I seeing things? The question should have been funny. Of course I was seeing things. What else did I think was going on?

Did I think my dead father was moving his paper sheet? Did I believe a Christ painting was appearing out of thin air?

The painting depicts Christ on the cross but there are no nails, no blood, no crown of thorns. The cross floats in a black sky; it is almost parallel to the lake beneath, the extreme angle providing fodder for all sorts of metaphorical interpretations but also inducing a sense of vertigo. Just like the stupid desk toy, the painting *lessens* gravity. It's the sensation of driving over a hill at high speeds and dropping into the descent when your stomach floats apart from your body. The queasy lightness that always made Phoebe sick. Had she suffered that feeling during the crash? Was she feeling it now, getting tests done, trapped in some dark place where machines whirred?

In the painting, Jesus was in the crucified pose, but his body slumped forward toward the lake, his arms straining behind him, his head bowed so only a mop of curly brown hair is seen. It was simultaneously a testament to his holy stature and a tear-inducing depiction of a man so cruelly destroyed. It was in many ways far more powerful than the traditional images of a bleeding Christ on the cross or a robed and crowned Jesus in crucified pose as if to prove his stature beyond mortality, like the sculpted Jesus in Saint John's church.

The print was almost the length of the wall from ceiling to floor. The light deepened the painting's shadows. One long shadow arm stretched along the middle board, what was called the *patibulum* to the shadow head at the far edge of the cross. The shadow looked bigger, out of proportion. Even accounting for the enlarged size of the print, the shadow was even larger than it should have been. A printing error, but—

It wasn't even there before. The walls were bare, blank, empty. The painting shouldn't be there—wasn't there.

The shadow rose, flexed larger and stretched back over the cross toward the middle, right above Jesus' bowed head and throbbed there on the center beam—what was called the *stipes*— a thing pulsing with life. This was a trick of my exhausted mind, a pre-heart attack hallucination, perhaps. Like father, like son.

The shadow melted down onto the sagging shoulders, up the sloping neck, and onto the ruffled hair. It seeped into the hair, water vanishing into cracks. I stepped closer, almost touching the gurney.

Jesus' outstretched arms shook as they must have during his hours of hanging torment. The arms sprang off the *patibulum* and joined together above his head, wrists crossed, a thick metal bolt appeared driven through those wrists and blood ran free to rain on Jesus' bowed head in plopping splatters.

In some faiths, it was believed Jesus did not die on a cross, but rather on a torture stake, a tree perhaps or a simple pole anchored in the ground. Some people believed the cross was actually a holdover from the pagans and worshipping it was a form of idolatrous demonism. Possessing a cross was feared to invite curses. Never mind wearing one around your neck.

Jesus' hair was moving.

It squirmed like worms heaped in a pile, twisting and curling. Two swirls became eyes and a dark spot was a hollow nose and beneath gaped a large mouth with a flicking black tongue.

I leaned closer, right over my father's body, the edge of the gurney pressed against my waist. Paper crumpled. The face was there and then gone, water draining back into the ground. I strained to see it again, like one of those optical illusions in which both a beautiful woman and an old hag coexist and depending on how you look at it you see one or the other, and when you see one it is impossible to see the other.

More whispering crinkles of paper beneath me as I leaned over even farther. Where was the face? Why couldn't I see it?

Because it's not there. The painting's not even there. You're losing it.

The head raised up to reveal a sliver of tannish forehead and then Jesus' head rose completely to face directly out of the image, to emerge *out of the wall*, to stare directly at me. His eyes sagged with crescents of blood and his mouth hung open, cheeks almost translucent, a fish yanked from the water, a dying man straining for one more gasp of air.

The face darkened. The eyes swallowed themselves into black hollows. The nose bloomed open at the tip like a grotesque flower made of skin and cartilage. The lips cracked, split. Teeth burst from bloody gums in crooked crisscrossing clumps, their slanted shapes like the cut-clasp nails used for floorboards.

I stumbled and the floor slid me backwards. I hit the folding chair and plopped awkwardly into it as if someone had shoved me there.

The toe tag swirled in that nonexistent breeze.

There was more writing on it. Beneath Cause of Death, in the same Sharpie, only scrawled in large block letters that crossed over the other lines, it read: DEAD PRIEST.

I looked back up. The wall was bare.

✝

I felt the egg of a scream in my throat wanting to crack. If I did scream, maybe the brown-haired nurse would fling open the door and come to my aid, asking what was wrong while that vein pulsed in her temple. But what if she didn't come? I might go on screaming until I passed out.

Don't leave me, please. Don't leave me alone.

Get a hold of yourself.

I looked at the toe tag again. Masters, Benjamin. Nothing more. Back at the wall: plain tan with shadowy mountain-peak patterns from the recessed lighting. I was overwhelmed, suffered a minor psychotic episode. Such things were probably more typical than people wanted to admit. I once officiated a funeral for a man who had died from complications after an awful bout of pneumonia. Such things don't usually kill thirty-three-year-old men, but it happens. His wife told me during the wake she kept thinking her husband was breathing. She stared at him in the open casket for hours and swore it looked like her husband's chest was rising and falling. An optical illusion, I told her. At the funeral, she started screaming her husband was alive, trapped in the coffin and she threw herself at the coffin, yanking off the flowers and clawing at the sealed edge; luckily, a relative grabbed her before she could knock the whole thing over. She was taken outside, and I finished the service. I wasn't crazy just as that poor woman wasn't. Grief does strange things. That's all. By the time we were in the cemetery for the burial, the woman was calm, resigned in her stroke of awful luck. Everything back to normal. Like now.

Only it's not.

The sheet was still pulled over my father's face. Maybe it had been that way the whole time. *Oh, really? You want to convince yourself of that, even after that whole bit about the reddish mole?*

I stood. My legs felt loose, something like rubber, but they held and I didn't wobble. The room had righted itself. Even so, I wasn't about to look back at the door. I stepped back to the gurney.

My father groaned.

It was a susurration of sound, a slight exhale, trapped breath, perhaps.

One pointed elbow stuck out from the paper edge closest to me, a pale bump, and a length of leg filled the gap riding down to the feet. He was naked under there. Not surprising, of course, people were stripped before going to the morgue, but if this room was designed as some kind of viewing room for family, why not keep the deceased clothed?

Another groan, a strangled rumbling. I was hearing things, of course.

Yet...

"Dad?" My voice trembled and that made all of this worse.

I reached out. My hand shook over his covered face. In some cultures, it was customary to wrap the deceased's face in some sort of holy cloth. Before entombment, Jesus was wrapped in linen. The Shroud of Turin was supposedly that cloth and prominently featured Jesus' imprinted face. This papery cover was as far from sanctified as you could get. I reached for a small wrinkled peak that might be right over my father's nose. I thought of cauls, the membraneous skin that conceals the face of some newborns and is believed to signify such babies are specially blessed, often gifted with sixth sense.

I lifted the sheet with thumb and middle finger. I could release it, turn around, and leave. I wouldn't even look at the door: go right for the door knob, get out of here, get back into that harsh, shadowless, antiseptic-stinking hallway.

I took a deep breath, as deep as I could anyway, and (*now, go light*) folded back the sheet.

My father's eyes were open. The blue in them had faded to foggy gray and the cataract floated like an ice floe.

Open eyes didn't mean anything. Sometimes funeral homes had to glue the deceased's eyes shut.

His mouth was slightly open. I leaned toward him, but not too close. I listened even though I knew any sounds would be a gas-inspired trick of my ears. The dead didn't speak and, in that moment,, neither did my father.

His eyelids slowly descended, the final curtain after a prolonged show, even featuring an encore or two. "It's okay," I said. "It's okay."

I'm not sure if I was speaking to him or to myself.

Those eyelids popped open and the muscles around his eyes stretched out, his forehead rippled in creases and his ceiling stare expanded into a shocked *I-don't-believe-it* expression. The eyes were marvelously blue, deep, dark ocean blue and radiating with life, the cataract gone, swallowed into deep blue. His mouth dropped open and he groaned—*just escaping gas, just gas*—but no, those were words, he was saying something, speaking from beyond the grave, drawing it out in one, long shivering exhale.

Black insect legs curled out of his mouth and around his lips and a bloated spider emerged. Light circled in its stacked eyes. Stubby black hairs stabbed at my father's lips. Fangs curved from its mouth and glistened with mucus. Only that wasn't mucus—it was poison.

I dropped back, hit the chair, snagged the side of it this time, my foot somehow tangling with it, and with the next move, I lost my balance and hit the tile floor hard. Pain throbbed up my elbow and across my hip. My scream cracked and rushed out, but I strangled it back with both hands.

Don't you want me to get better?

His mouth was closed. And his eyes.

My father did not speak, did not sit up on the gurney and turn to look at me. He was dead. Like Tamara. That was the issue here. I wanted to think it was okay he was dead—he was supposed to die—but death can not be rationalized that way. No matter what science says, death is not a biological event—it is an emotional one. In death, we face loss, complete finality, and we ask ourselves how we could go on. I had wept before my dead daughter, but it was only here, in front of my father, that all the pain could have an outlet. These horrors could not happen to my daughter—that would be far too much to handle.

The first people, primitive cave-man people, not Adam and Eve mud-people in paradise, must have been so baffled when they first saw one of their own die. What had they thought? They didn't, of course, think. They felt. And from that, more than from anything else, sprung our conception of faith. There must be meaning to this life. If not, all of it is one horrendous joke, yet rationalizing was futile—faith was visceral, felt and believed in the guts.

My father didn't move, and I didn't see that awful spider anywhere. Because it wasn't real. I was imagining things.

Or maybe it's hiding.

I got up and went to the door. It no longer looked so crooked, maybe only slightly and maybe not even. The doorknob felt good in my hand, solid. It grounded me and I did what we're all told to do in awful moments and got a hold of myself.

I turned back to my father. The sheet had settled flat against his body.

I started to turn to the door and stopped.

I should have left.

The paper sheet was back over his face.

✟

I returned, walking on shaky legs and fighting the rising insistence I might have to scramble for the bathroom, and fast. I never suffered actual sea-sickness (only that near-attack after staring at the perpetual-motion toy), but I had my share of stomach bugs, drunken purges, and food poisoning to recognize the numbing quake rising in my legs.

I slowed, even leaned against the wall near a garbage can with one of those peaked tops and swinging lids with the word TRASH on it. My head throbbed and heat rushed through me. I came close to tearing off that lid and heaving into the trash but slowly, very slowly, the urge to vomit lessened and my legs steadied beneath me. A tight, throbbing ball wedged itself in my stomach, threatening, a coiled snake.

Don't you want me to get better?

Maybe the nurses had been right yesterday when they said I was in shock. My pool dive when I was fourteen left me numb and cramping, heart loping and crawling in alternating bursts, but this was worse—my heart beat but I couldn't even feel it, as if it was outside my body, stuffed in a bag strapped to my back. I was lightheaded and would have sworn I was running a fever.

It was the thoughts spiraling through my mind that made this experience so much worse. Thoughts in confused fragments and awful, tilted images, and whirling, liquid paint that turned in tiny whirlpools that morphed into hollow eyes and a drooping, gaping mouth. Like a fish yanked from the water and tossed on a ship's deck. Not the kind of image I imagined when I envisioned Jesus and that made it even more horrible. I didn't put stock in the belief cursing or drawing offensive religious pictures stacked up the black marks in the GOING TO HELL column, but seeing that dangling mouth, cheeks stressed to translucence, a fish's maw desperate for breath or the empty cave of someone unable to scream, seemed very close to something so nasty and awful perhaps afterlife implications did hang in the balance.

It looked like the Toft kid when his parents found him on his bed in his Bills jacket with a *Thank You for Shopping* bag over his head, a plastic concave skin stretched across his mouth.

But I hadn't actually seen that. My image was pure imagination based on what my father had said. And I had no reason to believe the story was even true. Dad had been losing it. Maybe it was part of the ensuing heart attack or a stray thought flare in his decaying mind, but it didn't mean anything. Couldn't.

As the things I had seen in that room couldn't mean anything. They hadn't happened. I knew that and I also recognized they had been incredibly authentic, fully-realized experiences, much like dreams, so this was a matter of convincing my mind what it thought was real actually wasn't.

The problem was I couldn't wake from this. There was no way to assure myself it had all been made up.

Maybe you'll wake and it'll be Sunday morning and you can have cereal with Naomi and the girls and this time you'll drive your family home after the service.

That way you can all die together.

A papery sheet crinkled in my ears.

My legs gave and my knees took the hard smack as I crumpled to the floor and—*the bulbous, hairy black spider crowded Dad's open mouth*—my stomach squeezed and forced out a yellowy mess into a pile beside the garbage can. It stank of rotting things.

I'd been young, maybe seven or eight, when I was searching under my bed for one of my He-Man action figures, stretching my arm way under there, face pressed against the cold metal bed rail. I felt something stringy, fabric hanging down from the box spring, only no, I knew what it was, but the realization came a second too late. The spider crawled onto my fingers and bit the top of my hand. The pain was no more than a pinprick, but it was so surprising I screamed and pulled out from the bed and the thing was still on my hand, all black and fat and hairy. It stared at me with all those eyes, my pale face reflecting in eight orbs, and I screamed again, flailing my hand frantically. The spider hung on for a moment and I was sure it was going to bite me again, maybe scurry up my arm and try to go for my face, but it flew off and hit the wall and dropped onto my bed. It cowered in the folds of my comforter.

Even after my father found the spider and executed it, death by rolled newspaper bludgeoning, and my mother washed my sheets and cleaned out the web under my bed, I wouldn't sleep in my bed for a week. *It was only a spider,* my mother said. *Don't bother it and it won't hurt you.* Where it had bitten me, the skin swelled into two hard, red bumps, but a few days later vanished completely.

Vomiting on the hospital hallway floor, I felt that long-ago spider crawling on my hand and I slapped at its ghost.

When I was done, I sat back against the wall, breathing in short, hollow gasps. A man in jeans walked past, looking away when we made eye contact. Maybe he thought I was contagious.

My body shook and I didn't resist. I feared I might puke some more but that wasn't really what I was afraid of anyway.

At some point, an orderly in white with a curly grey beard over his black skin stopped his cart before me. He saw the congealing slop on the floor.

"You okay?" he asked.

"I'm sorry," I said, gesturing to my mess. My head throbbed.

He smiled in that way some people naturally have that conveys the perfect blend of empathy and reassurance. "Let me help you."

He held my arm as I stood until I was sure my legs were going to work, and he offered to walk me wherever I was headed. "Probably should be the ER," he said.

"I'll be fine. I'm sorry about the mess."

He stared at me as if evaluating like a doctor. "You're a religious man?"

My hand touched the cross. "A priest."

"Well," he said, "you look like you've seen the Devil."

Lavon and George stood and came to me as if I might collapse with my next step.

"Lucas, you all right?"

I laughed. They hesitated and I waved my hands as if all of this were part of some elaborate put-on. "I'm okay."

They helped me to the couch and sat opposite me, hands on their knees.

The same sad sentiments were repeated for the millionth and billionth times—I'm so sorry this happened; This is so awful; I can't believe it. I nodded through the repetition. There would be much, much more of this to come. The wake, the funeral, the burial.

Correction: the wake*s*, the funeral*s*, the burial*s*; that's burials with an "s."

I grabbed the tissue box on the table before me and squeezed the cardboard box into a crumpled mess. What I needed was to punch a wall, to break something, not to squish a stupid cardboard box. I needed to scream, to let it out, whatever this awful feeling was inside me. Everyone was going to give me his pity, his condolences, but what good would that do? I was a priest, the comforter, the assurer. If I couldn't find a way to get over this tragedy and get on with my life, what good was I?

I would disavow the priesthood. It would start as a sabbatical, a trip to the Holy Land, perhaps, a sojourn for renewed faith, and it would stretch longer and longer. I'd get a crappy little job somewhere working for minimum wage and live in a cramped apartment without TV and people would say I was lost, but those people wouldn't understand. How could they? No priest or religious leader would ever admit this, but regardless of the reason he (or she, as it may be in the Episcopal church) came into the faith, his steadfast service in the name of the Lord was predicated on the belief proximity breeds favoritism and protection. I will dedicate my life to bringing people closer to you, oh Lord, and in exchange you got my back, right? As Satan said of God's faithful servant Job, "he is faithful and pious because you built around him a hedge to protect him from the evils of the world." That's the deal, God. Build around me a hedge.

I failed to read the fine print.

Take my servant Lucas, a perfect and an upright man, one that fear God and avoid evil. Destroy all he has, all he loves, and stand not in awe as yet he worships me still.

"They were asking about insurance," George said.

"We told them what we know, but they may need your group number or something," Lavon added.

And the Lord said unto Satan, "Behold all that Lucas hath is in thy power, only upon his health insurance put not forth thine hand."

I started laughing and didn't care if the cackles resounded endlessly in that ugly hospital grieving room with Lavon and George staring as I twisted the tissue box into something a dog had eaten and regurgitated. I threw the box. It bounced stupidly off the print of the cornfield. I might have screamed, too, a desperate, squeaky scream full of anger and frustration and I wondered if anyone passing in the hallway paused to glance at the door marked PRIVATE. The brown-haired nurse, maybe.

Job again: "Shall we receive good at the hand of God and *not* receive evil?"

Yes, I would shout. *Yes, yes, YES! For the love of Christ, YES!*

Otherwise, what is the point?

✝

First, go light.
We were in Uz. But you didn't realize it.

When I was in seminary, along with the basic courses on Biblical studies, History of the Protestant Episcopal Church, and Teaching Scripture in a Congregation, there were the more abstract courses such as Spirituality vs. Organized Faith, and a course entitled, The Imaginative Officiant. It sounded like a class about using gimmicks in the church to engage congregants (something Professor Mable cautioned against in her course on homiletics, urging us toward intellectual introspection and away from evangelist preaching, use of video clips, helium balloons or cross-shaped confetti, all methods students had tried previously), but this had been a meditative-intensive course on embracing the imagination to strengthen one's faith. You had to see what you preached because if you couldn't see it, no one else would, either. We had assignments very similar to something students might get in a creative writing course: Imagine you are with Jesus at the Garden of Gethsemane and write a narrative of what happens, 1,000 words max.

Most of us saw this type of thing as amusing, a welcome respite from the arduous workload of religious history and Biblical studies, but a funny thing happened. We started to get into it. We wrote works that were one step from short stories, and we analyzed our choices: why did we imagine Jesus wouldn't notice us there among his disciples? Why did we see ourselves as Judas?

People don't think of priests as creative types. We speak truth, not fantasy. Depends to whom you speak on that one, friends. After that course, I appreciated my imagination as I never had before. In fact, I hadn't ever thought about it at all. The ability to imagine, to create something that while not tangible is still solid enough to see, to exist—that is a gift. If God made this world and all of us in it then He was the first to use imagination. Maybe that's all we are. Some call that blasphemous, but there are things worse than being a figment of someone's imagination.

Things much worse.

✝

It was late when a doctor finally spoke to me again. He was tall and slope-shouldered. Wrinkles twisted throughout his white coat. His name tag read, Dr. Noose. I had to look at it several times, really stare at the letters to make sure that was indeed the man's name. Dr. Noose. Suited for a job as warden of death row.

"There isn't too much to share," he said. "The swelling in your daughter's skull appears to be steady. That's good."

"Is it?"

"It means the swelling has not gotten worse. It may be quite some time before the swelling goes down and surgery may be unavoidable."

He had a good name for a school principal. *Mr. Noose is wonderful at executing pedagogical policies.*

The doctor looked at me curiously and I realized I was smiling. "Your name..."

The doctor stiffened slightly. "It's pronounced *Nuss.*"

I nodded. He seemed a little hung up about the issue.

"Your wife," he hesitated and I waited for it—*is dead, died on the table, sorry to say, didn't make it*—"is still in surgery. There were complications."

More nods and the doctor began explaining in technical jargon what was wrong with Naomi and why she wouldn't be out of surgery for several more hours.

Dr. Noose. Good name for a CEO. *Let's take care of this right now, people; you know I don't like having things hanging over my head.*

My giggling morphed into obnoxious, rolling cackles.

Keep control of yourself, buddy boy.

Hang in there.

☦

Phoebe was stable enough to have her own room. It was bland like every other room but at least it had a window. *Your shift nurse is Regan*, it read in purple dry erase marker on a small white board. Beneath was the date scrawled with slashes. Next to that was a laminated Pain Measurement Scale featuring a grinning smily face at one end and a comically distraught face with downcast frown and cascading tears at the other. The room smelled of disinfectant yet musty at the same time, a basement with Clorox-splashed floors.

Scratches and scuffs marked the plastic rails of Phoebe's bed. Who else had used this bed? Dozens of people? Hundreds? Of those, how many had died in it?

Tucked beneath what at least looked like a real sheet (the living get cloth, no paper on this floor), my little angel was so small her body vanished beneath that sheet, as if the body-like bumps were empty pockets of air I could slap flat.

IV lines ran from one arm, thankfully hidden beneath the sheet, and an an oxygen tube snaked from her mouth. *Intubation.* Strips of white tape held the tube in place and pulled her skin into clumps. Bruising shadowed her face in purples and browns. It sounds ridiculous, but she looked worse than Tamara. Red spots floated through the areas of pale skin, pallid seas filling the gaps between gruesome islands. Her head was cocked at an unnatural angle on the pillow. A kiss of blood had crusted on her chin.

The rail was cold in my grip.

"I don't know what to do," I said.

✝

I finally convinced George and Lavon to give themselves a break and go home. I pitched it with the implication if they didn't go, it was some kind of insult to me, a man who couldn't be with his family, not the way he wanted to, anyway, and George, having a wife and a grown daughter, went with a look of relief and gratitude, but Lavon hesitated. His wife had died five years ago, and they had never had kids.

"You sure?"

No, I almost said. *I'm not sure, but I can't keep you guys here, use up your time because I don't want to be alone. That makes everything worse. Adds to the guilt.*

"Yeah," I said.

I sat alone in that PRIVATE room for a while. People walked past on soft-soled shoes and squeaking rubber sneakers; pants swished, and people spoke in hurried phrases. People cried and people laughed. Something clattered on the floor, a clipboard, perhaps.

I relaxed, sunken into the couch, and fell into the print of the cornfield with the reddish setting sun. A slight breeze stirred the corn; it sounded papery, the sound of dead hands pulling a paper sheet over a dead face. The cornfield stretched into the horizon and the last of the daylight warmed my face. I smelled dried grass and the decay of things rotting in mud.

First, go light.

You were in Uz. But you didn't realize it.

It was nothing more than that lightless sensation that prologues a descent into sleep, a levitation of limbs, a weightlessness of self, yet I also felt that couch's slouching shape beneath me even as I lifted free from it.

Exhaustion, I thought.

But maybe not *only* that.

✝

Dr. Noose could not be located. He was on-call, sure, but he was busy or something, called off location, down to the ER, stuck in a consult—probably got hung up. Ha. Ha. The nurse, this one in blue scrubs with little Mickey Mouses running all over it, checked the computer and fumbled excuse after excuse.

"I want an update on my wife. Naomi Masters."

The nurse's station looked like one of those control centers featured in movies where Important People are charged with managing some national crisis. Multicolored folders lay in piles among flickering computers seemingly running through data by themselves.

"I'll see if I can find Dr. Noose," she said and grabbed the phone.

Don't kill yourself. Even at two in the morning, I could still crack a good pun. I should write them down, great sermon fodder. Heck, I could use it as an icebreaker for Tamara's eulogy. A priest walks into a hospital, meets this doctor named...

She couldn't find him. "I'll keep trying."

"Can you tell me my wife's condition?"

She glanced at the computer screen, up at me, back at the screen. "You'll need to discuss her condition with—"

"Can you tell me what room she's in? Can you tell me that at least?"

She looked long and hard at that screen, a hell of a lot longer than necessary to see where my wife had been placed like some biology experiment on a lab shelf, and then pitied me with a sympathetic stare.

"I'm sorry, sir, but I—"

I was ten feet away before she could finish. Her words echoed without form or meaning. The clack of my shoes sounded much more loudly. *Daddy's church shoes*, Phoebe called them. My hand went to the wooden cross dangling around my neck.

✝

I slept in a chair in Phoebe's hospital room and woke to Monday's first light with a painful crick in my neck and a cold throb in my back. I suffered no dreams. Maybe I was too exhausted. Or maybe I was storing up energy for later. As if part of me, a secret part secluded somewhere, sensed what was coming. Some people might call that intuition, sixth sense, divination, or even divine intervention.

I'm open to suggestions.

✝

What I thought of as The Grieving Party arrived before nine. They brought bagels and donuts and extra-large styrofoam cups of coffee. I drank the coffee and swallowed a glazed donut even though I'd had a stale egg sandwich from the hospital cafeteria. I felt ill but I ate anyway.

The entire vestry had come, including George and Lavon again, along with a half dozen church members and even ancient Vivian Colette, who wore all black and gave me a box of Richart Chocolates she said tasted so good it made you want to die, handing over the box and speaking without any trace of irony.

"You didn't have to come," I told each person in turn. People shook off my comment, said of course they had to come, and apologized. I'm sorry, so, so sorry.

Iris held my hands in both of hers and stared into my eyes from her own well of misery where her unborn child forever cried. *You thought you could help me through my grief*, those eyes said. *Well, Reverend Masters, what do you think, can anyone help you through this? They'll try. Even if you don't want them to, they'll try. But it's an exclusive membership-only kind-of-thing. They can't even get in. But you? You've been given premier status. Welcome to the club.*

"Have a chocolate," Vivian said. "It'll make you feel better."

✝

Gill Birchwood shook my hand and offered his best funereal face. He was in his mid-forties, married with two kids and worked at a financial giant in the city that had actually thrived during the recession. He was a vestry member, and a good guy, though a bit stuffy, like most financial guys, I suppose. "I certainly enjoy a day off work but not because of something like this," he said.

David Javan walked in behind him. He wore khakis and a striped collar shirt. "Whatever you need," he said. "I'm here. There's a lot at my disposal."

✝

I brought everyone to the PRIVATE room with the picture of cornstalks at sunset. I had come to think of this sterile grieving room as my place. I hadn't slept here—the couch would have been a great alternative to the chair in Phoebe's room—but I had come back here many times as a refuge. Phoebe loved playing tag and hide-and-go-seek. I'd chase her around the house and as I was about to tag her *It!*, she would hop on her bed or clutch desperately to the dining room table leg and shout, "Home base. Safe! I'm safe!" The PRIVATE room was my home base. In there, I was safe. I hated myself for not keeping perpetual vigil with Phoebe, but sitting there, staring at my poor baby girl was the most exhausting thing I'd ever done.

"Whatever you need," David said to me, hand on my shoulder, leaning in.

"There's nothing anyone can do."

"I'm here."

"This isn't your family."

That came out crueler than I'd meant, but grief was a solitary plight, and I wanted to suffer alone.

I deserved to.

✝

After more small talk, including a moment when Vivian announced someone ought to open that box of chocolates, they were from France after all, and the box was subsequently passed among us and each person carefully selected one (*do this in remembrance of me*), I took each person to see Phoebe, one at a time. *I can bring you inside*, I thought, *but you can't stay. This club is members only.*

✝

David and I stood side by side, shoulders touching, watching my daughter.

"I don't think I can do this," I said. I hadn't been aware I was even thinking that but once it was out, I had no urge to take it back.

David said nothing for a while.

Your father ... He is not well.

"What did you mean when you said my father was not well?"

"Not now," he said. "It doesn't matter now."

"What doesn't?"

"I'm so sorry, Lucas."

I waited for more, some explanation, something, anything, but he stayed quiet.

The bruising on Phoebe's face had spread and darkened to deep brown splashes. Her head was no longer as skewed as it had been and the creases around the strips of white tape holding the breathing tube in place had smoothed. Hair blotted her forehead in sweaty clumps.

The crook of her elbow where the IV line ran from was bulged red and swollen. Could it be infected? I had to tell a nurse. People got infections in hospitals all the time. Sometimes those infections were deadly. Her other hand rested on her chest, as if measuring her own breathing.

If I dared, I would have said she looked better, promisingly better, might-wake-up-any-second better. She'd moved her hand onto her chest, after all. Her arms had been beneath the sheet. Didn't that suggest progress?

But a nurse had done it, that's all. The whiteboard on the wall still said the same thing—*Your Shift Nurse is Regan*. So, Regan came in to check the IV line and forgot to tuck Phoebe's arm beneath the sheet again. She probably wiped my daughter's face with a washcloth, which was why her bangs were wet: water, not sweat.

All of that was possible, probable no doubt, but I didn't believe it. I didn't want to. Why would Regan-the-shift-nurse not only uncover Phoebe's IV-stabbed arm but also remove her other arm and lay her hand across her chest? There was no point. That was something a mortician would do.

Just getting her ready.

I stared at my daughter's bare arms and the image began to blur. No one had moved that sheet.

Phoebe had done it herself.

✝

"My father was not a religious man," David said.

His words startled me, and I blinked at him as if he magically appeared.

"But he was a caring man. He worked in the Peace Corps throughout his twenties and thirties, traveled mostly through Africa, and the first chance he got, he took me there. I was nine. It was us and two of my father's corps buddies. We went many places, but they particularly wanted to visit this tiny village a million miles from anywhere. They had helped the people, given them food, even defended them from a rival clan. My father asked many people and they pointed the way, though they told him not to bother. The place was cursed, they insisted.

"We found the village, what was left of it. Warlords had decimated it. They had come through in jeeps and trucks, kidnapped the children old enough to work and become part of the militia and they killed everyone else. Some were shot, but machetes were used on most. The bodies had been left strewn all over the place. Limbs, fractured torsos, bashed skulls. The dead were not buried because people in nearby villages were afraid. They didn't want the warlords coming after them. What was left of those poor people had been gnawed at by wild animals and bugs. Lots of bones, like an awful jigsaw puzzle. My father and his two buddies didn't say anything. They took the small shovels out of their backpacks and started digging. It took two days, but they buried all the bones they could find. My father even made me dig a little."

While he spoke, I felt like the floor had fallen away, felt as if I were floating.

First, go light.

"That's awful," I said. "But I'm not sure it's very helpful to me right now."

"After we left," David said, "I asked my father why he had buried the bones. My father looked down at me, I remember so clearly how the blinding African sun slipped behind his head and it was like an eclipse, and he said, 'There is only one rule in this world. If you can follow it, you will be better for it. No matter what anyone says, it is just one rule: love thy neighbor.'"

✝

Instead of Dr. Noose (must be hanging around here somewhere), Dr. Erica Qwan found me sometime later and asked to speak with me privately. I imagined standing up in the PRIVATE room among my gathered supporters and declaring, *These people have suffered with me. They deserve to know too.* Like this was some sit-in protest against the hospital for keeping my wife in a coma.

But, as I mentioned, grief is an alone kind-of-thing.

We spoke in the hall. Dr. Qwan had small, slender hands she used to direct my attention: to her name tag when she introduced herself, to her narrow chin repeatedly, tapping there in thought, to my own hand when she took it and explained what was happening, to the clipboard and the diagnosis on some official-looking document.

"I'm afraid," Dr. Qwan said, "your wife isn't going to make it."

Did she have an appointment? I thought with complete stupidity and fought off another laughing fit.

"I'm very sorry," she said.

✝

Everyone stood when I entered, even Vivian Colette. I waited for her legs to stiffen and keep her upright. I heard my voice explain what the doctor had said but it was as though someone else were doing it. The words—"subarachnoid intracranial saccular aneurysm"—sounded too scientific, "she's going to die," too absurd to be anything but a joke. I was thirty-three years old. How could my wife be dying?

✝

Naomi Patricia Masters died quickly. They had unplugged the machines, so there was no accompanying beeping that turned into an elongated, flatlined whine, but I heard it anyway the moment my wife was still, that steady, bleating cry.

My ear itched for her tug. She'd done that last night and we'd kissed. Our last kiss. When had that ear tugging started? It was an old joke, something from our dating years, some gag about always listening to a woman or risking her tugging something else and not in a pleasurable way. That wasn't quite it, but close. My ear warmed uncomfortably. I tried to remember the first time she snagged my ear and had it for a moment, had her full-teeth smile in a blaze of summer sun and the soft of her lips against mine—then it was gone, the joke, the memory, lost.

And with it, my wife.

Now she was with Tamara and Dad.

And only Phoebe was left.

✝

The room was still dark when I woke. At first, I thought it had been a dream that ushered me back to consciousness, but I couldn't remember anything. I felt strangely disappointed not to have suffered a nightmare. It was unfair I should sleep so soundly. Worse than unfair, actually—it was an insult to my wife and daughters.

Someone stood next to my bed. I felt the person's presence as I had felt someone behind me downstairs. *And how well did that work out for you?*

This time it had to be a nurse.

The rush of adrenaline pushed my heart into my throat, but I wasn't going to jump up and scream or lash out. The nurse was probably checking on Phoebe and decided to glance down at me too. She didn't deserve to have the shit scared out of her. She would leave in a moment and I could gradually calm enough to sleep again.

She remained. I felt her standing there.

I had fallen asleep facing my daughter, but I was now facing the window at the other end of the room. What at first looked like soft moonlight was actually the outdoor security lights casting the world in a hazy fog.

In a hospital, the lights never go out completely. The light from the hallway shone in as fractured white boxes around the window. It should have been enough light to keep away the black pall of darkness, but the boxes of light were more like hanging pictures, light magically arising out of the wall instead of shining in from the hall.

"Hello?" I said softly so the nurse wouldn't be startled into a scream.

She didn't respond.

Those white boxes remained undisturbed. My cot had been placed close to Phoebe's bed but because of the limited space, half of the cot was directly before the open door. The nurse should have been blocking at least some of that light.

You're barely awake. Your thinking is tangled. There's plenty of space for someone to stand next to you and be out of the light.

Still, the person remained. *Keeping watch.*

I pinched the skin on my hand, tenting it high off my hand until the pain was comically sharp. That didn't mean it wasn't a dream, did it? The mind controlled all things. When people suffered nightmares of falling, they genuinely felt the rapid pull of gravity and it was only in that last moment before impact when their eyes flew open, they realized it was all a dream.

"Hello?" I tried again. My voice wavered.

"Daddy, I'm scared."

Phoebe's voice was so clear and sharp and so small and frightened my own scream thundered inside me, vibrating ground threatening to split wide and release some trapped toxin. She couldn't be up. Couldn't be talking. She was in a coma, had that damn breathing tube shoved down her throat. *A dream, a dream.* My scream barreled up my throat and I clutched both hands over my mouth, squeezed my jaw hard and muffled the shout.

"Daddy," my daughter said, so close she could touch me. "Daddy, you promised."

I turned slowly. The cot strained beneath my weight. *She's dead. That's what this means. She died while I was sleeping. She gave up the ghost, as Jesus did on the cross, and this is her final goodbye. She's dead. My baby girl is dead and now it's only me. All alone.*

A dark figure stood over me.

The Uz Monster.

It has many names.

Golgotha, was one. The hill where Jesus was crucified. The place where his blood saturated the earth.

(*When he was thirty-three, just like you.*)

Abaddon was another name. A Bad One.

"Daddy," the figure said in my daughter's voice. But that was her hair flopping down around her face and a speck of light along the stub of her nose. It was Phoebe. She really was standing there.

"Honey?"

"Daddy?" she said and her face pushed through shadow and into light, as if emerging from a bog. Or a cave.

Light bathed her face but still I saw only her hair and the tip of her nose. The rest remained shrouded, masked beneath a veil that shouldn't be.

"Daddy?" Phoebe said again. "I'm scared."

"Daddy's here."

I reached toward her. My hand slipped beneath that black sheet and severed my arm at the wrist. *Just a trick of the light. An illusion like that old vanishing thumb gag Tamara had thought hilarious.* But the trick was too perfect. My arm didn't end cleanly in the straight edge of the shadow boundary, but had been truncated in a sloping, rounded stump indicative of professional amputations. My arm hadn't simply been severed at the wrist—the ulna and radius bones had been hacked away too, the tissue rounded, the skin molded.

Welcome to The Land of Uz.

Job hadn't been hacked into fragments. At least not literally.

But he suffered weeping boils.

A trick of the light.

Only it wasn't. I turned my arm and the amputation was complete; no matter the angle, my hand was gone. I pulled back from the shadow, from Phoebe's hidden face, and the darkness snagged me, held me. Something had my arm—*my hand, it has my hand*—and I yanked harder, but the grip tightened. A strong stench of awful halitosis gusted into my face. A mix of onion and meat gone sour.

It's eating me. The thought was clear and rational. *The Uz Monster is eating me.* That's why my hand is gone. It's eaten it, but instead of gushing streamers of blood and pain too immense for the conscious mind to handle, the monster swallowed what came into the shadow with clean, painless chomps and mended the remaining stump with medical precision.

My arm went further into the darkness. Flesh and bone vanished. My stump fell shorter. Now up to my elbow where a grotesque nub wiggled on the joint. I watched the darkness chomp off that lump that had been my forearm and move up my arm toward my shoulder. The bone vanished without pain, the tissue flexed over the injury and the skin healed as if observed through one of those high-speed cameras that document a flower from seedling through death and allowed you to watch its entire life cycle in one minute.

Darkness ate me, chomped at what remained of my arm. The humerus bone it was called and wasn't that ironic because what the hell was so humorous? It tugged me closer and closer. All that remained was another freakish stub of arm quivering beneath my shoulder.

"You have to help me, Daddy," Phoebe said in that same frightened voice. "You promised."

"I will!" I cried.

Pain, a whole goddamn frozen ocean of it, leveled me, and it was too intense, far too intense, and it was going to drag me down into the darkness where the monster could finish, only it wouldn't gobble me up whole, oh no—it was going to eat me, yes, but only my limbs, so I would wake and be Human Stub Man with four jiggling wads of tissue and skin where my arms and legs should have been.

"I'm trapped!" Phoebe shouted.

I tried to scream but it was too late—darkness swallowed me.

✝

I came to with a convulsive shake that rocked me out of the air and crushed me against the cold tile floor. The side of my face took the hit and pain bloomed through my cheek and along my eye. I thrashed on the floor like a damn fish. My face smacked the tile again and again. *My arms! It ate my arms!*

My scream was enough to pull me free.

I scrambled up and back, a frantic crab, and smacked into the wall. The artificial light filling the hallway washed over me. *My arms! My arms!* For a moment, they were gone, and I saw very clearly the awful way the remaining stubs wiggled in the bright light, the ends rounded, the folded skin creased like the sealed end of a sausage casing.

Then they were back as if blinking into existence and they flung wildly before me, a frantic drowning victim's arms. It took a moment to stop them, to realize I *could* stop them.

I sat pushed against the wall panting, heart racing, fresh sweat slicking my skin. The cot lay on its side. Phoebe was back in bed. She had never gotten out of bed. The whole thing had been one awful dream.

You have to help me, Daddy.

A nurse passed in the hallway but didn't glance in. If she had, there would have been a lot of explaining to do. Maybe a psyche evaluation for the bereaved husband and father. Perhaps I *should* have such an evaluation. Naomi liked to say anyone who went into the priesthood must have issues.

I'm trapped.

Slowly, I got up, my legs shaking, my heart thudding, and went to my daughter. Pins and needles stabbed at my arms. I must have turned over on my stomach and slept with my arms beneath me. That would explain the dream. Or explain at least enough of it to make the rest go away, though the image of my stubby arms wiggling at the shoulders, the skin folded into overlapping creases, refused to dissipate.

Phoebe's arms were beneath the white sheet.

That was okay, though, because the nurse had probably come in and remembered this time to tuck Phoebe's arms beneath the sheet. After all, what if she got cold?

I grabbed the single blanket I had used and turned to cover my daughter. It dangled from my fingers, the edge slumping onto her covered thighs.

But her hands had been exposed. I hadn't dreamed that. It had been earlier when I noticed, before Dr. Qwan shared her fears my wife wasn't going to make it. *Why does that scare you?* I wanted to ask. *Are you afraid of death or is this a quota-related issue?* If Naomi dies, Dr. Qwan goes over her limit for the month and she owes everyone on staff a coke.

Her hands had been exposed. I remembered the IV sagging from the tiny crook of her arm. Then they were covered. Then exposed again. *Peekaboo.* A nurse did it. Obviously.

But I knew better.

I dropped the blanket over her legs and reached for the edge of the sheet hanging off the side of the bed. My hand shook a little like Dad's hands sometimes had, but staring at it made the shaking worse and that made me worry I was losing it and that made the shaking much worse. What was I trying to prove anyway? I would pull back the sheet, go get some breakfast and when I came back, I would know for sure if... if...

What? If my daughter was playing peekaboo with me, only doing it from the depths of a coma?

Part of me knew I shouldn't even tempt it. Leave the sheet alone and get some fresh air.

I lifted the sheet and dropped it in the space between Phoebe's arm and chest. It folded into an albino flower.

Phoebe's white skin almost vanished against the stark sheet, like she had no blood inside her, like she was a victim of exsanguination. Maybe there was a vampire nurse or orderly around here somewhere, working the nightshift, and hiding in a supply closet during the day, hanging upside down from a closet bar. I could ask around about suspicious people, investigate a few janitor closets. The cross around my neck ought to protect me.

My hand went to that cross again.

Unless the cross is cursed.

There was something on her mouth, a dark spot, tucked between breathing tube and cheek.

A small black spider quivered there.

Another one scurried across her pillow and vanished in her hair. Two spiders. Small ones. No big deal. Wasn't it true over a lifetime people swallowed handfuls of spiders while sleeping?

Three more raced across the white sheet.

Maybe there was a nest under the bed, but as I bent to check, I saw more emerging beneath her pillow.

I lifted the edge of her pillow, her head lolling lifelessly to the side.

Dozens of tiny black spiders swarmed there and for a moment seemed to form some kind of symbol, a star maybe or even a pentagram perhaps, but that was my mind forcing meaning upon something so vile.

Your mind is concocting this whole thing. There are no spiders.

I slapped at them and they dispersed in all directions as if they lived inside the mattress. But they reemerged a second later, all of them moving in an avalanche of attack, gushing across the white sheet, onto Phoebe's neck, over her chin in a gruesome beard, and burrowed into her mouth, squeezing between tube and lips. A few spiders took the easy way straight up into her nostrils.

In a moment, they were gone. Inside my daughter. She hadn't flinched.

I gagged, throat itching.

There weren't any spiders. I was hallucinating. As I had been with my father, as I had moments ago when I felt someone standing over me, when I heard my daughter's voice. How could she speak to me with a tube lodged in her throat?

Grief hits in all sorts of ways. These freak images were products of my overheating mind—approaching the red line, entering the danger zone, rumbling with the threat of explosion.

I took several unsteady breaths.

Phoebe's fingernails were black.

For a moment, I thought a few spiders had stayed back like scouts, camping on her nails, but the black was uneven and streaked with purplish tints, dried blood blotting the cuticles. I imagined someone beating each of my daughter's fingers with a hammer. My own fingers throbbed.

Had the car accident done that? I supposed it was possible, but her nails hadn't been black before. Well, bruising sometimes took a while. Was that true or did it sound like something I wanted to be true? I wasn't a doctor. I was a priest. My speciality was prayer and in this situation was about as helpful as being a plumber.

I touched her hand, so warm, and turned it over. Black bruising blotted her palm but looked permanent like a scar, the way the skin folded in on itself, an irremovable stain, a sort of tragic birthmark, as if the black blotch was the vestige of a long-ago injury.

People might call that stigmata. Normally, people who bear the wounds of Christ do so in grand, bloody fashion, parading around hands forward like a zombie, but your daughter is very special—her marks are black, as if Jesus' blood is diseased.

I thought of my father's blackened hand, of the blood he smeared along the prayer railing.

"I'm so sorry, honey," I said, but I put her hand on the bed, palm down. I couldn't look at that mark anymore. Black as an angry storm cloud.

I watched her for a while.

At some point, I saw the smudge on my own palm.

The remains of a tiny squished spider. One leg twitched spastically.

✝

The Grieving Party returned a little after eight Tuesday morning. For a while at least it was the same crew, even Vivian Colette. She did not bring chocolates this time, though I'm sure I caught her looking around for the box she brought. I'd brought it to the nurse's station and casually asked about Phoebe's fingernails. The nurse, a woman with wide hips and a matching face, said it was actually pretty common when the body has suffered a traumatic injury.

I did not mention the spiders. After washing my hands and getting some fresh air, the whole middle-of-the-night incident faded to the remnants of dream, and with sun-up, it faded even further.

A hallucination. Had to be.

And why was that?

Well, because if not...

I thought very clearly, *Am I going crazy?*

Lavon parked a heavy hand on my shoulder and squeezed. I almost hugged him, more out of amusement because I thought he might back away, though that conclusion seems both unfounded and unfair. And, might as well be honest, I could've used a damn hug.

We gathered in Phoebe's room. Each person went to her and said something or bowed his head and prayed. Might as well have put her in a coffin and called it a wake. We stood and talked around and around the obvious. People were careful to step back from Phoebe as if she were a rare museum display with a tiny sign next to her, Please Do Not Block.

I heard little of what was discussed. I kept hoping Phoebe would sit up, yawn in dramatic fashion, smile, and say she'd never felt so rested.

✝

Doctors came and went, each one glancing at my daughter, saying as little as possible, and scribbling his or her name on the clipboard dangling at the foot of Phoebe's bed. Each doc getting a piece of the action.

We ended up in the PRIVATE room sitting around staring at each other's shoes. I was still wearing my shiny black church shoes, not to mention the same pair of sweaty dress socks. How long before someone mentioned I should go home, take a shower, put on some clean clothes? The more I thought about it, the more uncomfortable I felt in my clothes and the more and more sure I was the occasional whiff of acrid stench I detected emanated from my armpits, but it was a perk (if such a word can be applied) of being a grieving husband and father no one said anything. George's hand went to his face, however, after he had been seated next to me for a while, and I knew he was trying to block my smell while appearing to scratch the world's most persistent nose itch.

✝

Time creeps in rooms marked PRIVATE. It passed in the twitch of shoulders, the unconscious reflex of a swinging leg, the strain of lips in silent yawns. I watched these little gestures with the fascinated disinterest of an unbiased clinician, yet every eye that fell in sudden downcast amused me because what difference did any of this make? My wife, my daughter, my father—all dead, and Phoebe was playing peekaboo from the depths of a coma. Talk about absurd.

✝

After the Grieving Party left, I took a nap on the couch. It was a heavy and dreamless sleep that left me in a stupor, feeling worse than I had before. My legs and back ached, my feet throbbed, my head hurt, and now I was sure my body was wafting an ugly stink.

Phoebe was not in her room. Neither was her bed and after a brief, unnecessarily nasty cross examination of a nurse with pink, glitter-flecked lipstick, I learned Phoebe had been taken for more tests.

"But she's in a coma."

"She's stable," the nurse said. Her glittery pink lip quivered.

I waited in her hospital room. Without her bed in there, the room felt vast, a playing field good enough for whiffle ball or touch football. I sat in a chair and waited. Every time someone walked past, I sat up straighter, a leashed dog thinking every passerby is his owner, and the one time a bed rolled by with an old woman lumped beneath a shrouded sheet, I stood and then slowly sat back down.

Sleep, like a surreptitious hypnotist, slouched me to the side, slumped me forward, and sagged my chin onto my chest. I slept dreamlessly. Far as I know.

David Javan woke me up. He held two coffees in styrofoam cups, a small, crumbled brown bag, and a tentative smile.

"Any news?"

"Getting more tests done." I looked at my watch, but I had no idea what time it had been before I fell asleep. "I think I'm losing grasp a little."

"Stuck in this place," David said. He tested the cot with one hand before sitting. "Doesn't take long for hospital life to get to you. It's like prison. All routine. All waiting."

"I wish I could do something." The coffee tasted smooth and warm.

He offered the bag, the top crumbled shut. In it was a Glass Cross T-shirt with The Word of Christ Church building on the front, the cross peak a shining star, and beneath, *Behold the Glory*.

"Thanks."

"Thought you might want a change of clothes. Best I could do without invading your house."

"I probably smell."

"What's a little B.O. between friends?"

I held up the shirt, and then dropped it in my lap.

"You know much about The Word of Christ Church?"

"They host an expensive Bible Summer Camp."

First, go light.

"Indeed."

"And they have Reverend Roves. Made for TV, from what I hear."

"He likes to 'let the spirit take him.'"

"You don't sound like a believer."

"Not the kind of thing I believe in."

His was the face of experience with well-creased folds and graying eyebrows, yet something youthful shone there too, a stubborn kind of energy. "You're an interesting man, David."

He nodded, sipped his coffee. "The Word of Christ Church will pray for you and for your daughter. Reverend Roves will even come here, and we can have a good old fashion laying-on of hands. Host a tent revival in the parking lot, if you want."

"Do I get to pay a tithe, too?"

We laughed, and it felt impossibly good.

"I feel bad laughing," I said.

"No you don't," David said. "Nor should you."

I settled back into my chair. It sighed in a slow fart. "Tell me about yourself, Mr. Javan. If you're not a Roves disciple, why'd you end up there?"

"Paul Roves isn't a bad guy. In college, he studied acting before 'finding his calling.' Maybe he takes things a little far sometimes. He likes to get the people riled up, get 'em filled with 'the power.' I wonder, though, if he asked the congregation, would they rise up as a group and go after someone?"

"Go after someone?"

"Well, you get so filled up with the power, you need an outlet. Last Easter, Roves went all out. Three-hour service. They had dazzling preaching, healing hands, a thumping choir and a full horn section accompaniment. People stood almost the whole time. They clapped, cheered, cried out to the Lord. You can watch it on our website."

"See? He's ready for prime time."

"That night, a man named Tyler Tonst beat his wife so severely he broke her face in three places and cracked four of her ribs. Only hours earlier, he'd been on his feet, hands in the air, screaming the lord's name, his face bright red and straining for all that power. His cute little wife right next to him."

"That's awful."

"And it makes me wonder: how much effort would it take for Roves to get a really worked-up congregation like that into a single-minded army?"

"You have enemies?"

He sipped coffee. "Don't we all?"

I only have one, I thought of saying—*his name is death. Or maybe it's God.*

"I mentioned my father was not a religious man," David said. "That isn't to say he didn't believe; he just didn't care how he worshipped or with whom. When he took me to Africa, we prayed in different villages. I got to see all these different customs—something like that makes quite the impression. I don't believe there is one right way to worship or pray. If there were, we'd come with it build-in, an instinct.

"After my father and his buddies buried those bodies, we knelt around the mass grave and my father asked God to forgive him for lumping everyone together and then asked that God open His arms and His heart to these poor, decent people. My father cried while he prayed. I see that so perfectly, him speaking, eyes closed, tears rolling down his cheeks. I had never seen him cry before and never saw him cry again—not like that, anyway.

"My point is most people don't have such experiences. They plod through life, day to day, and nothing ever really strikes them. If you don't have a moment of profound faith, a genuine 'seeing of the light' Paul-on-the-road-to-Damascus experience, how can you ever know God or what faith even means? So, if the people at Word of Christ need Roves and his over-the-top methods to get them imbued with the spirit, I guess that's okay. But I wonder if Tyler Tonst had done what my father did, literally buried bodies all day and prayed over them, would he still have gone home and beaten his wife?"

I thought maybe Tyler Tonst might have beaten his wife with even more fervency and then put a bullet in her head. Maybe his own, too. "What happened to him, the wife beater?"

"He saw the light, you could say, and changed his ways."

"God's intervention?"

David shrugged. "Sometimes people need a little help to break from their prisons."

"Sounds like he should have been placed in a real prison."

"Not everything is always in our control. Even Tyler Tonst might have been a victim."

"Trying to make a point, David?"

"We can be trapped and not know it, and in such situations, we need other people to free us."

"Is this leading to an exorcism joke?"

He smiled. "You're the one who looks like he has a point to make."

"I never had such a moment where my faith became real to me," I said. "My father was a pastor his whole life and whether I was pushed or fell into it, the priesthood seemed to always be waiting for me. Not that I mind. I like being a priest. It worked for my father. Everybody loved him."

David smiled. "Oh, I know."

"You know how celebrities' kids get in trouble, brush with the law, end up drugged out and puking across the cover of the tabloids? Most people shake their head and say, 'Those stupid kids don't know how good they have it.' Well, I always feel bad for those kids. Can you imagine the pressure? The expectation to be like your parents?"

"Your father wasn't a saint."

"Does that matter if people think he was?"

"You're a good priest, and a good man."

I nodded but not because I agreed.

"My father was very strong in his faith. He was an intellectual, but not a doubter. I always find myself doubting and I wonder if I'm just playing a role. People look at me and want to see my father instead. You know, and this is awful, just awful, but there were many times especially during this past year when I hoped he'd have another stroke or a heart attack and that would be that."

"You think his shadow can't stretch beyond death?"

I'm all over this church, you know. My hands have been everywhere. My blood, my tears—all of it—given to this place. This place is me. I am this church.

"I've never had a moment of profound faith," I said.

Ironically, discussing religious conversion, the whole 'seeing the light' thing, never came up in seminary, and I wasn't even interviewed for my position at Saint John's. Ben Masters retired and his son was the most appropriate to fill his shoes.

"People assume Paul's conversion on the road to Damascus was a moment of divine intervention in which God sent an angel to save Paul before it was too late and his soul was forever lost. But Paul's conversion was slow, steady; it built up to that moment on the road. When he saw the light, it was the climax of a painful and uncertain journey. That's what faith is—something hard won over time, not an instantaneous thing. When I watched my father cry, I was seeing the culminating moment of his faith. You worry you never experienced such a moment, but Lucas, you're experiencing it now."

✝

Phoebe was wheeled back in and when I asked about the tests, a nurse told me a doctor would be in to see me shortly. Phoebe's hands were beneath the sheet again.

I did not fold back the sheet to look.

"Why did God send that angel down to Paul?" I said after the nurse left as though nothing had interrupted our discussion. "Why not let Paul come to his faith on his own?"

"Maybe he did. Maybe the angel is a symbol, a metaphor."

"How very Episcopalian of you."

"The good Reverend Roves would say God was rewarding his servant and each of us can know God's reward if we follow our own path to Damascus."

"Cute," I said. "You know what I think was going on?"

"I'm curious."

"I think God was flexing His muscles. He had all those angels, just hanging out, has to do something with them. Faith may be believing in that which can not be seen, but over and over again in the Bible, God shows His mighty power. He speaks from burning bushes. He commands His people directly. He sends angels to do His will. He even sends Jesus as proof of His almighty strength. I think God was bullying Paul. You better believe, because if you don't, boy oh boy, is there something waiting for you."

David laughed. "That's a unique take."

"I have my issues with the Bible."

"There's more than enough to go around."

"I always pitied those who believed the Adam and Eve creation story was real," I said. "I never came right out and said so, of course—we Episcopalians might not put much stock in original sin, but we don't go tromping all over treasured religious tropes. My kids watched those animated Bible classics just like anyone else's. If people want to believe God made man from mud and Eve from Adam's rib and that they lived in an authentic paradise, that's their right. For me, and for my father too, the creation story—either one; there's two if you read closely—was no more significant than the Iroquois Sky People legend or the Buddhist's primordial wind. How can anyone know what happened before people were around?"

David grinned, amused, or perhaps bemused. How could a priest be so flippant?

"So, there's Adam and his woman Eve enjoying life of total bliss and Eve encounters the serpent, who God created, mind you, and the serpent says, 'Why don't you take the fruit off that tree over there? Looks like tasty fruit.' Eve dutifully responds God forbade them from eating of that tree because it would kill them. 'Kill you?' the serpent says with a laugh. 'Surely not. God wants you to *think* it'll kill you because the big guy knows if you eat that fruit, you will be as a god too and know what is good and what is evil.'

"She takes the fruit and she and Adam eat it and it's good, but then they realize they're naked and they are filled with this awful emotion called shame. God calls down to them and they hide. Not only are they ashamed, they're scared. God is furious and thus the punishments commence. Bye bye paradise. Hello mortality and pain."

My voice cracked a little on pain, but David didn't notice. Or at least pretended not to.

"Nudists quote Genesis as proof God wants us to be naked. Jehovah Witnesses claim after Armageddon, the world will be restored to Garden-of-Eden plenty and, presumably, we'll all be nudists too. Catholics use Eve's transgression as the cornerstone of a faith constructed solidly on misogynistic ideals. Episcopalians? We watch cartoons."

"You don't give yourself enough credit," David said.

"You know, my wife would have told me to shut up about five minutes ago."

He waited. What could he do? My wife was dead, and I was talking about Adam and Eve.

"Why did God put that tree in the Garden at all? Did He want Eve to defy Him so He could toss them out into the harsh desert? On the heels of that, if God is omnipotent, didn't He know Eve was going to pick that fruit? Or, better yet, didn't God know the serpent was going to orchestrate this beguilement? Or, come on now, why did God make the damn evil serpent in the first place?"

"Demons have to live somewhere," David said.

"Demons? You know what I think? I think God designed us to fail. Perhaps watching Adam and Eve in complete happiness was unimaginably dull. Maybe the angels goaded Him into it. If you tempt them, they'll stray. Oh, you think so, huh? Fine. I'll create a clever serpent and he'll—ah, shit, Eve has no resolve."

We laughed again but it didn't come as easily, and it sunk down and away as if leaden.

"There's something else too. Why did the serpent want Eve to eat that apple? Did the serpent know what God would do and the snake wanted it to happen because anarchy rules? But after they ate that fruit, Adam's and Eve's eyes were opened. They *did* see. God wanted us blind and happy. The serpent wanted us to see and judge for ourselves. God casts Adam and Eve from paradise not because of their transgression but because He feared if they ate of the Tree of Knowledge again, they would know all, be gods themselves. Makes me wonder: who's really the bad guy?"

David's fingers scratched his coffee cup. "There are some African tribes that believe a god named Modimo created everything. All the good stuff, all the bad things. He was water and fire. He has no beginning and no end, like the Christian god. These tribes thank Modimo and fear him. In fact, only priests and soothsayers can say his name. It's interesting because we don't tend to recognize God created evil as well as good."

"Soothsayers?"

"Ever meet one?"

"Can't say I have."

"I've seen some odd things. Tell you about it sometime."

I expected him to get up and say he had better be going, but he stayed seated, fingers scraping at styrofoam. I stared at my daughter and tried to see through the sheet.

"You ever think about Job?" I asked. "How can we receive good and not receive evil?"

"Now, there's an interesting story."

"You know what? Of all the things I've wrestled with in my faith, all the seeming contradictions and conundrums in the Bible—why do bad things happen to good people?; why does suffering exist?; what happens after we die?—it is the story of Job that draws me back over and over. God calls Job His most faithful servant and then doesn't think twice about letting Satan kill Job's animals, murder his family, riddle his body with boils."

Anger bulged inside me, hot and filling.

"Why did God allow Satan to do that? To teach a point? Conduct a lesson? Prove he was the one true God? Be able to laugh before all the angels and say, 'See? I told you I am God.' That's what bothers me. Actually, it pisses me off. Job didn't deserve any of that shit storm God let Satan rain down on him. *I'm* Job. I'm His bait. His toy. Behold my loyal servant, Lucas. Look at his happy, perfect life. Fuck him. Let him suffer. That's why bad things happen. Why WE suffer. It's God's will—SO BE IT!"

I shouted those last three words and loved how my voice echoed out in the hallway. I jumped to my feet, my coffee spilling, and had David leaped up to stop me, I would have punched him. I've never hit anybody, but I would have hit him. The need would be too strong to resist. My chest heaved and my body flushed with heat. The anger had come on so rapidly and for a moment it surged inside me, another scream blooming in my throat.

David didn't move. He waited for me to punch him or grab something, my chair probably, and hurl it across the room, but gradually I calmed. I couldn't look at Phoebe. I was too ashamed. Thanks, Eve.

"Guess I should have gotten you decaf."

I started to apologize, and he stopped me. "Say what you need to." He hesitated a moment. "I know what it's like."

"Do you?" I sounded like a petulant kid.

"I had a son. Joseph. When he was seven, he was diagnosed with Hodgkin's disease. Lymphoma."

"I'm sorry."

I felt stupid, childish, and now ill. I sat.

"It was a long time ago. I know what you're feeling. I thought a lot about Abraham and Isaac."

In Genesis, God commanded Abraham to sacrifice his only son Isaac on the top of the Mountain of Moriah, so Abraham saddled up his donkey and brought his son to the top of the chosen mountain and together they built a sacrificial altar. "But where's the lamb for the burnt offering?" Isaac asked his father. Abraham said God would provide and then he grabbed his son and set him upon the altar and drew his knife to his son's throat but, luckily, God sent an angel to stay his hand.

"Can you imagine?" David asked. "Abraham so willingly takes his son up the mountain, but I can't imagine doing that. I'm supposed to believe that it was a show of love. I'd tell God to find someone else. I'd say, 'You want to see a son die? Send your own.'"

"Right," I said.

"Well, I don't get it. What was going through his head while he trekked up that mountain, while he and his son built that altar? What did Isaac think when his father set him on the altar and raised the knife? That's the problem with the Bible, you know, there's few details about stuff like that. It makes it sound so automatic, simple: God said do it, so he did it. Could cut out a lot of pages just writing that."

I imagined Abraham with red eyes, shielding his son from his tears, telling himself God had commanded him to do this and so he must. But what if that wasn't God's voice? What if he was going crazy? He could slice his son's throat and his men would find him on his knees weeping before his dead son and all Abraham would be able to say is God told me to do it.

Man Claims God Commanded Him to Kill Son, today's headline would read. *Crazy religious freaks*, someone would comment and flip to the Sports page.

"I'm sorry," I said again.

"People say in times of distress to turn to the Good Book, but I think that's a terrible idea. It's full of dark thoughts and false promises."

"I like that. Sounds worthy of a sermon."

"Probably not what people want to hear."

"You're right, I'm sure. Instead, I'll ask about Job. He loses his children, his land, his health and yet he is unwavering in his piety. How the hell did he stay so calm?"

"The priest in me would say, 'Faith,' but the realist? He says Job's a lame metaphor. If you reacted to all you're going through like Job, you'd need a psych evaluation."

"I'm so ... *angry*." I chuckled. Angry? What an inadequate word.

"I have one Bible quote I always turn to."

"'And God said unto the people, "Do not ask me why you suffer. I don't know everything."'"

"This is better. It's from Isaiah: 'Do not fear for I am with you.' I'm no god, but I'm here for you too."

My eyes burned but I wouldn't let myself cry. Not right now. I was sick of crying.

"Thanks. I appreciate it. I do."

I stood and went to my daughter. The plastic bed rail chilled my palms as if they had been keeping Phoebe in a freezer.

"That's when I abandoned my faith," David said. "I wouldn't say I lost it, I merely left it alone for a while. I went back to school, finished a doctor's degree I'd walked away from and decided I needed to put faith in something real."

"Helping sick children in Africa?"

"Helping anyone."

"But eventually you came back to the church," I said.

"I stopping fighting the link."

"Religion and medicine?"

"Both are avenues of healing. Took me long enough, but I finally learned that."

Behind closed lids, Phoebe's eyes were moving. I'm not sure if I said anything but I must have done something because David came to my side. "What is it? What's wrong?"

"Look."

Phoebe's eyes flexed back and forth beneath their lids, squirming bugs trapped in tissue. They wobbled all the way to the right, throbbed there. The edge of her lids vibrated, and bright white crescents shone for a moment before vanishing again. Her eyes tossed side to side, bulged against the lids. A seizure.

But only her eyes moved. Her lips didn't tremble. Her shoulders didn't twitch.

What about her hand? Dare to take a look? Play peekaboo?

"She's having a seizure," I said. "I have to get someone."

"No," David said. He grabbed my arm. "She's having a nightmare."

"A—nightmare?"

Her chest rose and fell rapidly.

"She's hurt. She's—"

"Put your hand on her. On her forehead." He sounded as if he'd done this a million times.

"My hand?"

He took it and placed in on Phoebe's forehead. She was cold. The little girl who always ran hot like a malfunctioning appliance was cold. *Because they were keeping her in a freezer. Pre-chilling her for the morgue table. Getting her ready for life after death.*

"She's cold."

"She's fine."

"No..." I started and couldn't finish, *you don't understand. She's never cold. Always hot. Some kids are like improperly set ovens—they run hot.*

"Tell her you love her."

"I—love her."

"No. Tell her."

Her eyes rolled and bounced and pulsed. I pressed my hand against her frozen forehead and willed my warmth into her. "I love you, sweetie. You're my angel. And I love you so much."

I said it again and again and then over and over in my head. *I love you so much. Please don't leave me. Please don't die. Please don't go. I'm sorry. I'm so sorry. Don't die! PLEASE!*

You were in Uz. But you didn't realize it.

"Lucas." David's calm voice tugged me back.

I fell away from the bed. "She's not . . ?"

"She's fine."

Her eyes had stilled. Her chest moved in slow, steady rhythm. A bead of sweat rolled down her forehead into the hollow of one eye. My hand pulsed with heat, like I'd been squeezing a hot pan handle. I wiped the sweat from her face.

"You're very close to her."

Yeah, she's my daughter, I almost said, but that wasn't what he meant. "What just happened?"

"You tell me."

"Nothing. I was praying, begging, actually."

"What did she say to you?"

"Say to me? Nothing."

David waited as if I were lying and he knew it, and then he fished a business card out of his pocket. It showed his name with *Incumbent* immediately afterward. Incumbent referred to a priest who had been given permanent pastoral responsibilities for a congregation. It was a title exclusive to the Anglican Church, known in America as Episcopalian. *It's not my church*, he had said. *Not that one.*

"I will be back, but call me sooner if anything comes up."

"Where are you going?"

"Someone I have to see." He squeezed my arm and left.

What did she say to you?

Say to me? Nothing.

But that wasn't true. She had said something to me. I was too scared to say it.

Help me, Daddy. I'm trapped.

✝

When I finally pulled the sheet back from her hand again, I almost collapsed to the floor, and might have if not for the railing gripped tightly in one hand.

Inky streaks stretched down Phoebe's fingers and across the back of her hand. Her knuckles were swollen large and purplish. Black lines wormed across her hands, but those weren't just lines—they were her veins and they were supposed to be blue. This wasn't bruising. This was blood poisoning.

I had no idea what blood poisoning actually meant, but if it didn't mean what I was seeing right now then Phoebe's condition had to be known as something even worse. Toxic sepsis infection, perhaps.

On one of those When Disaster Strikes television shows, a man had been cleaning out the crawl space under his stairs and hadn't noticed a colony of brown recluse spiders had taken up residence there. He was bit four times. (*It was only a spider. Don't bother it and it won't hurt you.*) The bite sites had started as small red marks and then bruised and turned black. As the poison spread through the tissue, black lines crisscrossed in his swelling muscles. The pictures of his swollen, black and bloody oozing wounds were enough to make any stomach turn.

He survived but his left arm had been amputated. The remaining stump of half upper arm wobbled at his side like something malformed and incapable. Naomi had asked why the hell I was watching that. I didn't know. Sometimes we can't look away.

I leaned close to her hand. More black lines stretched out over knuckles and under her hand. Gently, I turned her hand over. Her skin was freezing and slimy like thawing meat. The black filled all the palm lines as if someone had used Sharpie to play connect-the-dots. Her fingers crumbled inward, spider legs collapsing into death position. That stench of something sour and rotten, weeks' old garbage in a hot sun, came on sudden and strong.

It's her hand. It's decaying. Gangrenous. Like the spider-victim.

I had to grab a nurse, drag her in here, and demand she admit to me those black lines, those purply blooms, were not normal and something was very, very wrong here. Tell me what's going on. Tell me she's going to die. I can take it. Why not? What's one more?

Help me, Daddy. I'm trapped.

Instead of doing anything, I stood there and watched my daughter, praying God would finally deign to give me a reason to hope.

✝

I put on the Glass Cross T-shirt. It was an extra-large and sagged around my neck and billowed around my waist. I sat on the cot and watched my daughter. My feet throbbed, screamed actually, but I left the shoes on. I hadn't taken them off once. Not even while sleeping. I should keep them on, keep them on until I could no longer walk. Physical pain was preferable to what I was feeling, and it gave me something tangible to focus on.

I hadn't looked at Phoebe's arm, either. It stayed under the sheet and I strained to see the black shades beneath. For a while, no thoughts intruded, and there was only a steady, unpleasant hum of anxiety vibrating through my innards. I could stay this way. Like a man standing on a high-rise ledge who wants neither to jump nor return to life's drudgery, I tried to keep balanced, stayed still, breathed in slow, shallow breaths.

Nurses came and went. They checked Phoebe's vitals, changed her IV bag, but no one pulled back the sheet. A doctor I hadn't yet met came in, offered empty platitudes ("Still hanging in there"... "Best that could be expected"... "She's a fighter, huh?"), and scrawled his signature on the hanging clipboard. I said something about Phoebe's hand and the doctor glanced beneath the sheet (*peekaboo*), seemed to hesitate, and mumbled something about "keeping an eye on it" and then was gone before I could ask anything else. He may have introduced himself, but I don't remember. I honestly didn't care.

Time passed. I expected the Grieving Party to return or other people from church in ones and twos to offer condolences, but no one showed. Didn't want to intrude during this painful time. Lucas will be all right. He's a priest. He can handle it. Better to wait until the wake and the funeral.

Something I had yet to do anything about.

When people in my congregation suffered the loss of a loved one (Along with "I'm sorry," "suffered the loss" has also become another dreadfully pathetic and inadequate phrase.), I assisted with the funeral arrangements as early as the first visit with the bereaved. It's good to move forward; it offers much-needed closure. No one ever fought me on it—they knew it had to be done. In the absence of anyone pushing me to take that step, however, I was content to push it aside. Screw closure. I'm fine on this ledge.

The least I could do, however, was call Naomi's parents, and I got so far as to take out my cellphone before discovering I didn't have their numbers. In fact, I had never actually called either one of them. I should probably call the school, too, both actually, Phoebe and Tamara's and Naomi's. I had to call the newspaper, too. God wasn't about to take care of the death notices and obituaries for me.

I tried to sleep and couldn't. I tried talking to my daughter and barely made it past two words. What was I supposed to say? Everything's going to be okay? Could she even hear me? There ought to be a script for such occasions, something a nurse could hand over like a laminated menu. *Here you go; this should make it easier.* At least help me sound like more of a father and less of a bumbling idiot.

I wandered the halls for a bit. Each floor was a giant rectangle, so I walked around and around. Hospital life is long stretches of dull routine punctuated with bursts of barely controllable chaos. A woman cried quietly in one room. An old man snored in another. In a room at one corner of the floor, a man screamed for help in trios of spiking yaps and he began to sound like a dog: "*Yelp! Yelp! Yelp!*" A nurse looked in on him and walked away. When I passed his room, the man was laying flat, eyes closed, calling out to the ceiling. The TV played some soap opera where two people were caught in dramatic embrace. On my ninth or tenth trip around, a loud beeping noise went off in the old man's room and a voice crackled from every speaker on the floor, "Code neuro. Three North. Room three-one-two-five." The code repeated twice more. Sneakered feet thumped down the hall.

It was quieter outside the morgue.

The rooms marked with simple numbers 1 through 4 waited. Had Naomi been moved down here? Were Tamara and my father still behind one of these doors or were they on cold steel beds that rolled back inside refrigerated drawers, another couple bodies in a wall full of them? Were there locks on the doors? I could see myself checking the drawers for the name Masters, could hear the click of the handle unlatching, feel its cold metal in my palm.

Not that I could even get into the morgue. A large sign declared it a RESTRICTED AREA and a smaller sign beside double doors informed authorized personnel to use the card reader below for admittance. I could wait in one of the rooms for an employee to come by and grab whoever it was, knock him unconscious and steal his ID badge.

That might be interesting.

I stood outside room 3. Tamara's room. I could see myself going in there, standing before her again, crying my stupid eyes out because what the hell else was I supposed to do, but I couldn't lift an arm. I didn't want to see her again and, maybe worse, I didn't want to find the room empty.

Ben Masters had been in room 1. My body cooperated enough to take the knob in hand, but it would take a bit of willpower to push it open. Something tickled the back of my neck, but I fought the desire to scratch it or to even turn around. No one was behind me. *It's not me. It's the room.*

A haunted room in a hospital—especially a room intended as a pre-morgue body viewing room—sounded like a foregone conclusion. I didn't believe in such things; though, of course, like most self-proclaimed rational individuals, I simultaneously accepted Things Beyond Our Understanding happened all the time. The Christian faith centered around a man who healed people by touch, died, and came back to life. Some might say that sounded rather fantastical or that Jesus would be better called the Zombie Messiah.

I pushed open the door.

The gurney was gone and in its place stood a giant cross far too large to fit in the room. It was as if the inside of this room knew no boundaries and could stretch endlessly in all directions into darkness as thick as that in outer space. The cross was tilted toward me at an angle steep enough that it should have fallen. Someone was on that cross, the papery white sheet somehow sticking to him. I knew who it was, even before the sheet fell— the ground went slippery beneath me, a melting ice sheet on a lake, and the room's black walls orbed and flexed, stretched into tunnels echoing a distant sound that might've been a scream.

The sheet fell and there was my father, arms pulled tight to the nails in his palms, his ankles crossed on the foot rest, his pale body falling forward, the slumping underbelly of a bloated fish. *He's already dead, bloated with gases from decomposing tissue.*

His head hung forward, chin on his chest. Grey hair whirled.

"Dad?"

I might have screamed it. This was a hallucination and, as with a nightmare, maybe I could startle myself out of it.

His head lifted. Black spider veins crisscrossed throughout his face, into hollows where his eyes no longer saw, across a crumpled, rotting nose, and into a fallen mouth of toothless gums popping splats of blood across lips tearing like paper.

"*Lucas!*"

I slammed the door, stumbled all the way back to the opposite wall and screamed when my back hit it. My heart hammered and it could have burst, and I wouldn't have cared. For a moment there, the horrific illusion not yet fading from memory, I *hoped* for a heart-exploding death.

Slowly, reason returned. I made my way across the mile-long hallway to that door. No hesitating this time, at least not much, and when I opened the door again, steeling myself against any horror real or imagined—

The room was empty save for a single metal folding chair reflecting the subdued lighting. I closed my eyes, counted to five, and checked again. I stared at the far wall, at each wall, and at the floor and ceiling.

When I closed the door again, its click sounded strong and sensible.

✝

A skinny young man in a hospital gown stood before Phoebe's bed. He was slumped forward on crutches.

"Hello?" I said almost too slowly for it to make sense.

The man couldn't have been much older than sixteen or seventeen. Bandages partially hid lacerations around his eyes and one across his chin. One eye looked punched out and his legs shook even as he leaned on those crutches.

"I was walking," he said. "I found myself here."

"Are you okay?"

He laughed in a sad way, hopeless. "It wasn't a coincidence. I was looking for her."

"Who are you?"

"Jason Hicks. You're her father?"

"Yes."

"I was driving the car that hit her."

My urge to punch him came up so suddenly I stepped forward with fists before stopping myself. "What happened?" I sounded as stern as a detective questioning a suspected murderer.

The kid swallowed. "I was coming around the curve and we hit."

"You weren't watching the road."

"No, I was."

"Texting. Changing a song. Updating Instagram. Something."

The kid stared at me as if searching for a hidden meaning. "I had this awful nightmare last night. There was this metallic voice, like a machine talking, only I knew it wasn't a machine. It was real. Something alive."

"What'd it say?"

Abaddon.

"Nothing," he said. "I couldn't understand it, like it was in another language or something."

"What happened on the road?"

"That's not it, though, because I did understand it. I couldn't hear the words, but I knew what that metallic voice was saying."

"What happened on the road?" I stepped closer, hands tightening again.

"But when I got here, I knew I couldn't do it."

"Do it? Do *what?*"

He didn't respond for a long time and my hands relaxed. He was just a teenager, possibly troubled or some kind of user, and God only knew what this accident was going to do to him. How it was going to haunt him. I wasn't going to hit him, but I wasn't about to wish him freedom from what a guilty conscience might have in store for him either.

"Kill her," he said.

"Excuse me?"

"That's what that voice wanted me to do: kill your daughter."

"You should leave. You're obviously very traumatized."

"I'm not going to do it," the kid said. "I can't."

I spoke slowly and without ambiguity: "You. Need. To. Leave."

The kid didn't move. Maybe he wanted me to hit him. "I'm very sorry."

"I bet you are. Leave."

"But it wasn't my fault."

"How dare you—"

"I was speeding, but I was paying attention. It was the other car. It swerved over the line. It came right for me."

✝

I went home. Had to get out of the hospital. A quick break to wash up and get clean clothes. The house was dark. I sat in the driveway in my car thinking I should back out and return to the hospital, but my need to shower and put on clean clothes won out. As if that familiar act could keep the horrors away.

Besides, I would be quick.

Before my father moved in and my garage was converted into a bland hotel room, I had been able to keep my car in there and then enter the house directly, so when I reached for the garage door opener on the visor it was amusing and troubling to realize it wasn't there, hadn't been there in a long time. Funny, how you can forget such things.

It's okay. You've had other things on your mind. You're not going senile. Not yet.

Motion-activated lights lit the way to the front porch but the light beside the door was off and I fumbled with my key for a while before finally getting inside. To my left was the living room. The couch slumped in the darkness. *Ready, Daddy? First, go light.* Straight ahead was the kitchen and to my immediate right, the stairs leading to the bedrooms.

The entire house was just over two thousand square feet, but it stretched before me for miles in all directions. It was the room in the hospital basement with the liquid black walls that flexed and orbed. Only this was my imagination.

Meaning what happened in the hospital room was real? Maybe you are senile.

I almost called out, "Hello," but I was afraid my voice might echo, a rock bouncing off the insides of a well. The silence was something I would have treasured only a few days ago. Naomi took the girls to the store or to the movies and Dad was in his room and the house was mine. Get in some productive sermon-writing time. Now, I could have all the quiet writing time I wanted. That was my problem: I wasn't looking at the silver lining.

I felt sick.

I turned on all the nearest lights and stood in the living room doorway. The couch sagged against the opposite wall. Even with the lights on, slender shadows created gaps around the couch's back corners and in the crevices between cushions.

The chair where Dad had been seated while Phoebe and I were (*in The Land of Uz*) playing make-believe was opposite the couch. I went to it, touched its worn fabric. Wood almost protruded from the frayed corners.

I felt that familiar sensation of someone behind me and the back of my scalp itched in an arching ripple. My hand curled around the chair's cloth, but the sensation only got stronger. I didn't want to turn around, but not because of what might be there—I didn't want to turn around and find nothing.

The church is particularly silent when it comes to questions about the paranormal, which is odd considering the whole Jesus-rising-from-the-dead, father-son-and-holy-ghost thing, but if ghosts were real, I wanted them to be here. I wanted to turn and see my wife and daughter in the doorway, nearly transparent wraiths. We could sit together on the couch. They wouldn't even have to speak. We could stare at each other. That would be enough.

I turned and found nothing. The scalp itch lingered.

The stairs creaked in all the usual places as I ascended. The hallway light seemed dimmer as if the bulb were slowly dying. Speaking of, the lights in Phoebe's room did not go on, and only after flicking the switch up and down a few times did I remember how the bulbs had flared bright and burst out of existence. There had been someone in here with Phoebe when she was screaming her head off. Not just any someone, however.

Dad.

Of course he hadn't really been there. Never mind the impossibility of him walking up the stairs (or the unlikelihood he could squeeze my wrist so hard it hurt for minutes afterward, and do it with an infected hand), once Naomi had turned the hall light on, the image of a man, of my father, hunching over Phoebe vanished. A dream remnant lingering as a momentary hallucination.

Phoebe's night lights cast halos along opposite walls. One light was a cow stuck forever in a moon-leap and the other a glowing green cross that was one of those forever LED lights. She pleaded to leave them on, even though I was out to convince her she was going to be a teenager soon and teenagers slept with the lights off, like adults. And wasn't that a hilarious lie, considering the seashell nightlight in our master bedroom? I was the parent and I couldn't explain why I did certain things. Being a father was like trekking through a jungle and declaring you knew the way even as you were hopelessly lost and sinking into quicksand.

The room had been dark when I came in Sunday morning. Completely dark. I remembered thinking how odd both night lights had burned out, especially the green cross Naomi purchased, which came in a box promising in goofy print a "lifetime of light."

Sure enough, it was lit now. I started toward it and stopped.

Phoebe's stuffed animals were staring at me. A dozen or so creatures of different sizes congregated on the bed in a half-circle, all faces toward me. The bunny with beady red eyes appeared ready to pounce. Foppy.

In the faint night-light glow, it looked more like a panther. Assembled with the bunny was a stiffed-legged purple pony, a googly-eyed dinosaur with a long, sloping tail, a chipmunk with white sneakers and a heart held in both hands, a well-loved lamb whose coat had turned grey and clumpy, and a coterie of similar creatures.

They were assembled in a kind of welcoming party for Phoebe's return or perhaps as sentries in guarding position against intruders. Phoebe had obviously arranged them like this after making her bed before church. How many times had I walked into her room to find her stuffed animals in such an arrangement? Sometimes it was a bit freaky, that's all. Those plastic eyes staring at me. As if something were watching *through* those eyes. Like the eyes were magic mirrors—I had had that thought Sunday morning, and it came on now even more strongly.

I moved toward the bed. The animals watched me. I could imagine the bunny's haunches twitching in anticipation, preparing to pounce. I always thought the bunny had a weird science-lab vibe with its super-white fur and tiny red eyes, more like a mouse, just larger, a mutant. Its mouth was a stitched Y, but it wasn't completely closed the way I had thought, not simply a line of thread sewed in place—the jaw hung open slightly, and warped, curved fangs protruded over its furry muzzle. Bunnies didn't have fangs, not like this; they had fat buck teeth, perfect for chomping carrots. Who would make a stuffed animal bunny with fangs? Or red eyes, for that matter; this was supposed to be a kid's toy, not a prop for a haunted house.

The cow-jumping-the-moon night light flickered, faded, and went out. The eternal glow of the cross nightlight shaded the facing wall in a sickening purply green. Before I could turn to look at the cross light—confirm it was going to hold up its promise of forever illumination—it faded out as well. The light from the hallway slanted across the bed in a stretched rectangle, and my shadow dropped over the stuffed animals.

That feeling of someone standing behind me came on again but this time it wasn't behind me. I sensed someone—*something*—right there before me on the bed, just the way I could sense Phoebe or Tamara or Naomi in bed even if my eyes were closed.

It's strange how we can sense things we can't see. It makes us sound like soothsayers—(Like the ones David encountered during his trip to Africa when he watched his father bury dozens of corpses. *Love thy neighbor*, he said.) Maybe those "otherworldly" sensations were proof of God, a glimpse of His omnipotence. Knowing all things at all times was bound to feel strange. Enough to drive you mad, so we are given only glimpses here and there.

A soft, ruffling sound directly before me could have been Phoebe stirring in her sleep, but she wasn't there. She was in the hospital, in some sort of coma (*Help me, Daddy. I'm trapped.*), and I was tired and stressed. The sound was the stuffed animals arranging into a new position. Attack formation, perhaps. I would have laughed if it hadn't seemed so believable.

This is what had happened when Phoebe started screaming. She felt the presence of something else and when I entered, I saw a dark figure hulking over her, but that hadn't really been there. If it had, why would it look like my father?

Come back to reality, Lucas, my mother said when I was a boy and launching into some fantastical bit of pure imagination, alternate worlds with flying dragons and magic swords or things even more outlandish. *Quite an imagination on that boy,* she'd say as if commenting, *That's some haircut on you.* My father believed all good priests had active imaginations and that class in seminary complemented the notion. How else could you imagine God if you couldn't dream the impossible? But no matter what I could dream up—*Stranger things have happened.* Mom and her phrases.

The gentle shuffling sound of fabric and fur again. I leaned toward the bed and that good old active imagination offered an image of the bunny, mouth wide, those gnarled fangs jutting out, lunging right for my exposed neck. I could feel the soft pads of its fake paws pressing against my face.

I stepped to the side so the hall light shone across the bed. The animals hadn't moved. Not one inch. What a surprise. But just because they hadn't fallen into phalanx formation like Greek soldiers didn't mean they hadn't moved at all.

They're not moving because they're playing possum, my mind offered. *The moment you look away, they'll change position, like the toys in that movie. Or maybe they'll attack you. And are you sure that alien was on the bed before because doesn't it usually have a spot on the shelf behind you?*

I turned slowly toward the pink bookshelf. It had four drawers on the bottom and six shelves above. Dozens and dozens of stuffed animals stared back at me. Arms and legs jutted toward me. Furry faces peered out on top of each other. Wedged in among the animals were various knickknacks: the clear cube with a silver dollar in it she won in school for knowing all fifty states and their capitals, the music box with a ballerina figurine on top that spun lazily to a tune of high-pitched pops we got her for Christmas two years ago when she went through her dancing fad. A piece of pink construction paper folded into a comically large card sat on the top shelf, the one Phoebe could only reach by standing on a chair. Sprawling cursive filled the inside of the card, scrawled in thick black crayon.

The card must've been something she created years ago in second or third grade. Her writing projects, artistic creations, and even trivial tasks like Construct a Simple Sentence worksheets popped up all over the place: I found them in unmarked boxes, stuffed in the kitchen junk drawer, and taped to the wall in almost every room. Naomi said it was important we saved as much as we could because these years wouldn't last forever.

Like she knew what was coming.

I took the card down. A heart with uneven humps decorated the cover. A thick, jagged line broke the heart in half in a black lightning bolt. Phoebe had pressed very hard to make that line. Inside, the card read, *Dear Daddy*, and then it said the same thing over and over, filling the entire sheet of paper. Only one word.

Abaddon.

Over and over again. It must have been written thirty times, maybe more, the word overlapping itself in wild cursive loops, filling the folded crevice in tiny block letters, squaring off the corners with perpendicular precision.

Had Phoebe done this? Naomi or I would have noticed. Right? Could she have been seated at the kitchen table writing Abaddon over and over while Naomi and I went about our daily tasks? If only we had said, *Oh, honey, what's that you're working on?*

I reached to put the card back where I found it and Ben-the-bear stared at me with black eyes from that spot on the top shelf. His fat limbs seemed to reach toward me. I started, my heart cramming itself into my throat, and I forced a laugh. Forget playing possum; this was an ambush, but it wasn't like the thing had actual claws or even teeth, plastic or otherwise. It was a stuffed animal with worn paws and a ripped seam up one leg, not some hellish gimmick with sharp edges and a NOT SUITABLE FOR KIDS UNDER 5 sticker.

But you never noticed the bunny had teeth, either. And maybe it didn't, but it does now.

Something watched me through those bulging eyes. I could almost imagine it thinking, though not what its thoughts might be, like stumbling upon a strange animal during a hike through the woods and both of us caught in frozen stares, unable to know what the other might do.

They would be mad thoughts, the wonderings of a stuffed animal.

I hesitated only briefly before grabbing it around its mushy middle. Time to get control of myself. This little sidestep into the phantasmagorical was an especially elaborate way to avoid returning to the hospital where I would stare at my daughter and the tubes running from her body. And thinking about inanimate objects that had unexplained sentient powers was a B-horror movie cliché to distract me from remembering the teenager who (*kill your daughter*) destroyed my family.

The bear (*Ben*) stiffened with a solid skeleton and for a moment, I clutched it, trying to squeeze into its suddenly hard innards, and then I threw it against the wall. Its plastic eyes bounced off the wall with a dull *thwonk* and it fell face down on the floor.

The bunny watched me from the bed. Its fangs stretched below its chin.

As I walked out, both night lights came back on.

I took a shower and though it should have felt relaxing and invigorating, it was as mechanical and automatic as a thousand other showers. I tried to push the bedroom experience out of my mind, but it had burrowed its way in and the more I thought about it, the more it nestled in there. Maybe Phoebe hadn't written that card. Maybe someone else had written *Dear Daddy* to make it look like she was the author. Okay, sure, but who? Did Ben-the-bear know how to write?

No, not that Ben.

Don't you want me to get better?

I didn't want to believe it, but I could see my father going into Phoebe's room when everyone was out of the house and using her crayons to write that deranged letter.

I tried to laugh and couldn't. The sound of water pelting at my feet echoed in the bathroom while the fan in the ceiling drowned out everything else. The plastic shower curtain and the cloth one with the polka dot pattern on it obscured what little light there was, so showering was like standing in a cave beneath rain water trickling in through cracks.

It was the other car. It swerved over the line. It came right for me.

Had Naomi been distracted by the girls in the back? Had my father done something? For a moment, I saw it vividly: Ben Masters reaching over, snagging the wheel, and, what?, purposely turning them into the oncoming car?

That's what that voice wanted me to do—kill your daughter.

Someone was in the bathroom.

I was an expert at detecting people sneaking into the bathroom because when we were newlyweds, Naomi got such a kick out of furtively entering the bathroom while I was showering and yanking back the curtain to holler, "Boo!" A few times, I screamed, like a little girl on a roller coaster. She'd laugh until she cried. She called it a game. She stopped after the time I was so startled I slipped and almost cracked my skull against the tub spout, but the damage was done, psychologically speaking, and every time I've showered since, I've always sensed she was doing her stupid shower game again.

The thing about showering and sensing someone in the bathroom is you know, unless you have a wife like mine, there's probably nobody there, but because you're naked and enclosed, it's the ultimate vulnerability. It's ridiculous, but you begin to hear the *Psycho* music, but that's like most fears: they're ridiculous, remnants of childhood at which adults should chuckle, but people are killed in the shower, spider bites lead to amputations, and families die in car accidents. Even the wildest, most outlandish fears (*Uz Monster*) stem from the very real truth our world is not as safe and orderly as we like to believe. There is chaos always brewing just beneath the visible. It's why we slow down at car wrecks: we dare ourselves to glimpse that undertow of terror. Thank God the chaos didn't get us. We're okay. For now.

You know no one is in the bathroom. You know that from a logical mindset but the feeling of someone standing there intensifies. If you tug back the curtains and glimpse, you might be able to assuage your fears for a moment but giving in to them and looking grants the fear credence. Not looking until you're done showering, however, demands you think on other things and ignore the mounting certainty you're being watched, even stalked.

A shadow moved beyond the curtain but, of course, that was a trick of the poor light and the hazy double-curtain boundary. Naomi wasn't there. Neither were my girls or my father. If someone *was* there, it wasn't anyone I knew. *Or anything living.*

I tried to peer through the curtains and the water bleeding down the glass, but that shadow could be anything. My heart had decided that the shadow could be a threat and my mind could argue against it all it wanted but my body flushed with hot adrenaline.

"Hello?"

Speaking only made the sensation worse and I pulled back the curtain.

The bathroom was empty, but sometimes vision is deceiving. Think of all the germs and microbes floating all around us, all those invisible predators seeking entry.

✝

I put on jeans and a blue T-shirt and drove back to the hospital. The shirt featured the Episcopalian shield of a blood-red cross in honor of the church's Anglican roots over the left breast and a Saint Andrew's Cross in the upper-left corner comprised of nine white crosses. The Saint Andrew's Cross is really an "X" in honor of Saint Andrew who said he wasn't worthy of being crucified in the same position as Jesus. Like Saint Peter, who asked to be crucified upside down for the same reason.

I've always wondered if those requests were final attempts at converting potential Christians, selfless acts done in the name of the faith, or completely genuine gestures of contrition and unworthiness.

On the Mountain of Moriah, Abraham prepared to kill his son—

Is that the devotion God expects?

Where, one might ask, was love in all this?

✝

I went to the information desk and asked about the kid who'd been in that awful car accident out on Cliffside Road. The man at the desk asked for a name and for a moment I couldn't recall it and imagined grabbing the guy by the collar and yelling something about how my whole damn family was being taken from me and I didn't need any of this hospital bureaucratic bullshit.

"Jason Hicks."

The man's fingers made maddeningly annoying clicks across the keyboard and then he told me the room and handed me a flimsy cardboard Visitor's Pass. I yanked it from his grip even though I already had one. I'd been told to hold onto mine. For convenience sake.

The kid was on his crutches coming back from the bathroom when I came up behind him and shoved him hard toward his bed. His released a startled guttural noise, lost his balance, and crumpled to the floor.

His parents, both middle-aged and wearing jeans, jumped up from their chairs. Jason's mother screamed as if I shot her boy and his father puffed his narrow chest, eyes bugging, and said, "What the hell is the meaning of this?"

Jason was turning to see who had attacked him and I dropped to one knee before him. I grabbed his throat. The visitor pass crumbled between my hand and his throat and the edge of it wedged under the Band-Aid on his chin. He grimaced, eyes wide.

"Why were you lying?" I asked, my voice a harsh slap.

Come back to reality, my mother whispered.

"Why were you lying?"

"I wasn't." He struggled against my grip, face flushing red, but he didn't try to fight free.

"What happened on the road?"

"Hey!" the father yelled. He came up behind me. "Get off my son." He sounded more surprised than angry.

"Help him, Howard," the woman yelled. "For God's sake—help him!"

The man grabbed my arm, but I shook it off. "Why did you say you were going to kill my daughter?"

"Help!" the boy's mother yelled. "Help us, please!"

"I'm not," Jason said, straining to speak. "It's not me. Not me."

"*Stop lying!*"

The father grabbed me again and this time yanked me backwards. I snagged his son forward by the neck before losing my grasp.

You've lost more than that.

The man pulled me toward the wall as his wife screamed for help and a pair of nurses scrambled into the room with a security guard a few steps behind who almost knocked them down as he pushed into the room.

I raised my hands in surrender.

Jason Hicks stared at me with huge, horrified eyes.

It was the other car. It swerved over the line. It came right for me.

✝

David Javan was sitting on the cot in Phoebe's room, stationed there in a vigil. Maybe for Phoebe and maybe for me. Neither of us seemed particularly surprised.

"You look a bit harried."

"I almost beat up a kid."

"What happened?"

That's what that voice wanted me to do: kill your daughter.

"Doesn't matter. Kid doesn't know what he's saying."

"You want to talk about it?"

"One of Phoebe's doctors was there. He said I was under an unbelievable strain. When the kid's parents learned who I was, they backed off pretty quickly. Probably signing him out right now."

"What do you mean, who you are?"

"It was the kid who caused the crash."

Phoebe looked as she had, asleep and beaten, bruises floating on her pale face. I hesitated to touch her.

It was the other car. It swerved over the line. It came right for me.

We sat in mutual silence for a while.

"It's funny," I said eventually, "I've been sitting here and praying as hard as I can and yet there wasn't even a course devoted to prayer in seminary. And we're supposed to be the experts."

"When I was young, I was told to pray properly you had to be on your knees, back straight, hands joined, palm to palm, fingers pointed heavenward. You hold your hands anywhere from your heart to your face, close your eyes, and beseech God to hear your prayers."

"How very regimented."

"We can't have people praying willy nilly. How could God possibly keep track if there's no order?"

"How can we even know if God hears our prayers?"

"Jesus prayed, so I guess we should too."

"Worked out real well for him, didn't it?"

"Makes you wonder what the point is."

"Yeah," I said. "The point of anything."

David cleared his throat. "When my son died, people told me it was for the best. They said, 'He's with Jesus now. Take comfort in that.' I guess whatever works, but for me, that's such a lame explanation. Makes Jesus sound selfish. He needed another angel, had things for my son to do, blah, blah, blah. If that's all we are, future companions for Jesus, why not take us all now?"

"It was all Eve's fault, remember? She picked that apple and God doomed us to be mortal. I used to joke with my wife about that all the time."

"It wasn't Eve, though," David said. "It was the serpent."

"The talking snake. Right." I turned from Phoebe. David was leaning forward, forearms on his thighs, hands loose, head bowed.

"My son didn't die of lymphoma. The doctors will say he did, and maybe that's what took him in the end, but that wasn't the cause. Not the thing that started it."

"What was it?"

"When I was young, I was with this guy who called himself a 'traveling preacher.' His name was Henry Brahm, but he titled himself Reverend Pete. He took me under his wing as an apprentice. He knew my father, and I gave him a lot of credence because of that, which he probably didn't deserve. He always wore a full white suit, like he was Elvis, and when it came to faith, he loved two things: big crowds and desperate people. It took me a while to realize that, or at least accept it. He called me his 'chosen one.'

"I followed him through the south for years and eventually we made our way up into New York, out near Rochester. He had started as one man on foot, but he gained a rapid following and by the time we came up here, it was a veritable motorcade pulling into town. Like an old-prayer revival, we had a tent and giant banners written in old-fashioned script, promising *Reverend Pete's Prayer Parade is Come to Save One and All!* I was married and had a son, and I knew my wife was getting pretty tired of the life. She was home schooling Joe, but she wanted him to have some stability, make some friends.

"Reverend Pete did his thing, got the crowds riled up, promised God's blessing, accepted any and all donations— 'Heaven doesn't need money, but the realm of man does.'—and moved on. I knew my wife had been long in the planning to get away from Reverend Pete and his traveling prayer parade. I wasn't into it much anymore, anyway. I was thinking about going back to finish med school. My wife was a strong, wonderful woman. She finally pushed me to do what I should have done much earlier. Henry went on without me and we settled into small-town life. Place called Karras.

"My wife got a job as a secretary at a nearby college and I found work as an interim pastor at this little presbyterian church in town. Put off med school yet again. Joe started going to school and seemed to like it. We found a beautiful old house to rent. It was all working out very smoothly."

"That's when it all turns to shit," I said. "Just when everything is perfect."

"Joe started acting strange. Be real tired, exhausted, looked pale all the time. Started getting sick, too, a sniffle here, a cough there. The pediatrician said he was probably going through a growth spurt, something about the body tapping all its resources when it's about to rapidly grow. We fed him twice as much, but he didn't want to eat. We practically force fed the poor kid.

"That house had a full basement, completely finished, and Joe spent a lot of time down there playing. I went down there once and found him in the middle of the room with all his action figures and matchbox cars arranged around him in concentric circles. I asked him what he was doing, and he said, 'Protecting myself.' All the figures and cars were facing outward, miniature guardians."

I thought of stuffed animals arranged in a protective perimeter, of bunnies with curved, plastic teeth.

"He came up from the basement a few times looking so pale I thought he might pass out. We thought he was feeling better and just pushing himself too much. Joke's on us. When we eventually took him to a specialist, he pointed the way to pediatric oncology and I'll tell you, I can't think of anything worse than a place where children are told they're going to die."

He looked around—everywhere—except at me or at Phoebe. "You don't want to hear what happens there. I don't want to talk about it, either."

"I understand."

"I met your father there."

"When?"

"He said he was on a minor pilgrimage, touring the churches of New York and New England."

"He took me a few times."

"He offered prayers for my son and listened to our sad little story."

"Small world, I guess."

"Your father was a good man. I'm lucky to have known him. His faith was very strong." David hesitated. "My wife died in that town, too."

My throat dried in itchy patches.

"After Joe, my wife walked out of the hospital in Rochester and right into traffic."

"Jesus."

"Witnesses said they saw her stand at the curb, waiting, and when a furniture truck came speeding down the road, she stepped right in front of it."

I can sort of understand that, I almost said.

"I'm so sorry."

"My wife and son are buried in that town. I walked out alone, and I've never been back. Not that I went far. I've been all around the world, Lucas, but I can't bring myself to settle down any farther from them than here."

"You said your son didn't die of cancer. What did you mean?"

"There was something else wrong with him."

"What?"

"He was possessed."

✝

Help me, Daddy. I'm trapped.

"You think your son was ... possessed? As in, demons?"

"One night, before we finally brought him to a specialist," David said, "Joe came into my bedroom and woke me up. I took him in my arms, thought he had a nightmare, and he was so cold. Like he'd been playing in the snow. I asked him what was wrong, and he looked at me with such sad, scared eyes. 'The angels are hunting me,' he said. He always had a fear of angels. Sounds strange, but not if you think about it. They're these enormous creatures that radiate million-watt light and descend to do the bidding of some egotistical mogul in the sky. They're not human, nor are they gods, yet they can inflict pain as easily as heal. Some kids find it reassuring. My son did not."

Quincy Toft. *Quincy told his parents angels were hunting him. Big, bright lights, enormous things, horrifying.* Had to be the same story, but why would my father change the boy's name from Joe Javan to Quincy Toft?

"But it was only a nightmare," I said.

Awful nightmare, Jason Hicks had said.

"Maybe. Maybe not. At least not *only* a nightmare. I asked him how he knew the angels were hunting him and he said they told him. 'In your room?' I asked. 'No,' he told me. 'Downstairs.' I asked why he was downstairs and he started crying. Through tears, he told me they were whispering to him. They called him down to the basement in the middle of the night and tried to get him. I told him it was just a bad dream. He looked at me, and I swear I saw a glimpse of what he would look like in twenty years, deep-set eyes, firm jaw, exuding complete gravity. 'One of them touched me,' my son said. 'It said I was going to die very soon.'"

"You think angels killed him?"

"Angels, demons, ghosts? It doesn't make a difference, does it?"

"But that doesn't mean anything. That nightmare or hallucination could have been a construct of his own mind, a metaphor, a way to process what it sensed was wrong inside, like the body knew it had cancer."

"How very logical," David said. "After the diagnosis, Joe started acting very strange. More reserved. Talked to himself in this thin whisper."

"He was coping. Trying to, anyway."

David smiled in a sad way that bothered me, though I couldn't explain why. "He broke my wife's arm."

"What?"

"He grabbed her arm in both of his hands and broke it."

"He was ten, right?"

"And ill. Almost too weak to crawl out of bed some days."

Don't you want me to get better?

"So, what are you talking about?"

He stood, walked to my daughter's side. "When my son was dying, he developed other symptoms."

Sudden ability to speak Latin? Tourette's-inspired cursing? Projectile vomiting?

"What symptoms?"

"The doctors said it was a complication of the cancer. A sign of the body shutting down."

"What was it?"

"When he died, my son's arm looked like this."

He lifted the sheet to reveal Phoebe's blackened arm. For a moment, I didn't process what I was seeing. It looked like a fat snake was sleeping beside my daughter, but that snake was her arm. Her skin had thickened, turned scaly, and cracked in deep grooves where blood flowed like hot lava fracturing blackened ground.

A scream was barreling up my throat even as my mind insisted I wasn't seeing this. Her fingers had been black, her hand slightly dark, a minor complication of the coma, an infection or something, antibiotics would heal it, no doubt—that black, awful thing, that was *not* her arm.

In the hallway, I shouted for help. The nurse's reaction to the arm did nothing to calm me. Through the loudspeaker came "Code trauma two," and the room number and then a doctor was running in on shiny black dress shoes and the nurse was telling me to give them room, to back up, and David was grabbing me, pulling me toward the other end of the room.

There were no alarms or defibrillators (*Clear!*), or any sense of panic except the mad flutter in my throat that felt like I might vomit if I tried to say anything. Yet, I heard my voice over and over, a sound I recognized but couldn't control, saying, "My daughter! My baby! Help her! Please!"

Eventually, the doctor turned to me, took off his gloves. Blood dotted some of the latex fingertips. "There appears to be extensive tissue degeneration. We need to run some tests before confirming anything, but this is very serious." He looked confused as he spoke, like none of this made any sense.

"What is causing it?" I asked.

"I can't be sure, but I would guess it is some kind of bacterial infection. We will put her on a very powerful antibiotic and up her steroids."

"Will that fix it?"

"We'll give it our best shot."

It wasn't until after he walked away I realized who he had been. Dr. Noose, bearer of grim tidings.

✝

They took endless vials of Phoebe's blood and added another bloated liquid bag to her IV. She twitched at one point, as if reacting to something in a dream, but when I asked the nurse if she saw that, her pitying look was enough to silence my questions. Another nurse wrapped Phoebe's arm in layers of white gauze.

"I can help her," David whispered.

He had backed me up into the far corner and though he wasn't restraining me, he stayed in front of me, as if to stop me if I tried to get past.

I wanted to believe him, I did, but his promise of hope cut me deeper than a pronouncement of death. All things end. Every life owes a death.

"She's not possessed."

"There's someone you need to talk to," David said.

"My daughter was in a car accident. She hadn't been acting strange. She's in a coma, not in the clutches of some demon. You have any idea how stupid—"

"Lucas, listen—"

He raised his hands and I swatted them away. "No. I'm sorry your son died, but my daughter is not your son. You can believe whatever you want about your kid, but my daughter is not possessed."

"It's not like you think. This isn't *The Exorcist*. Possession is not how it is in the movies."

"Get out."

"I know this is tough, but I don't want you to lose your whole family."

"*Get out.*"

"There isn't much time. If we don't try, she will die. I guarantee it."

"Then she dies!"

My scream pushed him farther back then a shove would have. Behind him, faces crowded in the doorway. George and Lavon looked ready to jump David if I gave the signal. Iris held a white baker's box with red string knotted at the top.

The Grieving Party had returned.

✟

To their credit, no one mentioned funerals, wakes, or church services. They asked how I was doing, and I shrugged. They talked about current events in the world and I zoned out.

I stared at Phoebe. Could she be possessed? If she were, wouldn't she be squawking all sorts of nonsense and damning God? David said possession was not like the way the movies presented it. No pea-green vomit, no words bubbling up out of skin like internal tattoos. But saying her coma was the work of some monster sounded like the conclusion of medieval doctors who kept jars of leeches at the ready. A spirit has come unto you and made you ill. The spirit is invisible and untraceable.

Yeah, it's called germs.

I remembered thinking the other day of some TV show where a character contracted rabies, grew very ill, and was then miraculously better— *A miracle!* —before falling dead without warning. Possession would seem a very believable explanation.

But Phoebe hadn't been acting strange. She hadn't been ill, hadn't done anything destructive. *She'd been having frequent nightmares, though. You forget that? And what about all those stuffed animals? Set up as if to shield her.* As if she could imbue those cotton-stuffed creatures with enough belief to protect her from the Uz Monster.

Abaddon.

A Bad One.

Had she written that construction paper card? If not her, who?

Dad. He had been acting strange, more so than usual. He had grabbed me with enough force to bruise my wrist—grabbed me with a blackened hand. He had been ailing and then, miracle of miracles, gotten suddenly better. *Don't you want me to get better?*

And now he was dead.

He had died from a heart attack during the car accident, not from some demon eating him from the inside out, some metaphorical tumor.

This is how it happens.

What happens?

How you go insane.

That, at least, made sense.

✟

Dr. Noose visited me later and along with his blank expression, he might as well have had an actual noose slung over one shoulder. Should just as well get on with it.

"We are pushing antibiotics and steroids, but I must caution you—she is not responding the way we hoped. The infection seems to have stopped its progression, but it is not receding, not improving."

"So, it is an infection?"

"Oh, yes."

"Not psychological or..." *Supernatural*, I would have finished.

"It's definitely an infection, but we haven't located the bacteria or virus yet. We're still testing, but necrosis has set in. Tissue death."

"What do we do?"

"There's something we should discuss."

"She's going to die?"

"I certainly hope not, but the more immediate concern is this infection. If we are unable to eradicate it, it may spread."

"Okay."

"What I'm saying, Mr. Masters, is without immediate improvement, we will have to amputate your daughter's arm."

✟

The hospital settled into a post-dinner lull. As usual, Phoebe had a meal of liquid nutrients. I ate a bland sandwich of wilting lettuce on stale white bread cut in triangles.

I sat in the hospital room, watched my daughter and tried not to think of anything. That might have been possible before the accident and, in fact, Naomi often accused me of doing just that—sitting in the office at home doing nothing and thinking of nothing more substantial than clouds floating through my head.

Those days were gone, forever. Try all I wanted, but I couldn't simply sit there and think empty, puffy-cloud thoughts. Everything was dark and heavy. In my head, the sky had gone apocalyptic grey.

Amputate your daughter's arm.

There had been a news story a while ago about a woman who was a cancer survivor who had been diagnosed with a bacterial infection found in dog saliva. She lost both hands and feet. Then there was the teenage girl who contracted the flesh-eating bacteria while playing on a rope swing. Both women had been impossibly sunny in their recovery dispositions. The infections ravaged flesh, but the women and their families thanked the power of merciful God.

I had thought both victims were probably too stoned on meds to know what they were saying, and the families were in denial. I can hear Job: "Shall we receive good at the hand of God and not receive evil?"

There was something else wrong with my son.

What?

He was possessed.

Talk about denial. Possession, no matter how outlandish, was preferable to cancer. Better to have some demon screwing around inside your child's head than rapidly multiplying cells determined to eat up his insides. Demons at least can be ousted.

Exorcised.

What would David have me do, stage some elaborate ritual here in the hospital room? Bring in buckets of holy water, giant crosses, and strap Phoebe down in case the demon tried to animate her body. Then what? Preach the good word? Go all "power of Christ compels you" nonsense?

I should be clear on something. If I haven't come right out and said it before, I'm a bit of a skeptic which, I know, seems contradictory to my profession. I am not, however, one of those priests suffering a loss of faith. This isn't a story of how one man was shown the light and learned to believe again. There's an apt passage in Acts: "These [people] were more noble than those in Thessalonica [who believed without skepticism], in that they received the word with all readiness of mind, and searched the scriptures daily, whether those things were so."

Meaning, those people didn't just accept what they were told—they questioned, they searched.

That's me, searching, questioning.

When I was a little boy, I had a blue-and-white knitted blanket my grandmother made for me. I carried it everywhere, held it tight, even sucked on it like an infant or a kitten. It was my blankie. By the time I gave it up, the blanket was frayed, sagging in torn holes, and faded to pale yellowish white.

Adulthood brings its own blankies; they're just better disguised.

†

One of Naomi's good friends was a woman named Carolyn Pews. She was a teacher at Warrenville Elementary and a frequent guest at our home with her husband Jimmy. They had been to Saint John's a few times, but they were proud agnostics. I always told her that was a *non-prophet* organization. She was used to me saying such things or, *Mrs. Pews, would you care to take a seat?* To which, she might reply, *You know, when the cannibals ate the missionary, they got a real taste of religion.*

She stood in the doorway for a moment. She wore usual teacher attire: long skirt, blouse with shrouding blazer. A bloated leather satchel hung over her shoulder. "Lucas. I'm so sorry."

After a long embrace in which I lingered in her perfume, I apologized for not contacting her, but she told me to not be ridiculous. Lavon Solly had informed the school and news spread from there. She promised not to stay long (something even The Grieving Party were fond of saying, as if I wanted to sit and stare at my comatose daughter all by myself), just wanted to stop by and see how I was doing.

"I don't know," I said.

"This is so awful," Carolyn said. "I don't believe it."

"This is probably where I'm supposed to offer some biblical comfort."

"Naomi always said you were humble, but I think you've got an *altar* ego."

"Cute."

"Not very clever."

"It happens."

"I'm sorry, Lucas. I don't know what to do."

"Neither do I."

We embraced again and she cried a little against my shoulder.

"Isn't it considered uncouth to hug a priest?"

"It's okay," I said, "as long as you practice safe *sects*."

She laughed harder than the joke deserved, but it helped her get control. From her satchel, she removed a pile of different-colored construction-paper cards. "Her students made these."

She turned to Phoebe while I glanced through the sympathy cards seven-year-olds created. The covers featured sad faces and graveyards with lopsided headstones, stick figures holding hands around warped coffins and pale suns with frowning faces shining down. One of them, done on pink paper, featured a remarkably realistic bouquet of flowers. In fancy script beneath it read, *I'm SO Sorry!* I hesitated before opening it—*Abaddon, Abaddon*—but inside there were more life-like flowers and a child's simple, honest emotion: *I Miss You, Mrs. Masters.*

"Thank you for bringing these." My voice hitched a little, but I kept it in check.

Carolyn shook her head but didn't turn from Phoebe. She cried softly, gripped the railing. She stayed that way for while and when she finally turned and said she had to go, apologizing in a quiet, confused way, her eyes burned red and she seemed to stare past me. Like she was seeing something beyond this world. Something that haunted her.

✝

The sun set like something completely separate from reality—it bulged into the horizon and splashed into reds and oranges, but only the faintest stray light made it to the hospital window.

Phoebe slept without movement or noise.

That's because she's not sleeping—she's in a coma.

David called my cellphone three times; the third time I answered with the intent of telling him to keep his crazy possession theories to himself and, while he was at it, stay the hell away from me and my daughter.

He beat me to the punch: "I found Maggie Prescott. The woman who called the police after the accident."

I couldn't at first respond. "How did you know that?"

"Turns out, Maggie attends Word of Christ Church."

"Small world."

"She has something you need to hear."

"I'm not in the mood, David."

"Trust me."

"It's hard to trust anyone who believes in demonic possession."

"Catholics believe in it."

"I don't trust them, either."

A beat of laughter helped.

"I'm sorry I came on pretty hard before," David said.

"I'm, I don't know ... Lost."

"Let me help. That's all I want to do. You should hear what this woman has to say."

"I don't think I can take it right now."

He waited a moment. "She's already on her way."

✝

Maggie Prescott had the look of a woman who feared the sky might crumble if she glanced up. She stood outside her car in the hospital parking lot with a big wool coat wrapped around her, the collar popped around her ears and her hunched frame bending into the coat like a creature burrowing into a cocoon.

"I'm not sure what you'd like to know," she said.

"Everything."

It was Wednesday, a grey morning, three days since the accident. Sunday morning, I had been a priest with a wife and two daughters; now, I wasn't sure what I had left.

She squinted to see where David was watching from one of the benches outside the hospital entrance in a pool of fake light. A curl of grey hair rested on her forehead.

"When I saw, it was already over," she said and crossed her arms.

"What did you see?"

"I…"

"What?"

"Are you okay?"

"David told me you had something to say. Something important."

I stepped toward her and she backed up well out of proportion to my advance, but maybe she had good reason. For all I knew, I looked crazed. I felt like I was teetering on the peak of a slick roof and some inner weight was wobbling inside me and I no longer cared about keeping my balance.

"You can tell me," I said without any kindness.

"It's not anything. It's not going to help."

"Help? Is that what this is about? I don't need your help. What could you possibly tell me that's going to help? You found a cure for dead? Or maybe you know the secret to waking my daughter from her coma. Is that it? Can you save my daughter?"

My voice echoed around the lot. She turned from me and I thought she might get in her car and drive off, but the apology never made it past my throat—it tasted too bitter to do anything but swallow back down.

"You're right," she said. "There is nothing I can tell you that's going to change anything."

"Then why are you here?"

A glance past me again. "David thought you should know."

I waited.

"I was on Cliffside Road, coming around the bend where those evergreens are, where the branches stick out over the road..."

I nodded. I knew all this, knew what she was going to say. Cliffside Road's twisting mess of hills and steep drop-offs with roads that branched off it both up and down the mountain in blind curves shaped like tentacles. The road was notorious in Marguerite; teenagers called it Deathside Road because it claimed a teen driver every year, and my wife said she heard the yearbook advisor always kept the dedication page undesigned until the last moment. The advisor didn't have to wait long this year—only November and already the dedication could be designed.

It was the other car. It swerved over the line. It came right for me.

"I didn't know what I was seeing at first," she said. "Like it was a trick of my eyes or something. Then I realized it was a car accident." She shook her head. "It was awful."

"Tell me."

"I was sure everyone was dead," she said slowly, looking down. "I called 9-1-1, and then I saw."

"What?"

"A man stood outside one of the cars. The car was dented up against the trees. If it hadn't hit them..." *It would have toppled off the cliff and flattened my family*, I added to myself. "The other car was in the middle of the road, the front completely crumpled. I couldn't even see the driver. That poor boy ... The headrest was soaked with blood."

"What about the man?"

"He was old, grey hair, wearing a suit——"

"My father. He was in the crash."

"There was blood on his face, but he was moving well."

Don't you want me to get better?

"What did he do?"

"It's adrenaline, right? People can do all kinds of things when adrenaline is pumping through them."

"Do what?"

"The windows were shattered, the car compressed like an accordion. He climbed onto the trunk and reached through the rear window, stretched into the back of the car. He was like that for maybe thirty seconds, but it felt much longer. I couldn't believe what I was seeing.

"When he pulled the little girl out of the car, I finally got out of mine. I was running to him and yelling I'd called the police and I passed the other car and saw the kid at the wheel. I almost tripped—almost fainted, actually, but I kept running and I was trying to say something about not moving anyone because it could cause more damage, that's what they say anyway, but my words were all jumbled, and I probably sounded like a lunatic. But the man ignored me. He got down from the car with the girl in his arms, cradling her, walked a few steps, and fell to his knees."

"What was the girl wearing?"

"A yellow dress, like something for Easter."

Phoebe.

"Then what?"

"He was saying something, rocking back and forth, holding that girl, but I didn't know what he was saying. It was some foreign language, or maybe gibberish. It was like watching those videos of people in the Middle East hold the bodies of terrorist victims and scream prayers to God. The girl wasn't moving, arms and legs swaying as he rocked, head tilted back. The sun hit her face just right—it would have been beautiful."

Maggie Prescott had fallen into the world of memory and spoke in a detached, quiet voice, like she was recounting an out-of-body experience. Or having one. "He rocked her and said those words I didn't understand. His eyes were closed, his head tilting back and falling down again. I stood there. What could I do? Everything was so still, so quiet. Time passed so slowly. It could have been four hours before the ambulance arrived. Time is so strange like that."

"That's it?" I asked.

She paused and looked at me as if she forgot I was there. "He did say something I understood, at least a word I could say."

"What?"

"Abaddon." She said it slowly, emphasizing the sounds, *uh-bad-un*.

A bad one.

✝

I stopped where David sat on the bench long enough to tell him that what Maggie Prescott told me proved nothing. Changed nothing. In fact, if he had put her up to that little stunt, he should be ashamed. I told him to stay away. I told him to keep his crazy theories to himself. But there was my sermon haunting me again—the awful miseries strewn across Job's life like splayed roadkill.

David let me rant and walk away and he never said a thing.

As if he knew he wouldn't have to.

✝

It was a sound I've heard a billion times or more, a gentle rustling of sheet, the inevitable sound of repositioning in bed. I am a snorer, and on those nights when I was really honking, Naomi would do everything she could from yanking the sheets this way and that to elbowing me sharply (accidentally, she'd claim) in the back to stop my God-awful sawing. I can still hear the way her legs kicked against the sheets, pulled them taut, wrapped them around her ankles.

Had I been sleeping or even bordering on the edge of dozing, I might not have even heard that stirring.

Phoebe's blankets rippled and slipped along her body. For a moment, it was an illusion I couldn't explain. The sheet rose in odd, warped humps that trailed along her body toward her head and vanished as if nothing more than air pockets. I could have made a similar trick had I grabbed the foot end of the sheet and flapped it up and down, only not quite, could not have made such distinctive lumps.

Like something was crawling under there.

On the white dry erase board (*Your shift nurse is Regan*), one word was scrawled in frantic letters: Abaddon.

Her hand, bandaged into a gauze-white fin, shook off the sheet and rose gradually, an injured solider making to salute, a creature reaching out from an unquiet coffin. Her masked hand thwacked down on the railing, gripped it.

She pulled herself up in spasmodic jerks, half her body struggling forward while the other half hung limp with dead weight. *A stroke. She's having a stroke.* Her body convulsed, rocked forward, jerked upward, but her hand held with all its might on that railing, tendons pulling the bandage tight. The wrapping stretched across her knuckles and ripped, a cocoon tearing open to reveal something unnatural within.

She sat up, slumped forward. Her hair wet with sweat dangled around her face. Small tremors shook through her arm and across her narrow shoulders. Her name was on my lips but I couldn't say it. Was I even seeing this? It had to be a dream because if it wasn't … If it wasn't, it meant she was free of the coma.

Her head snapped to the side and then thrashed backwards as if slapped. Slunk forward, back arched, head back, and mouth open, she looked so pathetic. Worse, she looked abused, beaten, a victimized child surrendering to what's coming.

Her face rolled toward me. Hair streaked over her eyes. With both hands, she grabbed her breathing tube and tugged it rapidly out of her, her body shaking with the effort and mucus slapping against her chin. The tube seemed endless, a giant parasite feeding off her insides. She choked and coughed until it was out, and dropped the plastic thing on her lap, all slathered and spotted with blood.

"Daddy?" Her voice was soft and scratchy.

I couldn't speak, couldn't move.

"Daddy. Please, help me."

Her wide eyes peered through her hair. Something awful in those eyes. Something threatening.

Her other arm came up fast, the IV line stretching out, and her hand slapped on her wrapped arm. Her fingers dug into the gauze. *Amputate. Have to amputate.* Her hand pulled at the wrapping and the gauze tore in a long, zigzagging rip. Phoebe screamed. Blackened skin dangled from the frayed bandage hanging in her grip. Blood puddled in her ruined arm, splattered onto the sheet.

"Phoebe, no!"

I was there, right next her, as if I willed myself to her side without walking, and my stomach whirled, and my legs wobbled as if on an unsteady boat. My arms tangled with hers in an awkward mess. The torn bandage and skin plopped on her lap, and her hand went for the exposed flesh. She pushed against me with incredible strength. This was not an eight-year-old. This was something else. Adrenaline maybe. I caught her wrist, kept her stretching fingers from the gaping wound, but that hand came up, slapped me hard across the face.

"Help me, Daddy! I'm trapped!" Her voice rose and plummeted in unnatural octaves.

"Phoebe!"

She fought against me, slapped me again—hard. Her mouth dropped open in a snarl, her head snapped to the side, and she went for my neck. A nasty, heavy stink filled the room. *She shit herself.* I pulled back, pulling her with me. She stretched over the bed railing. Hands hooked into claws, she tore at the air. She hissed and growled. Yellow spit speckled her lips and chin and foamy phlegm bunched in the corners of her mouth.

Her IV ripped from her arm and bright red blood oozed in the crook of her elbow. A flailing arm smacked the IV stand; she grabbed it and flung it forward. It crashed against the opposite wall with a heavy, metallic echo. The thing was weighted at the bottom. She couldn't possibly have thrown that. *Not without help.*

A frantic machine *BEEPBEEPBEEP* went off and another alarm warbled around the chaos.

"Please!" I yelled. "*Please!*"

"*Fuck you,*" she said in a grainy baritone.

She yanked from my grip and grinned at me. *A nightmare. A nightmare. Has to be.*

"This is how it happens," she said.

The lights flickered, went out, blazed back on in blinding intensity.

Phoebe's hand slapped onto the open wound in her arm. Her fingers pushed into the fleshy meat. She could push right through, her arm so thin. Blood splattered across the sheet. And out of those puddles, tiny black spiders scurried free. They raced around the bed and over her body.

She tore a chunk of reddish tissue free from her arm with a liquid sucking sound. The tissue shook like Jell-O. She brought it to her mouth.

A woman's scream filled the room. A nurse stood in the doorway. Her face paled immediately, and I thought she might puke down her scrubs.

Phoebe—whatever was (*possessing*) doing this—grinned even wider and flung the glob of tissue at the nurse. It smacked her beneath the chin and wobbled down her body to the floor with a wet smack.

The nurse's legs gave out and she crumpled to the floor. She fell forward in a dead faint. Right on top of the chunk of Phoebe's arm.

"Daddy," Phoebe snarled.

Spiders swarmed over her face, filled the hollows of her eyes, and flooded down into her gaping mouth.

The lights snapped off again, flared super bright, one of them popping with a loud burst, and then eased back to normal brightness.

The machines continued their panicked alarms.

Phoebe's eyes, so dark but spiderless, rolled back to complete whites, and, as if yanking her power cord, she collapsed back onto the bed, and was motionless. As if she hadn't exerted any energy. Her breathing fell slight and shallow.

PART TWO

THE DEVIL VIRUS

Job suffered sore, oozing boils over every inch of his skin. His wife, spared the disease that tormented her husband, told him to curse God, but Job refused for how could he accept good from God and not accept evil? So, Job went off in his grief and bemoaned the day he was born, wished he had never known life, but he did not lash out at God who had blessed him and cursed him.

Job did not know that in some other world where angels congregated that the Devil had challenged God, claiming that pious Job would renounce the lord if God were to take away all of Job's blessings. With all the angels watching, God granted Satan the power to torment Job, to destroy all he had, save the very life God had given him.

"Do your worst," God said. "And we'll see what happens."

So, the Devil does his worst, writes a sermon of misery through Job's anguish, and all with God's permission.

If only Job had known.

—The Book of Job (paraphrased)

While doctors attended to Phoebe's arm, inserted a new breathing tube, and strapped her wrists and ankles to the bed, I went to the bathroom and called David. I didn't waste his time with apologies, and he didn't waste mine with "I told you so."

"We need to talk," I said.

"I'll be right over."

My hand shook as I placed the phone and his business card on the edge of the sink. I hadn't been sleeping well. Perhaps I hallucinated. But then why were doctors attending to Phoebe's injuries? But why would this be happening? Why to my angel?

I was the terrified witness outside a school shooting or a mall rampage, the one screaming, *Why? Why? Why?*

Because God let it happen—that's why.

I almost didn't make it to the toilet and by then I was shaking so much, I made quite the mess.

✝

I met David outside. We sat on a metal bench to the side of the hospital entrance where he sat that morning while I spoke with Maggie Prescott. A large halogen light buzzed over our heads.

I started to apologize, and he stopped me.

"Tell me what happened."

"I'm not sure."

"Tell me. All of it."

I started simply—words tumbling free in disjointed sentences that gradually gained inertia like a car rolling down hill—not going all the way back to Dad's heart attack and stroke, but only to Saturday night when I found Ben Masters on the toilet, and I was getting it out pretty well until I got to Phoebe's... event.

Whether it's grief or trauma or PTSD or some hybrid of all three, it's amazing how it creeps up on you. I was okay when I spoke about the car accident, about Tamara's body and Naomi's death, but my voice started doing this irritating shake when I was relaying what happened when I saw my father's body and then, well, by the time I told him what had happened, I'm not even sure I got the words out.

This is how it happens, Phoebe had said in that manic state.

Manic state? Try psychotic or insane or...

David let me grieve and I didn't apologize, though I wanted to. I knew I had to be strong, but first I had to give in.

Standing beside many deathbeds and comforting the bereaved, I had offered prayers as if such things could help. I hadn't really known, though. We don't know, not until it's our turn in the sweatbox.

I grieved and got it out, but you can never get all of it. Like the soap scum wedged between shower tiles, no matter how hard you scrub, you can't get it all.

But I got enough.

✝

When I was done, David's face had paled slightly and the fingers on his right hand bounced on his thigh as if tapping Morse Code. In the wake of silence following my purge, I watched people walk in and out of the hospital. Some faces hung with worry, others, disgust, and still others, tentative happiness. At least they had direction.

"I'm very sorry, Lucas. This is an awful thing."

"You actually think you can help?"

"We tried to help my son every way we could. Doctors pushed chemo, my congregation prayed, held vigils, we gathered around my son and laid hands on him and willed him back to health. But he only got worse. The infection in his arm spread. Doctors wanted to amputate, but they were in no rush. You know why? My son was dying. A lost cause. Either the infection or the cancer was going to kill him. When the doctors stop visiting your room, you know you've turned that last corner. Nurses checked every so often. Trying to estimate when my son was going to die, not that they told me that, but I could tell. My wife and I stayed beside him, held him, watched him go. Only he didn't go easy. He struggled. He thrashed in bed, cried out. Clawed at his infected skin. I held him down, but he fought against me. My wife cradled her broken arm in its new cast and cried. She didn't say it, but I knew what she was thinking. *Why won't he just die and let this be over?* I was thinking the same thing. There comes a point when fighting only makes it worse. No matter how hard you struggle, you will lose. In the end, we all go. We all accept it. But Joey fought. Except I don't think it was him fighting."

"You think it was…" I lowered my voice. "A demon?"

"You know much about viruses?"

"Viruses? What's there to know?"

"I know a lot."

"I'm sure, but what does that—"

"What does a virus want?"

"I don't imagine a virus wanting anything."

"Oh, everything that lives wants something. Humans are the most complicated of wanters, but when you go down the scale to the smallest living things, to the germs and the viruses, they still want."

"They want to make us sick," I said.

"They want to multiply. To reproduce. Like cancer. They want to thrive. So, a virus finds in a human a wonderfully cozy place to multiply. It reproduces rapidly and we get ill. Gradually, our body identifies the virus, forms T-cells, and fights back. Usually, our immune system wins. Our inner workings are astoundingly complex. If ever there is an argument for God, it is that we are so astoundingly well-crafted at the biological level. How could that craftsmanship be simple chance? Take fevers, for example. You get sick and run a fever. Do you know what a fever is supposed to do? It's the body trying to burn out the disease."

"What's your point?"

"What happens when our bodies don't win the battle? When no medicine helps. The fever can't get hot enough without damaging the brain and must be relieved. The virus keeps doing its thing, populating inside you at an accelerating rate. It is doing exactly what it wants to, its single-minded purpose. At the same time, however, it is crippling the very home it is inhabiting. If the body dies, so too does the virus. It found the perfect home and ruined it."

"Not unless someone else gets infected," I said.

"Exactly. The virus makes us cough, sneeze, snot all over the place. Give us explosive bowel movements. It must spread to other hosts if it wants to survive."

"So what?"

"Think how unique that is. The virus can multiply simultaneously in endless places, inside endlessly bodies, populate like crazy in every one of its homes and hopefully continue to spread itself farther and wider."

"So, it lives on."

"The virus does, but not the individual strains infecting individual people. It's like humans. We populate the earth and even as we die off, we still spread. Our offspring keep the mighty human infection spreading."

"Where is all this going?"

"Humor me for a moment. Take the virus again. Suppose there is an epidemic. How do we deal with it?"

"Immunize. Contain."

"Right. When the Swine Flu broke out in Mexico City several years ago, the government shut down the city. This caused world-wide anxiety, but in a few short months, the flu was completely under control. Some people with the virus died, some got better, but the virus was not allowed to leave the city. Eventually, it died out. That's the only way to handle an outbreak—quarantine and wait.

"Now, suppose, the virus were smart? Suppose the virus had some sense of what it was doing, and it could *choose* its victims, control its rate of reproduction. Imagine if it could consciously inhabit a host but lay in wait for the most opportune moment. It could plan its attack."

"Sounds like something the military would love to have," I said.

"Right. Something like that would be almost impossible to fight, certainly to contain." David sat forward on the edge of the bench. "I know you don't want to accept what I'm trying to say, but there's an awful truth here, and it's one I know very well. I know it as a doctor, as a priest, and as a father. There already are intelligent viruses. Call it The Devil Virus. Or call it whatever you want, but it comes down to the same."

"You mean possession?"

I couldn't believe I was actually engaging in this discussion. Could possession, as in from demons, even be real? Maybe Phoebe's freakout was the product of some brain embolism or the work of a bacteria infecting her nervous system. Maybe the doctors hadn't checked for that.

"Before my son died, when he was thrashing on the bed, clawing at me and at himself, trying to bite me, he said only one thing among endless, rambling gibberish. In an awful voice but one in which I still heard my poor boy, the thing that had my son said, 'We are legion.'"

"The men in Gadarenes," I said. "You must have told him that story."

In the Gospels, two men in the country of Gadarenes are "possessed with devils" and beg Jesus to heal them. Jesus says, "Go," and the demons are cast out into a herd of pigs that run violently off a cliff to drown in the water below.

"Even if I had," David said, "you think he would choose that as his final words? A ten-year-old boy?"

"Who knows what happens to the brain in those moments. He was scared. It kind of makes sense."

"You can try to rationalize all you want, Lucas, but the truth is a lot simpler. You don't want to accept it."

"Accept what, that demon possession is like getting the flu?"

"My son died in a mad flailing of limbs, his head whipping back and forth so hard blood vessels burst in his eyes. My wife grabbed him, screamed for him to let go, to let go and die. And he did. Then my wife walked out, and I never saw her alive again. You can say it was the guilt, that the last thing she said to her only child was he should die, and she couldn't live with that. But she said it out of mercy."

"David, I'm not trying to belittle your loss, but you have to under—"

"My wife walked into traffic, Lucas, because in that last moment, she was infected too."

✝

A woman started screaming in the lobby. People froze and then backed away in a hurry and a security guard went for the weapon on his belt, fears of gun-toting psychopaths rollicking through everyone's minds.

The woman grabbed at a man and the two embraced. They cried against each other and, after a moment, people went back to private concerns, walking around the grieving couple.

"You think your wife was possessed, too?"

"I didn't realize it at that moment," David said, "but I can recognize it now. She pulled back from our son as if shocked and something about her eyes. I don't know. I wasn't paying attention to her. My son had just died. But I know what I saw in that odd expression."

"Demons?" I said with a stab at sarcasm that fell flat.

"Madness."

"You think your son was possessed and that before he died, the demon jumped into your wife and she killed herself because she sensed what was happening?"

"It gets more complicated than that, but, I guess, that is what I'm saying. What your daughter has is another form of sickness. The Devil Virus is real. Phoebe is infected, but no doctor can help her. At least not only a doctor."

"Then who? Tell me: who could have saved your son?"

"There's someone you need to meet."

"Bring him here."

"Please, Lucas. It won't take long."

"Who is it?"

"Remember when I said I've seen some odd things?" He stood, offered his hand as if I were elderly. "Time for you to meet the soothsayer."

✝

I hadn't realized how shaky I was until we started driving and the heat warmed my hands into swollen slugs. Once I was calm enough to think clearly, I immediately regretted leaving the hospital, though part of me was pleased for another respite from Phoebe's room, and for several minutes I said nothing, those two emotions battling it out.

"Take me back. I can't leave Phoebe alone."

"I will, but not yet. Trust me, Lucas."

I didn't say anything, but trust had nothing to do with it.

"If you want to help Phoebe, you have to trust me."

"What do I have to lose, huh?"

"You know exactly what you have to lose, but I don't want that to happen."

The wheels hummed beneath us.

"Do you think it was wrong of me to teach that Jesus was real but that his miracles were not?" I asked.

David shrugged. "Water into wine? Healing the sick? Casting out demons?"

"Metaphors," I said. "Even the resurrection. All metaphors for faith, symbols of salvation."

"If that's true, though, what's the point?"

"What do you mean?"

"The point, Lucas. If all of those stories are metaphors and nothing more, what is the point? Why worship God? Why follow Jesus? Without the magic, what's the point?"

I paused, feeling a bit like the scolded student who dared speak his mind in class. "Magic, huh?"

"Have an open mind," David said. "You might be surprised."

✝

The Word of Christ Church pulsed in the night. David pulled onto the long road sloping down to the parking lot that could hold several hundred cars. Maybe two dozen took up spaces now. The main structure, the church, towered at three stories toward a triangle glass roof with a giant glass cross stretching off the peak. On clear, sunny days, I could imagine the flicker of sun reflecting off that cross. *Behold, the glory...*

Three black limos were parked out front.

"Is there a wedding?"

From above, the Word of Christ estate resembled an enormous cross with the church at the top. Perhaps that made it easier for God to know where to direct His attention. The complex sprawled across the land. When Phoebe attended Bible

Camp here, she remarked how the parish hall looked like a school. There was a large cafeteria in there and a full-service daycare. The place probably had a warren of offices with a built-in intercom and flat-screen TVs.

"I hope you didn't bring me here to pray."

"Funny thing for a priest to say."

"Reverend Roves going to lay his hands on me and give me the spirit? Or maybe he wants to visit Phoebe and stage a healing."

"We're not here to see Roves."

He drove to the back and parked next to a beat-up Subaru. The building before us would be the bottom shaft of the giant cross. Most of the windows were dark, but light streamed out from the far end where a walkway led to an entrance.

"When I was part of Reverend Pete's Prayer Parade, there was a woman there who used to read people's fortunes, palm reading and Tarot cards. She worked different fairs and carnivals and when Reverend Pete found her, he swore to me she was the real deal. Blessed with the gift of second sight."

"Preachers tend to be very skeptical of such things," I said. "Quick to denounce them as the acts of pagans. Burn them as witches."

"Reverend Pete might not have been the best of men, but he never questioned God's power or methods. He found this woman who could see things, know things she had no way of knowing, and he saw a miracle. When I told him I was leaving his ministry and staying in New York, he said he already knew. She had told him. After my son and my wife died, Reverend Pete called me. He said he had known this tragedy was coming too. He wanted me to come back to him. I hung up. Figured if she had told him all that stuff, she would have told him how I'd respond to his call."

"So, you doubted?"

"Actually, I was pissed. It was another thing turned me from the church back toward medicine. After all, if that woman had known, why hadn't she told me? Maybe I could have changed things."

"And?"

"Ever hear of the Cassandra Complex?"

"In Greek mythology, Cassandra was blessed to see the future and cursed never to be believed. No matter what she said or did, tragedy struck."

"This woman has experienced that Complex first hand. Something like that could drive a person crazy."

"So, she joined Pete's flock and, what, read palms?"

"Did her best to guide people toward God."

"A religious conversion or better pay?"

"A few months after wandering my way here, she showed up too. Said she was suffering so much grief over what had happened to me. She had seen it coming. She needed forgiveness. She needed a new path, one that used her talent for good."

"Yeah? How's that?"

"I'll let her explain."

He pointed toward the entrance. A figure stood silhouetted in the light.

✝

Cassie Angeca looked to be around forty-something. She wore a long black dress with a woven leather belt sagging off bony hips. A pair of large wooden hoop earrings that were miniature dreamcatchers swayed as she walked, and silver streaked through her dark hair. Deep creases scored the skin around her eyes. Her hand was incredibly warm when we shook.

"I won't waste your time," she said, leading us down a corridor of closed doors. "I want to help you."

"How are you going to do that?"

She opened a door and gestured us inside. "I'll show you."

Her office was spacious, a desk tucked in the far corner strewn with an array of knickknacks I couldn't identify, and weird, psychedelic pictures framed on the wall in an almost chaotic mess. The type of thing hippies would have stared at for hours while smoking a bowl. The room smelled not of weed, but of incense. Sticks of it wafted smoke from the window ledge. The only light came from lamps stacked on books in the corners.

A tan circular throw rug took up most of the floor with pillows tossed about it. Cassie invited us to sit and we sat cross-legged like little kids conspiring to play. I thought she might take our hands and start making the "om" sound Buddhists claim is the purest name of God, but she sat back-stiff and smiled in a way that cajoled my own.

"I'm sure David told you, I came to faith along a very strange path. I used to be a palmist and a Tarot card reader. I dabbled with astral projection, chakra healing, even telekinesis. I know, sounds ridiculous."

"I'm not judging." I said in a complete lie.

"You should. Anyone who claims she can see the future or project her consciousness through time and space ought to be forced to show some proof."

"I want to get back to my daughter."

"Of course. I'll try to be quick," she said. "I have a talent. It comes in degrees and seems to vary moment to moment. Sometimes it can be so strong it's overbearing, crippling. Other times, it's as small and helpless as a candle flame. When I joined Reverend Pete and met David, I felt a strong compulsion about him. I knew him immediately and I saw what was going to happen to his son and wife, but I had learned long before that telling people what is going to happen does not empower them to change the future. Knowing your future is debilitating. You know the story of Pandora, of course."

"More Greek mythology," I said. "Doesn't Christianity have enough of its own?"

"Probably. But in the story of Pandora and her box of miseries, everything escaped, disease, pain, terror, old age, everything *except* foreboding. If man knew what would befall him, he'd never be able to get up in the morning. I didn't tell David what I knew was going to happen because it's better not to know. I thought I'd done him a kindness. Afterwards, I thought better."

"You think he could have prevented their deaths?"

"Not by himself."

"So how?"

"I could have helped, and I didn't realize how much I could have."

"How?"

"You ever hear of someone with cancer suddenly getting better and yet the doctors can't explain it?"

"Sure."

"Even people riddled with tumors, people who should die in a matter of days, suddenly these people completely recover. The tumors shrink and vanish. We credit chemo. Or prayer. And, sometimes, people say they healed themselves. And what do we say about those people? We say, 'Good for them. Believe what you want. You're healed.' You ever been to one of those support group meetings for cancer patients?"

I shook my head.

"As part of those meetings, they sometimes practice guided mediation. They go inside their minds and heal themselves."

"Couldn't hurt, right?"

"Depends, but I'll get to that. I've run those mediation sessions. I've worked with cancer patients. I've seen patients heal themselves. Not all, of course, but more than a few."

"That's fine for cancer, but my daughter is in a coma."

Cassie and David looked at each other.

"When I saw what was going to happen to David's son, I thought it was an especially aggressive form of cancer. I thought his son would be too weak to fight it. At least that's what I told myself. He didn't have cancer and from what David has told me, your daughter isn't simply in a coma."

"What?" I said. "She's possessed? That's what you mean? Look, I don't want to sound like just another skeptic but—"

"I can save her," Cassie said.

We settled back for a moment. The sound of silence stuffed my ears.

"When I came here," Cassie said, "I knew only I needed David to forgive me and I needed a new direction. Together we worked to help the people in this congregation. It started with a young boy. I had been hired to work in the daycare, and I noticed this one boy, William, was somehow different from the other kids. He always stayed away from them. He cried for no reason. When I tried to read him, all I got was cold darkness."

"He was possessed?"

"Maybe. We helped heal him."

"How?"

"After that, we sort of became a team. We helped a middle-aged man heal his heart. An old woman lost her arthritis. And little miracles, too. Healed migraine sufferers. Healed bones. Healed anxiety. We've helped dozens and dozens of people."

"It's true, Lucas. I've seen it many times. Talk about magic."

"I wanted him to forgive me, but he did much more," she said. "David showed me the way to God."

"You're saying you're an instrument of God's power?"

"No more so than anyone else is. I'm no prophet. I'm not some mystical healer. I don't cure people. I'm more like a Sherpa. I show them the way. Show them how to heal themselves."

"That's great and all," I said. "But how many times do I have to ask? How do you do this? How do you help people cure cancer? Heal bones? Fix anxiety problems? How? How? *How?*"

My words did not shake her disposition. "It begins simply with something I call Prayer Construction."

✝

First, go light. Phoebe's voice, so soft, so serious.

"You're the prayer woman," I said.

"That's what many of the children call me, yes. I remember Phoebe. She took to prayer construction as if she already knew how to do it. It's not because you're a priest, either. I've known many clergy's children who didn't have an ounce of this kind of ability. It's amazing when a child can grasp something like this so easily. Often, it takes years to be a master, but I think your daughter learned it all in two months."

Phoebe and I sometimes played the Imagination Game. We put ourselves in a jungle or in a city or on a pirate ship and try to imagine everything around us. Once we had all the details, we started with the action. The stories were usually about her and her stuffed animals, morphed into giant, living things, and the adventures she shared with them. We'd come back to the same stories over and over. Who would have guessed the Imagination Game was a form of prayer practice?

"I know your church," Cassie said. "I run a group called Cognitive Introspective Release there on Tuesday nights. I hoped you would bring Phoebe at some point, but you never did."

"You were talking about prayer?"

"Kids have great imaginations," Cassie said. "And then we teach them to suppress it. But imagination is the gateway. The promise of imagination is the same as prayer: sanctuary and salvation. Everyone could use more of that in life, don't you think?"

"Salvation?"

Cassie smiled, slightly, a knowing smile. "Children are wonderful," she said. "Their minds are not restricted. Their imaginations are boundless. They are willing to believe anything because anything *can* happen, if you give it the right place to grow. It breaks my heart when a child loses that ability. Often, if it's found again, it happens in a church. Lucky for you."

That sounded like a self-help book: *Imagining God: How Imagination Can Strengthen Faith.*

"Lucky for *you*," I said.

"Some call it faith, others hope," David said, "but the reality is that it happens up here." He tapped his forehead.

I pointed to my chest. "Not here, huh?"

"The heart is a metaphor," Cassie said. "The brain is the gateway to God."

"Metaphor, huh?" I said and glanced at David. "How do we know we're not fooling ourselves? Believing what we want to?"

"Faith," David said.

We looked back and forth among the three of us. The light flickered almost imperceptibly, and the smell of incense thickened.

"Okay," Cassie said. "Let's give it a try."

✝

And she said it: "First, we go light."

We aligned our breathing into slow, steady inhalations and long, seeping exhales. Falling into that rhythm with David and Cassie was like slipping into a nap on a summer afternoon. Everything fell away except the sound of our breathing and the smell of incense. Time got lost. At first, I knew a minute had passed and then two and then I had no idea. I needed to get back to Phoebe, but maybe there was some answer in all this. Something to help. But that was denial. Prayer construction, mediation—none of it was going to help my daughter. I didn't want to leave yet because I hoped this might help *me*. Parents aren't supposed to be selfish. We're martyrs, letting ourselves be destroyed for the betterment of our children. Being a priest is like that too.

"Even as I speak," Cassie said very slowly, very quietly, "don't lose the rhythm of your breathing." Her voice jarred me as a slap might, and my breathing hiccuped. She waited for me to fall back in sync.

"Begin to imagine your entire body losing its mass. Your bones are no longer solid. They are hollow, transparent. Your muscles, all your tissue. It is as light as feathers. Let it all go. Feel the lightness travel up from your toes, up through your legs, into your chest. Feel yourself lift, lighter than air. Now, your head, your brain. It is not solid, either. It is you and you are as light as the wind. You can go into your mind and float there. You can be your mind and drift with it. Let yourself rise into it."

The perpetual skeptic in me said this was stupid. Worse than stupid, actually. Selfish. Phoebe was suffering and needed me. *What if when you go back to the hospital she's dead? How will you ever live with yourself?*

Simple: I wouldn't.

That silenced the skeptic.

I fell back into myself and that's exactly how it felt, like falling backwards off a step, that quivering uneasiness in the gut, the unnerving loss of balance tinctured with fear of pain and injury, a muscle spasm in the shoulders to throw out my arms, the cartoon character flailing on a cliff's edge, but I hit nothing: I fell and landed in a cushioned hammock of air.

It cradled me.

"There is darkness here," Cassie said. Her voice whispered through nothingness. "But there is something beyond the darkness, something beneath it. Find the edge, the corner, and peel it back like a label on a cold bottle. Brace yourself. The colors can be very bright."

It wasn't the corner of a moist bottle label, but it was a protruding slip of darkness, a mud flap with a glimmer of something bright beneath. I grabbed it, slippery and like rubber, and lifted.

Brace yourself.

I remembered talking with David about Paul's conversion on the road to Damascus. David said it wasn't a moment of sudden belief; it was the culmination of a long, painful journey of faith. But the descending angel, can you imagine? David's son saying the angels were hunting him, and something else too, another thought, but one I couldn't grab. But the brightness. I thought I could imagine it.

Wishful thinking.

As powerful as the noonday sun, light squeezed around the widening gap and pushed back the darkness, a starburst in space that burned everything in blinding whiteness. I dropped the flap, tried to, and pulled away, but the light kept pouring in. It flooded over me in brighter and more refulgent splashes. I grew warm immediately and then hot and quickly feared I would overheat, maybe even combust. The darkness tore back without a sound and the world baked in dazzling light.

"It's okay," Cassie said. "Keep breathing. The light will fade. I see you. Very good, Lucas. Remarkable, actually."

"I don't see—"

Only I did. The light dimmed and there was Cassie. She stood set in the light as if in a frozen camera flash. The face paled and then flushed with red swirls. When she moved toward me, her body wavered, heat waves rising off simmering pavement. She fell in and out of focus. *Better or worse?* I thought as if at the optometrist. The blurred edges of her skin pulsed in an array of colors. Tiny rainbows leaped off of her like sparks.

"What is this?" My voice warbled, echoing through static.

"I had a good feeling about you," she said. "Some people never even get here."

"Where is here?"

"It's a mutual place we are occupying, but it's my place. I made it as a waylay, a place I could gather people to prevent them going too far and getting lost."

"Lost?"

"It takes a lot of energy to keep this place going. A lot of concentration. It isn't easy. When people first go light, they are immediately drawn to their own place, whether they consciously created it or not. And when you go into that place, sometimes it isn't easy to come back. This place is safe."

"But we're not really here."

She reached out with one arm that shook and vibrated and smeared with rainbows, a water color bleeding in the rain. She touched my arm, which was as unsteady and blurred as hers. Her touch was solid and cool.

"We're in your office at the church," I said. "You're touching me in reality."

"What is reality?" she asked. "You see this place, you feel my touch—how is this not real?"

"My daughter never mentioned this place."

"I don't bring children here. Their imaginations are far too strong to contain. They construct their own place first, a place of good and bad."

"Bad?"

"If you don't consciously build the evil into your world, it will find its way in, and if that happens, you have no way to control it. Children bring it in and confine it somewhere. A prison, a closet..."

Abaddon.

God created the serpent in the Garden.

Another of my mother's sayings: *The Devil you know is better than the one you don't.*

"A cave," I said.

"Yes. Now, listen carefully." She was speaking loudly, and I realized it was suddenly windy, storm gusts on a beach, crashing waves, and she had to shout. Yet, I felt no wind, even as our bodies smeared into longer and longer amorphous streaks. "You must solidify this place in your mind. If we are to go from here, I need to have all my strength. I can bring you here, but you must find a way to stay. A way to come back. Use your own ability. You can do it. I sense it."

"Is this happening? You drugged me somehow. The incense?" I could still smell its sweet aroma. A hallucinogenic. Ayahuasca. A hippie thing, a druggy thing: Cassie was attempting to open my doors of perception. A trick, an elaborate one fueled with narcotics.

"Drugs can help," she said. "But they aren't an end in themselves. They can be a vehicle to a better place."

"So, I am drugged?"

"Try to hold onto this place."

"Did you drug my child? All those children?"

"I have to go, but this is the place. Remember it."

"Go? Go where?

"David didn't make it."

The wind gusted through us in a static howl. "Where is he?"

"I know. I'll get him. Make this place solid."

She let go of me and her body swirled with the next push of wind; it stretched into bands of revolving colors, whirled, and scattered, multicolored confetti spreading in all directions. My protest for her to stay dissipated with her body.

The wind worsened. It shoved against me, moaned through my ears. The golden sunlight intensified with the wind. *Only it's not sunlight. This is all in my mind. This isn't a place. This is a drug-induced hallucination.*

The light burned brighter and brighter. My face flushed with heat that got rapidly hotter and hotter. My skin pulled tight in protest. *Solidify this place in your mind.* But there was no substance here. How could I remember it?

Remember how it feels.

Cassie's voice only not speaking, a thought whipping on the furious breeze.

The smell of incense filled this world. Drug-induced. A crazy drug trip.

My fingers flew off in smears of red, blue, and yellow. My wrists followed and my arms up to the elbow and then—*may have to amputate*—all the way to the shoulders where colors swirled and flared as if eating my body.

Remember this place.

For Phoebe's sake, remember it.

✝

I came back (I hoped) to reality as if floating up from watery sleep. I had fallen over with my legs still crossed, and tight pain tweaked through my back and into my neck. Cassie remained in a posture-perfect back-straight pose, but her head was bowed, chin on her neck. David was sprawled awkwardly. His face lay pressed into the rug, pulling his mouth askew. A puddle of saliva congealed on the rug.

The incense continued to twirl gray smoke in dissipating whispers. She had drugged me. That at least made sense. But if it had been a drug, why would I come out of it while the sticks were still smoking? Cassie said drugs could be a vehicle to a better place, not a destination themselves. Maybe the smoke helped me get there but was too weak to keep me there.

Or maybe I was reading too much into it.

I felt lightheaded and a bit unsteady, which made sense, but I already felt my body returning to normal. My equilibrium balanced out, and my body cooled, though my face still felt warm, the skin tight, the tactile remnants of a dream.

But if it was a dream, how had Cassie been there? More importantly, how had she been speaking to me? Because she hadn't. A dream was a just a vivid hallucination. This had been a little of both. How could any of it be real?

A bit of an anomaly, sure, but stranger things have happened. I had thought the same thing when Phoebe's bedroom lights simultaneously burned out. Strange stuff happens. No reason to jump to wild conclusions. Like the lights in the hospital room, right? The hospital, one room in the hospital, suffered an electric surge at the precise moment Phoebe burst from a coma and started clawing and snarling like a rabid dog? Oh, right, because *that* happened, too. Was I supposed to accept all those odd events?

Faith, David said.

Yeah, look at him, drooling with belief, sprawled unconscious.

I moved closer to Cassie. Her breathing remained slow and gentle. A sweet smell swam around her, different from the incense yet similar. Her lips were moving. She was whispering. I leaned closer, nose almost touching her face. Her words slipped off her lips and were gone like the tails of the wafting smoke on the ledge.

"Cassie?" I asked very quietly.

In the corner, a stack of books shifted as if poltergeist-pushed and the lamp on top of them thunked to the floor. The light angled across David's sprawled body. It might have been windy where I'd been (wherever *that* was), but it wasn't windy here. Everything was perfectly still, the air unmoving.

I heard a scraping sound. On the wall hung a cross. It was one of those big wooden ones with metal folded around the corners in sharp edges like a weapon. It rocked back and forth in small arcs. The bottom of the cross dug a pendulum curve into the wall with each swing.

It didn't speed up; it kept sweeping back and forth. Back and forth.

I was still dreaming. Had to be.

"Cassie?" I asked louder.

The cross scraped the wall.

David erupted from his trance in a loud, heaving inhalation, a man breaking the water's surface, gasping for oxygen. His body contorted and flexed as if in seizure before he began to relax and sat up. He shook his head, ran his hand through his hair, and stared at me for a moment, confused.

"Didn't mean to startle you."

I had backed up toward the door in a rapid crab-walk. We both turned to Cassie, expecting her to explode from the depths of her own mind with equal drama, but her eyes slowly opened and she smiled. "Good. We're all here."

The cross stopped. The curved lines arcing up around it formed a demented smiley face.

✝

"Explain to me," I said slowly, "what just happened."

You were in Uz, Phoebe said. *But you didn't realize it.*

"Did you make the place real?" Cassie asked me.

"Real?"

"You remember how it felt there?"

"Bright and hot."

"It wasn't a hallucination," she said. "You might want to think so, but, if anything, it's closer to a shared daydream, only it's not a dream. It's another reality. It is completely real."

"And so are dreams, until you wake up."

"You remember your dreams?"

"Some."

"So, how are they not real?"

"Dreams don't do anything to you."

"Tell that to the people with night terrors. Tell that to anyone who runs from something hideous and wakes with a frantic heart and a cold sweat. Tell that to people who sleepwalk. Or people who die in their sleep. We always think that's such a peaceful way to go, but what if dying in your sleep means being killed in a nightmare far more horrific than anything that could happen in this world?"

"Doesn't make it real."

"I know you're scared. Fear is good. But it's going to be okay. We can help Phoebe."

"You said you showed people how to help themselves. Guided them like a Sherpa."

"Yes."

"My daughter is in a coma. How is she going to help herself?"

"Lucas," David said and pointed at me.

"What?"

He grinned. "Your face, Lucas."

"What about it?"

Cassie handed me a small silver mirror. I looked at my reflection with the hesitant curiosity of a child peeping between fingers during a horror flick.

A bright-red face glared back at me. Sunburned to the point of absurdity.

✝

"I usually have better control over the light," Cassie said. "Sorry. But you'll be able to control it yourself. You're very strong, Lucas. You have some of my gift, if I'm not mistaken."

"Great."

She stared at me with a curious expression I couldn't place, like she was studying me and wondering if she should share the findings. "There may come a time when you need to construct your own place, Lucas, and it's important you don't make it someplace real."

"Why?"

"I tell people it's okay to start with the outline of a home or a familiar vacation spot but then it must be changed, altered in significant ways—the more fantastically the better."

"Easier to remember?"

"It gives the creator more power. She can manipulate the environment, rule it as a god. And it keeps *this* reality safe."

"What does that mean?"

"If the world is completely authentic, down to the minutest detail, and the creator's power is strong, the actual world, *this* world, can be affected. Sometimes, though, it doesn't matter. The psychic energy spills over and things happen here."

She gestured at the lamp on the floor, the tumbled books. My eyes went to the smile gouged in the wall.

"A couple of books and a scarred wall isn't a big deal."

"Ever hear of astral projection?"

"More new-age science?"

"I can visit anywhere in the world without physically moving, so long as I can see that world perfectly or the person I want to visit. When I do that, I become like a ghost, unless the other person has the ability too, which makes us both like ghosts."

"An out-of-body experience?"

"Similar."

"What does that have to do with imaginary worlds?"

"David and I once tried to help this woman who refused to believe something awful was brooding inside her. She wouldn't come into my world, so I created a replica of her home and when she went under, we went to work. She resisted, wouldn't let us at what was in her, wouldn't let us free her, and the house, her actual house, crumbled around us."

"You mean the real house collapsed?"

"'Lack of structural integrity in the foundation,' was the official conclusion. We were lucky to survive, as was the woman. We were nearly crushed. On top of that, we failed to help the woman."

She looked at David the way conspirators might.

"What do you mean, 'when she went under'? You drugged her, right?"

"That isn't the point."

"Isn't the point? You're drugging people and tricking them into believing—"

"Your face is sunburned as if you were at the beach for twelve hours?" David asked.

"You have a talent," Cassie said. "I sense it, as I sensed it in your daughter. You can use this ability, but you need to know the potential dangers. Build a world too much like reality and everything is vulnerable. If you're going to do this—"

"I'm not some carnival-show freak."

Cassie nodded, thought over her next words. Before I could apologize, she said, "But there's always a risk. If you don't understand your world, you can get lost in it. Get trapped. It might start as make-believe, but a special place, a unique place you actually created from nothing often carries strong emotional attachment, and that's when it gets dangerous. The world can actually grow on its own."

"Sounds a bit crazy," I said. But, then again, didn't all of it? Heck, didn't a man being crucified and rising from the dead three days later ring a few bells in the crazy tower?

"A strong imagination is a wild-growing vine. If it isn't tended carefully, trimmed back, it will sprawl. Especially in fertile ground. And there can be accelerants."

"Excuse me?"

"The way poor diet exacerbates a spreading disease or alcohol destroys a liver."

"A disease? In your imagination?"

She glanced at David, sat a little taller. "Let's talk about demons."

"What about imagination?"

"We'll get back to it. As for demons—"

"David already told me: it's like an infection. A virus, right?"

"Easy enough way to think of it. Demon possession can be a highly communicable virus."

"Highly? So, how come we don't hear about demon pandemics?"

She smiled at me—ah, the wise-ass student.

"In the Bible," David said, "there's a lot of people infected with demons, right?"

"Sure."

"It's no metaphor, Lucas. Demons *are* everywhere."

"When the woman begs Jesus to cast out the demon in her child and he says to her he was not sent to help everyone, only the chosen ones, you expect me to believe the woman literally believed her daughter was possessed? She was ill, probably with cancer or plague or leprosy."

"And the men in Gadarenes?"

"We are legion," I said. "It's another fable. Might as well be Adam and Eve with the talking snake."

"People used to accept things they couldn't completely understand."

"And people used to hang witches in the town square," I said.

"Whether people once more easily accepted demonic possession or if the Bible simply brings it forward is beside the point. Demons are real. But they can be cast out."

"Your son died of cancer. My daughter was in an awful car accident and now she's in a coma. She's going to die too and talking about demons isn't going to do anything for her."

Even offering the rational response, I felt the absurd possible truth of what Cassie was saying. Wouldn't possession explain Phoebe's sudden burst from coma and her self-inflicted injuries? Wouldn't it explain what Mrs. Prescott said she saw at the accident site with my father?

"I don't know," I said finally.

"I know you struggle with this, but what must you see before you believe?"

"Take it all on faith, huh?"

"Please," David said. "I wish I could go back and help my son, but I can't. I'm here and he's gone, but I can help your daughter. Please let me do that."

"We're getting off track here," Cassie said. "But let me say this: Lucas, it doesn't matter what you decide. David and I have done this before, and we'll do it without your help. It will be easier with it, but we'll do it alone if we have to."

"Do what? Exorcise the demon out of her?"

"For lack of better phrasing."

I looked at both of them. "What do you want me to say?"

"Listen," Cassie said. "Demons are everywhere, and they may be responsible for a lot more than you'd think. In the Bible, people blame demons for things we might conclude are, as you said, naturally occurring: cancer, plague, perhaps even, maybe especially, mental disorders, multiple personality disorders, bi-polar syndrome. The thing is, in many cases, they may have been right. Demons might be the cause. They might be the cause of anything from the common cold to a tumor to schizophrenia."

"Well, isn't this revelatory?" I said. "Perhaps all my daughter needs is a little blood letting. Whose got the jar of leeches?"

"A twenty-year old shoots his mother in the face. He then gathers up some of his mother's guns—she's a survivalist, waiting for the end times, has the assault rifles she'll need for whatever madness the apocalypse brings—and then he drives to the elementary school where she works, and he executes twenty first-graders and six adults. You want to think a demon didn't do that?"

"Humans are plenty capable of evil without a demon's push. Blaming it on possession is an easy explanation for something that cannot be explained. It's a disowning of responsibility. Let's blame the Devil because God can't be responsible."

"Why not demons?" David asked.

"Why not God?"

"One without the other, right?"

"If demons are viruses, what about angels? Where are they? *What* are they?"

"I've seen them," Cassie said. "There out there."

Angels were hunting him.

"How do we know angels aren't the ones infecting people?"

"You already know that answer," David said.

"Because, like Satan, demons were once angels?"

"God creates the serpent in the Garden. God creates all His angels. Satan falls. Many follow. Angels protect us and demons hurt us, but maybe you're right: when it comes down to it, it may be impossible to tell the difference."

"So I'm right, now what?"

"Angel or demon: we can cast out that evil."

"Cast out the virus, you mean?"

"It is a virus and there's no way to know where it comes from or how many different strands there are, and, unfortunately, there's not a clear way to be inoculated."

"Isn't that the purpose of religion?"

"Religion is more of a blanket than a cure," David said.

"Try to think of demons in a different way from what religion and pop culture has depicted. Books and movies have portrayed them as singular beings. They can manipulate the physical world in limited ways, and they can usurp a person's body. A demon can jump from one host to another—if cast out or if the host dies—but still the basic rule remains: one demon can possess one person at a time."

"You're saying that's not correct?"

"We wish it were correct," Cassie said. "A demon can be like a puppeteer, the movies got that right; the difference is it can manipulate numerous strings at the same time. One demon can infect numerous people simultaneously."

"How do you know it's one demon?"

"I've seen it first hand. You'll see it too."

"See it? You mean, in that 'other' world? In the prayer construction place?"

Cassie nodded. "Demons are like germs, but not exactly— luckily."

"Someone gets sick, the flu, common cold, and the germ or virus goes through something like gestation," David said. "The immune system starts to fight it and you suffer the indignity of excessive mucus, pounding headaches, vomit and diarrhea. While you're suffering, you're also contagious, depending on the course of the germ or virus, and other people can be infected and endure similar unpleasantness. The virus or germ takes its course, the body handles it, and you recover. In that sense, a germ or virus can be in more than one place at once, but it's really not—it's essentially broken off pieces of itself that spread through the air or through touch and then they incubate in others and mature into full colds or into the flu."

"A demon births baby demons?"

"No. A demon cannot create spawn. That's something to be thankful for, anyway. But the way it works, from what David and I have been able to gather, is a demon may be powerful enough to spread itself into numerous hosts. It may go completely into one person and then, given the opportunity, reach out into someone else too. And then someone else and so on."

"How does it infect others?"

"Certain things make people vulnerable."

"Devil worship?"

"Maybe, but only because that might be the end product of what makes people susceptible. Imagination."

"Imagination? As in, people who are good at make believe?"

"The most creatively fertile minds offer the best playgrounds for a demon. There's a lot to work with and there's an easy entryway. This is why so many children are disproportionately possessed when compared with adults. It can be harder to occupy an adult's mind, unless there are certain open edges. Mental illness, super-keen intelligence, escalating rage. The broader and more creative the mind, the easier to infect."

"Super smart?"

"As intelligence goes up, so too does depression rates, and mental instability."

"Sounds like a great excuse to avoid homework."

"I'm not trying to suggest all bad behavior or illness is the work of demons. That gives them far too much credit. In most cases, a demon ends up being little more than a pest, and a strong creative mind sequesters it without even realizing. It's like the imagination has its own form of immunity defense. When that weakens, often with age, people try to fortify it with drugs and alcohol. Often that fails, but for some people, the defenses are very strong. Like the woman whose house collapsed. She confined her demon deep inside her and couldn't risk facing it to extract it. Sometimes though, the demon is strong enough to fight back. It can slip from the mind's defenses and do some damage."

"I'm getting lost," I said. "What does this have to do with contagious germs?"

"Anyone else in your family or of your friends who've been acting strangely?"

Don't you want me to get better?

"My father."

"He do something to you?" She gestured: I was rubbing my wrist.

I nodded and told her what happened Saturday night, in the church Sunday, and, from what Mrs. Prescott said, what happened after the accident. I relayed it with far less emotion than I felt. Perhaps that was what was meant by shock; no frigid pool water necessary. Cassie and David shared a confirming glance.

"It makes sense," Cassie said.

"What does?"

"If your father was infected, the demon might have spread its reach into your daughter because her imagination offered a more fertile habitat. But, this goes back to the germ comparison, unlike germs and viruses, when a demon reaches outside of one host into another or even several, its power in all of them weakens. Dispersal attenuates its ability to control."

"Which is a good thing," I said.

"For a time. It's not easy leaping completely free from one to another unless the people are somehow joined."

"Joined?"

"In the same mental dimension."

I nodded as if I understood.

"We'll get back to that," she said. "The simplest way for the demon to travel from one to another is by killing the host, and if it already has some of its presence in another person, it is then free to fully inhabit that person. I believe that's what happened during that car accident."

"The demon gave my father a heart attack?"

"Or maybe your father tried to fight back and the force was too much. We can't really know."

"And now it's inside my daughter?"

Abaddon.

She looked at David. "I believe so, yes," she said.

"But she's in a coma."

"Not entirely," David said. "She came out of it. That's why you called me."

"She attacked herself. Like she was crazed."

"The demon is trying to take control of her. Like a germ running rampant. A virus attacking all the organs."

"How does it take control of her?"

"It's in that other place, the place that exists only in your daughter's mind."

"The Land of Uz," I said. "It's what she called her prayer place."

"The demon is living there."

"I think I know its name. Abaddon. Does that help?"

"It might, but not me or David."

"Aren't we supposed to summon it out or something?"

"Forget what you think you know of exorcisms," David said. "This is nothing like that."

"It's easier?" I asked with a stupidly hopeful smirk.

Cassie and David didn't say anything for almost a minute. They communicated without words, just the slight flick of a hand and a gentle head nod.

"What happens when the demon completely controls her? She becomes evil?"

"Remember what I said about viruses?" David asked. "They want to live, to survive, but at the same time they are killing their host. That's why the demon spreads itself into several hosts. That way it can leap into a fresh host when the current one is no longer viable."

"Viable?"

"Demons might be clever, but they're still parasites and they can't stop what happens to their hosts. In fact, they probably speed it up."

"Her hand?" I asked.

"Anything to hurry death—sickness, suicide, or murder. Doesn't make a difference."

I laughed. It sounded horribly sad.

"We can help her," Cassie said.

"I was thinking about Job," I said. "When his wife says he shouldn't keep worshipping a god who would let him suffer, Job says, 'Shall we receive good at the hand of God and shall we not receive evil?' The hand of God. Coincidence?"

"Lucas," David said and grabbed me by the shoulders. "The demon isn't keeping your daughter in a coma. Phoebe is keeping herself that way because she knows if she wakes up, the demon will be able to kill her faster."

"Make her kill herself so it can be free," I whispered to myself.

"Her coma means there is still hope. She is protecting herself in her other world. We can help her."

Cassie and David watched me as if afraid I might attack them.

"Then show me how."

"Come on, Lucas," David said and stood. "There's something you need to see."

✝

David led me down the hallway, Cassie stepping softly behind me. All the other doors stood closed, many unmarked and seemingly identical. On the doors with nameplates were titles like Deacon #1, Student Pastor, Assistant Worship Arts Pastor, Church Planter, and Director of Contemporary Worship & Media Ministries.

The hallway ended in a wide square that, from above, was the center of the cross that formed this compound. A large sign read Reverend Roves with a painted robed arm ending in a finger pointing to the right. Glass crosses hung on the walls leading to a door. The corner office for Roves. Maybe his door nameplate read Reverend and CRO: Chief Religious Officer.

According to a detailed sign, to the left waited the daycare center, school house #1, and the gift shop. Had to have one of those—where else were you going to buy your Glass Cross T-shirt?

The actual church waited ahead.

Up a small set of stairs, a door opened into a sacristy as large as St. John's parish hall. Vestments hung in individual cubbies and couches and recliners formed gathering areas, a professional locker room. Stacked bibles and prayer books covered a long table. In one of the cubbies dangled a chain of numerous crosses and a shiny pair of black shoes had been set perfectly beneath the hanging cassock, the rope cincture draped loosely around the waist. At the far end were the blue choir robes and a wall of doors that opened to private changing rooms.

"Impressive," I said.

"You haven't seen anything yet," David said.

Several doors led out of the sacristy and into the church; we took the one that brought us out on the far side of the altar, closest to the sea of empty pews. Unlike any other large church I visited, all of which had been old, cathedral-imitation types, this church smelled fresh as if newly built and filled with promise, not musty with dried-up hopes. The altar was huge and dynamic with numerous paintings of glowing angels with open wings and outstretched arms and, of course, an enormous Jesus on the cross, bloodless, crown on his head, Heaven's eternal sun shining from him. But the church's claim to self-declared fame, was the peaked, glass roof. Even without a moon, the starlight was enough to rub a faint glow across square glass panels that tinted the whole church in gentle blue. Wall sconces formed little arcs of light, but they weren't even needed. I could imagine how impressive it was in here on a bright Sunday morning. A place where you could let the spirit move you.

I walked farther in on the unblemished wood floor. It did not creak. David had stopped ahead and now he turned to me and stepped aside.

Three coffins waited in the center aisle. The two large ones were next to each other and the child-sized one was before them, closest to me. The adult caskets were of a cherry wood, but the small one was so white it seemed to pulse. All three were set on wheeled coffin trucks; light winked off the metal frames.

Those limos parked out front hadn't been limos at all. They were hearses.

"No," I said.

The floor turned mushy beneath my approaching steps. The blue glow from above deepened, fell all around. *I'm still in that other place. In that dreamlike place.*

I staggered and David reached toward me, but I didn't fall. How was I supposed to react? Fall to my knees before the coffins and paw at them while screaming "Why?" or stand strong on stoic legs and clench my jaw to dam up the flooding tears?

Why had they done this?

"I'm sorry, Lucas, but we had to. There was no other way to be sure."

"Sure of what?"

Cassie approached from behind me, stopped short of touching me. "Even in death, there is a way to check for possession."

"You said the demon leaves the body at death."

"Think of it like an autopsy," David said. "The body still retains the evidence of almost everything that has happened to it. You can see where the bones healed from a tree fall decades earlier. Black lungs reveal decades of smoking. Organs speak of fatty meals and alcohol. And in the blood, all proof of disease, colds, and viruses can be found. I've tested their blood. Possession leaves a kind of phantasmic residue. It is detectable through modern science, but no one wants to entertain the idea. I'm lucky I didn't lose my medical license the few times I tried to push the issue. Couldn't even get my findings published."

"Phantasmic residue? Like a ghost?"

"More like a static memory of what was there. Blood can reveal it, but..."

"I can read it," Cassie said.

"How? If the person is dead ...?"

"Death isn't the end of everything," she said. "I thought a priest would know that."

She moved passed me to David, trailed a palm over the small, cherry casket.

"You 'read' all of them?"

"Yes."

"I'm sorry, Lucas," David said. "It was the only way to be sure. We actually have mortician facilities in the basement, so the hospital is very familiar with us. I spoke on your behalf, and I'm sorry I had to do that, but it was for the best."

"The best?"

"We would be glad to host the viewings and funerals here. As I said, we have all the facilities necessary to—"

"No. This is my family. I will officiate their services in *my* church. You had no right to do this."

"We had to."

"Bullshit. It was my father. Not my wife. Not Tamara. You didn't need to bring them here." I tried to go to the coffins, but my feet didn't move.

"You're right. They're clean. He is not."

I thought of Cassie touching Tamara's head and projecting herself into my baby's mind (*dead but death isn't the end of everything*), David standing beside her, eyes closed, trying to hitch a ride on her mental transport. They had no right. It was a violation on par with necrophilia.

"You were wrong to do this."

"Lucas, there's no time to argue."

"The longer we wait," Cassie said, "the harder it will be to oust the demon."

Oust, like the demon was some political incumbent. "What difference could it make? It's already been in there for several days, longer even, if what you said about reaching into other people is true."

What I'm saying, Mr. Masters, is that we may have to amputate your daughter's arm.

"It will take full control of her. She might even physically recover. But," Cassie said as a caveat, "if that happens, she will not be the same person. You might not realize at first, but there will be clues. You have to acknowledge them and not willfully ignore them. Eventually, though, the demon will be done with her and she will die. One way or another."

Don't you want me to get better?

"Phoebe is doing her best to help us, but the demon will learn all the little crevices in your daughter's mind. It will hide so well we won't be able to find it. If we wait, it'll be much harder to help her."

"Then why are we here? Why are you showing me this?"

"You need to know what to look for when we're in there," Cassie said. "You have to get the scent of the thing."

She gestured for me to join them, but I hesitated while they went to one of the large coffins. David started to open it and I stopped him. "Is he dressed?"

"He's covered."

David opened the coffin, the upper half of my father's body exposed. From my angle, I saw the white sheet concealing him up to his chin. I approached, keeping my eyes and hands from the other caskets.

The sheet covering my father featured a large stitched gold cross, the center over his chest. Even in the blue glow, his face had taken on a yellow haze. His cheekbones protruded over fallen cheeks that hugged his teeth, turned the front ones into tiny gravestones. His eyelids lay flat as if his eyes had been removed. Not removed, though—more like jellied.

"They have not yet been embalmed," David said. "The blood must be in them to get the best reading."

How many days before the bodies started to stink? How long could I delay the final services, the burials? Christ, I hadn't even called Naomi's parents. But when I made that call, I had to have an ounce of hope to share. If only for my sanity.

"Now what?" I asked. "We lay hands on him?"

"Not necessary," Cassie said. "I know the way. But we should sit."

As we had in the office, the three of us sat cross-legged, only this time a casket on wheels completed our circle.

"Before we go," David said. "You should be prepared for anything."

"Meaning?"

He looked uncertain. "Anything. Demons may be like viruses, but they are sentient. A virus may induce a fever dream, but a demon can create one especially tailored."

"What does that mean?"

"We're dealing with demons, Lucas, and we can get all theological about it, but the reality is far simpler: we're talking about monsters. And monsters prey on our fears."

What was waiting for me in that other world?

"Do you think you can find the place again?" Cassie asked. "Do you remember it well enough?"

Thinking on it for a moment, vertigo swirled in my gut. I nodded.

"I think of it as ropes," she said. "Each one leads me back to a place I've been. I find the one I want, and I climb back up into that other place. For some people, it's more like slipping off a cliff, but it's better to think of it as ropes. Offers more control."

"How do you know which rope to grab?"

"Think of your father and you'll find it. You may be able to smell it."

"Smell it? What's my father's rope smell like?"

She only stared at me. Some questions were best left unanswered.

"Is that damn sun going to fry me again?"

"Where we're going, there isn't any sun."

"What's that mean?"

She straightened her back, closed her eyes. "First, we go light."

✝

I tried to find the rope, but I fell instead. The floor gave way and I plummeted. The rushing annihilation pushed up through my throat, but I wouldn't let it out, whether scream or vomit. I had to know this sensation, had to remember it.

Blazing whiteness blinded me. A mid-day summer sun at first, warm, and a scalding ball of fire next, burning my face, melting my eyes. *They'll be jellied, like Dad's.*

The light throbbed brighter and hotter and the scream broke free. As if my shout was the secret control password, darkness dropped over everything, a heavy black curtain swooping a wave of air across me and something massive vibrated through me, as if a dinosaur walked nearby.

"I'm here," Cassie said in her melodious whisper.

"Thanks for not baking me," I said. "How do we go into my father?"

"We're already there. Do you smell it?"

It puffed gently, swirled passed me, and coiled my body in a stink that thickened from faint rot into heavy odorous flaps of wet, cancerous excrement. The smell clogged my nose and lodged in the back of my throat, something solid and awful. I gagged and choked. My stomach knotted, squeezed.

"Yes," I managed to say. "But I don't see anything."

"It's very close," she said.

"What is?"

She didn't respond.

The darkness moved around me with slippery silkiness and the smell worsened, got thicker, sewage lodged in pipes, all bodily fluids, decomposing food, and clumps of tangled hair.

That familiar sensation of someone watching me came on with the strength of a raging fever. The burst of fear that trembled with the sensation calmed—it was Cassie. She was here, even if I couldn't see her.

"What do you want me to do?" I asked.

She stood behind me with a solidity far larger than her actual slight frame. I felt her looming over me, growing larger, a shadowy something that breathed in long, deep inhalations, puffing itself bigger and bigger.

"Cassie?"

But it wasn't her. That smell wrapped around me with reeking tentacles. Breath hot with the same stink warmed my neck and scurried ice spiders down my spine. Whatever was behind me moved closer by slight gradations until only the slimmest space separated us and it slithered there with the grotesqueness of a serpent opening wide its jaws to consume cornered prey.

That's me. I'm the prey.

In a world without light, there is no direction. I ran and jumped and flailed but the thing, the beast, whatever it was, stayed right there, right behind me, almost touching but not quite, the hairs on my body pulling back with attractive static. Heat flushed through me and sank beneath frozen waterfalls. Over and over—roasting and freezing. Running and going no where.

A fever dream.

How long before the thing bent down and swallowed me? I could struggle against its throat muscles, but it would ingest me slowly, deliberately, and then gradually twist the life out of me. Or maybe melt me with stomach acid and the last thing I would know would be the pain of skin sluicing off my bones.

But that's not going to happen because I'm not really here. I'm in The Word of Christ Church, sitting cross-legged on the floor before my father, dead in a cherry-wood coffin. Nothing here can hurt me.

Sure, look at your sun-scorched face.

Terror trembled its way through my body and seized me, squeezed me like a balloon with one end bulging, thinning to transparency, threatening to burst. Things *could* hurt me here. If some crazy-hot sun could burn my face, then whatever monstrous thing hulked behind me might well swallow me. And what would be left of me in the church? A corpse, an apparent heart attack? Or would it be a gruesome spectacle filed under Mom's favorite rationale: *stranger things have happened*?

"Cassie? *Cassie?*"

I ran, hard as I could, but I wasn't moving. How the hell was I supposed to get out of here? Where was the rope? The hole to plummet free?

You fall down a rabbit hole—you don't fall out.

I thought of Cassie's place, the place of blazing sun and shimmering bodies, and willed myself back there. *Solidify this place in your mind.* I found the sensation and squeezed it, willed myself there with a terrible certainty I was never going to get there. I was going to die in this dark place and the coroner would say I had a stroke or aneurysm but really I had been consumed by something far more awful. Something tangible only in nightmare worlds.

✝

Gentle blue light misted through the dark. The desolate church and its sea of pews came slowly back. I was still seated as I had been, and my legs throbbed. Cassie had fallen over, body stiff, a mannequin. The blue light pooled in her open eyes. David was no where.

She stroked out and he fled. The thought was in the right realm but made the wrong conclusion.

My father was sitting up in the coffin. He had pulled himself up, so he leaned back against the head of the coffin, the lower half still closed. The sheet had fallen down into his lap to expose his bare chest with its tuffs of grey chest hair, but he'd pushed the sheet even farther down to expose himself.

He turned to me. Black eyes swallowed half of his pale white face. "Hello son," he said in plunging octaves. His skin crawled along his face, rippled, an army of ants beneath a tissue. His teeth were black, his tongue a slimy, flapping fish.

"This is how it happens," he said.

His hands, large and squirming with crooked fingers, clapped together and I jumped. He grinned, all liquid blackness and the stink of rotting fish. He reached down to touch himself. "Want to take a look, son? You know you want to."

He stroked himself, slowly at first and then faster. "Don't be frightened," my father said. "Just grab on and go." He laughed in rolling cackles.

"You're not real," I said, a defiant child staring down the Boogeyman in his closet.

He paused, head back and mouth agape in an exaggerated pose of pleasure and then rolled his head to stare at me with swirling black pits for eyes. His hands leaped onto the coffin's edge and I stumbled back, afraid he might pounce.

His laughter was metallic and grating.

He gagged, choked, whole body vibrating with the strain. His throat bulged like a snake swallowing a rodent. Whatever was in there was moving, pushing against the skin, moving upward toward my father's open mouth.

"You're not my father," I said. "You're not real."

His body shook, a violent ripple that started in his hips and rolled up his spine where his head snapped up and down, an animal choking on a bone and trying desperately to vomit it free.

A nightmare, I told myself. Monsters, demons—they existed only in nightmares, holdovers from caveman days. Residual fears.

Or phantasmic residue.

A fragment from some long-ago lecture in seminary came back to me: *The modern church avoids talk of evil, of the Devil, but how can we teach God exists and ignore the other half? It is the Job dilemma: How can we accept good from God and not accept evil?*

Something alien emerged onto my father's rotting tongue. I knew what it was before its first hairy legs stretched passed the lips and a bloated, multi-eyed spider head peered out as if from a cave. Its curved fangs glistened.

It was only a spider. Don't bother it and it won't hurt you.

Something scurried on my hand and I slapped bare skin. Miles away, something slammed, echoed. That putrid stench came back in a rushing wind.

"Lucas," a voice said from that far-off, echoing place. Cassie's voice. But she was frozen on the floor, eyes wide and bleeding blue light.

"Too bad," my father said, mouth too large, speaking around the spider's fat body. Black mucus oozed over his chin. "Don't worry. I'll see you soon."

My father's laughter thundered all around.

"*Lucas!*" Cassie's scream cut through the laughter. She stood at the far end of the church, a football field away and shrouded in darkness, and then she was next to me, nose-to-nose. Her skin smeared in rainbow streaks that stretched far back behind her like giant colorful rubber bands. "Take my hand!"

She held out a hazy, shimmering hand, and I hesitated only a moment before grabbing it.

My father's howling laughter followed me back to the same place.

✝

Cassie held my shoulders so I couldn't throw myself sideways into a pew and accidentally break my arm. Rollicking free from that other place was a slingshot propulsion where all my organs battered around inside me.

"It's okay," she said. "You're here. You're back."

David stared at me over her shoulder. He looked like he might vomit. *I could tell you something that'll make you puke*, I thought.

My father's coffin was closed. The rancid smell had retreated, the fading redolence wafting in the wake of a garbage truck.

"What the hell was that?" I practically shouted.

"Remnants," Cassie said.

"It didn't seem like a damn remnant."

"You're okay. But you needed to know."

"Know what?"

"What has your daughter. Now you've seen it, you can help us find it."

"That was a demon? That thing that looked like my father?" My eyes went back to the coffin. Lid still closed.

"We told you this was real," David said.

"But what are demons? Where do they come from? Why'd it look like my father?"

"What are germs and viruses?" David said. "Where do *they* come from?"

I started to object but words failed me, and I slumped back against a pew. I nicked my tailbone, but the pain stung somewhere over a distant hill.

"Whatever I need to do to save my daughter, I'll do it."

Cassie let go of me and looked at David a moment before turning back. "Let's get going then."

✝

Walking back into the hospital, I grabbed Cassie's arm. The bank of elevators waited a few steps away. People walked around us with their own worries plodding their feet. "How are we supposed to fight a demon?"

She'd gone back to her office but only to turn off her light and lock her door. She hadn't dug out an old leather case full of mystical accouterments, hadn't removed an ancient book of exorcisms from some secret cubby hole. A weapon wouldn't do any good, but there had to be something more—we couldn't go into Phoebe's Land of Uz and merely hope there was some way to save her.

"It must be forced out."

"How the hell are we going to do that?"

"I'll do it."

"No—tell me. This is *my* daughter."

She looked past me where David held an elevator open. "You believe in God, don't you?"

"Yeah."

"So, have a little faith."

✝

I expected a nurse or a doctor to stop me, but no one even said anything to us as we walked the hall and entered Phoebe's room, though a nurse stared at me for a moment and probably commented afterward to a colleague: *Poor man; lost his whole family, and a priest, too; goes to show you never know; maybe his little girl will get better; yeah, ask the patients in oncology about miracles.*

Then I remembered my sunburned face and realized she'd probably been thinking something more like, *Poor man, lost his whole family and then tried to fry himself in a tanning bed.*

Cassie went to the windows and closed the blinds. Phoebe was as she had been—calm, gently sleeping. Her shoulder ended in thick padding, a shoulder with no arm.

In a flash, I saw myself beating the doctor who had amputated her arm. *I was going to save her!* I would scream while I punched him so hard his teeth cracked.

Her black hand, still connected to her arm, lay on the sheet, fingers curled into the palm. Her arm had been wrapped with so much white gauze it blended into the sheet. Red blotches swirled in her cheeks. Her body was fighting back—she was struggling to heal herself.

Straps still prevented her from lashing out against herself, but her breathing tube had been removed and that meant she was getting better, breathing on her own, and wasn't that reason to celebrate? Joy mixed with fear in a queasy stomach roil.

"She's getting better," I said. "She's breathing on her own."

"It's the demon," Cassie said from across the room. "She's getting better because the demon is getting control of her. Her hand might even get better. She might even come out of her coma and seem perfectly normal. Like Sleeping Beauty."

"But maybe it's not a demon," I said. "Maybe she is actually getting better."

"Cancer that falls into remission is still there, biding its time, gathering its strength, waiting to attack. A demon is much worse because it has reason. It knows what it's doing. Phoebe might seem perfectly fine—a genuine miracle—and then the demon comes out."

"And does what?"

"Hurt you. Hurt Phoebe. It isn't going to reside inside her forever. It has something else in mind. They always do. Your daughter is a vehicle toward some other end. Eventually, it will want to be free and when that happens, Phoebe dies. We have to handle it now."

"If I let it run its course, and I let it leave my daughter on its own—"

"The only way to completely free itself is to kill its host. Listen to me Lucas: if we don't get rid of the infection, if we don't destroy this demon, it will kill your daughter. The only question is how much additional pain it causes before that."

"We just go into my daughter's head and fight it?"

"There's three of us and Phoebe is still in there. She is very strong. I feel it coming off of her, like heat. She will help us."

"I'll make sure we're not disturbed," David said and went into the hall.

Cassie approached Phoebe but stayed a few feet back, examined the space around her. She directed me to move the cot out of the way, and then suggested I spread the blanket on the floor. "Won't do much if things get bad, but at least we can be comfortable when we start."

"Isn't the demon in the other world?"

"A demon can manipulate the physical world, manipulate all available realities."

"How is that possible? If it exists in the mind, if it's like cancer?"

"It *is* like cancer—a cancer on everything around it. Have you had anything strange happen to you the last few weeks? Feelings of being watched? A sense that things were somehow a little off? Things even worse?"

I thought of stuffed animals with beady, watchful eyes. Of invisible spectators standing just out of view.

Cassie stared at Phoebe for a while. Her hands traced along the plastic rail. She touched the cloth restraints around Phoebe's wrists and ankles. "I remember her well," Cassie said. "She took to the Prayer Construction so easily. She told me about her world, but she didn't invite me into it. Sounds odd, imaginary worlds and whatnot, but most children want me to see what they've created. The thing is, most children can't create much. Their worlds are ephemeral pastiches of cartoons and fairy books. They collapse almost immediately. They draw pictures of goofy suns and stick figures. Phoebe did none of that. She built a genuine world. She could be trained to harness that power. Use it to help others."

"You mean be like you?"

"The world needs people like your daughter."

"So, you want me to lead the way? I'm not sure I've ever been there, either. I always humored her."

"You've been there. I feel it on you."

Hadn't there been a moment Saturday night after Phoebe's nightmare where the world fell away and I was in Phoebe's world? We were chasing the Uz Monster back into its cave. Chasing Abaddon.

You were in Uz. But you didn't realize it.

And I came out of it to see my father watching us. An animal spying vulnerable prey.

Cassie undid Phoebe's restraints. They dangled off the bed. Phoebe remained still.

"Is that wise?"

"We need her to fight. Hard to fight with your hands cuffed."

Cassie sat as before, and I followed. She left space at her side for David. She stretched her neck, her arms, like this was some yoga class. "You must stay limber," she said. "You know how in dreams you sometimes feel like you can't fight back? That can't happen."

I stretched as best I could.

"Aren't we going into an imaginary world? I mean, what does stretching matter?"

"It's not imaginary," she said. "All worlds are linked, connected, and your physical self stays here but its essence travels. Limitations remain."

"So, no flying over there, huh?"

"You can fly, as in really fly, but to do that you either have to have terrific talent or you have to go into that other world completely."

"Physically? How?"

"Simple," she said. "Go into the other place and die here. Even then, however, it might not work. Depends what world you enter. If it's your own, it will have to be immensely stable. If it's someone else's, you'll need permission."

"Permission?"

"No one gets into Heaven without God's approval."

Cassie straightened her posture, slowed her breathing.

"When I was in my father's world," I said, unsure of my phrasing, "you were there but David wasn't."

"He didn't go. He stayed in this reality."

"Because of what happened in your office?"

"He'll be okay," she said. "He will be strong."

"Why couldn't he follow? Where does he go?"

"David is a wonderful man. A mentor. But he's hurting. He blames himself for what happened to his wife and son. When he goes over, he visits Joey."

"How?"

"He built a place for his son. It's his own safe place."

"And if he goes there again?"

"He won't."

"But—"

David came back in, closed the door. "I told them we would be praying quite intensely. They looked at me like I was some injured dog in the street, but I don't think we'll be disturbed."

He dragged a wooden chair to the door and wedged it under the knob. He joined us on the floor and began stretching.

"This is ridiculous, isn't it?" I asked.

"Faith is never ridiculous," David said.

"Before we go," Cassie said, "there's something else you need to know. Being inside an infected world is like being in a room filled with poison gas. The longer you are exposed, the more vulnerable you become. I will do what I can, try to be a sort of gas mask for you, but I need my strength to handle the demon. It will try to evade us, lure us, trap us. There is the very real possibility you'll be struck. Remember my place and retreat there."

"If I am stuck there, what happens to me here?"

"You'll be in a coma," she said as if that were obvious.

"If being in an infected person is like breathing poison, why have me go into my father? Even though he was dead, something was still there."

"It was a test."

"Of what, whether I'd freak out?"

"When you went into your father, you encountered the remnants of what had been there, dying. It was attracted to you immediately and showed itself because it was desperate to live. It was essentially leftovers and mostly harmless, but it still wanted to live. Germs and viruses are selfish creatures, but they aren't completely stupid. They recognize their own and they work together."

"You mean because I'm my father's son?"

"No," Cassie said. "It's because you're infected too."

✞

"Possessed? You're saying I'm—"

"A demon may take up primary residence in one host, but it can still reach into others, remember. It must always have an escape plan."

"How come I feel fine? How come my hand isn't black?"

"Have you had any feelings of someone standing behind you? Any sensation of being watched?"

I didn't respond.

"You going into your father confirmed it. The demon is inside you as well, if only a fragment."

"How can you know any of this for sure? Aren't you guessing?"

"You can ask questions later," she said. "We have to get moving."

"If I'm infected, shouldn't we expel it from me first?"

"It's good you're infected."

"Good? Why?"

"Because it will be drawn to you, as the remnants were in your father. Your presence will bring it out. The beast will come right for you, and then I'll take it."

"And do what with it?"

Her eyes drifted for a moment. "Handle it."

"Okay," David said. "Let's get on with it."

✟

First, go light.

I fell back into Cassie's blazing bright world with surprising ease. The sun warmed my face, began to thicken my burn.

"See?" she said. "It gets easier and easier." Her body shimmered and smeared.

"Now what?"

"Take us to your daughter," David said. His face streaked long in multi colors.

Take us to your leader, I thought.

"What if she's not there? What if the place is gone?"

"It's there," Cassie said. "It's where the demon lives."

"I don't know how to get there."

"Yes, you do. Think of your daughter, make her tangible, and grab her."

I thought of a moment years ago when I was teaching Phoebe to ride a bike. She mastered the training wheels but, at four years old, she said she didn't want to be a little kid any more; it was time to ride like a big girl. She watched as I removed the training wheels, and I explained to her it might take a while to learn how to ride, but she shouldn't get discouraged. I was going to help her. And when she got on the bike in the church parking lot, her helmet falling askew across her forehead, she looked at me with all the seriousness of someone much older. "Don't let me go," she said. "Stay with me, Daddy."

I promised I would be with her the whole way, and I was at first, but she was doing so well. Perfectly balanced, pedaling smoothly, faster and faster I couldn't keep up even if I wanted. So, I let go of her seat and watched her ride straight across the parking lot toward the tree line. She knew how to turn, to stop—

she was a natural. But she was going fast, the plastic streamers on the handle bars fluttering across her arms, and when she screamed, my heart hitched into my throat. A huge oak loomed before her. I ran after her. "Turn! *Turn!*" She yanked the handle bars and hit the brakes, but she was going too fast and the bike slipped out from under her. She spilled across the gravel in three awkward thumps. She sat up with a dazed expression and when she saw me, she burst into howling cries. She held out her hands. The palms were scraped and bleeding, little pebbles lodged in among the soft tissue. Her knees were bleeding too, and one ear had been scoured. A thin line of blood trailed down her neck. "You promised you wouldn't let go," she sobbed against me. "You promised you'd stay with me, Daddy." I held her tightly against me, caressed her hair and cried right along with her. I had promised and look what happened.

She was in my arms again. I felt her familiar weight against me, and I squeezed her even more tightly. She smelled of the cocoa butter Naomi put on her. *I won't let you go*, I promised. *Never again. Daddy's here.*

And like that, I took flight. The scorching sun of Cassie's world dropped off and fell farther and farther behind. Cold darkness rushed around me. This wasn't exactly flying like Superman, more like rocketing through a tunnel, but my stomach wedged itself beneath my ribcage and I might have fooled myself I was airborne.

To do that you either have to have terrific talent or you have to go into that other world completely. Go into the other place and die here.

I felt the warmth of Phoebe's world before the first twinkle of starlight poked from the sheet of darkness. *It's nighttime there*, she had told me Saturday night. *But the stars are so bright it's like the sun's out.*

"This is the place," I said. "This is The Land of Uz."

Green hills verdant with crayon saturation rose up from nothing and glowed beneath stars that lit the world, so all shadows pushed off into the farthest corners. The hills bobbed up and down, flattened into plateaus, fell off into infinitely stretching valleys. Deep blue pools of water gushed from the ground and heavy vegetation sprouted and grew to towering, jungle-like heights instantly—life sped up through a time-lapse camera. Oak trees mixed with skinny bamboo trees with puffed, leafy tops. Enormous maple leafs blinked from green to yellow to red. Grass turned purple and blue, wobbled toward pink and flushed to orange. A child's conception of unbound beauty.

The land stretched on and on, flickering between endless color varieties. I had no idea how to stop moving, how to land, but the moment I thought it, I was on the ground. Cool grass poked between my bare feet. *But in reality, I'm wearing shoes*, I thought. *Yet, what is reality?*

A sign protruded from the side of a hill up ahead. It was not a green traffic sign, but a faded wooden sign that exactly resembled the one outside Saint John's, even down to the strips of peeling white paint along the edges. Instead of the name of the church, however, the sign read in Phoebe's careful, block letters: Rolling Hills.

"It's in here somewhere," I said.

"I can feel it," Cassie said.

She and David appeared as if slipping through a fabric screen made to resemble the surroundings. As if they materialized out of thin air. They stood solid, no wavering edges. They were barefoot as well. They looked around without surprise.

"She's trying to fight back," Cassie said. "Changing the colors, altering the landscape. She's a smart girl. She's trying to confuse it. She can help us. We'll find her."

"No, I have her." But my arms were empty. This realization hurt me in a terrible way. She had been in my arms. I had felt her weight. She brought me here. And I had lost her.

You promised you'd stay with me, Daddy.

"We shouldn't stay in one place," Cassie said.

"Why not? You said the demon would come for me."

"We need to take it by surprise. And it's not the only thing to fear here."

"This is my daughter's place. She's not going to hurt us. We're here to help."

"She can't control everything. There are other things here. Guardians."

Everyone is waiting for us. Braveheart and Pandy, Chip and Phillip, Sergeant and Foppy...

Her stuffed animals.

We give this place life.

"Guardians," I said not quite in disbelief.

"We must be careful," Cassie said. "She may be letting this place grow without restraint, letting it be the untamed vine."

"She's protecting herself," I said.

"Yes, and it'll be much easier for us to get lost here."

Trees loomed around us. They bled shades of gray and purple like oozing sap. Something heavy moved behind those trees. Its steps shook the ground. A sheen of white passed among the trees. A glimmer of pink. An orb of deep sanguine. Something huge, monstrous, impossible.

"What do you mean, 'guardians'?"

"Children value their places more than adults do. When a child builds a prayer place, she will also be sure it is protected. Some children booby-trap their places, others add sentries. Boys will have warriors with swords. Girls find inspiration in seemingly innocent places.

The ground thumped again. The huge thing of white stopped, watched us with that enormous crimson eye, peering through vegetation. A curve of white stretched from a blade of pink gums.

"It's her bunny," I said in almost comical shock. "Its name is Foppy."

"Doesn't seem very cuddly," David said.

"We're intruders," Cassie said. "It's only doing its job."

"How many could there be?" I asked.

"You would know best."

I thought of the pony, the dinosaur, the chipmunk with the white sneakers and the heart stitched between two paws. Of all the stuffed animals in her room. Of Ben-the-bear.

"They won't hurt us," I said.

"Unless the demon has taken control of them," Cassie said.

We looked at each other. Stars flared extra bright. "This can't be real," I almost shouted even though there was no noise other than the heavy steps of some monstrous bunny. "This is a delusion. Please tell me that's all it is."

"You can stay here and find out, but I wouldn't recommend it," Cassie said.

Another heavy thud vibrated through the ground. A deep, hollow crack sounded from the trees. An echoing collapse followed. Another tree fell and the ones before us shook.

"We need to go now," David said.

The trees shook and another one fell somewhere. David was right, but I wanted to see this thing. Was it really Foppy the bunny morphed into dinosaur size? Such things only existed in nightmares.

And what do you think this is? The Land of Uz IS the land of nightmares.

Another tree fractured and fell and there behind the closest line of trees stood an enormous bunny with dangling, floppy ears, and colossal red eyes potent with malicious life. We reflected across the convex surface of those eyes in sinuous ribbons. Fangs longer than our bodies curved down beneath its furry chin. Patches of fur were worn thin and faded to grey, like the stuffed animal. It opened its mouth and a pink tongue curled and it screeched loud enough to make my ears ring. It rose up on its mammoth back legs. Its front legs flailed, and gnarled claws sprang from the toes. It crashed forward against the trees.

We ran.

The trees thumped behind us and the bunny leaped into hopping pursuit. As its back paws sprung it forward and it thumped off the ground, the whole world shook so heavily, it was as if we were tossed up, the ground a trampoline.

It should have overtaken us immediately, and though it continued to pursue, we were outrunning it. My legs felt separate from me, fluid in their rapid motion. *Good thing I stretched.*

We ran up one hill of yellow grass and then another of brownish orange. Strange, twirling vines curled along the ground and seemed to race along with us. I thought of booby-traps, of venus flytraps trained in my daughter's imagination to snatch and devour.

"You have to find the demon!" Cassie shouted.

I was about to ask how the hell I was supposed to do that when up ahead the hill collapsed into a groove, a long rock slide, that led directly into a cave. Only it wasn't one cave—three rounded mouths gaped with equal black danger.

I ran toward it.

"Which one?" David yelled.

The ground thumped and tossed us off our feet again in cartoonish exaggeration. Somehow we landed in perfect stride and kept running.

"I don't know!"

"Three for three," Cassie shouted. "Find the beast and draw it out."

The cave openings shook, thick darkness wavering within. Which one had the demon? Better yet: which one hid my daughter? What if the other stuffed animals were in these caves? Certainly Ben-the-bear—bears lived in caves, for God's sake.

The ground dropped off, a continental slope that took out our feet and tumbled us down toward the caves on our backs, a slide into Hell. Behind us, above us, the bunny screeched with all its awful might. Its monstrous tumult shook the very air.

We slid faster. Our paths would decide for us which caves we would enter. Cassie swooped past on my right and David on my left.

With a rocky thud, I slid into the dark of the middle cave.

✝

The ground altered from smooth slide to rocky pool and my legs caught underneath me and tossed me forward in a painful second-base skid that slashed my face and bruised my ribs. I sat up and coughed out a clump of pebbles. My head squeezed with pain and wobbled like it might fall off my neck.

Even in the complete darkness of the cave, I could still see my hands and the blackish blood pattering onto my palms from my forehead. My hand glowed faintly blue. Maybe I had absorbed some of the starlight, like dream radiation.

Use the starlight, Daddy. Grab the starlight and send the Uz Monster back to his cave.

No running this time. No hiding.

I started walking. Sharp rocks stabbed at the soles of my feet. Pebbles made faint clacking sounds as I walked. The cave walls gradually closed in. Still, the darkness could not swallow my hands, now glowing blue.

"I'm here, honey," I said. "Daddy's here to save you."

My words should have echoed, but the moment they left my mouth, my words hit the ground and died. Or maybe burrowed inside the rock out of fear.

The cave narrowed from fifteen or twenty feet wide to ten and then five and then no wider than a doorway and even narrower in places where I had to squeeze sideways to get through. If the Uz Monster was down here, it certainly wouldn't be some huge, looming presence. At least I didn't have to worry about Foppy coming down here.

The cave ended.

I smacked the wall, backed up and smacked it again, a trapped animal confused by its cage's bars. I laid my hands on the wall. It was warm, the way Phoebe was always warm, and smooth, but completely solid.

I pushed against it, wedged my feet against the jagged ground, and pushed until I was grunting and panting. This couldn't be the end. There had to be a way through or around. Why would Phoebe let me slide in here if it was a dead end?

Because she's not in control anymore.

I punched the wall and screamed against the pain. "Phoebe! I'm here! I'm here to save you!"

A man's scream shook through the walls around me. David. Something had been waiting for him inside his cave. Something that in another world might be cute and cuddly, but here, in this bastardized version of existence, was a menacing, horrendous thing of fangs and claws and unrelenting hunger.

David screamed again. The wail faded back into silence.

I punched the wall. My middle finger snapped with a flare of pain. I waited for a similar scream from Cassie, but it didn't come. She knew what she was doing. She wouldn't be caught by surprise.

"Daddy."

Phoebe's soft voice came from nowhere and everywhere at once. "I'll keep you safe. I'll protect you."

"No, honey. I'm here to protect you."

"It's too late. This is the Land of Golgotha. The Land of Abaddon. He rules here now. But you'll be safe if you stay in here. We can be together."

"It's not too late. You just have to help us."

"Your friends are already lost. You can't fight Abaddon. He is *The Doomed* and this is his place."

Her voice now came from the other side of the wall. It hummed through the rock. I leaned against it. A sharp edge dug into my forehead. "No, honey. Listen to me. I'm here. Daddy's here. I'm going to get you out. I will do whatever I have to."

"I want you to stay," she said. "You promised to never leave me."

"I'm not: you're coming with me."

"It's not safe. Abaddon will get us. It got grandpa."

Just grab on and go.

"I know, honey. I'm so sorry."

"And Mommy and Tamara."

I smacked the wall and the fresh pain kept back the tears. "We have each other," I said. "Please, Phoebe. You're my angel. You have to be strong for Daddy. *Please.*"

She didn't respond for a while. Something rumbled around the cave, a slight earthquake tremor. "No, Daddy. I won't let Abaddon get you, too."

Another tremor rolled around the cave and behind me, rocks toppled from the ceiling. A scattering of rocks rolled down to my feet. The whole cave shook violently as if ready to explode.

"It's coming for you," Phoebe said. "I'll keep you safe."

"Don't worry about me. Protect yourself."

I slid to my knees against the wall. The demon was going to bury me alive or maybe reach through rock and seize me with a taloned claw and then eviscerate me. And in reality, I would collapse flat on a hospital floor, inert and unresponsive. *Looks like he went off-line*, a nurse would comment. Then they would fix me up in a bed and wheel me into a room with the other comatose patients.

The wall warmed rapidly but before it could burn my skin, it fell away, and I collapsed forward onto cool grass. Phoebe's bare toes wiggled before me. The way her pinkie toes curled across the adjacent toes almost made me cry. I got up and there she was: my baby girl in her blue and yellow Sunday dress with little butterfly clips in her hair.

"Hi, Daddy."

I hugged her and would have been content to die. Sounds extreme, but that doesn't make it any less true.

✝

The wall solidified. Sealed us in. No bigger than her bedroom, Phoebe's little cave had lush grass, a jade plant with purple petals, and a black ceiling twinkling with stars. I leaned against one curved wall and she laid against my chest. I kept one arm draped across her waist. My pain numbed and faded.

"You'll heal quickly here," she said.

I touched my forehead, the cut already clotted.

"He took all my animals. They're his now."

"I'm sorry, honey."

"But you're here, and that's what matters. We can live here forever."

You're infected, too, Cassie had said.

What had become of her? Had Ben-the-bear gotten her or something worse? Had she found Abaddon? And what of her and David in the real world? Were they prostrate on the floor? Were they dead? And what of me? Breathing but unresponsive?

"I'm so happy I found you, honey."

She nuzzled against me. "Me too."

"This is no place to live."

"It's perfect," she said. "We're safe."

I had no counter-argument. I settled back against the rock and held her tightly. My thoughts drifted from how to convince her we couldn't stay here to wondering why I wanted to leave anyway. What was there for us in the real world? Only pain up there. Only death. Only emptiness.

The stars blinked for me and whatever was meant by the world drifted off.

✝

Naomi's voice came from the darkness of my sleep: "You're not dead."

"I don't care. I have Phoebe. I have our daughter."

"You can't stay there. It won't let you."

For a moment, I had been in the car accident and Naomi was at my bedside in the hospital, cradling one of my hands, and whispering in my ear. "You have to come back," she said.

"I want to stay."

"Then it must be so Phoebe can be free."

And with that, I was no longer in the car when my father grabbed the wheel and steered it directly into an on-coming vehicle. What I wouldn't give to change reality.

✝

Stars coruscated across the cave ceiling. Blue light flushed in waves over us.

"How do you do that?" I asked.

"I just do," she said.

"It looks so real."

"It is real. Don't you believe?"

"That isn't the sky, honey. We're in a cave."

"It's like what you always say in your sermons."

"What's that?"

"Faith isn't easy."

My eyes watered.

"I love you, Daddy."

✝

A hair's tickle from my face, Cassie's voice: "Don't be stupid. This isn't your real daughter."

"This is my daughter and I'm never letting her go again."

"Look closely," she said. "That isn't your daughter."

But it was. I caressed her hair. It was a mop of curly brown, which was not hers, but must have been a trick of the poor light. "Right, honey? You're my baby."

"Yes, Daddy," she said in a hollow, phlegm-choked voice.

She shifted against me with leathery paper sounds and tilted her head back. Her hair fell onto her face and swirled there in spinning curlicues, a heaping handful of squirming worms. Black, hollow eyes spun in that mess and a large mouth drooped low in an exaggerated scowl.

I pushed her off and scrambled toward the solid wall that had also been transparent. I pounded against stone. "You son of a bitch!" I shouted. "Where is my daughter?"

"I'm right here."

I turned to face my daughter standing in the middle of the cave. I almost went to her, but black-blood veins snaked across her face and her skin pulled tight with the gruesomeness of a million facelifts.

"It's in you, Daddy," she said in that awful voice. "And it's in me, too."

"You're not my daughter. This is a trick."

"I am Phoebe. I'm what's left of her. I can be whatever you want. We can sit and watch the stars forever. Or I can be something more. I can make you happy in every way, Daddy. I can satisfy your every desire." She licked the fingers of one hand, one by one, and sucked long on her middle finger.

"Stop it, Phoebe."

She growled and yanked down her jaw with that middle finger. Her jaw snapped, popped, and hung crookedly. A fat black slug of a tongue wiggled in the gap. "You can fuck me, Daddy," she said in a voice full of gravel. Her body twitched, lurching a step toward me. "You can pretend you're fucking

Mommy. You can pretend you're fucking Jesus. Is that what you want? You want to fuck your savior? He's just a man. A man who can be fucked. Come on, Daddy. What do you say?"

"You are not my daughter," I said and slowly stood. The Phoebe-thing staggered forward a trio of steps. "You are Abaddon."

It smiled, broken jaw sagging.

"You are the demon and you're coming with me."

It laughed, if you could call it laughter the way the sound rolled in rocky cackles, and the creature posing as my daughter bent down like a runner at the starting line

—and pounced.

✝

It hit me with more weight than Phoebe's meager body and I staggered back, smacked the wall. My head bounced off the stone. *What's a concussion on top of everything else?* Only the wall wasn't solid, not completely. A direct hit would have cracked open my skull. It hurt but not as much as it should have.

The Phoebe-thing growled and hissed and clawed at my face. Hooked talons dug into the side of my face and tossed my head side to side. I beat at the thing, at my daughter's frail body; she was thin but solid, super-strength rope wound until it's as strong as steel—an organless body, something unnatural, something kept in a cage and hidden from light.

The stench of shit engulfed everything. The Phoebe-thing screeched into my ear and bit down right behind it. Teeth ruptured my neck and dug into the base of my skull. I howled with pain, smacked at her, punched her. We twirled, crashed against the wall again, a hellish, stumbling waltz.

The wall was softer still, like the green styrofoam florists use for flower arrangements, or well-beaten Play-doh, and I spun her around and into the wall, hitting it harder and harder. The Phoebe-thing tossed her body side to side, a beast trying to yank flesh from injured prey.

My fingers tangled in her long, greasy hair, and I steeled myself against the pain for a moment before I snapped her head back as hard as I could. The pain was a flush of heat that burst behind my ear and quickly spread down my neck. The Phoebe-thing fought against my grip, but I pulled her back, face to face. Her black eyes narrowed, somehow darkened even more, an oil slick at midnight, and her jaw snapped at me with the repetitive fervor of a rabid dog.

That's what she is, I thought. *An infected animal.*

"Cassie," I yelled. "Help!"

The Phoebe-thing, the thing that had once been my daughter—was still my daughter but suffering some horrendous infection, some Devil Virus—snapped at me, flailed in all directions. My arms burned with the strain. Her legs kicked at me, landed in the crotch, and she grinned at my face of shocked pain. Hot water swelled in my groin. Still, I held her back.

"This isn't you," I said. "You have to fight it, Phoebe. You have to be strong for Daddy and fight back. You can do it."

She stopped fighting, stood there, growling at me. Long streaks of bloody mucus trailed from her mouth. Her body shook with tremors that wobbled up my arms. She snapped at me and lunged, but I pushed her back before she could snag skin. She tried to maul me, dig her nasty claws into my forearms, but I pushed her back.

She stood hunched, heaving an awful stink of breath.

"Honey, it's Daddy. Please baby. I know you're still in there. Be my angel. You have to fight it. I'm here. I'm here to keep you safe."

The Phoebe-thing hesitated. Her mouth closed and her curled lips quivered. Her eyelids closed and opened again to reveal impossibly bright blue eyes. Her face twisted with confusion, the same face she used to make upon waking after sleeping in the car during long trips.

"Daddy?" Phoebe's voice came from the Phoebe-thing's mouth as if traveling long distance. Like my angel was imprisoned deep down inside this shell, a cave itself.

"Phoebe?"

"I'm scared, Daddy. Please help me."

She started to cry, and I took her in my arms, hugged her against me. "I'm so sorry, honey. I'm going to save you. I promise."

"Don't leave me," she said, but her voice dropped on the last word, a bronchitis-tangled sound.

"I'll never leave you again."

"Promise?" The word came out strangled in phlegm and filtered through rocks.

"Phoebe?" I broke the hug.

Blood tears trailed from black eyes. "Hi, Daddy."

I brought my hand up in time to save my face. She bit down hard across three fingers. Her cheeks stretched and cracked in jagged rips that tugged and frayed her lips. She chomped on my hand, gobbled it. My ring finger broke with an audible snap. Her hands swarmed around me, scraped my neck, sunk into my arms. I grabbed her hair and tried to pull her off my hand, but her teeth sunk deeper, right through my palm.

What was happening to me on the hospital floor? Was my hand breaking and bleeding or was all the damage internal? If my daughter devoured me, what happened to the real me?

This is the real you, I could hear Cassie explaining. *A demon can be in many hosts at once, but its central power can only be located in one. You can be here and in a hospital, but you're primarily here.*

Being killed.

"I command you to stop!" I yelled. "Christ commands you!"

Still chomping at my hand, the Phoebe-thing laughed in an awful, choking gag and bit even harder. Pain wound up my arm and into my head where a red-hot ball of it swallowed all other thoughts.

Cassie's voice, her *real* voice, circled me, calm but desperate: "Bring her out. Take her from the cave, and I'll do the rest."

We spun around, hit the wall again, but then we collapsed *through* the wall and hit the rocky floor of the narrow tunnel. The Phoebe-thing spit out my hand and appreciated it for a moment, two of my fingers mangled and dangling askew, and lunged for my throat. She clawed at me and bit my shoulder and tried to chomp hunks from my chest. We wrestled, rolling over the sharp rocks in awkward bursts, thudding against the walls, but moving, moving back down the tunnel, back toward the gaping cave mouth.

She tore my flesh and I fought against her. I smacked her against the rock walls and trilled a sound of victory even as my stomach lurched in nausea. *Not my daughter, not my daughter.*

Maybe not, but what was happening to the real Phoebe in the hospital bed? Was she being tossed about, a limp body in an invisible maelstrom or was she seemingly still, a ribbon of blood curving from one ear?

We rolled over a rocky hill and for a moment there was nothing—only that unnerving sensation of loss of ground, a car on a road's dip, a plane going airborne, the cartoon coyote standing past a cliff's edge on wisps of air—and then we plummeted.

Entangled and still fighting against each other, we dropped through a black tunnel with only the tightening panic in my gut to tell me we were dropping faster and faster, the sweat and blood and phlegm slipping from us like rain sucked back into the clouds. *Rushing annihilation*, I thought in hopeless recognition. *Only this time, I won't come out anywhere—I'll fall and fall and my body will be frozen in a coma. Or maybe there is a bottom and when I hit it, it's hello heart attack.*

"Grab the rope," Cassie said inside my head. "Grab it and come to me."

"Where?"

"Remember it. How it felt. It is solid. Go there."

Incense whirled up my nostrils and I tried to remember Cassie's place, the world of skin-scorching sun, the safe place, and for a second I felt sun and the tunnel began to lighten, but the Phoebe-thing buried its teeth in my neck, into my throat, and the rope vanished, yanked away up into the thick darkness.

We fell and I hoped there was a bottom, a rocky floor hard enough to kill us—both here and in that hospital room.

✝

In dreams, a fall is a short burst of terror in which the ground speeds toward you and smacks you free from the illusory world. I don't know if its appropriate to call those other worlds dreamscapes or nightmares, but I never saw the bottom before we hit it and the collision did not spring us back into consciousness.

I screamed myself into a sitting position. The hospital room blazed bright around me, only it wasn't the lights in the ceiling producing such intense brightness. The massive sun of Cassie's world glared down from some place far, far above. My body warmed immediately and began to sweat.

Phoebe lay twisted on the side on the bed, the sheet pulled tight around her in a cocoon. David and Cassie were flat on the floor, eyes closed. What if David was dead? Had Ben-the-bear killed him? If so, was he forever a vegetable?

This isn't reality, I thought without surprise. This is what it felt like in the church when my father sat up in his coffin. When that spider crawled up his throat. The world tilted and slipped, went foggy and sharpened to terrible clarity.

The wall with the small whiteboard (*Your shift nurse is Regan*) and the pain scale of smiling to frowning faces shimmered and revealed a world beyond, as if in the adjacent room, of multicolored hills and towering trees with enormous purple leaves. The wall swam back, solid, and rippled away again to show Phoebe's Land of Uz.

Something dotted all those hills. I thought at first of her stuffed animals, but these were all the same. Crosses wedged into the ground. And on each one, a human shape dangled in slow death.

Hundreds of crucifixions.

Welcome to the Land of Golgotha.

So proud in his pain. The thought was not mine, but it bloomed in my head just the same, and it felt terribly true.

Oh, Jesus, so proud in his pain.

You worship him and his cross, and it's all a joke.

Above, the ceiling went from solid to diaphanous so Cassie's sun could shine down, then solid again, and so on. The room wavered and rolled with a watery instability. Multiple worlds fought for dominance. I thought of the transparencies teachers had used when I was in school on projectors and how odd it looked when multiple transparencies were laid on top of each other, how my mind hurt with the effort to make sense of the overlapping chaos. I smelled incense and Phoebe's favorite sweet fruit candies.

This was not Cassie's safe place, but it wasn't far from it either. I felt it. But this was not far from Phoebe's world or far from reality. It was as if I had a choice. A sort of purgatory.

Or maybe this really was purgatory.

As if such a thing existed.

I went to the bed. The floor flushed from red to blue to orange to green in pools around my footsteps.

"Phoebe?"

She stirred as if shaking off a wake-up call, her body turned away from me.

"Phoebe, it's Daddy. I told you I wouldn't leave you."

I cupped her shoulder. Heat emanated through her hospital gown. Slowly, I turned her onto her back. A pale, bloated face lay against the pillow. Purple and black bruises clouded her cheeks and swelled her nose. As if she'd been beaten with a cinderblock.

Her mouth drooped open and a black tongue slid out. Only it kept sliding out, longer and longer, a horrible black slimy thing. A snake with no eyes, a giant parasite that had gestated inside my daughter and now birthed itself free. It stretched over her body, still pushing out between her lips, her front teeth indenting parallel trails along its slimy skin. It dropped off her tangled legs and onto the bright white sheets and hesitated a moment before lurching back toward her beneath the sheet. It moved fast. Phoebe's head bobbed as the snake propelled itself free and vanished under the sheet. It wasn't dropping off the bed, not slithering across my feet.

I grabbed the edge of the sheet, the damn thing still vomiting from Phoebe's mouth, and pulled it from her body in one hard yank. Her legs spun free and flopped flat on the bed.

The black eel-thing slithered between Phoebe's spread legs, up her gown, and the blazing sun shone through the fabric to expose the awful black thing worming its way back inside my daughter. The skin above her pelvis bulged. The thing squirmed inside her. Raping her. Killing her.

The Devil Virus.

Her limbs tensed, her whole body going rigid, eyes wide and unblinking.

The scream that came from my throat was not my own but something far less human and much more primal. The last of the black thing dropped from her mouth. Her arms yanked up and she grabbed the rail, snapped her legs up, and flung herself over.

The limb restraints dangled as if in mockery.

Not killing her. Controlling her. Owning her.

Phoebe's bare feet hit the floor a moment before the black thing slapped it with heavy wetness. Phoebe wobbled there, grinned. The black thing snaked up between her legs until the last of it was back inside her.

Blood plopped on the white floor between her feet.

But she's too young to have her period, I thought stupidly.

And how Naomi would have laughed at me in a wonderfully amused way, how much she looked forward to seeing me handle our daughters' adolescence, floundering in uncertainty with two teenage girls in the house. "Think of the hormones," Naomi had said with with a devilish grin.

Maybe she was hemorrhaging and bleeding out and—

Or maybe you're hallucinating.

Blood plopped in tiny splotches on the floor, each a kind of starburst.

She grinned.

And attacked.

✝

Ensnared in a hug, we tumbled back into the wall with those stupid pain faces and fell through it back into another world.

✝

We thudded onto cool grass. The hospital room hovered above us, David and Cassie levitating in a transparent box. What world was real?

Die in one, die in them all. Close enough, anyway.

"Your daughter's mine," the Phoebe-thing said in its awful voice.

The heavy thump of something huge vibrated through the ground. *Foppy*, I thought in a daze. *The goddamn bunny is going to eat me.*

The Phoebe-thing pitched on top of me, straddled me, the hospital gown pulling up past its waist. The end of that black creature protruded from her like a blood-slicked appendage. Something for a freak show.

The ground rocked again in a walking earthquake.

"This is it, Daddy," the Phoebe-thing yelled. "This is how it happens."

She dropped toward me, mouth gaping wider and wider, but something snatched her off. *Foppy*, I thought. *The real Phoebe is still controlling Foppy.*

Only it wasn't Foppy.

Cassie stood with the Phoebe-thing thrashing in both hands. Immense light flooded from Cassie's body, the sky cracking wide for the sun's brilliance. I squinted against the glare.

The angels are hunting me.

Cassie wrapped the Phoebe-thing in a hug, and it screamed and howled as if being consumed in fire. The light burned brighter and brighter until Cassie and the Phoebe-thing disappeared it its blinding surge and still the light grew stronger.

A supernova. She's going to explode and destroy everything.

I got up, slipping on the grass. The hospital room floated above me. I jumped for it and fell stupidly back to the ground. That wasn't how this worked. Wasn't the way free.

You have to believe, Phoebe, the real Phoebe said. *You have to have faith.*

Cassie and the Phoebe-thing had become a sun, a giant orb of monstrous light, paling everything around, wiping away all color, dissolving the boundaries among all worlds. My skin burned. My vision blurred. Tears smoked on my cheeks.

You have to believe. Have faith and come back to me.

The ground shook and a monster I couldn't see unleashed its wailing screech. The sun burned and burned and I shut my eyes against it and screamed into the tumult.

I screamed a prayer for salvation and hoped God was listening.

✝

My shout ground to a subway-car halt. The hospital room returned with concrete solidity. The hospital bed had turned over and Phoebe lay in a heap on the floor. Her IV lines had pulled free and a machine beeped madly. Ceiling tiles had fallen, and a large crack zigzagged across the floor like a continental fault. Around the edges of that crack, the floor had blackened, melted.

I went to Phoebe, turned her slowly over.

Sweat slicked her pale face and bruises throbbed across her cheeks but no tension tightened her forehead, no threatening twitch quivered beneath her eyes. She came awake slowly, as Sleepy Beauty would.

"Phoebe?"

"It's not over yet," she said in a dreamy whisper. "Not yet."

Behind me, Cassie screamed. I clutched Phoebe against me. Cassie rocked back and forth and flung herself against the wall with a hard thunk. Her hands came up to her face, clawed at the sides of her mouth. Her eyes were dinner plates. Her feet kicked up high, swung down, and bounced her whole body in an awkward, painful flop.

Cassie kicked David in the head where in lay on the floor, but he didn't move. He had gone to his safe place in some other world. Gone to be with his son.

"She can't fight it," Phoebe said against me. "She can't and it's going to come back. It's going to get me again."

Once you've had the Devil Virus, I thought, *you're twice as likely to be reinfected. Once the Devil has his claws in you...*

I clutched her but said nothing. No matter what happened, I was going to stay with her, be it here or in some other world.

Cassie made a choking, gaging sound that morphed back into a scream. Someone was pounding on the door, adding his own screams to the din.

Cassie's body jostled side to side, up and down, a poltergeist's plaything, and then she leaped up into a crouch, legs bent, back arched, hands still digging at her mouth as if trying to yank out her tongue. Or something else.

Her eyes rolled, focused on me.

I turned my body to shield Phoebe, but there was something other than predatory hunger in that stare. I saw a strange sort of courage in her eyes.

Cassie turned and sprang off David's limp body for the door. She grabbed the wooden chair wedged against the door and hurled it behind her. It hit the window and splintered the glass in spiderweb cracks.

A large man with shoulders pushing out his custodial uniform froze with one fisted hand in the air. Cassie screamed and barreled through the man head first. He stumbled back, hit something and a cacophonous spill echoed down the hall. Someone screamed.

"She only has one choice," Phoebe said.

It took a moment to register the resigned gravity of my daughter's words. I knew she was right but that didn't mean I wanted to accept it. I told her to stay right here, to not move, and I ran after Cassie.

This isn't how it happens, I thought. *This is how it ends.*

✝

I followed the sound of Cassie's screams and the shouts of shocked spectators. More things clattered to the floor. An old man was knocked from his wheelchair and another patient twisted his ankle and fell hard enough for me to hear something inside him crack.

Orderlies and nurses joined the pursuit. Heavy footfalls thumped down the hall and sneakered feet squeaked around corners.

Cassie took the stairwell. I entered soon enough to see her take five steps at a time in jumps that would make Olympians jealous. Her scream morphed into a frantic howl and warbled down to me.

I grabbed the railing and ran after her. My feet slipped off the edges of the steps, but I didn't fall. Up two stories and then the stairwell dead-ended at a door marked ROOF EXIT— EMERGENCY ONLY.

Cassie pushed the red exit bar and the stairwell filled with flashing red light and an emergency siren's *ERRN! ERRN! ERRN!*

I made it to the roof as Cassie stopped at the edge of the building.

"Cassie, no!"

She stepped onto the parapet and glared back at me. Her body trembled in self battle. Her hands tore at her face, ripped her cheek. Wind kicked up her hair.

"There has to be another way!" I screamed.

She hesitated only a moment longer before throwing herself backwards off the building.

PART THREE

THE DEVIL'S SERMON

Why did God allow Satan to destroy Job's life? Job had been such a pious servant. It seems almost God was being arrogant, even evil. Perhaps God wanted to impart a lesson. Perhaps God wanted to teach us faith is not something so simply understood. Or maybe He was trying to teach Job patience and appreciation. Like that phrase about best things coming to those who wait or being grateful for what you have.

In the Gospel of Matthew, Jesus assures his disciples, "Ask, and it shall be given to you; seek, and you shall find; knock, and it shall be opened unto you." He does not, of course, say when these answers will be given, found, or offered. They are somewhere, but it's unclear where exactly and if we'll even know it when we find them.

Our faith is rooted in that thought.

Yet, we keep asking.

We keep questioning

.

—Lucas Masters (sermon excerpt)

When I returned to the hospital room, David was awake and a nurse was helping Phoebe to her feet. I took her in my arms.

"It's all over," I said. "Everything is going to be okay."

Over her shoulder, I looked at David. Recognition of what had happened dawned slowly across his face. At least he had come back from his constructed world. I wouldn't have known what to do if he'd been trapped down there at his son's bedside. I would have left him there with his son.

But perhaps that might not have been such a bad thing.

The wakes and funerals came and went with the expected tears and left Phoebe and me as dazed zombies who were too exhausted to make sense but too stupid to lie down and sleep. We huddled on the couch and watched her favorite Disney movies. We ate popcorn and drank soda and didn't talk about anything that had happened. The color returned to Phoebe's hand and her self-inflicted injury healed remarkably fast, leaving only a hair-thin scar where she yanked out her own tissue. After a few days, all her bruising had faded away along with my out-of-season tan. My hand ached where the Phoebe-thing had bitten me, but I'd recover.

I marveled at Phoebe's arm and she shrugged.

"Healing is easy," she said.

"Many people might disagree with you."

She shrugged. "It's easy in The Land of Uz."

Naomi's parents visited through Thanksgiving. They stayed in separate hotels but were cordial with each other. They did not, for example, hurl turkey legs at each other across the table. They vied for time with Phoebe, but she only wanted to be with me. I promised them I'd stay in touch, call weekly, and they tried to believe me. Phone lines worked both ways, after all.

Nightly, I sat on the toilet with the door locked and the bathroom ceiling fan on and cried until the tears dried up. Or at least until I was too exhausted to weep.

✝

Naomi and Tamara were cremated. On the only occasion I could remember discussing after-death wants with Naomi, she said she did not want to be buried—the whole idea of being trapped in a box under ground to slowly decompose was creepy and, quite frankly, disgusting.

I bought separate urns but when Phoebe found me sitting at the kitchen table with the two silver urns reflecting the kitchen light glare, she picked up Tamara's and poured it into Naomi's. She smiled.

"That's better," she said.

✝

Benjamin Masters, retired and once-revered reverend, was buried in the plot he reserved years ago when my mother passed. It was in the town cemetery. As with Naomi and Tamara's services, I officiated my father's, stumbling my way through the motions and babbling on during the eulogies. I held it together fairly well considering.

"My father would not want me to be too literal," I said. "Those of you who knew him, which is most of you, know he preferred a long, outlandish tale ripe with metaphor to a sermon of direct religious instruction. He didn't like being told what to think—he preferred to find his way by himself. I could spin quite the tale for you today, but it would run rather long, not that that ever stopped my father."

Laughter trickled among the mourners.

"Some of you will want to believe my father has ascended, that he is in a better place. If so, please find comfort in that. As for me, I am comforted knowing that wherever he is now, my father is finding his own way. I hope his journey is full of fanciful sights and figurative adventures. And if an angel tries to show him the way, I hope my father is not too obstinate to accept a little direct assistance."

✝

At the gravesite, I stood over the hole as my father's coffin descended. Phoebe dropped a red rose into the hole. "Bye, grandpa."

Hey son, why don't you hop down here and join me? an adulterated warping of my father's voice said in my head. *We'll have some fun together. Jump down here and let those men in the overalls drive that front loader over and dump the burial dirt right on both of us. Heck, bring Phoebe, too. Come on, son. You'll be happier when you're dead. I can promise you that.*

Phoebe and I stood back when the front loader brought the dirt and two men in grey overalls shoveled it onto the coffin.

Come on, son. It's not too late. You can be happy. We can all be happy. We can be one big, happy family. Death can make you happy.

The dirt covered his coffin and muffled his words.

✝

The service for Jason Hicks took place at a funeral home. It was a closed casket. The teenager who had been driving the car my wife crashed into, and the kid I nearly beat up in his hospital room, had slit his wrists in the bathtub and then, to be sure, stabbed himself in the throat.

That's what that voice wanted me to do: kill your daughter.

I stayed in the back and said a few silent prayers.

"What a terrible thing," a woman said to me. She patted the corners of her eyes with a wadded tissue. "How do you know the family?"

"Jason was driving the car that killed my wife, daughter, and father."

The woman gawked. I hope she thought I was pulling her leg. Otherwise, that would be an awful thing to say at a kid's funeral.

✝

Reverend Roves and The Word of Christ Church gave Cassie Angeca a funeral worthy of a fallen queen. The service was full of readings and songs, lit candles and incense. Reverend Roves, dressed in a sleek black suit with his hair slicked back and his teeth incredibly white, delivered a sermon for the ages. Or at least one trying for such a title.

"There is hope in death," he said. "Death is not the end. Life lingers. It blesses us every day. It stays with us. Cassie is at peace, but the exuberant life she has left for us is our way to peace. In her way, Cassie helped us move closer to the mystical workings of our Lord. She has helped bring us peace."

What reality was Cassie in? Did she get to choose in those final blinks before her body crashed onto the street? Did she return to her world of perpetual sun and incense? Wherever she was, I hoped Roves was right, and Cassie was at peace.

No one gets into Heaven without God's approval, she'd told me.

I saw David before I left, but we didn't talk. He was kneeling in the front pew, hands folded, forehead pressed against them.

✝

Life lingers, Roves had said.
A kind of phantasmic residue, perhaps.

✝

Phoebe did not want to sleep in her room. I did not try to talk her out of it, did not try to get her to overcome her fears and be strong—I capitulated and maybe that makes me a bad father, but Naomi would have understood. My bed was too big without her.

Phoebe jumped into my bed with Ben in one hand and Foppy in the other, dangling by one pink ear. She nestled next to me and clutched her stuffed animals against her. Their cotton-packed heads bulged.

I petted Phoebe's head until her breathing slowed into its sleep-rhythm. I leaned across her very carefully and looked at the animals on my daughter's chest. The light from my nightstand arced across dark glossy eyes. Ben's protruding arms ended in harmless, rounded paws. No claws for mauling.

Foppy's swollen bunny face peaked in a scuffed pink plastic nose. It's Y-shaped snout sloped down to a stitched mouth that sagged with old-man jowls. I leaned closer. It smelled faintly of Phoebe's raspberry shampoo and something else, something sour. Its fur was matted in clumps and stained grey. Tomorrow, I would throw it in the wash. Along with Ben and all the other animals.

A kind of domestic purification.

Foppy's head turned toward me. Its mouth stitches tore apart with a loud fabric *rrriiippp* and narrow fangs dropped free, curving past its jaw. A trick of my tired mind, a shadowy illusion. I reached one finger toward the mouth and the bunny chomped it off at the middle knuckle. Pain exploded up my arm. Blood spurted across the sheets and blotted Phoebe's face.

I caught the scream at my lips as I jolted awake.

A large shadow figure hulked over me. It loomed with imaginary solidity. Its amorphous body wavered and shook with the moving night. Long cloaked arms stretched for me and a slender head protruded from massive shoulders. A hallucination. A remnant from a nightmare world.

Nothing more than residue.

Phoebe's warm body pressed against me. My hands went to her as black peeled away from the thing's face and moonlight rode along the ridge of my father's nose to bloom across his forehead. His skin hugged his bones and sagged beneath his eyes in bloody crescents.

"Ready for some fun, my boy?" His voice groaned and squeaked simultaneously in a stridulous mess that pinched my eardrums.

Just a leftover. Just unpleasant residue, black mold growing in the bottom of a garbage can.

I shut my eyes and squeezed my daughter. The room flushed with the stink of feces. Olfactory hallucination—nothing more tangible.

All in my head.

I felt the thing there, heavy yet weightless, a feather of lead, hovering, and willed it back inside my mind, back into some dark cave from which it had escaped. But the only cave I saw was the one in The Land of Uz, back in The Rolling Hills, and I would not send this thing there. It might look like my father and might even be him, some corrupted version of him, but he was not getting back inside Phoebe.

Nothing was going to harm her, not ever again.

It loomed closer and I squeezed Phoebe tighter. It couldn't hurt us, not here, not in the real world. Not if I pushed it back, sent it off somewhere else, anywhere except into Phoebe. But I had no other place. No mystical creation. No world of monstrous trees and rolling hills and labyrinthian caves.

I pictured the sacristy in Saint John's, the closet where the lay reader robes hung, and the procession crosses leaned against the inside left corner. The closet with the tiny safe holding the vital church documents. But the safe wouldn't work, too small. Across from the closet, however, behind a stained piece of half plywood, was the crawl space leading down to the cramped furnace room in what passed for a basement.

I saw the splintery edges of the wood, felt its rough surface where my father had long ago carved *Luke 17:21* like religious graffiti, smelled its faint odor of wood and spilled wine from an accident-prone Sunday years ago. I jammed my palms against the rough edge and pushed the door. It resisted a moment before pushing back several inches and falling off the track and wedging crookedly. A triangle of basement darkness shone through. It smelled wet and moldy down there yet emanated heat, rotting animal kill on a rain-slicked road.

Even when the board was completely pulled back, the hole barely accommodated a full-grown man, but this wasn't reality. Not *this* reality at least. *How could there be multiple realities?* That thought quivered through my head with a vibrating pain like a piercing arrow.

In the beginning was the Word, and the Word was with God, and the Word was God.

All things were made by him; and without him was not any thing made that was made.

God created all the worlds, and all the realities in those worlds, and nothing dreamed or imaginary exists without God first making it so.

God created all that was good *and* all that was evil.

He created this beast, this virus—this demon.

And He created the way it might be destroyed.

I could force this thing through the gap, if only I could get a hold. It was slippery and wavy and stinking of awful things and every time I tried to seize it, it squeezed free and loomed there, within reach but uncatchable. A black cloud, a slithery snake, a shadow man.

Because I'm not really there. I'm here, *and here it's nothing but a hallucination.*

"I'll be waiting for you, son," my father said.

I opened my eyes and his dead face pushed toward mine, mouth slung in a howl. His hands seized the sides of my face in ice clamps. *He's going to bite my face, tear off my nose.* I screamed to push him off, screamed with all the breath I had to push him away from me and my daughter, screamed him into a cramped basement I hoped existed in more than one world.

His hands squeezed my head and I flung my arms out. They passed through his shadowy arms and crashed against the lamp on the nightstand. It hit the floor with a ceramic shatter and a bulb pop.

Phoebe jumped from sleep with a shout and clung to me.

Slowly, silence settled around us.

"It's back," she said between rapid breaths. "It's back."

The shadow thing had vanished as if it scattered into the dark corners. Or was swallowed whole.

"I've got you. It's okay."

On the floor, moonlight lit the edges of ceramic shards and among the mess sat Foppy, its red eyes glowing up at me.

✝

Something watched while I showered.

The familiar sensation tickled all along my body and cupped my balls tight against me. No matter how hot I made the water, a cold chill hugged close. Even with the sun shining in through the little window and all the bathroom lights on, a figure shimmered on the other side of the plastic curtain.

"Phoebe?" I asked over the ceiling fan drone, knowing better but unable to help it.

No response.

No matter how often I had suffered that feeling of being watched, I couldn't fight against it, and eventually, I peeked around the side of the curtain at the empty bathroom. The moment I turned back to the water, I knew something was watching me again. It could have been paranoia, but that didn't make the cold any less real.

Like phantom spiders scurrying across the backs of my hands.

Drying off, I turned to the fogged mirror.

ABADDON was written in large, angled letters bleeding in condensation.

I smeared the letters away, yanked on some clothes and went into the hall.

"Phoebe?"

A cartoon played on the TV downstairs. Phoebe's bedroom door was shut. Ear pressed to the wood, I heard nothing. And was that some sort of surprise? Did I expect to catch Phoebe's Uz Monster pining away the daylight hours in my daughter's room? Even as I turned the knob so slowly it made no noise, I wondered if it was in there, perhaps sitting on the edge of the bed, leaning forward, fist under its chin—Rodin's Demon Thinker.

I hit a wall of stagnant waste. The smell was so intense I gagged and backed into the hall. Something had died in here and crapped out all its innards in the process. I covered my mouth but my eyes started watering.

The stuffed animals had congregated on Phoebe's bed in defense position, plush arms linked in a comical phalanx. I should have laughed, too, but all those plastic eyes made laughter impossible. At least not jovial laughter.

A box of crayons was on the floor, the individual crayons splayed out around it. Near the spilled crayons was a few thin stacks of colored Post-Its and beyond them the outlet with the night light cross and one of those fragrant Plug-Ins. The Plug-In was in the top outlet and the cross, upside down and glowing, was in the bottom. Naomi had installed them in the opposite way.

The upside down cross grated at me in a way I wouldn't have expected. It was just a symbol. Like a burning flag, it wasn't doing any harm, just insulting a cherished emblem. Still, though, an upside down cross bespoke hordes of anti-religious groups who lauded anything that ridiculed and demeaned believers.

I never considered myself one of the victims of such ridicule. My faith was more intellectual, not mired in biblical specifics. Everything was metaphoric, a symbology to encourage a peaceful, kinder existence.

The inverted cross was actually a Catholic symbol for Simon Peter who requested upside-down crucifixion out of humility. Not being a Catholic, however, I still needed that cross to be upright. Such a small thing, and yet, I guess, more significant than I ever would have wanted to believe.

Because now I do believe. Now, I believe it all.

The cross went dark as I pulled it from the outlet, and I removed the Plug-In. The stink of shit and rotting innards pushed through my pinched nose and sealed lips. I dared to open my nose and bring the Plug-In close. The smell was strong enough to usher bile up my throat.

I threw it across the room like a kid in a tantrum and my hand went to my chest for the wooden cross (*from the holy land*) but I hadn't put it on yet—it was waiting on my rolled socks in the top drawer of my dresser—and that filled me with an absurd panicky flutter.

Because now I do believe.

With the cross plugged back in correctly, its green halo fanned across the wall. Tons of Post-Its papered the wall. They overlapped each other and almost covered this entire wall, from baseboards to ceiling.

Naomi had been quite the hoarder of paper goods. The closet in her office was stocked full of copy paper, pens, pencils, loose leaf, and Post-Its. Phoebe knew of the supplies. She'd helped herself.

On each Post-It on the wall, the same thing was written: *Hi*.

I lifted one. Swirling crayon streaks marked the wall.

I lifted the few around it.

Crayon scribbles. Not scribbles, though—one word, scrawled in looping, childish cursive. I yanked Post-Its off the wall. Above the first discovered word was the word written again, this time in tiny block letters. And next to that, the word stretched from a small A to a towering, sagging D.

Abaddon.

(*A Bad One.*)

Written all over the wall. I tore down the Post-Its, snapping them off to flutter all around me. The crayon graffiti covered the entire wall, reached way up to the ceiling.

I could barely reach the top of the wall on my toes. Phoebe must have dragged over her chair. Must have been in some kind of hypnotic daze when she did this.

It's still inside her. It's making her do this.

It's taunting you.

I picked up a red crayon worn to a nub. *Abaddon* was written in all different colors, but mostly red and black. Some of the letters varied color within the name and heavy, curling scribbles filled gaps as if something had been covered up.

Pressing the crayon to the wall, I felt compelled to write, as if copying what I saw would prove this wasn't real.

I wrote the A and stopped. In tiny letters almost too small to decipher and crammed between several *Abaddons*, something else was written.

Revelation 9:11.

I'd been reading the Bible every night, religiously, you might say, but I hadn't started with Genesis. I wanted to know what came at the end. The Episcopal faith doesn't place much stock in Armageddon, and I'd never been interested in it. Not until I became a sort of Job and started walking my own road to Damascus.

Revelation 9:11.

And they had a king over them, which is the angel of the bottomless pit, whose name is Abaddon.

"Daddy?"

Phoebe stood in the doorway in her pajamas with her hair a tangled mess and sleep clouding her eyes.

"What are you doing to my room?"

The crayon looked foreign to me even as it finished writing the damn word on top of the same word. My hand cramped with the effort. I pulled it from the wall and dropped the crayon. My fingers ached.

The same hand the Phoebe-thing had bitten.

Black streaks tinged the fingers on that hand and dark veins bloated beneath the skin like cancerous worms. But that had to be a hallucination because the black was from the crayon. Okay then—why is there crayon on your hand? Well, because I ... I...

The infected hand of God.

No louder than the squeak of a surreptitious mouse, a faint voice chuckled.

"Daddy," Phoebe said, "it's back, and it's in *you*."

She started to cry and for a while I stood there watching.

I called David.

"If you didn't call by tonight, I was coming over."

"What do you mean?"

"I hoped it wasn't true, but it's too late now. When you're already sick, denial makes things worse."

"Tell me."

"Cassie didn't defeat the demon. She thought she'd taken all of it, but she didn't. We're both infected and it's trying to destroy us."

"The angel of the bottomless pit," I said to myself.

"What?"

"Never mind. What do we do?"

"We fight back."

✝

Phoebe and I ransacked her room for clothes, working fast and holding our breaths from the stink like the room was filled with poison. Which, in a very real sense, it probably was, as Cassie had warned.

Phoebe wanted to take a few of her stuffed animals, but I grabbed her arm and shook my head. She touched the head of her purple dinosaur and ran out of the room. I shut the door and wished I could padlock it.

When David arrived, Phoebe was organizing her clothes in piles. Ben and Foppy watched from the couch.

"Fall cleaning?" David asked.

"Taking a break from her room."

"I see." I expected him to ask about the room, even want to see it, but he didn't ask. He saw enough proof on my face.

Not to mention my hand, which even after scrubbing and washing and washing and scrubbing was definitely turning black. It ached dully and kept tightening into a fist as if my skin were getting taut and pulling the fingers inward.

We sat at the kitchen table and drank water from glasses that bled tears. David kept his infected hand in his lap. His nails had turned black. As we talked about things that made more sense than they should, my good hand went to the empty space over my chest: the cross had not been in my drawer. Not in any of them.

"If we're both infected, how are we supposed to fight back?"

David thought. He had not taken off his jacket and it made rumpled, leathery sounds when he moved. "Cassie explained how a demon is like a virus, only smarter, of course. It can infect numerous people at once but, unlike a virus, the additional infected will not develop a full infection. Or so we believe. If that's no longer the case, well, then I don't think there's much hope."

"So, that's it? Oh, well, we're screwed? The demon is going to make us kill ourselves or just straight-out kill us so it can be free?"

"Cassie believed, and I still believe, while a demon can reach into other people, it cannot spread itself too thin and must keep most of itself centralized in one host. It keeps a hold on others as a precautionary measure, so if its main host dies, it can leap into one of its other connections. When Cassie took on the beast in the other world, she thought she had it all. She had the ability to wrangle a demon completely into her and then sequester it. I saw her do it more than once."

"And what, keep the demon inside her, caged?"

"Exactly. But she underestimated this one. I did too. She realized immediately it was too much for her to control and instead of being its victim, she killed herself. She hoped that would end it. If the demon has nowhere it go, it dies. But she didn't destroy it because she didn't have all of it."

"Abaddon," I said.

"It's toying with you. Demons only have the names we assign them. Like viruses. They're predatory animals, fighting to live. Religion has given these particular monsters names and an entire mythology, but the truth is far simpler: demons exist just as we exist and just as viruses exist. In this chaotic mess of a world, demons are one more threat among billions."

"What about God? What about the religious significance?"

David sighed. "Honestly, Lucas—does it matter? This thing is going to kill us unless we stop it."

"But maybe the Bible has the answer. I've been reading Revelation and—"

"Remember when I told you what my father believed was the most important biblical teaching?"

"Love thy neighbor," I said.

"Right. Well, mine is 'God helps those who help themselves.'"

"I don't think that's actually in the Bible."

"The demon," David said, "nameless or Abaddon, doesn't matter, is inside us now. It must, however, be more centralized in one of us."

"How do we tell who?"

"There's only one way."

The weight of it settled on me: "Go back into the other place."

"Over there," David said, "we'd be able to sort things out. Find the damn thing and handle it."

"If it was too strong for Cassie, what are we supposed to do?"

"Assuming it's only in us, we could take it on fully and..." He looked away, slowly turned his glass.

Phoebe was talking to herself in the other room. Not to herself, of course—to Ben and Foppy.

"Then it's a matter of cleaning," David said. "Like a poison-filled room where the gas has been sucked out. Scrub the walls and disinfect." David smiled. "Problem is: I don't think we're the only people infected."

Phoebe giggled.

"I'm not making her go back there."

"I'm not taking about your daughter."

"Then who?"

"You ever wonder why some families are seemingly cursed? Why a child gets cancer and a father has a heart attack and a mother is in a car accident and ends up paralyzed? Why some families don't ever get lucky? Why colon cancer ravages an entire family tree until the last of the line dies and with him the family line?"

"I guess you're not talking about genetics."

"Genetics is a convenient explanation for things we're too afraid to understand."

"So, what, every bad thing is because of a demon?"

David shrugged, *if the shoe fits*. "What I'm saying is sometimes a demon, like a virus, like a genetic-born cancer, finds a host that is too perfect to let go. An ideal home. Now, if a family is big enough, a demon might live endlessly through offspring, but even then it can get overzealous. Everyone dies and it needs a new home. If it doesn't have one, it's lost, adrift. It might even die, microbes on the wind. Sometimes, it can underestimate what it believed a perfect home and can get trapped."

"You're losing me."

"The only way to get rid of a weed is to rip it from the root. We have to get to the root of this infection."

"And where's that?"

"Not far from here."

"What are you talking about?"

"Quincy Toft."

✝

"Who?"

But my father's words were coming back. *The Quincy boy killed himself. He swallowed a bottle's worth of Tylenol. Sat there in his bedroom with the pile of pills next to him and swallowed one after the next.*

"The kid who said the angels were hunting him," I said.

David grinned in a way I didn't like at all. "You know."

"Wait a minute, what are we talking about?"

"Part of the reason my wife and I abandoned Reverend Pete's Prayer Parade and settled in western New York was because Joey had made a friend. A skinny kid, the kind who might blow over in a mild wind. His name was Quincy Toft."

Kind of kid who fell over swinging a T-ball bat, my father had said. *Never had any friends. Followed kids, begging for them to let him be their friend.*

"They took to each other like best friends, even though Quincy was a bit older. He was small for his age. They hung out all the time. Played down in our basement. It wasn't long after Quincy killed himself we took Joey to the doctor and he pointed to oncology."

"And you met my father."

"The Toft family is the root," David said. "We have to rip it out, so we can get all of the demon."

"How can you be sure the thing didn't infect other people, too. If it infected my father and gestated inside him until he was too weak to fight back, how do we know it isn't spread across in other people too?"

"We don't. This thing might be strong, but if everything else I've learned adds up to anything, it isn't strong enough to spread itself so far and still wreak the kind of damage we've seen. It was in your father, then your daughter, and now it's in us. If we don't handle this now, it will take one of us and then the other. And then back to Phoebe. Once someone has been exposed, they are even more likely to be reinfected."

Once you've had the Devil Virus, I thought not for the first time, *you're twice as likely to be reinfected. Once the Devil has his claws in you ...*

"Like ants returning to an abandoned hill. The tunnels are already dug. The tracks are laid. The way is like memory. So long as this demon is living, your daughter is at risk."

I sipped my water and didn't like how my hand shook. "How do you know the Toft parents are infected?"

"We have to confirm."

"Drive up there and ask them?"

"It gets more interesting. Richard Toft killed himself. Drove head-on into a telephone pole at ninety miles-an-hour without a seatbelt. Chunks of him were scattered across the road."

"Bereaved from his son's death," I said.

"Or forced to do it by something trying to free itself from a human cage."

In the next room, Phoebe laughed. "Bad Foppy," she said. "Bad bunny."

✝

When I called Iris and asked if she'd take Phoebe for a few hours, she said she was ashamed she hadn't done more to help, she felt so awful for all I had been through, and Phoebe could stay with her for as long as I needed.

"A few hours," I said when I kissed Phoebe goodbye on Iris's front steps.

Phoebe's stuffed backpack protruded off her like a monstrous purple hump and Ben and Foppy nestled in the crooks of her elbows. "Be careful, Daddy."

"You too," I said.

✝

Karras, New York, sat west of Ithaca and we reached it with David driving in just under three hours. We kept our infected hands hidden and didn't mention the obvious: if we didn't do something soon, we weren't going to make it long enough to matter. In fact, we barely spoke during the ride. I talked around it, told him about Phoebe's room, about the sensation of being watched, about the shadowy figure in the night.

"Some people would say you have a poltergeist," David said.

"If only."

Wendy Toft lived on a street with wide oaks that wobbled shadows across the sidewalk. Hers was a small white home with an American flag hanging flat against the house near the front door, which was painted red. The day had turned cold and grey and her street was quiet. A red Toyota was parked in her driveway.

"How'd you know she'd be home?" I asked.

"Maybe luck is finally with us." He handed me a pair of leather gloves and I watched him put on his own pair, for a moment confused as to why. He pointed at my infected hand. I'd almost forgotten about it—the hand felt pretty good. "No reason to cause alarm."

I tugged on the gloves, following him toward Toft's front porch.

I grabbed his arm and pulled him back from the door. "What if something wants us to be together. That's the whole thing, isn't it? The demon wants to be free so it can completely infect one of us."

"Now is not the time to second guess."

"Sure it is," I said. "We go in there and who knows what might happen. If you're right, the demon will be reunited with itself. Shouldn't we prepare ourselves?"

"How do we do that?"

I had no answer.

"There's no way to prepare. Be conscious of any strange sensations. Like that sense of being watched. If you feel anything, give me a signal."

He started to the door and I yanked him back again.

"If we walk away now, the demon isn't going to give up," he said. "Think of Phoebe's room, of that damn shadow thing. Convince yourself it's a by-product of all you've been through. Tell yourself you've got post-traumatic stress and see a therapist. Read up on hallucinations and let that be the explanation. Write off all the other-world stuff as new-age mumbo jumbo. Pretend none of it happened. Believe God healed your daughter—an authentic miracle. You think any of that is going to help?"

Before I could respond, the front door opened, and Wendy Toft asked what the hell we were doing.

✝

We sat in a living room done up in a contrasting mix of dark woods and floral pastels. The more I looked around, the more jarring the place seemed, as if it had been decorated to give off the aura of death. Framed photographs of Quincy and Richard by themselves and with each other and complete shots with Mom included hung in dark-wood frames on wallpaper faded to a pale purplish blue.

Mrs. Toft wore clothes as faded as the wallpaper and her makeup clogged wrinkled crevices around her mouth, one particularly long and curved like an old scar. She sat back-stiff in a chair across from David and me on a couch with plastic protecting the cushions.

"I'm wondering if I should say it's good to see you, David," she said.

"I like the new house. How have you been?" he asked.

She offered a weak smile and a dimple of makeup flaked off into her lap. "I doubt you came up here without warning, with a man in tow, to see my new house and ask how I've been."

"His daughter is very sick."

"And who is he?"

I introduced myself. She did not offer to shake hands.

"I'm sorry about your daughter."

"She's okay now, I think."

"How nice for you."

"Look, Wendy—"

She cut David off: "It's Mrs. Toft, if you don't mind."

"That necessary?"

"Yes, David. It is."

He sighed, looked at his shoes for a moment. "I'm sorry, but I had to come up here. I know how hard things have been for you."

"Do you?"

"I lost the same."

She tilted her head, *how nice for you.*

"I want to ask some questions."

"You already have."

"Jesus," I said, "can we cut through this bullshit and get right to it?"

Mrs. Toft did not even flinch. "You can both leave. I'm not the one who barged into one of your homes."

"Sorry," I said. "I..."

"What?"

I turned to David. His look told me to shut up. "My friend is a little frantic, as I'm sure you can understand. His daughter suffered something we both know very intimately."

"What kind of cancer did she have?"

"Excuse me?" I asked.

"What other connection is there?"

"I thought your son..."

"Killed himself? Why yes, he did, but not until after the doctors told him he had to have chemotherapy and when he asked what that was, they told him it was poison that would kill all the bad stuff inside him. He believed right until the hours after the first treatment when he was violently ill. Before the next treatment, he killed himself. So, let me ask again: what type of cancer did your daughter have?"

"She—"

"You know that's horse shit," David said. "He wasn't diagnosed with anything. My son was. After yours swallowed enough Tylenol to kill twenty people. Our sons were sick with something medical science can't explain. Or at least won't."

"Well," Mrs. Toft said. "Each man believes his own truth, doesn't he?"

David stared at her.

"That's what snake-oil salesman Reverend Pete used to say. Come in and find Jesus on Reverend Pete's Prayer Parade but, oh, gee, forgot to mention, Jesus is on vacation and he isn't taking calls. And miracles? Cures for diseases? I hope he died of intestinal cancer, shitting himself stupid in a hospital bed."

"I'm not here to make amends," David said.

"Oh, even better. Here to rip open old wounds, then?"

"There's no reason for you to be so hostile."

"Isn't there?" Her mouth clamped shut and more makeup droppings fell. Like scales. "I assumed that's why you're both wearing gloves."

"Ignore the truth if you want, but it isn't going to help anything."

"The truth? What, pray tell, is that, Reverend Javan?"

"Were you in his church?" I asked.

She looked at me as if disgusted. "I hope you're not a protégée."

"*Enough!*" David yelled. "You know why we're here."

"Why is that?"

David stood, tore off his glove to expose his blackened hand, and jabbed a finger toward her. "*Because of demons!*"

She grinned and burped a small laugh.

✝

Halfway back to the car, I stopped David. "Was that true about her son? Did he have cancer, too?"

"Don't be taken in by her show."

"Her show? You mean her yelling at two guys who pop out of nowhere to tell her her son died because of a demon?"

"It's in her."

"You know what's in her? A lot of buried pain and a shit load of understandable anger."

He grabbed the top of my shoulder and curled his fist with my jacket, as if to pull me forward for a sucker punch in the gut. He spoke slowly. "Parents who lose a child go through far more emotional fluctuations than any other bereaved survivor. They fly through moments of rage and helplessness. They suffer immense guilt."

"No shit, David."

We stared at each other and my body tightened. He slowly let go of me. "Sometimes parents fall into emotional pits from which they can never escape. Other times, often times, they find the only way to have any shot at any kind of life is to build really strong walls to protect them against anything and everything. Shield them from all the pain."

"Yeah, and when someone tries taking a bulldozer to those walls, they get a bit testy."

He leaned in and spoke more softly. "When someone constructs walls like that, they do it to protect themselves from being hurt, right?"

"Yeah."

"What if those walls are actually the bars of a prison keeping something trapped?"

In the car and heading back to Marguerite, David reiterated his belief that somewhere inside Wendy Toft was a piece of the same demon that was inside us. We couldn't just go inside her head and search it out, though—we had to be active extractors.

"What does that mean?" I asked.

"Why do you think Mr. Toft killed himself?"

"Immense grief."

"Or recognition of what was in him. Like my wife. Like Cassie."

This isn't how it happens. This is how it ends.

"Or the demon made him do it. It got its claws in him the right way and found a way to free a piece of himself."

"You're asking me why Mrs. Toft doesn't do the same, right?"

He shrugged. Up ahead, a sign marked the entrance to the highway.

"Because she doesn't believe she's got anything wrong with her?"

"Because of her emotional walls, Lucas. Think about it: most people suffer dark thoughts from time to time. They hear their infant child cry for the billionth time in the middle of the night and they think in a flash of drowning the kid in the bathtub or tossing the baby out the window. Or they're commuting home from work and wonder in a dark moment what it would be like to steer into oncoming headlights. These thoughts bubble up from our subconscious all the time. Some people chastise themselves for thinking such awful things. Other people hear those thoughts and push a stranger in front of a subway train. Some people keep those thoughts buried so deep they aren't even whispers. But they're there. Waiting to escape. To explode out."

He passed the entrance to the highway and immediately turned into a supermarket parking lot and grabbed the nearest spot. I was thrown side to side and pawed at the door handle. I started asking what the hell he was doing, and he told me to shut up.

"You want to know how I can be so sure, right? How I know she's infected?"

"Yes. I want proof because all I saw was a woman who's been hurt too many times to dare let herself get hurt again."

"Remember what I said about demons finding a good home and sticking with it. Who knows why but they find a good host, like a virus finding the ideal immune system to ravage, like destined lovers—"

"What's your point?"

"Wendy Toft is my sister."

"My sister is an incredibly strong woman. Civilized people call it stoicism, but the truth is she's a heartless bitch."

I remembered David telling me about his younger sister who had mauled her cheek with Daddy's straight razor and who wore a lot of make up these days. Had that been the act of a demon? Testing her out, perhaps?

"Where did the demon come from, originally?"

"Where did any particular strain of virus come from?"

"Don't give me that shit. You know. Least you think you do. So tell me."

"In Africa," he said. "When my father and his friends buried all those bodies. If there has to be an origin, it's there. He prayed over the skeletons of people who had been torn limb from limb, hacked up and left in bloody clumps for the animals to feed on. People warned my father not to go there. They said it was haunted, cursed. They said the Mbwiri lurked there."

"Should I even ask?"

"It's a demon. I told you, names don't matter."

"What happened after you got home? What happened to your father?"

"He turned abusive and nasty and hateful."

"He kill himself?"

"He went back to Africa and we never saw him again. I tried to find him, twice. Once on a missionary trip with other pastors— your father wanted to come along but couldn't manage it—and once as a doctor."

"Healing the sick children."

"Yes. I did a lot of that. Immunizations. But I also went looking for that destroyed village. I asked around. People either didn't know or pretended they didn't, which amounted to the same. I thought I was going to get lucky one day when I was helping this old man who was very sick with some mysterious illness. He told me the Mbwiri was in him and he wanted to die but he warned me. 'When I die,' he told me, 'the demon will be loose. Do not be around me when I die.' I told him about my father and the village. He looked at me with these yellow eyes and said, 'When you hunt the demon, it also hunts you.' Two days later he died."

"Were you there?"

"No. But when he went, a nurse was with him, holding his hand. Pretty young thing. A week later she came down with the same mysterious illness. She drowned herself."

"They were infected," I said. "They could have passed it on to you."

David shook his head. "I was already infected. From my father. When that nurse died, that's when I started putting it together, this Devil Virus. That's when I realized what had happened to my son and my nephew. I tried finding a cure, but it led nowhere. I became a joke. So, I wound up at Word of Christ and if not for Cassie, I might have given up all hope of ever finding a cure."

"Do we know there's a cure?"

He looked at me. "Prayer," he said as if that were obvious.

"So, your father vanishes, but he leaves a piece of the demon behind?"

"A little in each of us, I think. But we were from strong stock. I remember nightmares. Sometimes I'd hear voices that sounded metallic telling me to do bad things. To hurt my mother and sister. My mother had a nervous breakdown. And then there's my sister."

I saw it on his face, something hiding beneath a layer of sand. "What aren't you telling me?"

"He raped her."

I lost my breath for a moment. I started to apologize, and he waved it off.

"That's what started it, her wall building. She cut herself with Dad's straight razor but after that, she didn't try to hurt herself again. She trapped whatever my father had given her deep within her. She couldn't face it, but she could conceal it. When my wife and I and our boy came to Karras with Reverend Pete, my wife had long been working toward reuniting me with my sister. A broken family is no way to live, she told me. With both of us close to each other, the demon had the strength to get my nephew and then my son. It fed off them, grew stronger and spread into your father, maybe when he offered prayers at Joey's bedside. Maybe it didn't happen exactly that way, but it's the best I can figure out."

"No it's not."

He looked at me.

"A year ago, you and my father went on one of those pilgrimages, only you came back here, right? You, Cassie, and my father. You tried to get the demon out of her. When she resisted and you tried anyway, her house collapsed. That's when it got my father. Maybe it had first spread into him when your son died, but it was a year ago when it found a better grip inside my father."

"I'm sorry, Lucas."

"His heart attack? His stroke?"

David shrugged in a pathetically awful way.

"You dragged my family into this."

"Your father wanted to help. He thought Cassie was almost a prophet."

"This isn't about him. This is about me and my daughter."

Cars passed on the road.

"When I met Cassie, she showed me how to keep the monster sequestered," David said. "She opened my eyes to the true miracles of God's world. It's a lot vaster and more awe-inspiring than people realize. We helped a lot of people together. Healed a lot."

"Surprised you still bring God into this."

"Remember the business card I gave you? I'm an Incumbent of Saint Paul's Episcopal Church in Karras, New York. A permanent fixture. When my father never returned from Africa, my mother started bringing us there. It saved her during her breakdown. It gave me hope. I can't turn away from that."

"Paul on the road to Damascus," I said.

For a moment, the desperate gravity of our exchange lifted, and things felt better. Hopeful.

"We tried to help her but she resisted."

"You should have all died," I said. "Then I'd still have my family."

"It won't be like that this time."

"What won't?"

"You should be with your daughter."

"Why? What are you going to do?"

"This is a family matter, Lucas. I need to handle it. I know what needs to be done. And when it's done, you will know because you will feel it. It will come into you more fully, but it will also stretch out of you for a place it knows well—Phoebe. You must be with her to protect her. Go back into her Land of Uz and help her fight the monster."

"What are you going to do?"

"Tear down some walls."

✝

Outside his sister's house, I asked him, "What's 'tearing down some walls' really mean?"

"Worry about your daughter. Protect her."

"Shouldn't I stay here, stay away from her?"

"It's not going to matter. When it's free, the demon will come on strong."

"Possess me, you mean?"

"Or try to free itself from you. Make you crash your car."

"Then it'll be in you, right? What then?"

He didn't respond.

"I'm not letting you kill yourself."

"There's something else you need to worry about."

"What?"

"Demons travel from subconscious world to subconscious world, but they can also hitch rides on inanimate objects. Like germs and viruses. I saw it in Africa. The old man who said he was infected had a polished stone clenched in his hand, said it was some kind of charm. When the nurse who was at his side when he died drowned herself, that stone was lodged in her throat."

"Meaning?"

"It's already infected Phoebe and will be much easier to reinfect her, return to an old home. You could stay away from her, but it's already got her. Objects close to you are marked, infected."

"Her stuffed animals," I said. "They're infected, carrying the virus."

David was shaking his head.

"What then?"

He pointed at my chest. "Where's your cross?"

✝

I drove alone. At times, I was speeding at almost ninety and at others, I was drifting below forty. Thoughts spun and whirled through my head. Should I have left David alone to handle his sister? What was he going to do? Sneak into her subconscious and blow up her damn walls? But what did that mean in reality?

No matter the feelings tugging at me and telling me to turn around and go back, I had to get to Phoebe. Had to protect her. We would go back to Uz and stand our ground and wait for the beast to show itself. Then what?

Trap it somehow. Destroy it, if possible.

I thought of Saint John's sacristy. Of the little basement with the wooden slat where my father had etched *Luke 17:21*.

Of my father's words: *I am this church.*

Something rode with me in the back of the car. I sensed it there, some *other* thing, and almost caught it in the rearview mirror—a fleeting dark shard of shadow, a fragment of pale skin. Eyes back on the road, I felt it back there again, right behind me.

I waited for cold hands to reach around the headrest and seize my face, for fingers to stab my eyes and wrench my mouth, for my father's dead voice to whisper behind my ear: "Don't you want me to get better?"

All in my head, of course. Every sensation of being watched, every moment Phoebe's stuffed animals seemed to stare at me with plastic eyes that were also real, the visions in the hospital body-viewing room, and the spiders scurrying into Phoebe's mouth—all hallucinations. Not real, not in this world, anyway.

I saw all those things because I'd been infected since the beginning. The virus had been in me, maybe for years. Gestating. Biding its time.

My father infected me, and I infected Phoebe.

Now, it was up to me to make sure she would be safe forever.

✝

When I stopped at a hardware store, I called Lavon Solly and asked for a favor.

"What is it, Lucas? What's going on?"

"I need you to trust me."

"You sound a bit frantic."

"I need your help."

"Anything."

"Meet me at the church in an hour. Bring your truck."

I could almost see that license plate: MILK MAN. Something vivid. Something that might stay tangible no matter what reality I traversed. I hoped so, anyway. For Phoebe's sake.

"You sure you don't want me to bring someone else? George maybe?"

"Just you, Lavon. Please."

"Why do I get the feeling we're not going there to pray?"

"Oh, we're going to pray," I said. "It's all I've got left."

✝

Halfway to the car, my purchases swinging at my side in a plastic bag, my cellphone rang. It was David.

"Where are you?" he asked. He was breathing hard, forcing out each word.

"I'm almost home."

"Good."

"What happened?"

He chuckled and the sound made my skin go slick with cold sweat.

"Tore down some walls."

"What did you do?"

"It's spreading up my arm, the infection," David said. "Trying to devour me. I feel strong, though. Amazingly strong. It wants me to die, Lucas. You know what that means?"

"It's coming for me."

"Be ready."

"Fight it, David. Fight back."

"There's no point. I can't do anything. You protect your daughter. Do whatever you have to to keep her safe. I'm going to see my son."

"Wait, David—"

He ended the call.

He killed his sister. The thought was clear and completely crazy, and completely correct. I imagined him choking her with his blackening hand, bashing her skull against the floor until she passed out, and then strangling her until there was no more breath.

And now he was going to kill himself, try to suffocate himself, or maybe stab himself, and once he did, the virus would be free to come for me.

I'm going to see my son.

As if Heaven would admit a murderer.

✝

A half hour outside of Marguerite, I was speeding again and coming up fast on a double tractor trailer. My infected hand felt okay, strong actually, and I was driving with it, periodically squeezing the steering wheel. Squeezing it hard enough to choke someone. The black skin was charred and flaky, pulled tight across the knuckles.

On the back of the last trailer in block print, it read, BE KIND, BE CAREFUL, BE YOUR BEST SELF. In a smear of dirt, someone had finger-etched, *Wash me!*, and in the bottom corner, scrawled in bleeding spray paint, *Follow Me for Blowjobs.*

"So much for being your best self," I muttered. "Maybe you ought to clean your truck."

Staring at those motivational lines got me thinking. Who the hell was this guy in his obnoxiously large truck to tell me how to behave? What empowered him to instruct me, a random traveler, to be my best self? Especially with his truck covered in dirt and defaced with graffiti.

So, teach him a lesson.

The thought was a strong push on my driving foot, hard enough to almost ram into the back of the truck. I hit the brake a little too hard and almost went into a spin.

Getting distracted by the writings on a truck was not exactly fortuitous for the kind of concentration I would need to protect Phoebe. The truck company was trying to spread a good message. What was the harm? Still, though, if trucks could do it, didn't that, in some small way, negate my role as preacher, as in shaper of morals and teacher of good behavior? Wasn't it, when looked at in the correct light, a kind of insult to me?

Then put him in his place.

How was I supposed to do that, make him pull over and berate him on the highway shoulder for daring to spread precepts that fell solidly within my authority?

No time for a lesson. Just a quick, admonishing slap.

I sped up on the side of the trailers. Across the sides of both, it read in huge letters, KANE *is able!* And wasn't that a little too much to my point, considering Cain killed Able? Cain was the first murderer and, in a very genuine sense, the one who got the whole miserable party of humanity going.

"Cute pun," I said, speeding up even more. "But I could teach you something about religion. You want to know just how able Cain was? Allow me."

I was almost at the cab.

That's right. Run this arrogant asshole off the road. Better yet, hit him and send him careening into the concrete struts of the overpass up ahead.

That would work very nicely.

I rode along side the cab, waited for the right moment.

In the backseat, something laughed, a metallic, grating cough of a laugh. *Go ahead,* that laugh said. *Push this trucker off the road and maybe even kill him. That'll teach him to steal your priestly thunder. You show him who's really able.*

I surged forward, angling toward the front of the cab.

That's it. Teach this bastard. Teach him good.

I sped up even more. My black hand squeezed the wheel with immense strength.

Don't just give him a slap, though, oh no, really teach him a lesson. Crash right into him and send him barreling into the overpass up ahead. Leave no doubt who's boss.

My hand swerved the car away from the truck to get a steeper angle of attack and—

Do it. Teach him, preacher man. Teach him good.

I hit the brake hard and fishtailed across the lane and spun to a sloppy, squealing stop. Car horns blared passed. The truck kept moving, passed safely beneath the underpass, and was soon well ahead.

I shut off the car.

It took a while for me to calm my breathing. I had to peel my hand off the wheel a finger at a time, as if it were glued there. Once free of the wheel, I had a clear thought it was going to form into a fist and punch me.

I stared at my hand. The fingers jiggled and I wasn't sure if I was doing that or something else was. But it stayed there on my lap.

You'd like to attack me, wouldn't you? I thought. *Choke me to death if you could, but it'd be easier to drive me straight into that underpass.*

David was dead and the demon was loose, but it wasn't coming to fully infect me. It wanted me dead, too, so then it could be totally free, a complete organism hunting for a favorable host.

Headed right for Phoebe and the fertile lands of Uz.

You think you have a plan? that voice said from behind me. *Go ahead. Try what you want. We'll be waiting. You forget— We are Legion.*

"I'll be ready for you," I said.

Laughter followed me all the way back to Marguerite.

Before she even broke my hug, Phoebe said she was sorry about David. I knelt before her on the front walkway with Iris standing in the doorway, her children running around inside and shouting, "You're it!"

"What do you know about David?" I asked.

"He's with his son."

"How do you know that?"

"It's back, Daddy."

"I will keep you safe, honey. Don't be scared."

"I'm not."

Iris still stood in the doorway. I nodded, waved, and lifted Phoebe into my arms. With her backpack, she weighed more than I expected, and I almost toppled down the stairs.

"Don't be worried, Daddy," she said in the car. "I'll protect you." Ben was tucked against her.

"Where's your bunny?"

"Foppy was being bad. He's in my bag thinking about what he did."

"What did he do?"

"He said mean things."

"What did he say?"

"He wanted me to hurt the other kids. Push them down the stairs and hit them with a rock."

✝

I drove to the spot on Cliffside Road where Naomi crashed head-on with a speeding teenager. *It was the other car. It swerved over the line. It came right for me.* I slowed and turned onto the narrow shoulder. Black splotches marked the road and several fractured trees held vigil with bowed, mournful heads.

"No, Daddy. There's nothing here."

I turned back on the road, but she touched my arm and I stopped.

A yellow sports car sped around the corner and went wide, tires squealing over the double yellow and then it was gone, howling down the road.

"Okay," Phoebe said. "It's safe now."

Cassie's words: *Phoebe built a genuine world. She could be trained to harness that power. Use it to help others. The world needs people like your daughter.*

✝

I pulled into the Saint John's parking lot. Gravel kicked up beneath the car. Lavon's truck was parked next to the spot reserved for Reverend Masters. The rear license plate was crumpled at the corners and metal veins crisscrossed through his vanity plate as if he'd backed into a lot of things: MILK MAN. Lavon came out of the church and waited on the porch. Dust streaked his green overalls.

"We can't go home yet, honey."

"I know, Daddy."

"What do you know?"

"It's time to fight."

"It's going to be okay. I'm going to get it."

"You can't do it alone."

"Lavon is going to keep you safe."

"No, Daddy. Only I can do that."

"Do not go into your world. Don't go back to Uz."

She looked at me with a face Naomi had made millions of times, particularly after one of my dumb jokes or false ultimatums—*seriously?* She was going to look like her mother one day. Assuming my plan worked. "You're not strong enough to make your own place without me. You need me, Daddy."

And that's how it's going to get us both, I thought.

But she was right. I did need her.

Phoebe hefted her backpack into her lap and unzipped a side pocket. Foppy's pink ears protruded first and then his squished face popped free. I clenched my stupid startled scream, but I couldn't stop my heart from kicking up a few notches. It was a stuffed animal, not some talisman of the possessed.

Black cord wrapped around the bunny and tied directly against its furry chest was my wooden cross. *It's authentic, right from the holy land.*

Authentic and infected, too.

She held Foppy out to me. "It's okay. He's learned his lesson."

Nothing but stuffed cotton in my palm, though it felt warm and the cross almost hot as if it'd been in an oven.

As if it held all kinds of power.

✝

"Having a slumber party?" Lavon asked, glancing at the stuffed animal.

"Not exactly. Thanks for your help." In my other hand, swung the plastic bag of stuff I'd purchased.

"Of course. So, you want to tell me what's going on?"

Phoebe had gone inside the church. Her footsteps echoed.

"It's complicated, but I need you to do something for me."

"Short of killing somebody, I'm your man."

I must have gone a little pale because he started to apologize. "No, it's my fault. Things are a little nuts right now. All I need you to do is stay in your car and wait."

"For what?"

"Back up."

"What is going on, Lucas? You can tell me."

"I need you to trust me on this. Stay out here and be ready in case anything happens. First sign of anything, you come in, grab Phoebe and go. Just get her."

"What is this? First sign of what? What's going to happen?"

"I need to know you'll protect Phoebe. *Please*."

"You know I will. I don't want you doing anything stupid."

"Me neither. Be ready if things go bad."

"How will I know if things go bad?"

I hesitated. "If there's an earthquake, come running."

✝

The hanging lights cast a sickly glow on the empty pews. Twenty-four wooden pews split evenly into Gospel and Epistle sides; twenty-four pews as old as the church that sheltered them; twenty-four pews worn away on the corners where people grabbed when standing or passing and the rounded seat edges where people had slid from sitting to kneeling millions of times; twenty-four pews coats and coats of fresh stain couldn't completely rejuvenate, especially not where people always sat, like Mrs. Colette, year after year in the same spot of the same pew, the wood worn smooth into a shadow of her narrow posture.

"Dad?" Phoebe stood at the railing encircling the altar. The large hanging Jesus-on-the-cross stared down at her with painted eyes.

"Sorry, honey. Daddy got lost for a moment." I walked to her across blue carpet that had been replaced fifteen years ago but had long been beaten flat in the path up to the altar.

"You're not lost. I see you."

"And I see you. So, I guess we're okay."

We hugged and I held her a little longer than usual. She did not protest.

"If we go back to Uz, I can keep you safe."

"I know, honey, but I need to keep *you* safe."

She thought for a moment and her fingers flared off her hands as if saying, *Presto!*

"Have a lightbulb moment?"

She smiled. "Do you know what your world is going to be? Can you see it?"

I looked around—the old pews, the beaten carpet, the hand-crafted Jesus. "I see it perfectly."

"We should get started then."

I told her one moment and went into the sacristy. The room was not much bigger than a walk-in closet, certainly no where near the spacious locker-room size at Word of Christ Church. But we didn't need fancy cubicles and luxury accommodations. My father often said all a church needed was people. Everything else was for show. That included Bibles and prayer books.

As to underline the point, my father had carved a reference to his favorite Bible passage in the half-sheet of plywood blocking the entrance to the basement, which was nothing more than a cramped room made of cinderblocks stacked around a furnace grown considerably louder in recent years.

I caressed the engraving in the wood. *My hands have been everywhere. My blood, my tears—all of it—given to this place. This place is me. I am this church.* Into the wood, my father had etched the location of his favorite biblical passage—*Luke 17:21.* "That's all anyone needs to know," my father told me when I was struggling to write a sermon about the very purpose of collective worship, a priest's bread and butter. I took his hint, as well as his advice that "a metaphor is a sermonizer's best friend" and wrote a pretty damn good sermon. Now, however, I hoped everything I had written in that sermon was completely off the mark. No metaphors, no symbols: I needed it all to be literal and true.

At least in a certain reality.

The edges of the plywood stabbed at my hands as I tried to yank it back on its wooden tracks. It moved a half inch and jammed. I smelled old wood and a faint trace of wine I spilled years ago, its faded handprint stain along the closest edge.

On the next push, the plywood moved another few inches. A rectangle of darkness wavered behind it. Hot, moist air puffed out, the last breath shaken free from a corpse's throat.

I tried again and the wood slid back two feet, maybe more, before I got over eager and pushed hard enough to snap it off its track and wedge it at a steep angle. My right hand slid up the jagged edge and splintered bits porcupined me. I cursed and Phoebe called for me. I yelled I was okay, but her rapid footfalls approached, and I grabbed the bag of stuff I purchased and tossed it through the hole. It hit the hard floor with a dull thump.

The door opened. "Daddy?"

"Sorry, honey."

"We need to go now," she said and turned backed to the church.

I adjusted the thermostat by the door that led to the parish hall and the furnace rumbled to life. "Let's get going then," I said to myself.

I glanced back at the space where plywood had been yanked back to reveal a fracture of darkness. Nothing but a furnace down there.

For now.

✝

We set up before the altar. Phoebe laid out a blanket depicting a landscape very similar to her mythical Land of Uz. Purple ponies pranced across lush green hills. She sat cross-legged with Ben in her lap and I sat across from her. I started to put the cross-tangled Foppy next to me, but Phoebe said I had to keep him closer. "Better to be safe," she said.

"Should I tell you about my place?" I asked.

Phoebe sat back-straight, eyes closed, breathing slowly. "I'll find you, Daddy."

She could be trained to harness that power. Use it to help others. The world needs people like your daughter.

"Okay."

I closed my eyes, found the rhythm of my daughter's breathing, and waited for her to say the magic words. Eventually, she did.

"First, we go light."

✝

No matter how many times I've been on a plane or on a roller coaster, that liftoff sensation or imminent plunging-gravity punch always takes me by surprise. Moving over to the other place was no gentle slip into warm waters this time—the floor fell away, and I fell with it, down in a vertiginous tailspin that wedged my stomach in the back of my throat. I tried to call out to Phoebe, but my lungs hitched with pain, and I was helpless to stop the plummet.

"I'm here, Daddy. Find my voice and grab it."

Phoebe's words whispered in the cyclone of darkness and spiraled around me in flashing rings of rainbow colors. Wind whistled. I tried to grab those colors, but I couldn't reach. I threw myself at them but didn't move. As in every dream I ever had where I'm fleeing from some monster or fighting off some intruder, I tried to move and found my limbs stuck in thick mud.

You must stay limber, Cassie had warned.

"Just grab on," Phoebe said in pulsing colors.

Like your daughter says, my father's choked voice said, *grab on and go!*

I can't! I tried to shout. *I can't move!*

I fell faster. Dizziness roiled bile inside me and even with my eyes closed, the world spun and spun; it tossed me around as easily as a rag doll.

Or a stuffed animal.

"Grab on!" Phoebe shouted.

The weight in my hand, far too heavy, made me open my eyes and there was Foppy, perched in my palm, my wooden cross strapped to its chest.

My legs whipped around beneath me and then beside me and above me, spinning as if no longer a part of me. My fingers bled crimson tendrils that were swept into the spinning world, my blood vacating a sinking vessel.

"I'm here!" Phoebe shouted. Her small hand cut through the whirling dark and her fingers snagged one of Foppy's ears. "Hold on!"

My fingers pushed against the invisible mud and I screamed with the force. Heat flushed through me and sweat slicked over my body. My fingers dug into Foppy's back and stomach until they were almost touching inside him through the fabric.

Like a plane hitting turbulence and banking hard left, I was thrown to the side into the swirling void. My legs stretched around me and down endlessly as if made of elastic. The darkness chewed up my legs and sank its teeth into my torso. Wind screamed all around, pushed me into the swirl, but I clutched that stuffed animal so hard my forearm cramped, and I thought I might lose my grip. My other hand whipped around me, so far away.

I managed a scream that roared into my daughter's name.

The world swelled with the smell of those fruit-shaped candies Phoebe loved.

I love you, honey.

The darkness took me.

✝

My head thwacked against the hard altar floor and my spine went numb. In football, they call those stingers, which I finally understood. The world wobbled and shimmered back to me in degrees, but even when it returned to normal, the edges crackled and crumbled, paper slowly burning, as if I had done permanent damage to my periphery.

Jesus loomed far larger then he should have on his cross, at least three or four times larger than the real one—or at least its counterpart in a more familiar world. This one had no face, either: heavy brown curls draped off his head over his face. The curls twisted with unnatural life and behind him, a dark sky swallowed the wall and sunk back to a swirling horizon. The Dali painting given new life.

The altar was smeared like a picture of something moving too fast to catch. The altar drape might have been hastily colored in with forest green crayons. The altar candles towered high and tall flames flickered at their peaks.

"You shouldn't have done this, Daddy." Phoebe stood apart from the world, a vibrant cutout traipsing over a still-photo background. She looked around, clearly troubled.

"It's okay, honey. I know what I'm doing." I managed to take my eyes from the looming Jesus. *I hope so, anyway*, I added in my mind.

Wasn't all of this in my mind?

My head hurt with the thought. It was the kind of question a madman mumbled about wrapped up in straitjacket and bumping into padded walls.

Phoebe started to speak, and something rumbled beneath us. The floor shook, threatened to topple us. I reached for Phoebe, but she was standing strong in surfer pose. The ground vibrated for several seconds and stilled.

"It takes a lot of energy to keep the place solid," Phoebe said. "I'll help you, but we can't stay here long."

"I'm supposed to be saving you," I said.

She shrugged. What did I expect? Adults couldn't do half what they thought they could. Even fathers had limitations.

Something moved behind us in the rows of pews. Something watching. I spun around. It moved along the floor several rows back with slick, papery smoothness. Something with weight, which I couldn't possibly know but I did.

Because this is my world. This is in my mind.

I hadn't created the monstrous Jesus or the towering candles, and I certainly didn't add whatever was moving among the pews.

"It doesn't work that way," Phoebe said.

"You know what I'm thinking?"

"You built this place in your mind but once we came here and gave it life, it became part of something bigger."

"Bigger?"

"Building worlds is a dangerous thing. You should have been more careful."

"It's make believe," I said, though I knew better.

"Now, it's real," she said. "And real places are dangerous."

A pew near the back jolted as if hit with a sledgehammer. The vibration traveled through the floor into my feet. I stepped off the altar onto the blue carpet that looked almost purple, and approached the middle aisle separating the pews.

Long and black and thick with predatory life, a massive snake slithered across the aisle. Its black scales glistened. It must have been seven or eight feet long. Maybe longer. That thing had come out of my daughter's mouth and then gone back inside her.

I stepped to the first pew. The carpet squished beneath me as if soaked. That faceless black snake was the demon inside me, twisting and oscillating its way through my thoughts, slipping from my grasp and circling around my feet in a perpetual taunt.

The snake looped around another pew and slid back over to the other side. Maybe ten feet long and as thick as the width of an inflated tire. A pew on the Epistle side thumped forward and settled back. In reality, the pews were bolted to the floors, but I'd forgotten that detail. I hoped such small things wouldn't matter.

The Devil's in the details, my father said.

The pew rocked forward again and when it settled back, the thing hissed, an extended *ShhhThhh* that backed me up, an arm reaching for Phoebe.

But she had stepped around me and forward to stop where the pews ended before the pulpit. "We'll have to move fast," she said.

"Wait—what?"

The thing hissed louder—*ShhhTHHH!*—and the pew thumped forward hard into the one before it, which toppled against the one before it and the rest dominoed forward with successively louder crashes and yet among the cacophony arose the distinct, but incredibly magnified sound of a snake's rattling tail. It was something close to the sound of maracas but deeper and rising in intensity, building to a sound unlike any percussion instrument.

The black serpent rose up amid the crashing pews to more than fifteen feet high and looked at us with a sloping arrow head completely black without eyes or a mouth. But it didn't need eyes or a mouth. It could see perfectly well because it was in me and had learned the way around and it needed no mouth because it could eat me with its thoughts. This thing was a parasite from Hell that had gorged itself on my fears.

A virus, I told myself. *And viruses can be killed.*

It moved fluidly, side to side, rising higher yet toward the ceiling that should have been blue, but which radiated an oily blackness. With the cascading pews headed right for me, I stood before the snake-thing like a stupefied spectator before the monstrous swell of a tsunami.

Phoebe ran down the aisle past the snake. She left rainbow streaks in the air, like sun spots behind closed eyes. I screamed for her and followed. The snake swung around behind me and destroyed the pulpit with a direct hit. Giant wooden shards exploded across the church, rattling across the pews and thwacking my back. The snake thumped against the wall, shaking the entire building, rattling the windows.

Phoebe hit the doors and fell into darkness. Without Cassie, there was no blinding sun, no over-powering rays to push away the dark. I ran right after my daughter and into a crayon-black night as the serpent careened down through the Gospel-side pews to shatter some and topple the rest.

I tripped down the stairs and hit the gravel on my knees. Phoebe's purple backpack glowed, and I pawed it desperately. She turned to look at me, her whole body radiating a pale hue, a human nightlight.

"Daddy, look."

She pointed back at the church. I expected the snake to burst through the roof and rocket toward us like some radiation-enhanced beast from a B-horror movie, but she was pointing at the towering trees almost engulfing the church. They stretched hundreds of feet into a sky so black we shouldn't have been able to see them, but they were each a different color or even multi-colored and pulsed with those shades, pink and orange and yellow and colors far more exotic, things with Crayola names like Blizzard Blue and Cerise and Mauvelous and Jazzberry Jam and Laser Lemon and Purple Pizzazz and Screamin' Green. Leaves as large as cars swayed in an absent breeze, illuminating the darkness with colors that lighted a child's imagination.

The night smelled sweet, an early summer sweet.

The trees surrounded the parking lot. This was the entire world. Nothing lay beyond except an abyss where unknown things hissed and groaned and clawed and cried. I heard those sounds and it was as if we were meat in a box tossed in a lion-filled den.

Building worlds is a dangerous thing. You should have been more careful.

Right where he sat in a more-familiar world, Lavon waited behind the steering wheel of his truck with the same vanity plates. The buckles on his overalls sparkled in a lemony light. He stared through the windshield at the church as if he heard something. He shimmered out of focus, a TV going fuzzy, and came back again.

I approached him but Phoebe stopped me. "He's not really here. He's like a ghost."

As long as he was real in one place, that would be enough. I hoped.

"It's here," Phoebe said.

At the far end of the parking lot, shrouded beneath the kaleidoscopic leaves of unnatural trees, stood a small white house with a concrete porch, an American flag hanging flat against the vinyl siding next to the red front door.

"You know whose house that is?" I asked.

"It's Abaddon's now," she said.

We ascended the porch steps hand-in-hand. In her other hand, she hugged Ben. I had left Foppy and my cross behind. I'd have to hope that wasn't a mistake. Phoebe didn't say anything about it, which I took as a good sign. Then again, I wasn't the soothsayer here.

The front steps should have been solid concrete, but they felt mushy and even cupped around my shoes like mud. By the top step, the concrete sucked at our feet and we had to make large, exaggerated steps that stretched the concrete in elastic strings like melted cheese. Once the strings snapped free with loud pops, they melted back into the porch where the concrete rippled.

Coming to life. Testing its newfound sentience.

But this was in my mind, so wasn't I giving life to everything around? Whether I meant to or not, everything in here drew power from me, an unwitting psychic generator. But I knew that truth only stretched so far. Phoebe was the real power source— it pulsed off her in heat waves and warmed my hand until I thought my fingers might burn. *Some kids are like improperly set ovens*, a doctor told us. *They run hot.*

Wendy Toft, née Wendy Javan, lived behind this door. I had not placed her here, however, so there was no assurance what was waiting for us. I built this world, hastily but built nonetheless, and something else had brought this house here. I hoped that something else was David.

I waited for the door to vibrate or ripple with preternatural life, but it stood solid. Phoebe squeezed my hand and nodded— *Get on with it, Daddy.*

My fingers hesitated around the doorknob as if afraid what might happen once they touched it, like poking at an animal that isn't as dead as it appears. The knob was freezing, and I turned it quickly and pushed open the door.

A short set of steps led to the main living area, which Wendy had decorated in dark browns and awful fading pastels. In the real world—*other* world—her living room was one third of a larger box that included her dining room and kitchen, but here, the stairs led directly to that living room with the plastic-covered cushions on the couch and encroaching darkness hid everything else.

This room was all there was.

For a moment the room was empty, levitating on a black cloud, and then a woman's high-pitched scream ripped the air and Wendy Toft flickered into existence on the floor with her brother on top of her, straddling her chest his hands wound around her neck. His black hand clenched hard enough to almost flatten her throat. Purple streaks trailed up her neck and across her face. Her lips darkened from blue toward black.

"You have to die," David said. *"You have to die so it can be free."*

I moved toward them, thinking I could stop this, but this murder had already happened, and the moment I reached toward the scene, the two of them vanished. Nothing more than a flicker through the imagination.

A step beyond, David appeared again, shimmered there, down on his knees, hands together as if in prayer. He clenched a long carving knife in that prayer grip. The blade stretched ten inches high.

He angled the blade toward his throat.

"David, no—"

The blade shot forward and sunk with a thumping squish, and the image vanished before David fell to the floor.

"David knew what he was doing," my father said.

He was dressed in full priestly garb and sat alone on Wendy's couch. He was looking even older than when he died, as if death aged him further, less hair, more wrinkles, and even a patch of moss had sprouted beneath his chin. A small beetle trundled along the side of his head and investigated his ear.

A rotting, talking corpse.

"We're finally all together," he said. His teeth were black, and he spoke as if through a throat of dirt. "One big happy family."

"You're not grandpa," Phoebe said.

He grinned at her. The beetle burrowed into his ear.

"You're not getting Phoebe. You're not getting my daughter."

"We already have her. The moment you brought her here, she was ours."

Phoebe squeezed my hand.

"No," I said. "You don't. If you did, I wouldn't be here."

The thing posing as my father laughed in a trio of high-pitched barks: Ha! HA! *HA!* "David killed his sister and then himself because he wanted too. I didn't make him do it. Heck, I'm not even human. I'm some virus. I can't make anyone do anything."

"You're a demon," I said. "Abaddon."

His smile grew larger, stretching his skin until it ripped in places to reveal the bones beneath, a cheekbone, a sliver of jaw. "No," he said. "I'm your god."

"You are no god," I said.

The Ben-thing crossed his legs, joined his hands on his knee. They were black, the skin dangling free as if flayed. "You know what must be done, Lucas. But you have a choice, of course. What would any of this mean if you didn't have free will?"

"I'm going to destroy you."

"We are eternal. We are legion."

Phoebe pulled my arm. "Daddy, look."

She held up her stuffed animal. Ben-the-bear squirmed with life. Its legs wriggled and its harmless paws flailed and its plastic eyes gleamed a rich violet. It reached toward the thing posing as my father.

The Ben-thing's smile waned. "If you want to save your daughter," it said, "you have to die. Do what Abraham was too afraid to do: kill yourself and prove the scripture true—'Greater love hath no man than this, that he lay down his life for another.'"

"You know nothing of scripture," I said. "You're a bastardization of God's will."

"And yet God made me as surely He made you and your daughter."

"Daddy, the bear—"

"Or kill *her*," the Ben-thing said, smile returning full. "Yes, that sounds more like it, doesn't it? Kill your daughter. Use your hands as David did. The strength courses through you. You can feel it. It is right. It is what should be done. Kill her and you'll know true love and with it, godly power."

"No," I said but couldn't say anything else.

It did make sense. The Ben-thing was right. I *should* kill her. In fact, killing her would be a kindness. If I killed myself and the virus infected her, she would be its pawn, but if I killed her, she'd be spared that misery. She was just a girl. She didn't deserve the cruelty a demon would inflict. She was strong but not that strong. I could save her. I could take on the demon myself. I was a priest. I could battle it back with God's true word. No metaphors. No symbols. Just God's pure, unadulterated Word. I would make the ultimate sacrifice and God would see fit to bless me.

"That's right," the Ben-thing said. "It's the right thing to do."

My blackened hand came up, fingers tensed into a claw. My other hand squeezed Phoebe's hard enough for her to cry out and try to squirm free. "Daddy, you're hurting me."

"Do it," my father said. "Don't make her suffer. Do it now."

I turned to Phoebe. She was crying, pulling away from me. "Daddy, no."

"I'm sorry, honey. Your grandpa is right. It's for the best. I'm actually saving you. It's God's will, my angel. It'll be quick, I promise."

My diseased hand pounced onto her throat. She shook with the force, her small body almost snapping in half.

"Do it," my father said. Now standing next to me, whispering into my ear. "Kill her and you'll save her soul. You'll be a saint."

Yes. I would be a saint. I would be a divine figure, a true holy man. The Reverend Benjamin Masters was revered, but he was no saint. I would surpass him. I would be elevated onto the highest echelons of piety. God would look down and declare, *You are truly my most devout servant and all the glories of this world and of all others will be yours.*

Phoebe collapsed to the floor. Her eyes went huge, threatening to erupt from their sockets. Her skin paled and then flushed red. Her lips bloomed blue. My hand squeezed tighter.

"Finish it," my father hissed. His words warmed my ear.

"I love you, Phoebe. I love you so much."

Recognition flickered across her face but not of her imminent death. It was of salvation. She swung her arm up hard and Ben-the-bear flew from her hand. It smacked the side of my face but instead of simply bouncing off harmlessly, its limbs dug into my skin with thick claws and tore a gash in my cheek and the pain was immense, a raging forest fire of pain, as if the bear had sliced me with an acid-soaked blade.

I released Phoebe, my black hand lurching for the bear, but it was moving, gouging my ear, and climbing up the back of my head with razors like mountain-climbing ice axes. I stumbled back trying to get at the animal, but when I smacked into my father, the bear leaped from me and latched onto him.

He howled in pain.

The bear tore at my father's face. Spiked claws stabbed his eyes and blackish muck squirted onto the bear's fur. It slashed my father's nose and ripped open a gaping hole in his cheek, the skin flapping loose.

My father screamed, mouth huge, and the bear thrust itself into the opening. My father's scream was immediately muffled. The bear's legs worked up and down as if swimming and then it was all the way in my father's mouth and his throat was bulging, stretching bigger and bigger, the skin going translucent, the bear's eyes gleaming from inside.

The bear's head ripped through the skin with a papery, liquid plop. Ben-the-bear smiled at us with a fabric-stitched mouth.

Seizures knocked my father backward. He collapsed back onto the couch, back arched, mutilated mouth sagging skyward, and with a seizure vomited out a cloud of black muck that hung suspended before it, like someone purging his own diseased soul.

Or the evil possessing him.

The black cloud was thick and oily. It squirmed, a cancerous-ameba, and stretched toward me.

That's the demon. That black mass is the demon in its purest form. Not Abaddon the Destroyer or the Doomed, who lives in a bottomless pit—merely a diseased thing seeking a host. Nothing more than a virus.

Phoebe grabbed my hand.

"Daddy," Phoebe said in an urgent, husky whisper. "We have to go."

She yanked me from the reaching cloud. *I tried to kill her*, I thought. *No, I practically had killed her.* Yet, she still trusts me. Still wants to protect me.

So much for what I thought I knew of love.

We ran for the stairs, but they were gone, and only darkness surrounded us.

✟

"This way," Phoebe said.

The Ben-thing lay motionless on the couch. Ben-the-bear pulled himself free from the mauled neck. For a crazy moment, I thought the stuffed animal had waved at us.

The cloud stretched for us with elongated arms.

"Hurry, Daddy."

Phoebe ran head-long into the darkness, only it wasn't simply darkness. It had formed into a swirling tunnel that spun rapidly around us making me dizzy and almost fall. We started running and that made the dizziness worse, but I managed to keep my feet, though I thought I might vomit.

Behind us, the stand-in for Wendy Toft's living room fell farther and farther behind us. The black cloud filled the end and came for us.

"This way," Phoebe said.

"Where are we going?"

In the dark, maybe wrapped in the tornado swirl, things watched us and hissed and growled. *ShhhTHHH!*

And another sound, something heavier, a loud CLACK CLACK, as of something walking. Not walking, though—scurrying.

CLACKCLACKCLACK.

And there it was trying to push out of the spinning tunnel and get us: an enormous spider. Its bulging eight eyes reflected my silent scream.

"*Here!*" Phoebe shouted and yanked me hard.

The spider's monstrous fangs pierced the tunnel.

We fell.

✝

A faint white light pulsed far down at the bottom of a well. I felt Phoebe falling with me, but I couldn't see her. We floated above it and yet fell simultaneously, or perhaps the sides of the well rushed up past us.

It will find us here, Phoebe whispered in my mind. *It's coming to get us.*

I'll protect you. I promise.

The floor smacked into us or vice versa but the pain was numb, distant, and we got to our knees in a room without walls where only the gentle white glow from a Batman night light offered illumination. David sat in the only chair facing the only other thing: a twin-sized bed with wooden head and footboards and a black and blue comforter featuring Batman in various superhero postures. The comforter was tucked neatly beneath a young boy's sallow, sleeping face. Two extra-large pillows with comforter-matching slipcovers barely gave beneath the boy's head.

David leaned forward, elbows on his legs, and dropped his face in his hands. I slowly stood and helped Phoebe up. Bruises had formed on her neck in the shape of fingers. My black hand twitched at the sight.

Wouldn't it feel so good to slip your hand back around her slender neck? Place your fingers over those bruises, right where they belong, and squeeze.

"You shouldn't have come," David said through his hands, both normal.

"We need your help," I said.

He laughed like someone about to be executed. "There's nothing I can do. Nothing you can do, either. This is where I need to be."

Phoebe and I stepped to the foot of the bed. Joey Javan's body was a mere ripple in the heavy comforter. His head looked painted on the pillow among the batwings and flying punches.

"I'm sorry, David."

He rubbed his face and looked at us. "Everyone is always sorry. It doesn't mean shit."

"Without your help, I would have lost my daughter."

"And then you'd know what I feel. Then maybe you'd be sorry."

"I *am* sorry."

"Goes back to Job again. God lets Satan screw with him hardcore and Job proves his steadfast devotion, so Satan slumps off in failure and God restores Job to his previous plenty and then some. But you know what God didn't do? He didn't apologize. He didn't say, 'Gee, Job, I'm sorry about all that shit, dragging you into my mess with Satan and all, but I had to prove to all my angels no self-righteous dickhead could get the better of me.' And you know why He didn't apologize, don't you, reverend?"

"Because He's God," I said.

"Ain't that fucking right." He touched the comforter and gripped it in two fists.

"You don't need to torture yourself." I wiped sweat off my face and was mildly surprised to find blood. That bear had really cut me. I patted my face and found a gaping gash stretching from ear to mouth. The injury had hurt incredibly, but now it felt numb and wasn't bleeding much.

"Torture myself?" David said. "That's what you think I'm doing? You think I'm here because I feel guilty for what happened to my son?"

I said nothing.

"This is my world. I built it. Nothing elaborate. No fancy colors. No sprawling landscapes. Just a small corner for me and my son. A place where we can be together. This place is mine. You have no right to be here. None. Here, I am God. But you know what the real bitch of it is? I can't do anything for my son. I tried, Lucas. I tried so hard but he just sleeps there, forever on the brink of death. I lean over him to hear the soft whisper of his breathing and it's so slow that with every breath I think it's finally over, but the next one always comes. He can live forever here, but he lives in a sleep. He can't speak. Can't even look at me. You feel sorry for me now?"

"This is no way to be," I said.

"You're right—it's not." David spoke with his head down.

Phoebe slipped her hand from mine and walked around the bed opposite David. She stopped at Joey's head and watched him like someone appreciating a sleeping pet.

"All that Abraham and Isaac crap, remember? How could Abraham so willingly bring his son to the top of Mount Moriah and place him on a sacrificial pyre? How could he put his knife to Isaac's throat? What are we supposed to say? Abraham had blind devotion? He trusted in the Lord?"

I said nothing. My hand twitched again.

"The story has its priorities out of whack. Just because God commands you to do it, isn't it still murder? God tells me to kill my son, you know what I say? 'Fuck off!'"

His scream echoed as if we were in a grand hall and his fists twisted the comforter into messy bunches. He laughed a little mournfully, but I was looking at Phoebe. She reached toward Joey, one skinny arm impossibly steady.

She shouldn't do that. She shouldn't try to wake the slumbering beast. I had to stop her. In fact, I had to stop her once and for all. I had to prove who was boss, who was the Dad around here, show her *I MEAN BUSINESS.*

My hand clenched into a fist.

Yes, show her you mean business, Dad. Punch her hard in the face and then strangle the little bitch. Do it now.

Phoebe looked at me from the bed, concern blooming there, and her hand cupped Joey's forehead.

"'Do not fear for I am with you,'" David said. "You remember when I told you that was my favorite quote? That's why I won't abandon my son. I will stay here forever and watch over him. He will never have to fear because I am with him."

"Phoebe, stop," I said. My fingernails were stabbing my palm, drawing blood.

The little bitch is going to ruin everything.

David looked up and his eyes went wide. "What are you doing? Why are you touching my son?"

"This isn't your son," she said. And only to me, speaking into my mind, she added, *It's the last shred of the Uz Monster and I'm going to let it free.*

"Phoebe, no," I said aloud.

Let her do it, a voice said. *Let her do it and then you can kill her, wrap your hands around her little throat and—*

"Don't," I said again.

"You can't do this to me," David said. "*Please.* Look at my son." He pulled the comforter off the bed in a slow, slithery tug.

What laid on that bed was not a sickly boy in Batman underpants but the remnants of a person who had suffered the cruel indignity of the body's unfair fragility. The muscles had withered and the flesh clung to knobby joints and slender bones. Liver spots blotted the narrow chest and speckled across the twig legs. Yellowish bruises splotched his sides as if someone had hugged him too fiercely.

David stood and the comforter piled over his feet. "Get away from my son."

"You have to help us," Phoebe said. And to me, she said, *Get ready, it's coming.*

"Get away from my son."

"He says he's not your son," Phoebe said. Her hand slid off Joey's forehead and covered his mouth. With her other hand she pinched the boy's nose.

"You little bitch. Get away from him or—"

I snagged his arm before he could jump on the bed. My black fingers buried into his forearm. He squealed and tried to pull free, but I had him and my feet stood strong, solid.

"He says his name is Legion," Phoebe said. "Because he is many."

"No!" David screamed. "*No, you little bitch. No!*"

The frail boy's chest was still.

Phoebe let go and backed up, staring at the boy curiously. *She killed another person*, I thought. *My baby, my little girl—my angel—is a murderer. I must be in Hell.*

"*You BITCH!*" David screamed. "*YOU KILLED MY SON!*"

"He's not your son," Phoebe said. "He never was. Your son died a long time ago."

Joey's eyes opened to reveal black orbs and I released David. He went to his son, crying, begging for him to be alive. Bed springs clanked beneath him. He took his son up in a hug.

The boy's mouth dropped wide as blackish sludge gurgled out and over his chin. The stink was immediate and thick. Phoebe fell back, ran to me.

We have to get out of here.

(No, we have to die here.)

Not yet.

Joey's body stiffened, more muck vomited over his chin and onto his chest, and he growled like a cornered dog. The boy's hands flapped around David's neck and he buried his face against his father's cheek with a wet smack. For a moment it was a sweet, if slightly gut-roiling moment, the dim light glowing gently around them, and then David screamed so loudly it filled his entire world and thundered down the cavernous halls of darkness around us.

He stumbled back to the edge of the bed with his son clinging to him like some giant parasite, hands ensnared around his neck, mouth clamped firmly on the side of David's face. Bright blood spurted on Joey's face. David managed to get his feet on the floor and kept his balance, but when he turned toward us, his feet tangled in the comforter and he toppled back onto the bed in an awkward sideways sprawl.

Joey shook his head side to side, which elicited more desperate screams from David, and he pulled back, stretching David's cheek, and tore the flesh. Joey turned to us with a flap of his father's cheek caught in his mouth. He grinned, the ruined skin sticking to his chin.

We have to go now, Phoebe said. *Before it becomes one.*

The Joey-thing laughed in a mad chitter and swooped its head back down onto David. This time, it bit off David's ear, spit it onto the pillow in a bloody splotch, and tossed itself at David again. David screamed once more when the thing only resembling his son all these years clamped its teeth around David's nose.

It needs to come with us, I said. *We need all of it.*

(*No, we need to die. We need to let it be free.*)

No, Daddy.

I'll keep you safe.

David did not try to fight off the Joey-thing and his arms and legs kicked now out of reflexive nerve injury as Joey tore open the side of his father's neck and blood pulsed across the white sheets. David's eyes rolled back to all whites and he offered only a weak moan of protest.

The blood spilling from David's wounds splashed across the bed and the headboard and darkened to black. The liquid came alive and trailed onto Joey. It slimed up his frail body and poured into his mouth and up his nose and into the corners of his eyes. He fell off his father and sprawled arms-out on the bed. The black liquid poured into him and his little body shook with violent tremors. He cried out in the voice of a frightened boy and his chest expanded in a balloon. His ribs pushed against his sides, growing larger and larger. His limbs puffed and his skull bloated into one of those alien heads with Joey's eyes disappearing beneath the sloping forehead.

This is gonna be big.

Get ready, I told Phoebe.

The Joey-thing's chest burst like a turkey stuffed with a cherry bomb. The black gunk splashed into the air and hovered there in a cloud. Joey's head cracked wide and more of the stinking darkness joined the levitating cloud over the bed. His legs and arms popped one after the other, hissing out more black cloud, and all that remained was mutilated corpse.

The cloud throbbed with awful life. Faces floated in there, hundreds and hundreds of them, faces of people screaming and of things less than human, things with fangs and insect wings and black hearts. It moved toward us.

I waited until the last moment and offered it my hand.

Now, I said. *Go light.*

✝

This time it didn't feel like falling at all. It felt like we flew. I thought of the image I had been keeping safe since I saw it and focused on it completely. I hoped Phoebe was beside me or flying after me and hadn't sought safety in her Land of Uz. I thought only of the license plate and the sweet smell of summer night.

Gravel dug through my pants into my knees. Lavon's crumpled MILK MAN license plate shone before me in the illuminating flux of multicolored trees—pale yellow to dark purple to neon green to blizzard blue. My head pulsed with the vacillating light and I thought I might pass out. I grabbed the bumper and the cold metal grounded me. I had touched the bumper, meaning the truck was real, meaning either I was back in the "real" world or the truck had come here.

I stood and stared through the back window into the cab: empty.

Phoebe was gone too.

Wherever you are, stay there. I projected the thought out as hard as I could.

Behind me, Wendy Toft's house shimmered in heat waves. The large oak out front flickered and vanished. The sidewalk crumbled away into darkness. The Toyota in the driveway dropped into a crevasse and the entire driveway fell after it. The front door bulged, pushing out like elastic and sinking back, pushing out further and receding—a rectangular heart, but what pulsed inside that heart was not blood.

A splintery crack lightninged through the door and it exploded in shards that vanished before they could hit the ground. The black cloud gorged with faces and alive with sentience funneled out the door and quickly concealed the entire house. The mass rotated and whirled, grew larger. Heads and hands pushed from the sides as if people were actually trapped in there but the cloud snapped them back in their prison. The fluctuating colors played along the cloud's surface and vanished into it, eaten by it. The thing made almost no noise, a whispery howl no louder than a rough breeze, but its stink spread out rapidly, a larger cloud than itself, invisible but thick.

I stepped around the truck so the church entrance was directly behind me and faced the cloud, a western showdown between man and monster.

"You want me?" I called to it. "Come and get me!"

The cloud spun around itself and elongated toward me. A giant face with hollow eyes and a cavernous mouth screamed the attack. The cloud moved as a worm, only faster, stretching itself out and pulling itself back together.

Not like a worm, though, I thought. *Like something much worse.*

The trees flickered vibrant colors, bleeding across giant leaves. *Transplanted right from Uz. Only place they'll grow.*

Something surged toward me and when I turned back, the cloud was almost on me. Millions of faces screaming for me.

I ran up the church steps, grabbed the door, and—

The doors wouldn't open. I yanked on them and they gave an inch or two but no more. The cloud flexed toward me, bulged itself sideways, stretched above the church roof and down to the ground where it ate away the gravel into a widening pit. An abyss. I threw myself at the doors thinking they might fracture but they bounced me off and almost back down the steps. I pulled on the two handles with all I had—*open goddammit, open*—and the entire world shook in a quaking vibration that dropped me to my knees.

The world was crumbling and if it collapsed before I got inside the church, all of this would be for nothing. I'd be stuck in some coma and the demon would have free reign to do its worst in the infinite realms of my subconscious. It would kill me and go after Phoebe.

(*Then save some time and pain and kill yourself.*)

I tried the doors again and my arms felt sluggish, and I thought of dreams where I couldn't move my arms and awoke to find I had rolled onto my stomach with my hands trapped beneath. *You must stay limber.* The more I focused on pulling those handles, the less my arms cooperated. They fatigued, slipped off the handles, dangled at my sides, palsied.

For a moment, they weren't even there. Just useless wobbling stubs jutting off my shoulders.

The world trembled again. Not an earthquake. Something approaching. Something huge. *THUMP.* Gravel leaped high all across the parking lot around the black cloud that had stopped short of Lavon's empty truck. Trees broke in loud cracks and collapsed. *THUMP.* The church porch wobbled as if it might crumble. The air itself seemed to shake. *THUMP.*

A monstrous, deafening howl from the throat of something enormous and preternatural, a prehistoric thing from an alternate world of horrors, erupted as if from every corner of this world. To the right, the trees shook, several cracked and thudded to the ground. Through the trees shone the grey-stained fur and the pink lining of the sagging ears.

An exclamation of disbelief barely escaped my mouth as Foppy's giant head pushed through the leaves. It stood at least two stories high with a head as large as a small car, its red eyes blazing headlights. Its hard-plastic pink nose twitched with tissuey life and its mouth opened wide in another thunderous howl. Giant buck teeth protruded off the top and bottom of its mouth and long fangs hooked down and over its chin in sharpened sickles.

Foppy was being bad. He wanted me to hurt the other kids.

There are other things here, Cassie had warned. *Guardians.*

The bunny thundered a scream and from beneath it, Phoebe burst through the tree line riding her bike, pedaling madly. Plastic streamers fluttered back from the handlebars.

You promised you wouldn't let go. You promised you'd stay with me, Daddy.

She headed right for the cloud.

"Phoebe, no!"

The black cloud seemed to shudder from the bunny, backing up behind Lavon's truck and stretching vertically down to the ground to form a wall, and Foppy bent forward and unleashed that thunderous screech again. Phoebe looked toward me from her bike—riding like a big girl—and it was her only older, maybe in her twenties or even thirties and she was wearing not a Sunday dress but a reverend's cope with a vibrant purple stole and pedaling furiously as if late to officiate a service—then Foppy leaped from the trees on massive hindquarters rippling with muscular strength. Mouth wide, Foppy launched at the black cloud, stretching above Phoebe to chomp at the diseased thing.

It's going to kill it. It's going to devour the virus.

It bit into the cloud and the faces swarming within silently screamed. Those fangs sliced through the cloud and Foppy looked ready to tear the black mass into tatters, but the cloud swarmed to engulf the bunny's head in a jaw of its own. Phoebe, still riding fast and right for the cloud, brought up a hand as if to wave to me and then she was gone into the blackness as well. Swallowed. Foppy collapsed forward into the cloud and it ate all of it as completely as a black hole ingesting an entire planet.

I screamed.

The cloud flexed and circled into itself and vibrations trembled through it. The church porch shook and the entire building shuddered in an earthquake. Something crashed inside, a fallen light, a thrown pew.

The church doors banged open and Lavon ran out. Phoebe was in his arms, her hands wrapped around his neck. He ran fast enough to pass me in a blink, but he slowed as he passed, like he was in a movie I could slow down, frame-by-frame.

Lavon was fuzzy, out of focus, ghostly, but Phoebe stood out with magnificent clarity. She looked at me and I felt every moment I had ever shared with her, every bedtime story, every hug, every laugh, every roll of the eyes, every crying fit, everything we shared from a bedtime story or a stupid joke to a magical world that existed just for us, every little thing that made me the most important man in her life and she the most genuine angel I would ever know.

I love you, Daddy.

She reached for me and I for her and she dropped something in my hand, and for a moment she was older again and in priestly garb—*She could be trained to harness that power. Use it to help others. The world needs people like your daughter.*—and then she was gone, tucked beside Lavon in his truck as it backed up and turned to go out so fast it sprayed gravel across the porch. The rocks vanished before they could hit me.

The truck drove off through the trees. A thin tail of exhaust twirled and disappeared. In my outstretched hand, Phoebe had dropped the wooden cross with the hemp rope. I clutched it and put it on, pressed it to my chest.

"Greater love hath no man than this," I said.

The cloud came for me again. I turned and the headless black snake bobbed in the open doorway. It watched me without eyes, as if it knew my soul.

The snake spit forward and I dove under it, over the threshold into the church. All the pews had been knocked about and destroyed into cracked fragments. The stained window glass detailing the stations of the cross were shattered. The pulpit stood in a split firewood mess as if massacred with an axe. The altar was karate-chopped in half and Jesus-on-the-cross had tumbled off the wall onto the pile. The wall behind wavered with living darkness, a lake's surface at midnight. The building shook. A fan fell from the ceiling onto the broken pews. The blue ceiling crumbled in giant jigsaw pieces that shattered on the floor.

The missing blue pieces spelled out a giant word: ABADDON.

The snake threw itself at me, collided into the wall, and slithered at my heels. I ran up the far side toward the sacristy, leaping debris, and chanced a glance over my shoulder. The snake was right behind me and right behind it, the black cloud plumed into the church. The faces within grinned rictuses of mangled teeth.

I shouldered through the door and into the sacristy. The window over the sink that drained directly into the ground had shattered and all the vestments had vomited out of the closet. The safe had tumbled across the floor to the plywood sheet that was pulled back enough to reveal the room beyond.

I tossed the safe aside and grabbed the plywood to yank it farther back. Its splintery edges pierced my palms and warm blood pushed between my fingers. Etched in the wood, *Luke 17:21* loomed large as if it had always wanted to be bigger than the small carving my father had done.

The quote was about the kingdom of Heaven and where it truly resided. I wasn't sure I knew much about Heaven, but I could write one heck of a sermon about Hell.

The snake careened through wooden debris, sending it flying in all directions, and hurtled directly for the sacristy. I pulled on the plywood against arms beginning to palsy, the black hand going almost completely numb, and the wood gave enough for me to squeeze through and drop onto the hot concrete floor. The furnace groaned, running hot and shaking with the effort.

As I'd hoped.

The snake thudded into the sacristy, smashing into the far wall and swooping back to fill the plywood gap. With no expression on its face, I still knew it was smiling as it hovered there in the entrance.

I turned to grab the bag I dropped in here earlier, and my father stood before me.

✝

He looked remarkably well, no longer an animated corpse, but alive and flushed with vibrance: eyes clear, skin smooth and bright.

Concerned I'm getting better?

"Hello son." Blazing light shone from his mouth as he spoke like he'd swallowed a sun, Cassie's perhaps, and I had to squint and look away. "No time to be shy," he said.

I started to speak and he seized my throat. His hand was fire-hot and clenched my neck so tightly I could barely breathe and somehow couldn't move, his touch numbing my entire body as immediately as ice-cold water. *He's just in shock.*

It's time for a lesson, he said without opening his mouth, speaking directly into my mind. The words were metallic; each one the high-pitched, piercing *TING!* of hammer against metal. *It's time for you to know the truth about your God.*

A sopping dishrag in scummy water swirled in my gut. I was going to vomit, but my bones shook, so maybe my whole body was going to split wide with the next piercing reverberation of clashing metal. At least it would be an end, and I wanted that badly.

I deserve one last sermon, my father said. *Don't you think so? You know how well-regarded they always were. I'd hate for you to not know the truth before you die. Are you ready? Good. The title of my homily should get the point across: The Devil's Sermon.*

Your precious Job is an ecclesiastical joke designed to evoke guilt and shame. He is a pathetic waste who bowed when he questioned God's motives and God said, "Where were you when I made the Earth?"

And what does that mean? He made the Earth and everything in it. SO WHAT?

HE made YOU.

HE made ME.

Where is He NOW?

The words *screeched* and *PINGED!* and *clanged* inside my head, and I couldn't escape them, but I wasn't sure if I wanted to anymore. They sounded right. Truthful. As if the answers had always been inside me; they just had to be pried loose.

But I had to get the bag. I had to finish this and hope it'd keep Phoebe safe.

(*Safe in death.*)

And what about His great son, Jesus? that awful voice said. *Was he not as much a fraud as his father?*

Jesus was a plainclothes magician.

Proffering mundane miracles.

Thousands of birds took flight from a desert plane in my head, only it wasn't birds flapping in liftoff I heard but thunderous applause, filling my head, echoing throughout the world.

And these words were making sense. They really were. Maybe he was right. God was playing with a loaded deck, shamelessly cheating on every hand.

The night before he is captured and sentenced to die, Jesus leads his disciples to the Garden of Gethsemane where they pray. Jesus removes himself from the disciples and prays, saying, "Father, if thou be willing, remove this cup from my lips: nevertheless not my will, but thine, be done."

It's Job all over again, the voice said in amusement. *Now, however, it is the SON of God begging HIS misery not happen, begging Judas not betray him and Pilate not sentence him to crucifixion.*

"And being in agony he prayed more earnestly: and his sweat was as it were great drops of blood falling down to the ground."

Here, Jesus prays with such fervency he could be sweating blood.

That is your symbol of faith—be thou unwilling, be even ungrateful, yet pray hard enough to purge blood and the way will be shown to you.

Oh, Jesus, so proud in his pain.

(*So proud, ah yes, and that phrase so familiar.*)

(*In my mind. This thing, this disease has been in my mind for years.*)

(*How to kill a virus?*)

You worship him and his cross, and it's all a joke.

All of it was foreordained, all the misery set equally upon the loyal and the hapless.

When the priests in the temple turned against him, Jesus said, "When I was daily with you in the temple, you stretched forth no hands against me: but this is your hour, and the power of darkness."

Everything was decreed and destined. Some people find comfort in that, tell themselves God would not heap any more miseries upon them than they could handle, but Judas killed himself and the wild crowd chanting for death found satisfaction in Jesus' agony.

Found, in fact, a bloodlust God had fostered.

Is THIS how God wanted it? He gave the Garden of Eden to Adam and Eve, yet he also gave them the serpent that would start the whole awful parade of misery marching. All I wanted to give them, all I ever offer, is truth. God PUNISHES you for wanting truth. He gave Abraham a son and made him believe he would have to sacrifice him. He gave us Jesus, our supposed SAVIOR and DAMNED us to DESTROY him.

GOD IS A SADIST.

And I thought, *YES! God is a sadist.* That made perfect sense. Otherwise, why would there be so much suffering? Why would we be so cruel to each other? Why would we decay and die?

If God were loving, why wasn't He *actually* loving?

He loved His son so much He condemned him to die.

Was that really love?

A strange yellow light lit the room. It was coming from the cross, glowing against my chest.

(Naomi and the girls handing it to me wrapped in tissue paper: "It's authentic, right from the holy land.")

It brightened more and more. The light washed over my father's face and that awful smile wavered. Where the cross rested against my chest, my skin rapidly warmed. It was going to burn me.

Use it, Daddy, Phoebe said. *USE THE CROSS.*

But the Devil wasn't done.

(*It's not the Devil. It's a disease. A VIRUS. You can kill it.*)

How? How to kill a virus?

(*You know how—do it.*)

A *dark vein pulses poison blood through the doctrine you have taught your entire adult life*, that metallic voice said. *The Word of God is a bloody word, one full of VIOLENCE and MURDER. Anywhere it's opened the Bible offers a tale of woe: Eve defies God and all of mankind is subsequently punished; Job's life is destroyed; Abraham is told to murder his son; Jesus offers hope in miracles but knows it will all be for naught— eventually, the blood spills.*

Use it, Phoebe said. *NOW!*

But I can't move—

Only I could. My hands came up easily. I hesitated only a moment before seizing the cross and yanked it off the hemp rope around my neck.

Maybe it is not so surprising how warped religion in practice becomes, not so shocking how easily zealots take the pulpit and preach fear and damnation and then sin exhaustingly behind closed doors, beat their wives and rape their children, not so startling how people will scream and fight and kill in the name of God. Look at the Bible. It is your Pandora's box. And once the miseries were let loose, it was already too late. Hope is the ultimate joke. Your God doesn't care. In the end, you're all DOOMED. Unless you choose A NEW GOD!

I screamed against the weight and rightness of those awful thoughts, (*because they're your thoughts, not a demon's—it's a virus, an infection eating your mind, nothing more*), against the metal squall of its voice, against its need to rationalize and belittle God. I smacked the glowing, burning cross flat against my father's chest.

His mouth dropped open with that magnificent light—*the angels are hunting me*—and he screamed with all-too human pain.

"'*The kingdom of Heaven is within!*'" I shouted, my father's favorite biblical passage echoing in the cramped furnace room.

He let go of me. I hit the floor hard, my knees snapping painfully, but it didn't matter. I crawled quickly and grabbed my bag. I took what I needed and turned to the furnace. It was an elderly thing that should have been replaced and which hadn't been burning completely clean in many years. A repairman said it would hold out for a while, he could clean it, but he wouldn't push it forever. The chimney liner was accumulating ash—ash could cause a fire.

I grabbed the flexible metal chimney liner, much like a snake itself, and tore it free from the fitting that was shaped like a T. Burning scars destroyed my palms. I wedged the starter log, still in its packaging, into the furnace gap and squeezed a load of lighter fluid onto it. I wedged the liner back so it was almost touching the furnace.

I flicked the grill lighter and its flame flickered three inches long.

My father was gone.

The cross glowed on the floor. I grabbed it with my diseased hand and froze, flame threatening to wink out.

In the opening to the sacristy, the snake no longer swayed. In its place stood an enormous black spider. Only its grotesque face could fit in the opening, the rest of its bulbous body stuffed into the sacristy. Black hairs jutted at all angles and basketball-sized eyes shone my warping reflection like mirrors in a funhouse. Black slop—poison—sluiced off its curved fangs.

It hissed at me, loud and vibrating, and opened its awful mouth wide.

This was the truest form of Abaddon, the truest form of the infection, the truest form of the virus infecting my soul.

It was the black spider under my bed that had been haunting my dreams for decades. The evil I forever feared and never wanted to confront.

"*You want to be my god?*" I yelled. "*Make me.*"

The spider lunged forward, squeezing its head through the gap, the wood splintering, and I touched the flame to the soaking bag. It caught instantly, flaring up into a blowtorch, and then the spider was busting through the wall, wooden shards scattering everywhere, and it crashed into my chest and torpedoed me back against the wall. The fire jumped into the chimney liner and it caught in a *WHOOSHING* blaze that raced up through the wall along the sacristy and up to the chimney cap on the roof. I could imagine fire spewing from the roof of Saint John's as if the Devil himself had conquered a piece of Heaven.

Not this time.

Spider legs hard as tree trunks and sharp as spears pinned me against the wall. The spider's mandibles worked rapidly up and down, a chomping machine preparing to feast.

We are Legion because we are many.

The shadow man from Phoebe's bedroom, the black cloud of millions of faces, the black serpent with glistening skin and no face, and this awful spider from the corner of my nightmares.

And now me.

Everybody's here.

The top of the furnace warped with a metallic warble as if smacked with a hammer and black, charring streaks crackled and bubbled across the metal.

Do you know what a fever is supposed to do? David had asked me. *It's the body trying to burn out the disease.*

(*Some kids are like improperly set ovens—they run hot.*)

The monster, the demon, the virus Phoebe called Abaddon, towered before me. Its fangs pushed in and I raised the glowing cross between us.

We are many. We are far, far too many than you could ever comprehend. The spider, the virus, the demon—it spoke through me and its words came from me, screamed from my mouth. *And now you'll be one with us. Because YOU ARE US. You'll be with all of us forever and ever and we'll eat you alive and you will eat others and you will lust for the taste of souls. You will be one with us. One OF us. We are Legion. And now you are too. And together, we'll get your daughter. She was so good. So tasty. You'll be the one. You'll get her, infect her, and kill her. Together, WE'LL EAT HER SOUL!*

Cross first, I punched the spider in the mouth and it swallowed me up to the shoulder.

My scream of protest roared into one of triumph.

With a metallic screech and a rushing howl, the furnace exploded.

EPILOGUE

THE KINGDOM OF HEAVEN

And the Lord said, "Where were you when the world was born?"

And Job knew his folly and humbled himself before the Lord and admitted his sin of pride and begged forgiveness. The Lord said unto Job, "You have proven yourself a most loyal servant. I will bless you now and for the rest of your days."

Job enjoyed great prosperity and a new family and lived a hundred and forty years.

So Job died, being old and full of days.

And after death, did Job ascend? For truly it is written: No one gets into Heaven without God's approval.

—The Book of Job (paraphrase)

In the beginning, God created the heaven and the earth. And the earth was without form, and void; and darkness was upon the face of the deep. And the Spirit of God moved upon the face of the waters. And God said, *let there be light*: and there was light. And God saw the light, that it was good: and God divided the light from the darkness.

At first, there was nothing, only darkness and absence of feeling. Then the cool ground soothed my flaming hands and a smooth rock wall gave me a place to lean. I thought of cartoons that mocked purgatory where people waited in endless, amusement park-style lines or sat interminably in waiting rooms where the magazines were decades out of date.

So, this is the afterlife.

The first light winked into existence not as a blooming sun but as the gentle glow of a distant star. Its light was a slight, pulsing blue, far up there, yet somehow very close, as if I could reach out and touch it.

I want to stay.

Then it must be so Phoebe can be free.

"Are you?" I asked the twinkling star. "Are you safe and free?"

The ground softened and cooled further. I slid my hands beside me through instantly sprouting grass. More stars flashed into existence and the collective blue light revealed my familiar cave.

A tendril of vegetation pushed out of the ground and curved upward, thickened into a sturdy plant trunk and bloomed a knot of tangled branches with thick, oval leaves that were unnaturally bright purple, the way Phoebe always wished.

"You saved me," I said. "Daddy's are supposed to do the saving, remember?"

Was it true she saved me? This was her place, her Land of Uz, but maybe I had brought myself here. Maybe she was gone. Or maybe dead. Maybe the virus got her, some stray molecule that slipped free, some devil microbe floated off and infected her.

"Are you safe?" I asked.

Nothing, just the stillness of an artificial night with a solitary blue star.

"Phoebe? My angel?"

The air shimmered as if in a mirage induced by heat exhaustion and Phoebe stepped into existence. Or maybe out of it, depending on how you looked at it. Reality or imagination? Was there any difference anymore?

For a blink, she was older once more and dressed as if for mass with a purple stole like a scarf hanging over her shoulders, and then she was young again and wearing her Sunday dress, hair done up with the butterfly clips.

"Peekaboo," she said. "You'll be safe here."

Go into the other place and die here, Cassie had said. *Even then it might not work. Depends what world you enter. If it's your own, it will have to be immensely stable. If it's someone else's, you'll need permission.*

"But are you safe?"

"The church was destroyed. Lavon said they're going to raise the money to rebuild."

A sense of accomplishment settled onto me like a heavy coat, one that is at first comfy and then too warm. But it had worked.

"Abaddon?"

She shook her head.

The church had been destroyed and with it Abaddon. The fire had eaten it up, a fever devouring a virus. Or maybe it had been cast back into its bottomless abyss—every last shred of it.

And God saw what Lucas had done and was pleased. And though he died, God saw fit to give Lucas life afresh and bless him to live a hundred and forty years, and watch his children, and their children, on and on for four generations.

So Lucas died, being old and full of days.

But did he ascend?

Unless you're delusional and this isn't really happening. Maybe you'll wake up in a hospital bed with third-degree burns all over your body and Lavon will be there to say he saved Phoebe, but she's been acting weird and has this strange black mark on her palm. Like some kind of infection.

My own hands looked normal, healed, and I felt no discomfort. I couldn't even detect where Phoebe's bear had mauled me.

"I'm sorry, Daddy. But you have to stay here if you want to survive."

"You're safe," I said. "That's what matters."

I reached for her and she took my hand. A moment later, we embraced. She radiated heat. I laughed and it triggered tears. After the hug, I hugged her again, but then something occurred to me, a storm cloud rolling out in the distance.

"If they rebuild, you must make sure none of the original wood is used. Burn it all. Spare nothing. He had his hands on all of it. The demon infected everything. And the house, too. You shouldn't live there. The virus can live on objects. Grandma or grandpa will come for you. They'll take you away. Don't go back into the house. Don't take any of your stuffed—"

"It's okay, Daddy. Everything is going to be okay."

After a moment, I asked, "Are you here? Am I?"

Her smile faltered. "People say you went crazy. They say you couldn't handle losing Mom and Tamara and that you tried to kill me. Blow me up with the church."

"Stranger things have happened. What does Lavon say?"

"I tried to take him here for a visit but he couldn't make the leap."

First, go light.

"I almost lost you, Daddy. I almost lost you forever, but I found you. I brought you here."

"You saved me."

She smiled.

She took my hand and guided me to my feet and across the cave. I was barefoot.

"Do you believe in Heaven?" she asked. We stopped at the wall where fallen rocks had dammed the way.

"Isn't that what this is?"

"You don't have to stay in here," she said with a smile. "You can come out and lay under the real stars."

"Real?"

"What is it you priests always say?"

"You have to have faith."

"Ready?" She squeezed my hand.

I could have stayed like that forever, standing there holding my daughter's hand with blue starlight painting her nose. "Ever think about what you'll be when you grow up?" I asked.

She smiled. Of course she had. What kid hadn't?

"You'd make a wonderful priest."

And there she was again, older and dressed as a priest—so beautiful, smiling just for me.

"Mom is waiting," Phoebe said, somehow older and younger simultaneously. "And Tamara."

"You brought them to Uz?"

"Grandpa's here, too. He's like he used to be."

"I love you, honey."

"Can we go now?"

"Sure."

She closed her eyes. "You know what to do."

"First," I said, "we go light."

Our bodies lifted as one and we passed through the wall and swept up the tunnel and emerged out the cave mouth into a world of rolling hills and the lush land beyond where multicolored trees glowed in eternal summer night and the stars never stopped shining. We flew and gave this world life as surely and completely as if God's magic were our own.

THE END

ABOUT THE AUTHOR

Chris DiLeo is the author of *Calamity, Blood Mountain, Hudson House,* and *Meat Camp* (co-authored with Scott Nicholson). He is also a high school English teacher in New York. Connect with him @authordileo and authordileo.com.

ALSO FROM
BLOODSHOT BOOKS

From a crater lake on an island off the coast of Bronze Age Estonia...

To a crippled Viking warrior's conquest of England ...

To the bloody temple of an Aztec god of death and resurrection...

Their presence has shaped our world. They are the Riders.

One month ago, an urban explorer was drawn to an abandoned asylum in the mountains of northern Massachusetts. There he discovered a large specimen jar, containing something organic, unnatural and possibly alive.

Now, he and a group of unsuspecting individuals have discovered one of history's most horrific secrets. Whether they want to or not, they are caught in the middle of a millennia-old war and the latest battle is about to begin.

Available in paperback or Kindle on Amazon.com

http://amzn.to/1peMAjz

**FINALLY IN PRINT AFTER MORE THAN THREE DECADES,
THE NOVEL MARK MORRIS WROTE <u>BEFORE</u> *TOADY***

EVIL NEEDS ONLY A SEED

Limefield has had more than its fair share of tragedy. Barely six years ago, a disturbed young boy named Russell Swaney died beneath the wheels of a passenger train mere moments after committing a heinous act of unthinkable sadism. Now, a forest fire caused by the thoughtless actions of two teens has laid waste to hundreds of acres of the surrounding woodlands and unleashed a demonic entity

EVIL TAKES ROOT

Now, a series of murders plague the area and numerous local residents have been reported missing, including the entire population of the nearby prison. But none of this compares to the appearance of the Winter Tree, a twisted wooden spire which seems to leech the warmth from the surrounding land.

EVIL FLOURISHES

Horrified by what they have caused, the two young men team up with a former teacher and the local police constabulary to find the killer, but it may already be too late. Once planted, evil is voracious. Like a weed, it strangles all life, and the roots of the Winter Tree are already around their necks.

Available in paperback or Kindle on Amazon.com

http://bit.ly/TreeKindle

There's a monster coming to the small town of Pikeburn. In half an hour, it will begin feeding on the citizens, but no one will call the authorities for help. They are the ones who sent it to Pikeburn. They are the ones who are broadcasting the massacre live to the world. Every year, Red Diamond unleashes a new creation in a different town as a display of savage terror that is part warning and part celebration. Only no one is celebrating in Pikeburn now. No one feels honored or patriotic. They feel like prey.

Local Sheriff Yan Corban refuses to succumb to the fear, paranoia, and violence that suddenly grips his town. Stepping forward to battle this year's lab-grown monster, Sheriff Corban must organize a defense against the impossible. His allies include an old art teacher, a shell-shocked mechanic, a hateful millionaire, a fearless sharpshooter, a local meth kingpin, and a monster groupie. Old grudges, distrust, and terror will be the monster's allies in a game of wits and savagery, ambushes and treachery. As the conflict escalates and the bodies pile up, it becomes clear this creature is unlike anything Red Diamond has unleashed before.

No mercy will be asked for or given in this battle of man vs monster. It's time to run, hide, or fight. It's time for Red Diamond.

Available in paperback or Kindle on Amazon.com

http://bit.ly/DiamondUS

January 12, 1888

When a day dawns warm and mild in the middle of a long cold winter, it's greeted as a blessing, a reprieve. A chance for those who've been cooped up indoors to get out, do chores, run errands, send the children to school... little knowing that they're only seeing the calm before the storm.

The blizzard hits out of nowhere, screaming across the Great Plains like a runaway train. It brings slicing winds, blinding snow, plummeting temperatures. Livestock will be found frozen in the fields, their heads encased in blocks of ice formed from their own steaming breath. Frostbite and hypothermia wait for anyone caught without shelter.

For the hardy settlers of Far Enough, in the Montana Territory, it's about to get worse. Something else has arrived with the blizzard. Something sleek and savage and hungry. Wild animal or vengeful spirit from native legend, it blends into the snow and bites with sharper teeth than the wind.

It is called the *wanageeska.*

It is the White Death

http://bit.ly/WDKindle

ON THE HORIZON FROM
BLOODSHOT BOOKS
2019-20

What Sleeps Beneath – John Quick

The Cryptids – Elana Gomel

Dead Sea Chronicles – Tim Curran

Midnight Solitaire – Greg F. Gifune

Dead Branches – Benjamin Langley

The October Boys – Adam Millard

Clownflesh – Tim Curran

Blood Mother: A Novel of Terror – Pete Kahle

Not Your Average Monster – World Tour

The Abomination (The Riders Saga #2) – Pete Kahle

The Horsemen (The Riders Saga #3) – Pete Kahle

other titles to be added when confirmed

BLOODSHOT BOOKS

READ UNTIL YOU BLEED!